Visionary

by

Michael Hallford

TUMBLAR HOUSE
' Bona Tempora Volvant'

Arcadia
MMVIII

ISBN 978-0-9791600-6-6

©2008 by Michael Hallford

Cover Art by Jef Murray

Tumblar House
PMB 376
411 E. Huntington Dr. #107
Arcadia, CA 91006
www.tumblarhouse.com

Acknowledgments

Throughout the numerous revisions and transformations this story has passed through since I first imagined it while on a year hiatus from Rice University in 1978. I could never have brought it to completion without the encouragement of so many people along the way, and to them this book is gratefully dedicated. First and foremost I wish to thank my beautiful wife Victoria, who has supported me enthusiastically and unconditionally, through the whole process and whose patience and forbearance have inspired me. For so many others who have read the manuscript and generously given their feedback, among them Eric M, Eric G, David R, and C.J., I am fervently thankful. Thanks to Jef Murray for the beautiful cover. Thank you Stephen Frankini for having the courage to publish it. Thank God for every blessing among so many blessings that He has brought into my life, especially my children whose support has also been exceptional.

PART I

And it shall come to pass afterward, that I will pour out my spirit upon all flesh; your sons and your daughters shall prophesy, your old men shall dream dreams, and your young men shall see visions. (Joel 2:28, Acts 2:17)

Chapter 1

Jim had gone to bed late the night before after fighting an anxious insomnia, which filled his mind with incessant what-ifs, and though he would never have said that he felt regret, he wondered what his life would have been like had he been born to different parents, chosen different friends and placed his trust in different people. He pondered all the decisions that he had made, which had led inextricably to his present circumstances, and which left him indifferent to all the mundane details of his life.

When he stopped caring, he could not have said, but the evidence of his apathy lay all around him. His apartment resembled Troy after battle, with books and newspapers slaughtered across his floor and soiled clothing tossed wherever he removed them as if from an army in hasty retreat. There were half-eaten meals, which he had abandoned in mid-digestion and which in their concealment he had forgotten to toss out, and on his walls hung artless posters, some newspaper clippings, and several weird prints, all unbalanced and misaligned.

In the midst of this chaos stood only one refuge of coherency: In the corner of the room sat a small walnut chest, polished and spotless. Inside its rigid walls, Jim protected his treasures, an unfinished novel, several college papers he seemed satisfied to keep, and a small locket he had worn as a baby. The locket occupied the place of honor in this shrine; it sat in its own case atop his novel. Years before he had locked the chest, and the key he misplaced somewhere in the clutter. He would have to dig through weeks of neglect in order to find it.

The alarm rang at eight o'clock and he struggled against waking. He growled as his arm searched aimlessly to turn off the earsplitting buzzer. In the shower he growled again as the hot water pulsated against his back. He preferred the water almost unbearably hot and steam filled the stall making it difficult to breathe. After thirty-five minutes, he emerged from the shower, war-weary and purified for another round of battle. As he shaved, he read the words of a poster of Murphy's Law which hung on the bathroom wall. The words from the poster echoed like a mantra in his head, "Whatever can go wrong will go wrong."

He had learned the tough road of a struggling journalist. Moving from smaller papers to larger ones, he had been settling and unsettling in a spider's web across the northeast. Finally, he had accepted a permanent position as a staff reporter for a small daily paper. In this city of 200,000, true journalism seemed an impossible fantasy. He covered small town news when once he dreamed of being a network commentator.

Jim spent ten minutes searching for his shoes beneath clothing and newspapers before he remembered he had left them in the kitchen sink. "I should clean this up," he said to himself. But he was rushed this morning with a story to cover. He pinned a press badge on his collar and combed his hair. This day he would cover his first real story: Nigel was coming to Hadleyburg.

The city was a furor of activity this humid morning. From children waiting impatiently for ever-tardy buses, to the cacophony of traffic noises as people hurried to work at factories, Hadleyburg was filled to overflowing with Americana, with its specialty shops, its variety stores, and fast food franchises, all strung as pearls along the main drag. At the end of the drag was a town square around which Carver Avenue was wrapped as a comforter. Nelson Carver had been mayor in Hadleyburg for twenty-two years until his untimely death at sixty-seven from cancer. In Hadleyburg, four streets and six buildings bore his name.

In the center of the square sat City Hall, a monument to the kind of Romanesque architecture in vogue at the turn of the century. The town founders had built it in red brick with a gaudy dome on top. Atop its dome waved an American flag and beneath it dangled the state flag, fold upon fold. Both were worn from twenty years continuous use. Across from City Hall stood the post office and behind it was the Carver Civic Center built as a memorial on the tenth anniversary of the mayor's death, and behind it was the newspaper, "The Hadleyburg Times," which boasted on its marquis "Circulation of 100,000. Serving best as the town deserves." Here Jim eked out his meager existence writing whatever his editor dictated. He had covered everything from city elections and the town's annual strawberry festival, to a referendum to fluoridate the town's drinking water. This day Reynolds dictated that he covered Nigel, who would be speaking at the civic center at 11:00 that morning. A crowd was expected to meet him.

At eight thirty, people had already begun to gather around the ticket booths to purchase fifteen- dollar tickets to hear him speak. Others had come to speak before, but no one like Nigel. Hours before, the network news had arrived with their vans. A legion of journalists armed with cameras and microphones loitered impatiently, hoping to ambush him as soon as he arrived. Mayor McGovern had requested assistance from the state police and they were dispersed in key positions around the square. Thousands were expected to fill the square, some in protest, others pledging complete loyalty to the enigmatic little man, and others who for only curiosity's sake sought to discover what the commotion was about. They came for a multitude of reasons. Rumors of his healing a small child in Cleveland and of his gift of foresight in helping a young widow find her son were told and retold among his admirers, no matter how much he tried to dismiss them. At a time when technology seemed more god than servant, many longed for something to believe in, and Nigel inspired profound hope in them. Sociologists and psychologists tried to explain it, but all their speculation proved unconvincing.

In Baltimore, three months before, a young woman was overtaken by police as she struggled to reach him. Screaming, "Let me touch him or I'll die," she kicked and twisted against overwhelming opposition and jumped on stage into Nigel's arms. Trembling in surprise, Nigel held her while she cried uncontrollably. Because of incidents such as this, the sponsors of Nigel's appearances instituted stringent security procedures wherever he spoke.

By ten o'clock the crowds were beginning to grow around the square; they looked like patches of wild flowers in bloom. Those near the doors resembled a high school football team in forward formation. The goal line became the double doors at the front of the auditorium. Jim arrived at 10:15 as a second string running back trying to fight his way through the defensive line. He made it as far as the ticket booths before being pulled out of bounds.

"Jim," a voice called to him. "Over here."

Burgess Kingman, holding a camera in his hand, pulled him behind the ticket booths.

"I tried calling you last night. Don't you answer your phone any more?"

"Not if I can help it."

"Reynolds gave me a list of a few points he wanted you to emphasize in your copy."

"I know how to write a news story."

"He's not telling you what to write. He just wants you to understand the paper's position on this?"

"Alright, let me see it."

Burgess handed him a small piece of paper which he glanced at a moment then folded and put in his pocket.

"Maybe I'm missing something, Burg. There must be four thousand people here. What's the attraction?"

"People want to believe in something."

"Hell, I'd like to believe in something, but you have to grow up and face reality someday. You're born, you suffer, you die. That's the cycle of life."

"How long have you been in this mood?"

"I stay in this mood." He paused. "I hate this town. I hate everything about it, from the courthouse to that gazebo over there. (He pointed to the town square.) God, I want out of here."

"Calm down, Jim."

"Calm down? Hell, I haven't even started yet. What's wrong with these people? This is the twentieth century. You can't be chasing after everyone who sets himself up as a prophet. People like this Nigel just raise people's expectations only to destroy them. It makes me sick."

His friend began to snicker nervously and shake his head.

"We've got a little time," Burgess acknowledged, looking at his watch. "Would you like to get a bite to eat?"

"Yeah, I could use a cup of coffee."

The two men forced their way through the wall of people until they found sanctuary in a small coffee shop at the corner of the square. Once inside Jim groaned in relief as they both sat down in a small booth near the front windows. A waitress approached them to take their order, but before she could speak, they could see through the windows that a fight had broken out between Nigel's detractors and his supporters and the state police were attempting to disperse and separate them. Two men were exchanging punches a few feet from the storefront and the patrons had arisen from their seats to watch them through the windows. Jim also approached the windows.

"Sometimes I think the whole world's gone mad," he turned to Burgess and told him. "I pray that I'll wake up some morning and this will all be some horrible dream and I'll be someone else."

"I thought you weren't a praying man," Burgess rebutted.

The waitress returned to their table to take their orders.

"What can I get you both?" she asked them.

"I just want a cup of coffee," Jim responded.

"I'll take a couple of eggs scrambled and some toast." He paused. "You know you shouldn't report on an empty stomach."

The waitress returned a few minutes later with Jim's cup of coffee and Burgess's plate. Jim downed the coffee in three huge gulps, while Burgess meticulously cut his eggs and toast with a fork and knife.

"Everything important in life is in the details," he said as he put the first bite into his mouth. Jim watched him as he cut each piece with a surgeon's precision and methodically chewed and swallowed them.

The waitress brought the check, which Burgess graciously agreed to pay. Then both of them left the coffee shop to fight their way back across the square.

"We should probably start making our way into the auditorium," Burgess said while looking at his watch. "You write a few words and I take a few pix and it will all be over before we know it."

After making adjustments to his camera, Burgess disappeared into the crowd. Then Jim stood motionless as he stared into the square. It was saturated with humanity. Before his eyes was Hadleyburg in microcosm, and a perplexing uneasiness came over him when he looked across the crowd. Soon the doors opened, and parents with children, the affluent and the poor, pulsated through the doors into the auditorium. They came to see what others had seen and heard—Nigel. Jim walked in formation with the rest of them, though he told himself that he was not one of them. Despising extremists of any persuasion, he found Nigel's critics as nauseating as his fans were maudlin. He wished to walk a tightrope of moderation against what he saw as the strong winds of public caprice. He was determined not to be affected by anything that he might experience inside.

When he entered the huge double doors to the auditorium, he was almost deafened by the noise of the audience. He put his fingers in his ears to make it more bearable. Leaning his shoulder against a metal support beam, he could feel it vibrate from the noise of the crowd. Even with his finger in his ears the sound was unnerving and made it difficult for him to concentrate.

"A little loud isn't it?" Burgess shouted in Jim's ear.

"A little. This must be what hell is like."

"I've got some news for you. Guess who's here."

"I don't know."

"Julie. She's standing on the other side of the auditorium."

"Then I've gotta go."

"Come on, Guy. It took me fifteen minutes to find you and I was looking. She'll never in a million years spot you in this crowd."

"Where's she sitting?"

Chapter 1

"On the left side three rows from the end."

"Let me see your camera a second."

Burgess handed him the camera and said, "Be careful with it. It's brand new."

Jim scanned the auditorium through its lens until he found her sitting where Burgess had seen her. She sat quietly with her hands folded across her lap and with her brunette hair pinned back behind her head. She turned her head to look around the room and Jim dropped the camera to his side.

"You're right. She's here. I can't let her see me here."

"You can't keep running from this girl forever. Worse comes to worst you can wear a paper bag over your head."

"I'm not running away from her. But she's the last person I want to see right now."

"Hey, it's not my life. But if I thought I had to confront her sooner or later, I'd rather get it over with now."

"It's not your life."

Burgess took the camera back and disappeared into the crowd as suddenly as he had appeared. Jim retreated and hid himself behind a pillar.

The houselights began to dim and the curtain at the front of the auditorium slowly opened. Two tables sat on stage, one near the front and the other a few feet behind it. On each of the tables sat a vase with a single red rose. A microphone stood at the center of the stage with a dim light above it. Nigel sat at the rear table with his hands cupped on his face, hiding his nose and mouth. Jim couldn't keep from staring at him.

"Is this the man they're making such a fuss about?" he asked himself. "He looks so sad."

Dressed in a white shirt and gray slacks, Nigel carried his eighty years well. Yet he hardly looked the part of prophet or seer. There seemed something strangely familiar about this aging little man.

James Jamison and Governor Michael Wilson were sitting at the front table. They looked like what they were: businessman and politician. Jamison got up and moved toward the microphone.

"I think it's about time we began," he said. "Nigel isn't feeling well, but he's agreed to talk for a little while."

He turned to Nigel and nodded. With an expression of what seemed like pain, Nigel pushed himself up from the table and limped slightly on the left leg as he walked toward the microphone.

"They tell me there's four thousand of you here, and even more outside."

His voice was hoarse. "I can't for the life of me figure out why you're here. Go home. You must have other things to do."

"What's he doing?" Jamison said, as though taken by surprise.

"I've been all over this fair land of ours on these talks and everywhere I go people come to me for solace. I'm not God."

Jim noticed that Jamison and Wilson were leaning over to each other and whispering as Nigel was speaking. He couldn't stop watching their lips that he might catch what they were saying. But the lights were too dim and they were too far away from him. He could only make out a word or two.

"I think there are some things you ought to know," Nigel began to speak more forcefully. At this moment the chatter between Wilson and Jamison seemed more frenetic, and if not for what followed, they both shuffled hesitantly and seemed intent upon interrupting him. But then in mid-sentence, as Nigel was asking the crowd why they came, his legs grew weak; he grabbed the back of his neck and he collapsed in a resounding thud on the wooden platform.

This scene was not what Jim expected, and like the others he stood motionless with his gaze fixed on the stage. Wilson had jumped up from his seat and was checking Nigel for a pulse.

"Is there a doctor here?" he shouted through the microphone with a profound sense of urgency. Taking off his jacket, Wilson rolled it up into a ball and placed it under Nigel's head. He loosened Nigel's shirt and took his shoes off his feet. Burgess stood next to the stage and took one picture after another of the drama as it unfolded.

"Damn," Jim could hear him say. "What a story."

For what seemed almost an eternity the crowd gasped silently until a doctor emerged from the audience and began to examine Nigel. After a few seconds of examination, he said, "It's not a heart attack."

"What is it then?" Michael Wilson asked him.

"I don't know yet. Has someone called an ambulance?"

Jamison left the stage to get a phone.

"Is he a diabetic?"

"Not that I'm aware of," Wilson answered him.

In the heat of the moment, without even realizing it, Jim had moved from behind the pillar and was standing near the front of the auditorium. Julie, who was standing only a few yards away, discovered him. A smile covered her face and the skin around her brown eyes wrinkled. But she forced a more serious demeanor and tried not to betray that she noticed him. An ambulance arrived a few minutes later and two paramedics carried Nigel away on a stretcher. The whine of the siren had ended what had been anticipated as a "media event."

When the excitement subsided, Julie began to look expectantly for Jim, but he had disappeared as suddenly as she had discovered him.

"Julie," Burgess startled her as he spoke. "It's good to see a familiar face in this hole in the wall town."

"Oh, Burgess. You're here too."

She hugged him.

"Yeah. Me and Jimmy boy, we're both trapped in historic Hadleyburg."

"I saw him. How is he?"

"A real mess. Dumbest thing he ever did was push you out of his life."

Her lips turned down into a frown, but she forced a smile.

"You look well, Burgess."

"I'm surviving. But how about you?"

"Jim would be proud of me. I'm working as an editor at Newsmaker magazine." She paused. "So much has changed, hasn't it?"

"Yeah. I'm losing my hair. "He rubbed his hands through his thinning scalp." But I guess everything changes. But what brings you here?"

"I came to see my father." (Julie's father was James Jamison, one of the men who sponsored Nigel's talks.)

"I'm going to the hospital in a second. Why don't you come with me?"

"Won't Jim get upset?"

"Probably. But he's in a real rut right now. It wouldn't hurt him to get a little upset."

"No, Burgess. It's not the right time. But you can tell him I said 'hello.'"

She hugged him again and then she too disappeared into the crowd.

Chapter 2

Parkland hospital was a war zone with reporters strewn across the lobby as victims of its aftermath. Jim stood off in the corner and watched the others as a scout searches his enemies for their points of weakness. He had been there for five hours huddled against the floor, while his stomach growled for nourishment. Burgess had been gone for what seemed like hours to get something for them to eat, and he could hardly bear the waiting. He wanted to leave, but he knew that Reynolds expected him to stay. So he sat. He stared at the walls and at his hands while he waited for some news of Nigel's condition.

Near the two steel doors through which the paramedics had carried Nigel, stood the "big name" newsmen. There were Frank Glen of *Newsmaker* magazine, Thomas Miller of the *New York Times* and Bob Bigelow of *America*. They spoke in what seemed to him muffled whispers and he occupied his mind by pretending they were acting out various outrageous scenes from *A Midsummer's Night Dream*. He kept sighing and shaking his head.

At four thirty, Burgess returned with chicken for both of them. "Anything happen while I was gone?"

"Not a thing, Burg. Remember, this is Hadleyburg. It's like a big black hole which sucks up anything interesting within a hundred miles."

"What are they talking about?" He pointed to the trio at the double doors.

"I think they're the center of the black hole, Burg. Nothing could possibly be going on over there."

"Let's get a little closer. I'm anxious to hear what they are talking about."

"Let me eat my chicken." He took a bite out of a drumstick.

"You go. I couldn't bear to hear them."

Burgess moved a little closer to hear what they were saying.

"Come on, Frank. You can't believe this psychic crap," Thomas Miller was saying. "This is the 20th century. We're not some primitive tribe in Burma with its shamans and its witch doctors."

"Then you explain how he does it."

"We've been round and around this one," Bigelow jumped in. "Foretelling the future is the stuff of fairy tales and gypsies."

"You've missed the point. He's never said he could see the future."

"He doesn't have to," Miller jumped back in. "Any guy who believes his dreams predict the future has a few cards short of a deck."

"And you, Frank, former writer for *Paranormal Magazine*, and the man who started all this nonsense, are ready to declare him a prophet."

"That's not fair. All I said was that he has a following like that of a prophet, and I'm not responsible for this."

"Some following," Miller chimed in. "They're all a bunch of kooks and social misfits. The same people who believe in UFOs and Poltergeists."

Burgess had heard enough, and moved back to the wall where Jim was sitting.

"Well, Burg, what did they have to say, as if I need to ask?"

"You're right. It's the center of the black hole."

"It's because of those yo-yos that people give this Nigel a second hearing. They run across the country following him like a bunch of puppy dogs and then complain that he has a following. They made him so they can sleep with him."

"I probably should take some pictures."

"Go. I think I'll take a nap."

He slid down to the floor with his back against the wall. From the far corner of the lobby, an explosion of noise startled him, as he had almost drifted into sleep. From behind the double doors, the doctor had finally emerged and a wall of flesh soon surrounded him. With microphones thrust into his face, he began to speak.

"Nigel is conscious. I just finished talking with him. At this point we're not entirely sure what's wrong. We're still running tests. I will keep you posted. As for his spirits, they're good." He paused. "Nigel has told me he wants to give an interview, but not to any of you. He wants to talk to James Jacobson."

"Who in the hell is James Jacobson?" Miller asked.

"Is there a James Jacobson here?" the doctor shouted.

Jim began to realize that his name was being called, and he finally stepped out into the hallway.

"Yeah, I'm Jim Jacobson. What do you want?"

"Nigel wants to talk to you, Mr. Jacobson."

"Why me, Doctor? I don't want to talk to him."

"He didn't say. He just asked for you."

"No, forget it. I don't want to talk to him."

"Am I to understand you're turning down this interview?"

At that moment Burgess leaned over to his ear and told him, "Mr. Reynolds just called down here. It appears Nigel called him personally and asked for you to give this interview. He advised me to tell you he considers this very important. I wouldn't turn it down."

"But I want no part of this," he whispered back.

"Reynolds said 'either talk or you're fired.'"

"Alright, I'll talk to him."

"Then come with me," the doctor snarled, gesturing with his hand. "As for the rest of you, this is a hospital and you'll have to leave now. Don't force me to call security."

The doctor gestured for Jim to follow him, and then both went through the double doors.

"Good luck, Jim," Burgess said as they left.

"I'm Dr. Namath. (He paused.) Before we go upstairs, I'm going to lay out a few ground rules. You do anything to upset Mr. Fox, you cause any disturbance, or you go anywhere you're not supposed to be, I'll have you thrown out. You're not going to turn this hospital into a circus, and I'm not going to baby sit you. Do I make myself clear?"

"Yes."

"We've got a very sick man here, and I want you to treat him as gently as you would your own father."

"I understand."

"Do you know how he got my name, doctor?"

"That you'll have to ask Mr. Fox."

"Why does he want to talk to me?"

"Look, I know as much as you know. Ask Mr. Fox."

The doors to the elevators opened and Dr. Namath remained inside.

"I have other patients to see. He's at the end of the hall." After the elevator doors closed behind him, Jim wavered a second. He even thought of pressing the button so that he could go back down. But something kept him from doing what he felt inclined to do. Perhaps it was curiosity, or so he would have like to convinced himself. But he began to walk, deliberately, as though his next step might propel him into the abyss.

It would have been difficult for him to put into words all the emotions that battled inside of him as he began to walk down that hallway. Perhaps it was in seeing Julie that all these unresolved impulses found a suitable catalyst to bring them to the surface. 'God, what am I getting myself into' was the only thought he recognized. He wanted to turn back, but his legs kept moving in the same rhythmic stride, almost as if they carried him of their own volition.

Posted outside Nigel's room was a bodyguard. He didn't say a word as Jim passed by him, like a statue, immobile and impassable. Jim nodded to him and said "Hello," but the guard would not respond to him. Then Jim slowly pushed to door open to enter Nigel's room.

It is difficult to capture in words the sense of surprise which Jim felt when he pushed open the door and had his first glimpse of Nigel's room. Filled with flowers of every description and large gift boxes, it looked nothing like a hospital room, with its customary blank walls and bare unimpressive furniture. One of the beds had been removed and Nigel sat on the other one with his head supported by a soft down pillow.

"Thank God you've come," were Nigel's first words. "I'd get up to greet you, but I'm not supposed to be out of bed."

"That's alright, Mr. Fox."

"Call me Nigel. Take a seat and relax."

Jim nervously set himself on the edge of the nearest chair.

"I'd offer you something to drink, but all I have is water. Do you like the flowers? They're all gifts, quite a haul for an old television salesman."

"They're very pretty."

"Pretty? They're gorgeous. Please make yourself comfortable."

"Hospitals make me uncomfortable."

"They don't thrill me. But if I have to be here, I'd rather be comfortable, than uncomfortable." He paused. "Are you sure you don't want anything?"

"No, thank you."

"I'm not the monster they paint me out to be. Relax."

Jim slid back on his chair. He seemed misplaced in the midst of so many flowers.

"What do you know about me, young man?"

"Just what I've read in the papers."

"Then you don't know much. Your colleagues out there think this is some big game. Do not pass go. Do not collect two hundred dollars. They have no idea what is really happening."

"What is really happening then?"

"You wouldn't believe me. Not now. There's a great deal more at stake than they care to imagine."

"Like what?"

"I can't say yet. Have you ever felt like your whole life you have been living in a dream and you suddenly wake up and realize everything is different from what you once believed?"

"You speak in riddles," he spoke with a hostile edge in his voice. "What about your powers?"

"I have no powers. I had five horrible dreams which came true. Was it coincidence or providence, or a glimpse into the hidden weave of the universe? You must decide."

"I don't believe in the supernatural."

"Natural and supernatural. Such distinctions are meaningless to me now. Everything we can explain is natural and real. Everything we can't explain is supernatural and unreal. In my experience, some of the things we can't explain are more real than the things we can."

"I understand where you're coming from. But did you ask me here to argue philosophy?"

"No. I want you to help me."

"Me, help you? Why would I do that?"

"After you understand what's at stake, I'm certain you'll help me."

"How do you know that?"

"I know a great deal about you, young man."

"You have me at a disadvantage. I know almost nothing about you."

Jim looked more uneasy as they continued their conversation. He didn't look at Nigel, because Nigel's eyes seemed to pierce through him every time he turned Nigel's way.

"I intend to remedy that."

Dropping his arms to his side, Nigel stopped speaking and began to cough. Jim turned his head to look at the old man. He could see that Nigel looked pale and he had dropped his head to his chest. Nigel closed his eyes a moment, took a deep breath and then opened them.

"Are you alright, Mr. Fox?"

"I'm OK for a dying man." He paused. "I injured my leg in the Second World War, and it seems a small bone chip has broken free and has lodged itself here." He pointed to the back of his head.

"Can't they operate?"

"They will. But I'll probably die."

"That's terrible."

"When I first heard about it, I reacted to it badly, like I've reacted to every other tragedy in my life. But I've accepted it now."

"When are they going to operate?"

"Tomorrow morning."

"Then this could be your last night."

"It could be. Would you mind spending a few hours with a foolish old man?" Nigel spoke with earnestness in his voice.

"OK. But I'll have to make a phone call first."

"Sure, take your time. I'm not going anywhere."

Nigel adjusted the pillow behind his back as Jim rose to leave the room. He walked to the nurses' station at the end of the corridor. While he was looking at the floor, he reflected on his whole experience as a journalist. All the stories he had covered from prom nights to store openings rushed at him in a flurry of forgotten memories. He had always dreamed of covering a "big" story, but not this big story. This fulfillment of his life long dream brought uneasiness instead of satisfaction.

"May I use your phone?" he asked a nurse who seemed not to notice him at first. "May I use your phone?" he repeated.

"I'm sorry. It's not for personal calls. There's a pay phone in the corner." She pointed with indignation at a payphone near the stairs.

Jim searched his pockets, but could not find a coin.

"Do you have a quarter I can borrow?"

"Alright, here." She slid a quarter across the counter.

Another nurse who had been working quietly on the other side of the counter turned to him and asked, "Are you Mr. Jacobson?"

"Yes."

"I just came on. How's he doing?"

"Fine," he answered with ambiguity in his voice.

"I heard him speak in Baltimore. He was wonderful."

"Yeah, I heard about it."

"What's he like?"

Jim didn't feel comfortable in responding to her question. He hesitated a moment and then said, "He's not what I expected."

"Do you like him?"

"I have to think about it."

"What's to think about? I like him."

With this remark Jim disconnected, "I came to use the phone."

"OK, but please be good to him, Mr. Jacobson."

He found the phone in the visitor's lobby, where a man was sleeping there on a makeshift cot. Dialing slowly, he stared out the window and saw a news truck parked five floors below. He knew they waited to hear his words about Nigel.

A woman's voice answered, "Hadleyburg Times, Laura Greene speaking."

"Laura, It's Jim. Is Reynolds there?"

"No, he's been called home on an emergency. I heard you're interviewing Nigel. Your big break, huh?"

"Yeah, my big break. Is Burgess there?"

"No, he's at the hospital last I heard. Some girl called down here this evening. Let me see if I can find her message."

"That's OK. Tell Reynolds if he comes back, I need to talk to him."

"Sure thing, Jim."

He hung up the phone and quietly left the lobby. When he returned to the room, Nigel was sitting quietly and reading with his face looking more troubled than before. He didn't seem to notice when Jim entered the room.

"Mr. Fox, I'm back."

"I'm sorry for my inattention. Did you make your phone call?"

"Yes, but nothing came of it."

Nigel took a deep breath, the kind of breath one takes when some deep longing of the soul cannot find words to express itself.

"I don't want to die. There's so much I have yet to do. I had it all planned, what I would say to you. But how does one break through that deep soul-wrenching cynicism which takes control of the best of us? Before all this began, I had a private dream of fame and the power that came with it. That was my weakness."

"What are you getting at?"

"There are men out there capable of such great evil that your mind cannot conceive of it. I never believed that. I was like the next man thinking that everyone was basically good. I thought I was a pretty good fellow. But I have some part in this."

"Please excuse my confusion. But what are you talking about?"

"I've taken a great risk in asking you here. I'm sorry to put you at such risk, but I have no choice."

"What do you mean put me at risk?"

"Your presence here entails some risk."

"Do you mean danger?"

"Yes."

"Why in the hell do you involve me in this?" Jim snapped at him and rose to leave.

"One thing you must do is remain calm about this. Don't leave."

"How can I be calm? You're scaring the hell out of me?"

"He must not suspect that you know anything."

"Who, Mr. Fox?"

"Alright, I'll tell you. Michael Wilson."

"The former governor? You've got to be kidding. Is he your man of incredible evil?"

"You don't believe me."

"I know a little about Michael Wilson. He raised millions for famine relief. He fought for civil rights and has backed other causes. Before he became involved with you, he was one of my personal heroes."

"I know that.   You worked as a volunteer in his first gubernatorial campaign."

"How do you know so much about me? And why?"

"I can't tell you that now, but trust me, please."

These words spoken with vulnerability echoed in Jim's mind. He had heard them before, coming from another's lips, and they returned him in a moment of anamnesis to five years before when Julie had said these same words to him.

"I find it difficult to trust anyone."

His face became flush and he fervently fought the tears.

"You know there's a lot of stuff been bottling up in me for a very long time."

"I understand."

"Since you seem to know everything else, you must also know my mother died when I was in college. (Nigel nodded.) It nearly destroyed me. My father was such a mess. He couldn't do anything. I had to make all the arrangements. Shortly after the funeral, I was going through some of her papers, and I found the adoption papers. They never told me. Something as important as that, they never told me. To this day my father doesn't know I know." He paused. "For some stupid reason, I wanted to find my real parents. I wanted to know why my real mother gave me up. I traced everything back through the adoption agency and I found that I had been abandoned on the steps of an orphanage with a note saying, 'I don't want him anymore.' This left me empty inside. After that my life seemed to fall apart."

"Perhaps your parents kept it from you, because they loved you and they knew it would hurt you."

"Yes, but I trusted them, and they lied to me."

"We all have our private hells, we have little courage to speak about."

"Listen to me," Jim interrupted. "I sound like some afternoon soap opera. You're dying and I'm whining like a baby."

"You needn't feel uncomfortable with me about anything."

"How do you feel?"

"A little weak. What time is it?"

"Ten thirty."

"I've missed the local news. I wanted to hear what they say about me."

"It's probably not good."

"You're right. Could you help me out of bed, young man?"

"Are you sure? You're not supposed to be out of bed."

"Just help me to my feet. I want to walk a little."

He carefully held Nigel, while he lifted himself to his feet, and Nigel began to walk around the small island of space between the bed and the door. Nigel limped on his left leg and his face cringed in pain as he stepped.

"Is your leg OK?"

"I'm in a lot of pain. A souvenir from the Nazis."

"You fought in Europe."

"No, I was in the Navy. Let me sit down."

Jim rose from the chair and let Nigel sit down.

"Go sit down on the bed. It's not that bad."

Jim stood beside him and did not sit down.

"I'm sure you must have questions, young man? This is an interview. Why if one of the others were here they'd never stop with the questions."

Jim was silent.

"What about my powers? Am I a psychic? Can I read minds? When did I first realize I had my powers? These are the questions they would ask me. Am I lonely? Am I afraid of death? Am I ready to face eternity? These questions would not interest them in the least."

"Why did you bring me here?" Jim finally asked him." And why have you bothered knowing so much about me?"

At this question Nigel's voice hesitated, "I can't answer that now. It would take too much time, and damn it I don't have any more."

Suddenly, the door swung open in a loud clash and a nurse came into to the room. When she saw Nigel sitting in the chair, her voice pierced the air in a loud shriek, "What are you doing out of bed, Mr. Fox? Dr. Namath told you to stay off your feet."

"I'm sick of that bed."

"It's ten-thirty, you were supposed to be asleep an hour ago. Dr. Namath is not going to be pleased. As for you Mr. Jacobson, you have overstayed visiting hours." She paused. "I have no choice, Mr. Fox, but to give you a sedative."

"I don't want a sedative. I'd like to talk to Mr. Jacobson."

"As for you Mr. Jacobson. There's a phone message at the desk. Someone named Reynolds."

"Go return your call, young man. I'll handle her."

Jim noticed as he left the room, that the bodyguard who had stood watch there before had disappeared. The long empty corridor remained with its rows of doors like prison cells with invisible bars. Behind each door was hidden tragedy and human suffering, concealed by whitewashed walls and polished floors. Technology had not destroyed death; it just made it easier to ignore.

"Do you have a message for me?" he asked the same young nurse to whom he had earlier talked.

"Yes, Mr. Jacobson." She handed him a folded note. "Are you related to Mr. Fox?"

"No I'm just here to interview him."

"Then he's completely alone. How terrible."

"Can I use your phone?"

"Sure."

She pushed the phone toward him and he grabbed it with his left hand. The phone rang five times before someone answered it. "Hello," Reynolds began.

"Mr. Reynolds. It's Jim Jacobson. I'm sorry to call so late."

"That's fine. So where are you?"

"I'm still at the hospital with Nigel. Burgess said he talked to you. I need to know what you want me to do with this story."

"Burgess is a liar. I've been home all afternoon on a family emergency. My boy was hit by a car while riding his bicycle."

"Is he all right?"

"He's got a slight concussion. It could have been a lot worse." He paused. "As for the story, did Burgess give you the note I gave him?"

"Yes."

"Find out something about his powers. I'll look at it in the morning. Look. I have to go. I'll look at it in the morning."

He ended the conversation with a hesitant "Goodbye."

"So much for context. Thanks for the phone."

After he pushed the phone back to her, he began to walk down the corridor with little idea what he would write about once this ordeal was over. He realized that Burgess had coerced him into an interview he could have evaded. Yet, he wasn't angry with him, and he didn't know why.

When he returned to the room, he found the nurse gone and Nigel sound asleep in bed. He noticed how labored Nigel's breathing seemed and how commonplace he looked, nothing like the prophet some believed him to be. Feeling a deep disappointment that he could not talk to him again that night, he reluctantly took a seat beside his bed. There he sat for a few minutes before he could no longer subdue his curiosity, and he began to look around the room.

For the first time, he observed with a reporter's perception the things that Nigel had brought into the room. He noticed books and magazines of assorted slants and biases depicting Nigel's story in radically different perspectives. There were worn photographs of people Jim could not recognize, some with a much younger Nigel before age had wrinkled his face and neck and whitened his hair with its slow corruption. He saw what looked to him like religious art. But his eyes passed these with detached indifference. There was a small porcelain doll wearing a costume he did not recognize, which he lifted up a moment to examine, but then set aside. The thought passed his mind how confused and unconnected all these things seemed, and how at first glance he had learned nothing from them about this enigmatic man. Obviously these things were important to Nigel, but their secrets would remain forever silent to him. His gaze darted randomly across the room until a scrapbook, which was balanced on a table, caught his attention. Worn and frayed at the edges with the name "Beth Fox" written in a feminine hand across its front, this book enticed him for investigation. He reached for it several times, but pulled his hand back in pangs of conscience. Finally, he snatched it firmly and with a boyish mischief returned to his chair to discover its contents.

On the first page was taped a single wedding announcement, yellowed with time, and held precariously by amber cellophane. The second revealed wedding pictures with a younger Nigel and his bride. She had long black hair and huge eyes which betrayed a gentleness he had not seen in anyone. On the next few pages he discovered baby pictures and a single photograph of Nigel with a small baby in his arms. Each new photograph he examined became a new piece in this elaborate puzzle which he didn't have the pattern to reconstruct. On the next few pages he saw pictures of London Tower and Buckingham Palace. He began to ponder the possibility that Nigel had left it there for him to find. But he dismissed the thought as paranoid. He turned page after page, which displayed image after image, with no captions to explain what they meant. Finally, on the last page, he found a playbill, awkwardly folded and torn at the edges. He opened it to reveal a photograph of Nigel, wearing a turban and gown, with words beneath him reading, "Come see Nigel, The Seer. He will dazzle you with his never before seen psychic powers."

"My God, he was a stage mind reader."

This discovery made him even more confused than before. He placed the scrapbook on the table, and returned again to his seat. With a deep sigh, he relaxed his back and looked around the room again.

"You're a bag full of surprises. I'll give you that, Nigel. I'll have a lot of questions for you in the morning." He stood up again. "I've got to think."

He nervously paced the hospital room. His body, fatigued from the long day, demanded sleep, but his mind rushed forward unbridled. He could not make sense of it all. His eyes wandered from object to object, from impression to impression, as a bee moves from flower to flower in search of pollen. His attention changed erratically from flowers to the sound of rain tapping on the window glass, from Nigel's words to the sight of him lying as dead on the stage of the civic center. He walked to the window and stood. There he watched the network news vans parked five floors below. In his youth these symbolized all his highest aspirations, now he felt only uneasiness about them.

"Look what I'm doing, I'm losing my objectivity," he coached himself. "I must keep a cool head about everything."

He drew the curtains closed, dimmed the lights and returned to his chair. After only a few minutes of sitting quietly, he drifted into an uncomfortable sleep. Outside the gentle rain became a thunderstorm.

Several hours later Jim awoke to the sound of a thunderclap which rattled the windows of Nigel's room. At first he did not realize where he had been sleeping. Both sore and uncomfortable from a chair too rigid for his back, he rose to his feet in a mighty lunge forward. He rubbed his eyes and forehead with a desperate precision. The room, a treasury opened before him with awesome mysteries, seemed as a carnival house of mirrors. Jim had diligently searched the room for its secrets, but instead he saw only his own reflection.

The air seemed heavy and oppressive and Jim decided to leave the room for a few moments, only to catch his breath. But as soon as he had entered the corridor, he was on his way away from Nigel's room. His steps were uncertain at first, but he regained a regular gait as he approached the elevators. Without a thought of its consequence, he was inside the elevator and on his way to the lobby five floors beneath him. When the doors opened, he knew they would give him his freedom.

When the doors opened, he discovered an empty lobby. Not a soul remained where total chaos had been. He noticed the vinyl furniture which had earlier been hidden by a mob. The room seemed sterile with its red plastic couches, its plexiglass tables with magazines strewn randomly atop them, and the plants in fake porcelain planters. Outside, the wind roared in the canvas sidewalk covers which encircled the ground floor, and pushed against the glass making a rasping sound as though the building gasped for air. He was drawn to the windows with a childlike fascination. He stared into the darkness with the same awe at nature's violence that he had experienced as a boy.

"I must go back," he finally resolved and he returned through the doors back into the lobby.

His journey back to Nigel's room was more purposeful than his departure. With a firm conviction to endure whatever ordeal would befall him, he pressed the button, and he waited quietly while the car moved up its five floors. His heart was calm for the first time that day.

When the doors opened and he had begun his walk back down the corridor, he had not gone but few steps before the young nurse rushed into his path and blocked his way. On her face he saw despair.

"No, Mr. Jacobson. Don't go back."

"What's happened?"

"Nigel has died."

"What?" The news hit him with the force of a hurricane. "He was fine when I left him."

"We found him out of bed. He apparently got up, and on his way back he hemorrhaged."

"Dead?"

"We haven't had a chance to move him yet. Please go."

"Let me see him," he said as he tried to push her aside. But she began to cry and blocked his way with what seemed like inhuman strength.

"It's not a pretty sight. Please go downstairs."

"Please let me see him."

"No, Dr. Namath is looking for you downstairs."

She pulled him back into the elevator and the doors closed behind him.

"No, No, No," Jim shouted as the sealed box dropped floor by floor to the lobby. His heart beat with such intensity he could hear it in the silent box. He began to sweat profusely and his hands began to tremble. When the doors of the elevator opened on the lobby, he had been overcome with sorrow, and tears flowed as a torrent down each cheek.

"I've got to get a hold of myself," he kept reciting as a mantra.

When the doors opened, he saw that Dr. Namath and Julie were standing in the lobby. They were talking seriously and did not notice him at first. When they discovered him, both were silent a few moments, then Julie finally spoke, "Jim, where have you been? I came down here to talk to you before you hurt him. But it appears I am too late."

"I didn't hurt him."

"You left him."

"He was asleep."

"Dr. Namath says if he had stayed in bed, Nigel might still be alive."

"It's not your fault, young man," Dr. Namath finally spoke. "She asked why he died. I made a conjecture."

"Do you know why he got out of bed?" Jim asked.

"Apparently to write you a note. We found a pen in his hand."

"Did you find the note?"

Dr. Namath dug around the pocket of his jacket and found a small piece of white note paper. On it was a phrase written in Greek letters.

"I don't read Greek, doctor. Why would he write to me in Greek?"

Jim took the note from the doctor's hand and put it into the pocket of his jeans. His face was pale and his eyes were dark from too little sleep.

"What does it mean, Jim?" Julie asked him.

"How in the hell do I know?" He paused. "What time is it, doctor?"

"Six o'clock."

"Is there anything else I can do?"

"No, not really."

"Well, then I'm going home."

"Home, Jim?" Julie asked him. "Are you sure?"

"I've had roughly two hours sleep. I feel like hell."

Chapter 3

The news of Nigel's death flowed quickly through a web of capillaries which carried the information from Bangor to Seattle as quickly as the microwave and as dependably as the electron could transport it there. The early morning papers and the breakfast news programs began to condense the bad news into two minute blurbs in the same prepackaged portions as the breakfast cereals people ate. His critics believed that after he was gone his followers would most certainly forget him like yesterday's newspapers. Yet despite the pervasive cynicism of the age, there persisted in many of them a longing for spirituality that could not so easily be tossed away.

A paperboy tossed a newspaper on the doorstep of Jim's apartment. It landed awkwardly against the door and waited for Jim to find it. Inside, in the midst of Armageddon, he slept, still clothed in the jeans he had put on the morning before. He had collapsed in bed shortly after entering the apartment, and his phone lay unplugged on the floor with his shirt tossed on top of it. The whole morning had passed and nothing could have wakened him from his stupor, until afternoon when he turned over on his back.

At one o'clock, a loud knock finally startled him from his sleep, and he staggered as though sedated to the front door.

"Who is it? What do you want?" he shouted through the door.

"It's me, Jim. Open up!" Burgess shouted through the door. With unresponsive fingers he struggled with the lock, until he finally opened the door.

"You look terrible," were Burgess' first words.

"I feel terrible."

"You're in a hell of a lot of trouble. Reynolds wants that story from you. He had me scribble down a few words for today's cover story."

"I feel sick."

"Reynolds has been calling you all morning. I made up some story to cover for you."

"You and your stories. That's what's gotten me into this mess in the first place." He paused. "Come inside."

Burgess seemed reluctant to accept his invitation, but entered anyway.

"I've been asleep, Burg. What time is it now?"

"One twenty."

"God, I've been asleep all morning."

Jim cleared a space on the couch for him.

"Sit down, while I get something to drink."

Burgess reluctantly sat down, while Jim struggled to find a coffee pot.

"How long has it been like this?"

"The apartment? Six, no seven weeks."

"How can you live like this?"

"I don't live. I exist."

Burgess picked up a stack of papers from the floor to make room for his feet, and a key fell from between the papers and into his lap. He was about to put it back into the papers when he called to Jim in the kitchen.

"I found a key here. Where does it go?"

"It's probably the key to my chest. Just stick it in the lock for me."

Burgess got up from the couch and scaled the debris until he reached the chest in the corner of the room. After placing the key into the lock, he watched the chest lid pop open to reveal some of its contents.

"What's in the chest, Jim?"

"Just some personal things," he said as he walked back into the living room. "You wouldn't believe what happened to me last night. It was the weirdest night I've ever had. Aside from Nigel dying, which was a real shocker. It was like he was prepared for me. He had come to this town just to talk to me."

Burgess' curiosity had overcome him and he was searching through the chest to uncover its contents.

"Hey, what are you doing in my chest?"

Burgess pulled the small locket from the chest and dangled it in front of his face.

"What's this? It looks like some religious artifact."

With his free hand, Burgess pulled a notebook of poetry from inside the chest, rifled through a few pages and then balanced it on the edge of the chest. Jim rushed quickly across the room and snatched the locket from his friend's hands. He pushed Burgess away and Burgess returned to his place on the sofa. Then with the stealth of a burglar, he returned everything to its place and locked the lid of the chest. He stuck the key in his pocket.

"I'm not one of your stories. So leave my things alone."

"I never would have figured you for poetry. Why you're a soft touch."

"Burgess, what do you want?"

"Come on, Jim. Don't get upset with me. I got Reynolds to wait till six o'clock. I came to give the message. Now I can leave."

"Don't you want to hear what happened?"

"Not especially. I'll wait to read your story when it comes out."

Burgess scanned the room once again in disbelief.

"I see you still haven't joined the computer age. You're still writing your stories on that old electric typewriter."

Burgess dusted off his pants and almost as abruptly as he had arrived, he was gone. Jim was a little disappointed that he had not been able to share his confusion with his friend. But Burgess was often brusque with him, and he had learned to tolerate his lack of courtesy.

After a brisk shower, Jim had pulled a typewriter from his closet and had cleared a place on the table to work. The pizza which had been sitting for three days on the corner of the table, he tossed into an overfilled trash can in the kitchen, and he picked several of his soiled shirts and tossed them into a laundry hamper. This was his first effort at cleanliness in over a week.

He sighed as he returned to the table to write. 'What do I write?' was the recurring theme of his thoughts. But after several aborted attempts to put pregnant words to paper only ended in frustrated thrusts of the paper from the platen, he became so frustrated with himself that he almost tossed the typewriter in the trash. He took the folded note which Nigel had written him, and laid it beside the typewriter. But this gave him little satisfaction, because he had not the faintest suspicion what the Greek letters actually meant, and he could not understand what purpose it served to write a note to him in a language he did not understand. Certainly, if Nigel knew as much about him as he claimed to know, Nigel must certainly know he did not know Greek. The thought occurred to him that he was being toyed with, but why would a man risk his life to toy with him? All these questions and others made it impossible for him to do what he knew as a journalist he must do—to find a perspective, a framework in which to place the events of the past twenty-four hours. He lacked a clear foundation to say anything coherent and his inability to concentrate finally forced him from the table to his feet, where he stood and watched in a nervous shuffle. Then he remembered the words of one of his professors, 'If in doubt, imitate.' So, he decided to leave the apartment for a while to find another newspaper and see what they were saying.

When he opened the door to leave the apartment, he discovered the newspaper which had been tossed there earlier. But sitting beside it he found a small package wrapped in brown paper, measuring six inches by five inches by ten inches. His name was printed in bold letters across the top. He immediately took the package inside.

At first, he hesitated in opening it. He thought of package bombs and Ted Kaczynski. But he finally tore off the paper and lifted the lid of the box to reveal its secrets. Inside, he found fifteen cassette tapes, numbered one through fifteen, and a short note which simply said, "I hope this answers any questions you may have about me."

He chuckled a moment when he realized what he held in his hands. Inside the box, he also found a small cassette player with stereo headphones. He opened the first cassette placed it in the player, and turned it on. He listened.

"It's a difficult thing to sit down at a table and talk into a machine about my life," Nigel's voice began. "But I know my time is short, and I probably won't have the time to tell you everything I wanted to. But I will try as honestly as is possible to tell you about myself. I hope you will be patient with the rambling of an old man and will forgive me any lapses of memory that time may have created. I will try to tell as much as I can remember and may God forgive me if I remember it wrong."

Chapter 4

I was born on October 18, 1918 in the house my grandfather built on a dairy farm in Wisconsin. I remember it as a red brick house with cedar floors and a thatch roof. There was a white picket fence which I had helped my grandfather paint as a boy of five and there were always flowers in a line of beds which every spring my mother planted around the house. It wasn't a big house. It had no indoor bathrooms. But it was where my earliest memories of childhood were minted. I used to try to hurdle the fence as a young boy, and I remember how proud I became when I was finally able to clear its planks at eight years old.

As childhoods go, mine was a pleasant one, filled with the incessant tasks of milking and feeding, of shoveling manure and hay. But I never liked the farm. I hated milking cows early in the morning, and I despised the smell of animals.

My father was a simple man, uneducated, yet wise in the ways of life. There was nothing he didn't seem to know about cows and corn and when to plant and when to reap, and if I had let him he would have imparted to me all that he had learned. But I was too much like my mother who lived in faraway places, wherever the illusions of books would take her. She had named me Nigel and my brother Reginald because she was captivated by Victorian novels, and I had often thought that she longed to live in the English countryside rather than where the fates had put her.

"Nigel," she used to tell me as I sat in the kitchen while she snapped green beans. "Don't be afraid to see the world, if the opportunity comes your way."

My father thought her a silly woman, but loved her as much as anyone I've known. Her name was Martha. I guess I've forgotten to tell you, my Father's name was John.

Jim turned off the player and put the earphones on the table. He went into his bedroom and searched through his drawers until he could find a notebook in which to write. He returned to the table and wrote on the first page their names, John Fox, Martha Fox and Reginald Fox. Then he put the headphones back on and continued to listen to the tape.

Some say that as you grow older, the memory necessarily recedes and whole decades can disappear as if stolen by amnesia, but I still have clear memories of childhood and my recollection of the later years is as lucid as yesterday. I remember the McIlhenry farm, a mile or so down the road from us, where Dennis Allerby and I used to play. Mr. McIlhenry had signs posted all over his barn and stable saying, "No Children Allowed." But Dennis and I never heeded them. One day he caught us both inside his stable trying to steal rides on two of his ponies, and he chased us home, shooting his shotgun in the air.

"Get out of my stinkin' stable," I can almost hear him shouting. "Can't you see my stinkin' signs." Both of us, we couldn't have been more than twelve, ran frantically across his wheat field and through his vegetable garden, trampling a row of cabbages along the way, while he ran behind us. He was cursing, reloading and shooting in the air. He must have wasted ten cartridges before we escaped across the creek.

"What do you think?" Dennis asked me as we both collapsed under a sycamore tree. Struggling to catch my breath, I responded, "I think we're crazy. We should leave his farm alone." But the unrelenting boredom of the moment seemed to encourage more such mischief. Sometimes, I'm surprised I survived my childhood at all.

When I was twenty years old, the year was 1938, I was engaged to be married to a girl named Florence Scrapper. She was blond with fiery hazel eyes and she inspired in me more passion than emotion. Her father, William Scrapper, had been a boyhood friend of my father and they had hoped in our marriage a kind of business merger. Her father grew feed-corn and my father bought feed-corn for the cows. I'd like to say that I loved her. But at twenty years old I knew little about what love entailed, about sacrifices and suffering, about joy in the midst of sorrow. What I loved was that she knew how to kiss! And kissed we did, in barns, under bridges, in the back of the movie theater in town, wherever we could escape for a few minutes without chaperones.

Had it not been for unpredictable circumstances, I probably would have married her and when the luster of lust had faded with age I would have regretted every minute of it. But that October when it was bitterly cold, I caught rheumatic fever and everyone thought I was going to die. My father who had depended on me for so much up to then, found himself without a helper. So he turned to my brother, Reginald, five years my younger, but stronger and more disposed to farming than myself. During the course of the few months from October to March, when I spent most of my time in bed, their relationship grew deeper, and I think my father began to realize that in his younger son he could find a more compatible partner than in me, because Reginald always loved the farm. When I finally regained my strength that following spring, I discovered that my younger brother, like Jacob, had usurped my place as heir to the family title. From that time on it would be he who would receive the blessings of my father's wisdom.

My mother and I had always been close, but we grew much closer then. Though the memories of much of that time have been blurred by time and the weakness that I felt, I remember how she read to me book after book about faraway and enchanting lands, all the places she had wished to see, but my father found ridiculous. Those places excited me far more than cows and corn, and when I recovered I realized my passion for Florence had also subsided.

It was in late March of that year that my father, thinking I would lose all interest in the farm, brought home a calf, a young milk cow and said to me, "I have hopes of entering her in the livestock show in September. I want you to raise her. I raised my first cow when I was fifteen. Way I figure you're five years overdue."

I could not argue with him at the time. So, whether I wanted to raise the cow or not, I raised her. I fed her and cleaned her and affectionately named her Milly after this great-aunt I couldn't stand.

Of that whole period of my life, one conversation I had stands out in my mind. It didn't concern the farm or my mother's books, and at the time I wouldn't have thought it important enough to write down, but later I remembered it.

I was sitting on the front porch, as was my habit in the evening. I looked across the corn fields, which my cousins had planted a half a mile away. It was close to dusk, and the sunlight painted streaks of amber across the field, and ears were ripe, ready to be plucked. My mother came up beside me, placed her hand on my shoulder and said,

"What are you looking at?"

"The corn. It's amazing how much can grow from such a little seed. Maybe it's not so bad after all to stay on the farm?"

"I had a dream about you, Nigel."

"Another dream."

My mother had an intense preoccupation with her dreams, unlike anyone else I've ever known.

"You were standing just as you're standing now, looking across a field of corn which seemed to stretch for miles in front of you. And the ears were larger than any I have seen. Then before our eyes the field of corn became a field of human faces, as numerous as the corn we see. But there was something terribly wrong and I couldn't help you."

"Why do you worry about these dreams? There aren't that many people in the entire county. If I took seriously every dream I have, I'd always be upset."

"Don't tell your father. He'll think I'm silly."

"You've been on the farm too long, mom. Maybe you should get him to take you to the city this week and see a picture show."

"You know your father doesn't like the city."

"Yeah, too many people. I've heard it all before. Let me take you there. We can go to Woolworth's and have an ice cream cone."

"And have your father miss his supper? I'd rather not."

"It won't hurt him to miss a meal."

"In twenty-five years of marriage, he's never missed a meal."

"You're not his slave. This is the twentieth century."

"No, but he needs me. He expects me, like the sunshine in the morning, the spring harvest. I've always been there for him."

"Someday, I'd like to take you away from here and let you see some of those places you're always reading about."

"Not as long as your father is alive, and I don't think I could survive without him."

I could hear my father calling, "Martha," from inside the house.

"That's sweet," she said and she kissed me on the cheek.

"Your father's calling me. Who knows? Maybe you'll get to see the world. There's nothing to say you can't leave the farm someday."

But I thought my mother was wrong. If I would even mention the idea of leaving the farm, my father would go into a rage and scream at me, "You can't leave the farm. I need both my boys to help with harvest. I can't afford to pay for outside help."

And he couldn't. It had been hard enough to save the farm from foreclosure during the most difficult years of the depression. From March through August of 1939, I kept myself busy, along with my other chores, raising Milly and reading in the evenings. Occasionally, I took my mother to the picture show. I had taken to reading Jules Verne novels and Jack London. I remember reading a Charles Dickens book, but I do not remember which one.

By September, the leaves had begun to turn and the time of the fair drew closer. Milly had begun to demand almost all of my free time. But she had grown to be a beautiful animal and I understood why my father believed she might win a prize at the show.

When the day for the fair finally arrived, after what seemed like years of preparation, the county park was like a carnival, with tents and pavilions, and foods of every description scattered between the trees. My mother had baked two chocolate cakes and an apple pie for the baking contests. She asked Reginald to carry a quilt she had made of swatches from my father's old shirts, and I dragged Milly, with a leather harness into a pen in the livestock pavilion. Soon Reginald was busy cooking sausage on an outside grill, my mother was sitting at a quilting party and my father was sitting with other men, discussing their crops, playing cards and drinking beer. Nothing about it seemed to interest me. So I spent most of my time with Milly.

My mother came into the pavilion that afternoon and saw me washing Milly with a brush.

"Nigel, why aren't you with other people?"

"I'm not interested in tractors and plows."

"But there are plenty of young women here. Mary Parker has been asking about you."

Mary Parker was the preacher's daughter. Petite and attractive, I might have had an interest in her had she not had the annoying habit of using thee's and thou's when she spoke and quoting bible verses as freely as others cursed.

"You know Mary makes me uncomfortable."

"But she likes you, Nigel."

"I think she wants to save my soul."

My mother smiled, because I think she knew I had no interest in the religious life.

"I think you should talk to her."

Shortly after that Mary also found me in the tent.

"Why don't you come and join us, Nigel? They're starting a tug-of-war in about ten minutes."

"My life is already a tug-of-war."

She smiled at my half-baked attempt at humor. She was wearing a gray dress which was tightly cut and followed every curve of her well-proportioned frame. It seemed a little provocative for a preacher's daughter.

"God bless, Nigel. Don't be so persnickety."

"OK, I'll go."

I dropped the brush and followed her out of the tent. That afternoon I was in a tug-of-war, a three-legged race, a cake walk, and a horseshoe tournament. We had a lot of fun. And at the end of the day, we sat beneath a tall fir tree overlooking the lake, and we ate a cherry pie.

I could see she wanted to be kissed, but I couldn't kiss her, because I remembered how Florence and I had begun, also with a kiss. One kiss would lead to others, and as naturally as the corn grows, I'd find myself engaged, then married. All my hopes and dreams of seeing the world would wither as the corn withers after the harvest, and at fifty I would be like my father, talking about plows and fighting my son because of his dreams as though I had never dreamed at all.

"We should go back," I said. "The judges are picking the best livestock."

"You'd rather be with Milly than with me?"

"Of course not. But they'll begin to talk about us."

"Then let them talk. Old busy-bodies."

"You can't mean that. You know what vicious tongues they have."

"It's not that easy being a preacher's child," her voice became more serious. "My father expects so much of me."

"Have you ever thought of leaving here?"

"I couldn't. My family's here."

"I've often thought of going away. If I had the money, I think I'd go to New York, and there I'd find my fame and fortune."

"New York. It's so far away."

"It's not so far, not like Paris or London or Calcutta."

"You always dream about such exotic places."

"Why just dream? Why not go?"

"How would you do it?"

"I'd just get on a train and go."

"And where would you stay when you get there?"

"You ask so many questions. Mary. Where did Lewis and Clark stay? Columbus? Or Juan Cortez? They didn't ask such questions. They just went."

"It was dangerous."

"They found a whole new world."

Then my mother came and called us back. Milly had won first prize. FIVE HUNDRED DOLLARS. I had never seen so much money in all my life. It was my ticket out, and I was determined even if it meant fighting my father, I would use that money to leave the farm.

I cannot describe the sense of euphoria I felt at the end of the day. It was the closest I had come to happiness in what seemed like ages. My father seemed even more euphoric than myself, because he had been hoping to buy a new tractor, and this windfall made possible the realization of his desires.

When they awarded the prize, he stood beside me. I knew that he presumed I would give him my winnings and he would buy the tractor. After all, he had paid for the animal in the first place.

I really don't think the thought crossed his mind that my mother wanted otherwise, and I don't think I realized then the depth of her desire for me to make a name for myself in the world. Years later, she told me it was she who had encouraged my father to give me Milly in the first place.

That evening my mother invited Mary to supper with us, and it was during the course of dinner conversation that the issue of the money finally came up.

"I don't want to tell you what to do with the money, Nigel," my father began. *"But we could certainly use a new tractor."*

"How much did you pay for Milly and her feed?" I asked him.

"About seventy dollars, more or less. Why?"

"After I repay you the expenses, I'd like to use the money for something else."

"Like what, Nigel?"

"I'd like to go to New York."

"No, absolutely not." He turned to my mother and said, *"Martha, I*

*know you like to encourage these kinds of fantasies, but the time has
come for him to learn responsibility. Someday, he'll have to take over
the farm."*

Normally that would have been the end of it. My mother almost
never said anything to counter him. But she said something at the time
that I didn't understand.

"Remember the circus, John."

Mary and I looked at each other. We were confused, because we
could not remember a circus. I presumed it must have been before we
were born or when I was too young to remember.

Then as firmly as he had been before, he said, "Alright, he can do
with the money what he wants."

I did not understand till many years later what the full import of
that remark entailed, and why at the mere mention of a circus, he made
a complete about face on his position. But I realized something about
their relationship. It was far more complex than I ever imagined. After
he said this, he reached over and squeezed her hand, as if to thank her
for not going deeper into the issue. Then he did something which was
unlike himself.

"Martha, let's go into the city tomorrow."

She smiled and said, "Sure."

It would be nearly ten years after his death that my mother finally
explained to me what was going on at the time. Then I would feel so
foolish for being too quick to judge, when I knew neither the complete
circumstances nor true motivations behind his actions.

I remember the day as I left the farm as vividly as yesterday. It was
October 10th and a light rain had been falling all morning. My mother
took me into town and waited at the station with me. My father would
not come and I did not argue with him for fear of having him change
his mind about my leaving. Mary Parker met us there and we sat and
talked for what seemed like hours, about trains, and farms, and all the
people we had known.

My mother had insisted I buy a round trip ticket, so that if things
went badly for me, I'd have a way home. I had the ticket in the back
pocket of my trousers. Then the train came and with a hug and a kiss
from both of them I was on my way.

"Don't forget, no matter what happens, you're special, Nigel," my
mother said as the train pulled away. I felt like I had lost my childhood

and fought back tears. In a strange way, it felt like death.

There was silence for a few moments longer and then the tape clicked off. Jim took the headphones off his head and laid them on the table. He had filled several pages with assorted phrases, but still nothing tied them together with any degree of clarity. They were like musical notes without a staff to give them harmony. He remembered having seen the photographs and the ticket stub, but everything else seemed in a fog. "I wish I had taken more time," he thought. Then he wrote "New York" in huge letters across the page. The clock on the wall chimed four o'clock and he was no closer to a story than when he began. He flipped the tape over and placed it back into in the player. Then he returned the head phones to his ears so he might listen to the second side.

Chapter 5

I sat on the train, concentrating on the hum and the click as the cars rolled on the rails. I can't remember what town we were in, but about two hours into the trip, as I was sitting near a window and watching trees blend into a brown blur as we passed beside them, the oddest feeling took hold of me. I had forever altered my destiny with what seemed to me an act of pure impulse, yet ironically, there was something uncomfortably familiar about what I was doing. It was not the first time I had experienced this feeling and it would not be the last. But just as there seemed a certain logical progression as we moved from city to city, the rails seemed more than just a way of passage for the train. Just as the wheels were held firmly in place by the rigid steel of the rails, there seemed a certain inevitability about the path I had chosen, almost like the rails, which patiently guided the train to its destination. I was never one to believe in déjà vu, and if you had asked me at the time to describe what I felt, I probably wouldn't have had the words to describe it. But I looked out the windows with a childlike preoccupation at the way objects would approach and recede as the train moved passed them, and I told myself I was afraid.

People would come and go. Their faces all seemed familiar to me. This one looked like my Uncle Mike. That one like my Aunt Jane. So many faces with so many shapes, yet all possessing a common humanity. I thought a lot about what I would find when I arrived. Yet, every image of New York I could visualize seemed in a fog, as though I struggled to see through a dark curtain held in front of my eyes.

There were a number of people who came into the seats beside me and who left when they reached their points of destination. With some, I tried to make idle conversation. With others, I was silent, afraid to say a word. We would sit for hours beside each other without so much as a hello. One elderly woman talked to me about her grandchildren, and showed me their pictures, and there was a bible salesman on his way to Cleveland who gave me a small pocket bible. Finally in Cleveland another young man boarded the train and sat beside me. He was also on his way to New York.

He was taller than I was and his hands were smoother than mine, which had calluses and scars on them from all those years of farm work. I noticed them because he sat there looking at them for what seemed like hours.

"What's your name?" I finally asked him. "Mine is Nigel Fox."

"I'm Leonard Matthews."

He didn't seem to want to talk to me.

"Well, where are you going?" I asked him.

"New York. I have a job there with my uncle."

"Doing what?"

"I don't know."

"I'm not trying to pry. I'm just bored to death. I've been sitting here for hours."

"I'm never bored. Have you ever noticed how the hands work?" He bent his thumbs across the palms of his hands. "The opposing thumb. Because I can do this, I can hold a hammer. I can turn a screwdriver. Things are possible for me that are impossible for the other animals. What an amazing feat of engineering in a simple pair of hands."

I thought he was a little strange.

"Is that what you've been thinking about all these hours?" I asked him. "Some anthropologists argue that because we can do this, (He folded them again.) We developed technology."

"Technology. I've never heard that word. Is it new?"

"I guess it is."

"What does it mean?"

"It's the ability to take an idea here, (he pointed to his temples) and realize it in a concrete form. Like for example this railroad train. Someone had to think about it before it came to exist."

For some reason that phrase led to others and soon I could hardly keep him quiet. He told me all kinds of things, about physics and anthropology, most of which I didn't understand, and then he talked about his family.

"My dad works for the telephone company in Cleveland," he told me. "He repairs telephone wires."

He reached into a satchel over his head and pulled out a book. "The Principles of Electricity," *I read the title.*

"I've been reading this book. My plan is to get settled in New York and then to begin learning all I can about electricity. I'm hoping to get a job with the telephone company. My mother was a little frightened for me. But I think it's a good plan. I learn quickly. I should be able to pick it up in no time. What about you, Nigel? What are your plans?"

"My mother has a cousin she hasn't seen in years. I'm supposed to get in touch with her as soon as I'm in New York."

"My uncle has this job for me. Maybe if you can't find anything else, he can help you." He copied down an address for me. "It's in Brooklyn."

We talked for a little longer and then he began to read his book. We had so little in common and our lives seemed to be moving in such different directions. When we parted company after a few minutes of conversation on the platform at Penn Station, I was convinced I'd seen the last of him. I had no idea at the time that this young man would later become my closest friend.

To describe New York to someone who has never seen it is a little like trying to describe colors to a man born blind. It would be easy to say that it was not what I expected. But I had no expectations concerning it, save one: it would not be like the farm and this expectation was quickly confirmed. When I emerged from the bowels of Penn station, New York and Wisconsin seemed like two different worlds, and I felt like Marco Polo, seeing the orient for the first time.

Towering over the city was the Empire State Building and I stretched my neck to see its spire. I remembered having gone with my mother into Green Bay to see King Kong *when it had played there six years before. I could almost picture that huge ape, standing on its top and swatting airplanes with his hands.*

I reached into my pocket and retrieved the paper on which my mother had hastily scribbled her cousin's address. A cold and brisk breeze blew through my body. I struggled to read it, while the wind threatened to tear it from my fingers. Once I was sure of its content, I began what would become a day of erratic wandering. By mid-afternoon I was seriously thinking about getting back on the train and going back to Wisconsin. It seemed hopeless that I would ever find the address. I kept forgetting if the avenues were numbered east to west, or west to east, and everyone who I stopped to asked directions seemed as confused as me. Later, I would realize that there were many people in the City who never ventured beyond the narrow limits of their neighborhoods. In those few blocks they called home, they were born, they worked, they married, and they died. Invisibly circumscribed by pavement and concrete, each region held captive its own atmosphere and culture. In that respect, the only difference between New York and Wisconsin was that we had more room.

The wind had become more violent as I stood on the corner of Fifth Avenue and Eighth Street. I had been all over the East Side looking for the address. This was the edge of the Village, as it was called, and it had become a kind of artists' colony, a haven for the "avant-garde." I learned that word from a street vender from whom I asked directions.

There were outdoor markets and fruit vendors and newsstands. Newspaper boys were selling copies of the Post on street corners. They shouted vigorously about the headline of the moment. There were butchers and tailors and delicatessens. All stretched out along a block of row houses four stories tall.

The woman I was looking for, my mother's cousin, was Melissa Wilson Brubaker, Wilson having been my mother's maiden name. My mother had talked about her often. She had married a painter and they moved to New York to find fame and fortune. She said the most recent word she had heard from her cousin was that her husband had died and that she longed to see someone from home. My mother had written her a letter telling her I was coming. But neither of us knew what to expect, nor even if she was still willing to see someone. Yet in a city as large as the City, one relative, even a distant one, seemed better than no relative at all. By my own calculation Mrs. Brubaker was approaching fifty, which at the time seemed ancient to me, although my mother never actually told me her age.

I knocked on the door of the second floor walk-up and an older woman nearly sixty opened the door a crack and said, "Whatever you're selling, I ain't buying."

"I've come to see Melissa Brubaker."

"Mel ain't here."

"When do you expect her back?"

"Look, buster, she ain't here!"

She slammed the door in my face, but I was determined, so I knocked again. She opened the door again.

"If you don't scram, I'll call a copper."

"*I'm Melissa's cousin from Wisconsin. I've come a long way to see her.*"

"*Mel's never mentioned any family in Wisconsin.*"

"*I've got her letter somewhere in my bag.*"

I searched through the bag and found the envelope and held it up for her to see."

"*Mel's at work. Come back later.*"

"*Where does she work?*"

"*What do you think I am, an information bureau?*"

"*I'd appreciate it if you'd tell me.*"

"*You'd appreciate it if I'd tell you. How genteel! She works at a place called 'Frankie's' four blocks west of here on the left.*"

I had problems with east and west as I mentioned before, but soon I found myself in front of Frankie's. It was a dinner club and I could hear music from the street. I had never been inside a dinner club. They had no such things in the county where I grew up. Like so much of what was to follow, it both frightened and excited me.

Inside, I discovered a small stage and rows of small round tables. A young woman heavily made-up and wearing a dress which was cut so low I wondered how she kept it from falling off, was singing a song which sounded very much like talking. I found a seat near the rear of the club, and I sat down at the table.

A young woman dressed in a black evening dress approached the table. She was without expression, looking much like the mannequins I had seen in Macy's windows. She laid a fork and napkin in front of me and without changing her expression ever so little, she asked me, "What's your pleasure?"

"*I'd like to talk to Mel (I struggled to keep from saying 'Melissa.') Brubaker.*"

"*You're not going to order anything?*"

Her face became agitated.

"*Do you have soup?*"

"*Yeah, we have soup. What Kind?* "

"*Chicken, if you don't mind.*"

She turned around and left the table. Soon another young woman about thirty-six or thirty-seven, with short chestnut hair pinned back behind her ears, approached the table. I pondered if my order had so agitated the previous waitress that she decided to send another. Then she spoke.

"Yeah, I'm Mel, What do you want?"

"You're Mel? I had expected someone much older."

"Who are you?"

"I'm your cousin, Nigel, from Wisconsin. Didn't you get my mother's letter?"

"Yeah, I got it. But I don't know what I can do. I got no room and my land-lady don't take too kindly to guests, especially men."

She had a rough edge to her voice, much harsher than I expected.

"So you can't put me up for even a few days."

"I can't put me up for a few days. I'm two weeks behind on my rent as it is." She paused. "Come on. Order something. It costs to eat and sleep in New York like everywhere else."

"I ordered some chicken soup."

"Order something else. The manager's watching me."

She turned and looked at an older man sitting at the bar.

"Alright, what do you recommend?"

"The fish is the only thing edible."

"OK, I'll have the fish."

She seemed a little uneasy about how long this was taking and she told me, "Look, I'm off at nine. We can talk then."

When she left me sitting at the table, I listened for a while to the singer who sang one sardonic song after another. At the time I could not recognize the style of music. Experience later enriched my musical vocabulary and I recognized the way that the rhythm and the harmonies blended together with a chant-like melody to form what I would later call "the blues".

Her voice was ambiguous and tentative, and when she spoke her dialect was distinctly Midwestern. I sipped my soup, nibbled on the fish, which was heavily seasoned with garlic, and contemplated what dream had carried this young woman so far from home. Was it ambition? Was she motivated by the same desire for change as I was? Was she happy that she had made this choice? But these were questions without answers.

I pulled out the small pocket bible, which the salesman had forced upon me on the train. I was motivated not by a sincere interest in the scriptures, but boredom. I thumbed through the pages, read a little of Job and Jeremiah, but nothing interested me, and I put the bible back in my pocket. I remembered how animated the man was when he gave it to me. It was an odd problem I had always had. Religious zealots seemed peculiarly fascinated with me. I conjectured it was my face or some mannerism which attracted them. For whatever reason, I was continually confronted by those who wanted to save my soul.

Then a curious thing happened to me. This young man who had been sitting across the room came up beside the table and began talking to me as though he knew me. I did not know quite what to do. He finally looked closely at my face and realized his mistake. "I'm sorry," he apologized. "I thought you were someone else."

He excused himself and went away. This happened to me several times in that first few weeks. I still cannot explain it. Later, Mel came by and gave me my check. She chatted with me a few moments.

"You're crazy coming to this Godforsaken place. If I had the bucks, I'd be on my way home tomorrow."

"It can't be that bad."

"It's like Oz. I don't know why I let David talk me into this."

A hard edge masked the profound sadness in her voice.

"Look, you pay my two weeks back rent and you can sleep on the floor. But that's it. You've gotta spend your days someplace else."

"Thank you."

"And as soon as you can find your own place, you gotta leave."

"I understand."

After she left me to serve another table, I reflected on all that had happened that first day. I understood on a superficial level what she meant about Oz, but it would take a greater maturity for me to understand the deeper meaning of her statement. I had seen the film and thought it rather silly and contrived. But there was something mythic in its portrayal of that uniquely American impulse, to dream of a paradise where dreams do come true. I genuinely believed that we only need dream with tenacity and our dreams would come true. This same impulse inspired the Wright brothers to fly, Bell to invent the telephone, and my own people to endure tremendous and unceasing hardship to settle and build a life for themselves in Wisconsin. But at twenty-one, I did not understand any of this.

After finishing my meal, I walked around the neighborhood for an hour or so and tried to become familiar with all the landmarks. Then I decided I would write my mother a letter and tell her I had arrived.

As I walked south toward Washington Square, I was frightened and unsure of myself, though I never would have admitted it at the time. I sat down on a bench and there began to write. I wrote about the train, about Leonard Matthews, about the bible salesman and finally about Mel. My tone was hopeful yet cautious. I told her I was OK and that she need not worry about me. When I finished the letter and placed it in my bag, it was after dark. I sat anxiously on the edge of the bench and looked up at the cold night sky. The thought never entered my head that within a few weeks, I would come to regret my decision and in a fit of despondency think of ending my life.

Those first few weeks were difficult. At night, I slept on a rug on the floor, with a blanket wrapped around me, and my bag propped beneath my head as a pillow. In the morning I would wake early, sore and hungry, and I would begin an arduous day long search for work. I first read the newspapers to find advertisements for whatever unskilled-labor positions were available. Most had been filled by the time I called them, and the two or three remaining positions I would visit in the morning, ended always in disappointment. By midday, I was usually dog tired and hungry. Four weeks would pass, and my money was dwindling, and I still could not find work. To save money, I was only eating one meal a day, which usually consisted of fruit, raw vegetables, and white rice, which I bought for a quarter from a Chinese restaurant on Fourteenth Street. In four weeks, I had lost fifteen pounds. I was hungry all the time with a kind of hunger I had never known on the farm.

From the little I saw of Mel, I thought she was coping all right, but there were several times, I came home and found her crying, though she always pretended not to be. Once she sat up all night in a small wicker chair, staring at a photograph of her husband and sobbing almost inaudibly. I quietly watched her for most of the night, pondering what I might say to her to console her. But I had no capacity to understand the loss she was facing, nor the wisdom to know what to say.

One morning she asked me to find something for her in her closet. She seemed reluctant to go inside herself. I discovered she still had his clothes and shoes there, and all his paints and brushes just as he left them.

"Someone else could use these," I told her as I lifted up several

brushes in the air. "I saw people selling them in the market on Fourteenth Street." She rushed over and put them back just as I had found them.

"No, I couldn't," she responded. "I just couldn't."

Several of his paintings hung without frames on the walls, and there were a dozen or more others leaning on top of each other in every corner of the room. Though I had never possessed a critical eye or any aesthetical sensibility, the works seemed good to me. They were mostly landscapes and studies of various sights around the city. Then there were several nudes that he had painted of her, which she had tried to hide from my inspection. But the apartment was so small, I could not help but see them.

Mel was reluctant to say anything about her husband. Whenever I broached the topic, she would immediately change the subject. Though on one occasion when I was walking her home from Frankie's, she showed an unusual willingness to talk about him.

"You know, New York wasn't that bad for me when David was alive," she began. "It was his city. We used to go to the park and have picnics. He would draw portraits in the park. We laughed so much. How was I to know it could not last?"

"How did David die?"

"He was smacked by a bus on 42nd and Fifth Avenue. He never knew what hit him."

"It must have been hard to take."

"The hardest thing was having to identify him. Seeing his body laid out like that. I can't put the image out of my head. Hard? It stinks. He drags me up here and then he checks out."

I could sense the anger in her voice and I tried to say something positive. "I wish I could understand. But I've never lost anyone close to me."

She smiled.

"What are you gonna do with your life, Nigel? This isn't the circus."

"I'm not thinking that far ahead, I just want a job."

"Nigel, you're nuts. Go home to Wisconsin."

But I couldn't bring myself to accept that I had made a mistake, that the whole adventure had become a nightmare and that with each successive day my situation only worsened. Still, I was determined to

*make the best of it, to wait out what I believed was a short slump. I kept
telling myself that I could somehow make things better for both of us,
once I inevitably found a job. Then like a dam bursts or a volcano
erupts the whole arrangement with Mel came to an explosive end.*

*I didn't realize or understand what a volatile and dangerous
situation I had created when I allowed myself to stay with Mel. I simply
didn't understand the forces that were at work within her. Then one
morning, it was a Tuesday, I suddenly felt something on top of me and I
woke to Mel kissing me.*

*Had our ages been closer and had she not been my cousin, I might
have found the experience a pleasant one and even encouraged her to
continue. But I felt violated. Not only had she barred me from the
apartment, except in the dark cover of night, but she attacked me while
I slept.*

*I tried to stop her, but she kept kissing me with a ferocity I had
never experienced and she tried to unfasten my clothing. Finally, I
pushed her off of me and shouted, "Damn it! Stop it! Leave me alone!"*

*I grabbed my bag and ran out of the apartment. At the corner I
caught a bus and sat there in the back for what must have been several
hours. The bus made its consistent cycle around Manhattan, while my
mind jumped aimlessly from image to image and from memory to
memory. 'How could I have been so stupid?' I kept repeating to my
mind's ear. I was broke and I knew I could not go back to Mel's.
Nothing had worked out as I had planned. Mel's question kept
haunting me, "What am I going to do with my life?" I felt like a failure
and I seriously considered suicide.*

*Then I decided to get off at Central Park. My eyes were fighting
back tears as I stood on a corner overlooking the park, and then it
started to rain. At that moment if I could have clicked my heels together
like Dorothy and gone home, I would have gladly gone.*

*What a pathetic sight I must have been, this twenty-one-year old
farm boy, standing on the streets of Manhattan in the rain.
I would have laughed at myself had the situation not seemed so
hopeless. If I had been a religious man, I would have prayed, but I did
not believe any outside power could save me. I was convinced I was a
victim of my own decision and that there was an inherent logic to the
punishment. In every man's life there comes a time when he must face
the senselessness of fate. A man of character accepts his plight. But I*

was angry, deeply angry at myself and I could not accept what had happened to me. So I resolved to end it all by throwing myself off a building. After I crossed the street, I began to walk. I stared up at the tops of buildings as the water soaked my hair. With my eyes blurred with tears, I resolved that I would use my last dollar to ride to the top of the Empire State Building and throw myself off in one last gesture of defiance. Then I heard something drop from my pocket and hit the pavement. When I looked down, I discovered the little pocket bible lying on the ground. Before I could even bend my back, an arm reached down to pick it up for me. When my face met his, it was Leonard Matthews, who I had met on the train.

"Nigel, is that you?"

He stared into my ravaged face.

"Yes, it is."

"You're going to catch a cold out here. Where's your umbrella?"

"I haven't got one."

"Here. Take mine."

He handed me the handle.

"I've wondered why you haven't looked me up," he said. "I figured you must have lost my address. Look. Let's get out of this rain and find a place to talk."

There was a diner not far from there and we both went inside. A hostess led us both to a table where we sat down.

"You wouldn't believe what kind of job I've got. I work for my uncle at a small theater. It's like vaudeville. I operate the lights and curtains." He seemed excited to tell me what he did. "And what about you?"

"I haven't found a job," I said with desperation in my voice.

"Let me give you my address again. No, better yet. Let me take you there. I'm certain my uncle can find something for you to do." He paused. "It's strange meeting you like this. I wouldn't have even been this far, if I hadn't taken the wrong train."

I was stunned. I didn't know what to say.

"Would you like something to eat?" he continued.

I was afraid to admit how broke I was.

"No, I'm alright."

"Come on. Eat something. I'll pick up the tab."

We ordered something and a waiter brought it to us.

"Eat," he said and I ate. If you've never known hunger, you cannot know what it felt like to eat again. I had taken several glorious bites, and then I began to cry. I tried to wipe the tears which ran down my cheeks.

"God, you don't know what I've been through. Before you ran into me, I was this close to killing myself."

I held up my fingers.

"I told you to look me up. Why didn't you look me up?" Then I began to tell him all that had happened since I had arrived in New York, finally culminating in our meeting that afternoon. When I finished, he was silent and his silence frightened me. But then he began to tell me something which we hadn't talked about on the train.

"I didn't tell you why I left Cleveland," he began. "I didn't think you'd understand. (He bit his lip.) At home I stand in my brother's shadow. He's the brightest and most talented guy I know, the kind of guy who wins everything he tries, and I'm just his kid brother, who keeps running behind him like a little dog. I never quite measure up to his stature. Well, I'm sick of it, and come hell or high water, I will make a name for myself in New York. I've had a few setbacks too. But I'm not going to let them lick me. No way." He paused. "And you shouldn't let these setbacks upset you either." He paused again. "We live in exciting times, Nigel. In the next fifty years, a world as different from our world as ours is from the cave men, will be born. The possibilities are endless, and it will all be transformed by electricity. I went out to the World's Fair, and I saw a device which can transmit pictures through the air, just like radio. They call it 'television.'"

Then as he had done on the train, he began to explain to me in very technical language what he saw as the possibilities for such a device. In that one short conversation, he was more of a prophet, than I have been in these past months.

As we were talking, I had that same sense of inevitability that I had felt on the train. I have often thought about it, though I cannot prove it, that there are bonds between those of kindred spirit, which like one magnet is drawn to another, bring them together and that even if I had tried to avoid Leonard, I would have met him somewhere else.

Chapter 6

The first tape clicked off and Jim removed the headphones from his ears. He could hear a loud knocking on the door. Setting the headphones down on the table he got up and answered it.

"What's gotten into you, Jim? Are you asleep again?" asked Burgess, who was standing in the courtyard.

"No, I was occupied."

"I've been knocking on the door for fifteen minutes."

"What time is it?"

"Don't you know? It's seven thirty."

"Damn! I missed my deadline. Tell Reynolds. I'll get something down to him by nine o'clock. I just got to put some notes together."

"That's not why I came down here. Reynolds knows the story will be late."

"How does he know that?"

"If you'd just shut up and listen, I'll tell you."

"The paper received a letter this afternoon from Mr. Fox. Apparently, he wanted you to write his biography. He sent a ticket for you to go to New York tomorrow morning."

"And what did Reynolds say."

"He said 'go.'"

"Did the letter say why in the hell he wanted me?"

"I don't think so."

Jim ran his fingers through his hair in a nervous thrust. "I don't know about this. It's all a little too weird for me." He paused. "Look, come inside a second. I want to show you something."

Burgess followed him inside, and they both sat down at the table. Jim picked up the box of tapes and handed it to his friend.

"So what are they?"

"They're tapes."

"I can see that! Tapes about what?"

"About Nigel's life."

"You mean that old fart dictated his life story to you on tapes. Give me a break."

"Yeah. That's what he did."

"I suppose he's gonna brag about all those powers. I must warn you. There's a whole gaggle of those geese round the corner from here, waiting to snatch you as soon as you're out the door."

"The press is here?"

"Yeah. They all want to know if he made some deathbed confession or last-breath prediction. You know the tabloid stuff. I wouldn't let them know you got those tapes. You'll never hear the end of them."

"I guess not."

"I wonder who gave you that box? Now that's a story."

"I haven't the foggiest."

"Does this place have a back door?"

"Yeah."

"Then use it." He paused. "I hate to be a bearer of bad tidings. But I gotta go. And By the way, Reynolds wants to talk to you before you leave."

After Burgess rose from the table and left the room, Jim sat there quietly and stared at the note pad in front of him. 'I don't want to go to New York,' he thought aloud. Then he placed the cassette back in its case and back in its box. Then he decided to plug the phone back in and placed it on the table in front of him. He dialed a number and listened to it ring a few times. Finally, an older man answered the phone.

"Hello."

"Dad, it's Jim."

"What's wrong this time?"

"Do you have a few minutes to spare? I have a problem."

"I'm preparing my lecture notes for tomorrow, but I can spare a few minutes. I hope it's not a question about economics. I'm sick to death of any more questions."

"It's about Nigel."

He held back a chuckle.

"What do you have to do with that old medicine man?"

"You haven't read the papers?"

"You know I don't have time to keep up with all that nonsense."

"He apparently wanted me to write his story."

"You? How in the hell did he get your name?"

"I know it's a tremendous opportunity. It could be that big break I've always wanted. But I don't want to do it."

"I can't tell you how to live your life, but I couldn't do it."

"Normally I'd agree with you, but there's something gnawing at me about this and that's what I can't figure. I think maybe I should go. It's a free trip to New York after all."

"Sometimes you have to trust your instincts. I don't know, Jim. I don't have all the factors."

"Dad, thank you."

"Have you come to a decision then?"

"Yeah, I think I'm gonna go."

"Then, good luck."

"Yeah. I'll need it. Goodbye."

He hung up the phone and as soon as it touched the lever it began to ring. He looked at it while it rang a few times and then he finally picked it up.

"Hello."

"Jim, it's Julie. I'm sorry about the way I behaved at the hospital, but I need to talk to you. Can we go somewhere to talk?"

"I'd love to, Julie. But I have to pack and then go down to the paper."

"Where are you going?"

"I'm going to New York."

"Then you're going to the funeral?"

"I didn't say anything about that. I hate funerals."

"Nigel's funeral will be in New York on Wednesday. Maybe I'll see you there and afterwards we can go for a bite to eat."

"Sure, if I'm there."

"Well, I don't want to take up any more of your time. It was good to talk to you again. Goodbye."

She hung up the phone and then he unplugged his phone from the wall jack. He stared at the notes a few seconds longer and then he began to pack.

When Jim finally arrived at the paper to pick up his tickets and talk to Reynolds, it was nearly eleven o'clock. He walked into the office with a comfortable gait and placed a bag on his desk, which unlike his apartment was neat and well organized. Reynolds a man in his sixties, who looked more like an accountant than a newspaper man, noticed that he had finally arrived and gestured through a glass window for Jim to come into his office. After filling the bag with several tablets, pens, and a tape recorder, Jim closed the bag and entered the office.

"Take a seat, Jim."

He sat down.

"Quite an eventful twenty-four hours. Not your everyday news."

"Yeah. You could say that."

"I guess I won't beat around the bush. I know how you feel about all this Nigel stuff. But I have to ask you to do this, for the paper."

"Alright, I'll go."

"That was easier than I thought."

"I've already made up my mind, Jack. Hell, it's a free trip to New York, for God's sake."

"I want you to try to be as objective about this as possible. I don't want your obvious negative attitudes about this man to come across in your writing."

"I'll be fair. I promise."

"You have to be more than fair. I don't want you to offend all the religious subscribers, yet I don't want it to come across as the *National Enquirer* either."

"Did Mr. Fox say in his letter how he got my name? Why it is he wanted me to do this?"

"No, I don't think he mentioned it."

"Can I see the letter."

"Sure." Reynolds went to his desk and returned with the letter.

Taking it from Reynolds hand, Jim began to read.

```
Dear Mr. Reynolds,

     I'd like if possible to have a writer
of yours named James Jacobson to accompany
me back to New York upon my return from
Hadleyburg.  I have decided to put my own
story  down into words and I cannot think
of a more suitable candidate for the task
than Mr. Jacobson.  Enclosed I have
provided a round trip ticket and I have
arranged for a room at a hotel for him in
New York or should he so desire he can stay
in my own house upon his arrival.

Sincerely,
  Nigel Fox
```

"That's it, Jack."

"That's it."

"Doesn't give many clues, does it?"

"Not many."

"Well, I guess I better get some sleep. I'll need it."

"Jim, be careful who you trust."

Chapter 7

As Jim sat in his airplane seat, a flight attendant approached him.

"Can I get you anything to drink, sir?" she asked him.

"No, I'm fine."

He was reading one of the in-flight magazines which he stuck back into the seat flap in front of him. He picked up the tape player which was beside his leg, and again put on the earphones. Through the window, the ground below looked like a model railroad layout with tracks stretching out in both directions, and tiny buildings tossed across a green canvas. He picked up the tape labeled number two from a box atop his lap, put it in the player, and turned it on. "On my first tape I got as far as my lunch with Leonard," Nigel's voice began. "I can see this will take much longer than I anticipated."

After Leonard and I had finished lunch, he took me by train into Brooklyn to show me where he worked and lived. The building was long ago torn down and replaced by a cooperative, but I sometimes go there to remember what it was like.

It was a small theater, what once must have been a vaudeville house. Though not particularly attractive, it did have atmosphere. Leonard obviously loved the place and he gave me a grand tour.

"This is the light board," he said. "Here I control the spotlights, and house lights." He moved several levers which alternately turned on and off various lights around the theater.

"One day, we'll be able to do this with a box this small" He held his fingers together about three inches apart. "Of this, I'm convinced." He took me beneath the stage and demonstrated to me the trap doors, one by one opening and closing them. His face seemed animated by every movement of these mechanical devices. "I've been thinking about putting electric motors on them," he told me. "But I have to figure out how to muffle the noise." Then he took me upstairs and showed me the curtains and pulleys. I felt like I was on a museum tour as he explained to me every detail of the building. To be frank, I thought it looked like

a dump, but I didn't have the heart to tell him what I really thought. Even when he asked me bluntly, "Well, what do you think?" I answered with a cautious, "The place has character."

His uncle had gone on an errand that afternoon, so Leonard couldn't introduce me to him, but he did introduce me to Marty who managed the acts and to Glenice who handled the tickets and who kept the books. They both were friendly and I felt comfortable there for the first time in weeks.

"This is a revival house," Leonard explained to me. "On Thursday, Friday and Saturday nights, we have various acts, from magicians to tumblers, to singers and to comedians. But you just have to see The Great Bartholomew."

Even then I saw in Leonard that same sense of childlike wonder at life that would become the driving force behind so much of his later success. Leonard was like no one I have known since. He combined a childlike simplicity with a keen scientific mind, and he was also the best gin rummy player I've ever known.

Jim felt a tap on his shoulder and he turned his head to see who touched him. Sitting across the aisle was a man dressed in a long black robe, with a full beard and his hair long and tied in a pony tail behind his head.

"I'm sorry to bother you. But my prayer rope fell beneath your seat."

Jim reached down beneath his seat and found a knotted black rope, which he immediately gave to the passenger. The man began to chant rhythmically in a soft voice in a language he did not understand. Jim put the earphones back in his ears and continued to listen.

Later in the afternoon, Leonard's uncle returned. He was a tall man, about Leonard's size, sixty-five or sixty-six and balding. He wore eyeglasses which had slipped down on the bridge of his nose. When he walked in the door, Leonard approached him and I could see both of them talking in the doorway, but I couldn't hear what they were saying. Leonard seemed animated, his arms moving in marching rhythm as he spoke. His uncle stood passively with his arms folded in front of his chest. He kept nodding as Leonard spoke. Then both of them approached me.

"Leonard tells me you know about animals."

"Yeah, a little."

"I get a number of animal acts in here. I think I can use you."

"Thank you."

"I can't pay much. But twenty-five dollars a week is reasonable."

"I'll take it."

"Then you can start in the morning." He paused. We shook hands.

Leonard's uncle Bob never said very much and I often wondered what he really thought about things. He was a hard man to talk to, because he rarely revealed anything of himself. I had an uncle in Wisconsin just like him, my mother's brother Jack. Whereas, most people reveal their opinions on various subjects, I can't remember one issue where he took a position one way or the other. When others would argue fervently over which crop to plant or which fertilizer to use, he would smile and say something obvious like, "Isn't the weather warm this summer?" or "It's very hard to keep from getting wet in the rain." In that respect Leonard's uncle Bob reminded me of my uncle Jack.

During the course of the next few weeks, I learned a lot about the theater. Leonard explained to me about curtains, and sets, and lighting. We watched many of the acts, some good, some not so good. At night we'd drink a little wine and play cards, and Leonard would drill me on various aspects of electricity. Though I was not as quick as he, we both gained a basic understanding of watts and voltages, of resistance and capacitance. It was in one of these sessions that Leonard first told me about his dream.

"You know, Nige," for some reason he began to call me that. *"We should open a radio shop. We could sell radios and phonographs. We could buy old ones, repair them and sell them. I think we might make a pretty good living."*

"That would be great if we had the cash to pay for it."

"We won't be broke forever," he always told me. And like so much else of what he said, he was right. But I'll talk about that later.

My duties at the theater included watching after animals and cleaning up after them whenever an animal act played. I cleaned the floors after performances and sometimes I ushered, if there were no animals in the back. I had the opportunity to see many of the acts and like Leonard, I had grown particularly fond of The Great Bartholomew.

He was a stage magician and illusionist. He would perform various *standard magician tricks with cups and balls and rings and hats. He would close his act with a demonstration of his powers of psychic prediction. He called himself a "mentalist" and he performed some of the most amazing feats of psychic illusion we had ever seen. He would ask people to hold up various objects and while blindfolded, he would describe what they were and explain what significance they had to the person holding them. It was truly an amazing thing to see. Bartholomew would dress in a long purple robe and matching turban, looking very much like an Indian Fakir, though his accent betrayed a southern dialect from South Carolina or Georgia. Leonard and I had a running wager as to who could discover his secret first. The winner would treat the loser to a steak dinner. Even I, to satisfy my curiosity, held up the pocket Bible during one of his performances, and he was able to describe what it was and to tell me it had been given to me on a train. At the time, I found him as amazing as the others did.*

In retrospect, I look at those months as one of the best periods in my life. There would be much better times, and times which were much worse. But I would have said I was happy if anyone had asked.

After a couple of months there, I was beginning to develop a crush on Glenice. She was friendly and attractive in an unsophisticated sort of way. She reminded me a little of Mary Parker, whom my mother wouldn't let me forget. Her hair was cut short which was the fashion of the time, and she wore dresses with pastel colors and lace collars. But Glenice had a hopeless crush on Leonard, and would never take notice of me. Her whole face would light up whenever he entered the room, but he was too self-involved to notice her.

The only damper to my spirits came in mid-January. It was during one of Bart's performances. (Leonard had nicknamed him "Baffling Bart.") A woman held up a corset and with his erudite charm, he proceeded to tell us what it was and where it had been. There was a chuckle from the audience. Then he grabbed his chest and collapsed on stage. It was such a surprise that we all thought he was faking it. But when we discovered that he had died, we were stunned. Both Leonard and I cried.

After the funeral when Bart's daughter, Thelma, came to pick up his things, she asked Uncle Bob to throw away his equipment. She blamed his constant touring for her father's untimely death.

I remember overhearing her say, "I don't want the sight of those things in my house." Bob honored her wishes and threw everything out for the trash. But Leonard retrieved the robe and turban and kept them hung on his wall as a memento.

"What do you want with that ridiculous robe?" I asked him. "You never know when it might come in handy," was all he said, and he would take that robe and turban with him whenever we moved.

During this whole period, I was writing my mother once a week, though I never had the heart to tell her about Mel. In her letters she kept me informed on the various goings-on at home. I learned that my father had reluctantly hired another man to help him, and that Reginald was seeing Mary Parker's sister, Martha, and that Mary Parker was frequently over at the house asking about how I was doing. From the tone of her letters I could sense how much she missed me, though she would never ask me to come home, and I probably wouldn't have gone home even if she asked, because things seemed to be going much better for me in New York. But then the bottom fell out again.

Attendance at the performances had begun to dwindle even before I had arrived and I was not privy to the financial struggles which Leonard's uncle had been experiencing for a number of years. By April it was not unusual for only a handful to come to any one performance. There were a number of reasons why this was happening. Just as television eventually supplanted radio, the motion picture had supplanted vaudeville. The theater simply could not compete with the inexpensive entertainment provided by the movie houses. Faced with bankruptcy, Leonard's uncle finally decided to put the theater up for sale, and though he tried to keep us all working, he finally had to let us go in May. Then for the first time, Leonard seemed worried. If Leonard, the eternal optimist was worried, it became for me a cause of great concern.

For five desperate weeks, we both looked for work, with none to be found. Again I found myself hungry and afraid. I struggled with the same feelings of hopelessness and of deep regret which had haunted me before. New York can be hell if you don't have any money, and I was so broke that I often went two days before I had a bite to eat. Then one day Leonard had a brainstorm. He took us by train to the Bronx and we inquired about work at the zoo.

"It is a natural decision," he explained to me on the train. "You know animals after all."

"I've worked with farm animals. I don't know anything about zebras, and lions and the rest."

"A zebra's a horse with stripes and a lion's an overgrown tom cat. You've dealt with horses and cats, haven't you?"

"Yeah, I suppose."

"Then you can handle these."

"I'm flattered by your confidence in me. But I don't know if I can handle it."

"It's worth a try, Nige. The worst they can say is 'no.'" I thought about it and agreed with him.

"Alright, I'll give it my best shot."

When we arrived at the zoo, Leonard again did most of the talking. The field manager asked me a number of questions about animals and feed, and I answered them to the best of my ability. Then he asked Leonard several questions about electrical repairs. To my surprise, he hired us both on the spot.

Leonard and I found a small one room apartment near the zoo. We would walk to work every morning about six, and we would not leave until six in the evening. Leonard drilled himself throughout the day with mathematical formulas and electrical terminology. He explained to me about coulombs law and about ohms and magnetic fields. Though as hard as I tried to understand, I did not have his gift for scientific thinking. Sometimes he called me "farm boy" whenever I was reluctant to continue in the drills.

My duties included a number of tasks, but primarily I looked after the African exhibit. I insured that they were fed properly and I kept their pens clean. I was so preoccupied with the moment that I failed to see the irony of the situation. I had left the farm and had come so many hundreds of miles, yet I was doing many of the same things I would have done at home.

Of this period, two different events stand out in my mind. The first was rather trivial, but amusing. It concerned a zebra I had named Hal. Among the half a dozen zebras in the exhibit, he was the most temperamental one. He refused to eat with the others, and whenever it rained he would splash mud all over himself. We had been having several days of rain, and he had completely covered one side of himself with mud. So, I decided to wash him down with a hose. When the water sprayed onto his back, the strangest thing happened, he began to run around the exhibit at a full gallop. He circled it three or four times and then he stopped to eat his feed. Out of curiosity, I did it again, and the same thing happened. Whether it was a trained response or something entirely of his own volition, I could never discover. But as predictably as the sunrise, whenever water touched his back he ran around the pen and then he ate. When I showed Leonard what had happened he found the whole thing very amusing. I'd never seen him laugh so much.

"Nige," he told me. "Only you could find a zebra with a sense of humor."

The second thing that stands out in my mind was a conversation Leonard and I had about the Great Bartholomew. We were talking one evening in July. Leonard was sitting at his desk with a book about circuits opened before him. He turned to me as I sat in my chair with a magazine, and then he tossed the turban in my lap and said, "How do you suppose he did it?"

"I don't know." It really wasn't a pressing concern of mine.

"It fascinates me. I know it was a trick. It had to be. But I can't for the life of me figure it out."

"Maybe he was psychic after all," I said to agitate him. But neither Leonard nor I believed in the supernatural.

"If you look at an electric wire, you can't see the current flowing through it. But you can measure its effects. We saw the effects. I want to find the current."

"Why are you so concerned about this? He was just some silly stage performer."

"I hate to be confounded. I'll figure it out."

If anyone could figure it out, Leonard could. When he put his mind to something, he almost always accomplished his objectives. But for me the issue was a senseless one. Even if he could figure it out, what good would it do? But I didn't have the heart to tell him that.

While we worked at the zoo, Leonard saved every dime he could spare to buy electrical equipment and the tools necessary to repair radios and phonographs. He would often go on fasts in order to have enough money to buy wire and batteries. I had never known someone with such single-minded dedication, and together we learned to test circuits, to repair capacitors and tuners, and Leonard explained to me the nature of frequency and of amplitude modulation. When summer waned into autumn, we had begun to buy broken radios, and we repaired them and resold them. We were able to buy even more equipment with the proceeds from the sales.

Our room had begun to look like Dr. Frankenstein's laboratory, with wires and lights and radios on every available protrusion. I found it a little amusing and sometimes would bow down and pretend to be Igor, saying, "Master, shall I fetch a brain for you?"

Leonard would usually chuckle beneath his breath, but wouldn't say anything. He was far too busy to engage in horseplay. Of all the days of my short life those days seemed the most peaceful, of this I was convinced, but then the dreams came.

The first came in mid-September, on a humid night when I had trouble sleeping. I had gone to bed exhausted, having spent the whole afternoon cleaning animal pens. I remember it vividly. It began like a pleasant dream. I was sitting in a meadow at what must have been springtime, because there was a carpet of wild flowers, of red and blues and royal purples, stretching out in all directions as far as I could see. In the distance, jutting out above a line of trees, was a huge domed building with a golden cross on the top. I surmised it was a church, but I had never seen a church like this one. I remember walking through the flowers which rose to almost my knees, and there kneeling in the clover was a young black-haired woman; she was crying.

"What's wrong?" I asked her. "Why are you crying?"

She turned to me with eyes full of fear. "They're dead!" she said. "They've all been killed."

"Who's dead?"

"My father, mother, and my brothers."

Then she grabbed me and started screaming. "They're dead. They're all dead." When she raised her hands, they were stained with blood.

I woke up from the nightmare and I was sweating heavily and trembling. Then Leonard told me I had been shouting in my sleep those very same words, "They're dead, they're all dead."

During the rest of the day, I could not put the image of her bloodstained hands out of my mind. Leonard would have thought it childish that a dream should bother me as much. So, I didn't talk about it. The next night I had the dream again, this time more vivid and with greater detail.

I saw dozens of soldiers, gathering up the men of the village, some pushing and shoving them with the butts of their rifles. They lined them up against a wall and I could hear a bell ringing with a deafening clang. Then the soldiers lifted their rifles, and with frightening precision, shot them all dead in a moment of gunfire. I saw their lifeless bodies scattered like newspapers on a blood-stained street. Then as though I were behind her, I saw this same young woman with jet-black hair and she was crying.

Again, I awoke in a cold sweat and told Leonard about the dream.

"Maybe you're not sleeping long enough," he told me. "Sometimes that can cause bad dreams."

"I don't think it has anything to do with that. It's like I was there watching it happen."

"Don't be silly, Nige. Get a good night sleep and the dreams will stop."

The third and the fourth and the fifth soon followed, each more horrific than the ones which preceded it, and each time I told Leonard, he told me the same thing, "We all have bad dreams. Forget them."

But I could not forget them. They were images of such intensity that I could not push them from my mind. I began to think I was going crazy. Then details like the pieces of a puzzle began to fall into place.

The soldiers became German soldiers. I recognized their uniforms from a picture in the paper. The villagers spoke another language which I could not recognize and the young woman also shouted in this unknown dialect. "Could it be," I began to ask myself. "That I'm sharing someone else's dreams." I couldn't even consider the possibility. Because if my suspicion proved true, then everything I believed was wrong, and I couldn't deal with being that wrong. It would shatter everything twenty-one years had built.

Finally, the sixth and final dream came. After everything else had happened, I saw this young woman running into the forest with a young boy ten or eleven years old, running behind her. Then the two of them hid beneath a fallen tree.

In our waking hours there are certain fixed points of reference. We can regain our bearings if we get knocked off-balance. But in dreams the mind creates its own points of reference, and logic need not have part of it. Past, present and future can merge as one, and what is

*impossible to imagine while awake becomes routine while dreaming. I
know, God willing, if I should live another day, there will be sunrise
and sunset, both the natural and the created rhythms which give my life
stability. But if one morning the sun should not rise, or the seasons fail
to change, then my whole relationship to the world would shatter and
I'd go stark raving mad. As the steady rhythm of my heart gives my
body life, so these rhythms make me sane.*

*What disturbed me most about the dreams was the eerie feeling they
conjured in me. I sensed that the points of reference belonged to
someone else and that I was an intruder in another's dreams. Yet to
preserve my psyche, I suppressed such thoughts. I convinced myself
not to worry about them.*

*But the dreams were trying to tell me something, but I was too
selfish to listen. While I complained about my lot in life, a life filled
with abundant blessings, there were people dying at the hands of brutal
killers all around the world. But like so much of America, I was too
asleep in my own concerns to give a hang about the rest of the world.
It's taken me fifty years to understand what John Donne said so long
ago, that each man's life touches mine. If I had listened then, I'm
certain, I wouldn't have to endure this now.*

*In every man's life there comes a chance to make a real difference
in this world. I missed my chances more than once. God, if I had
possessed the courage to act, when I had the strength to act.*

The tape was silent for what seemed five minutes, and then Nigel's voice
began again.

*So much for an old man's regrets. Sometimes, I get carried away. I
think I should talk about something else.*

*There was a Greek man who lived a floor above us. His name was
Demosthenes Phronizis. I remember him, because his English was not
so good and because he used to offer us Baklava which his cousin
made for him every Saturday.*

*He used to tell me how beautiful the Greek islands were and how
much he longed to go home to Ellada. Like so many Greeks he came
here to earn a living but his heart was back in Athens.*

*Leonard found him annoying because he kept making verbal
mistakes. He would often substitute similar sounding words for each*

other.

"If he can't use the words properly," he would tell me, "he shouldn't use them at all."

Leonard would often correct him when he made mistakes, but I didn't have the heart.

"Greece," Demo said, "is like a flower. How do you say, delegate and frugal. My village was a paradisos, and the women beautiful."

The way he always talked about Greece, it made me wish to go there. I could see the Parthenon and the Acropolis, the islands and Ionia. But Leonard said, "He's exaggerating. No place can be as beautiful as he says."

Years later I would have the chance to see Greece and confirm that Demo didn't lie. But then I had only my imagination to fill in the gaps.

Demo would come downstairs to talk to us. During the day he worked in a sweatshop cutting cloth, and at night he struggled to learn English. He said it helped him to practice with someone. One night he came down to read to us a letter he had received from home. He struggled to translate it from Greek into English.

"My faithful son," he began. "It is with sadness I tell you of our situation. We pray everyday for peace, but we know the Nazis will come someday soon.

Costa and Themi want to fight. But we are so weak and they are so strong. Our people have..." He paused. "I don't know the English for this word. I think you say 'suffer'. But it means much more. Our people have suffered much pain in the past. Please pray for us that God watches over us. In the love of Christ, Your mother Athena."

He finished reading and folded up the letter with tenderness. He placed it back in his shirt pocket.

"Should I go home?" he asked me.

"Why would you want to do that?" Leonard interrupted. "I'm glad there's an ocean between me and them."

"Nigel, I trust you," Demo continued. "What should I do?"

I didn't know what to tell him, but I thought about my own mother, and I knew if she were in danger I'd want to go home.

"If it were my family, I'd want to be with them. But I can't make your decision for you."

"Then I go. Thank you."

When we came home the next evening, he was gone. He could have moved, or he could have gone back to Greece. I never knew what became of him.

There are so many people who I met during that time. I wish I had the time to talk about all of them, because from each of them I learned something which enriched my life. But time only permits me to talk of a few.

There was Willy the plumber who told me all about pipes, and Agnes who sold flowers on the corner and Peter who painted signs. All of their faces, like a gallery of portraits are hung before my mind's eye.

The tape clicked off and Jim took the earphones off his ears. He reached into his pocket and pulled out the note which Nigel had written in Greek. He stared at the letters and tried to make sense of the sounds.

"What are you trying to tell me, old man?"

He placed the note back in his pocket, turned the tape over and began to listen again.

In January 1941, Leonard and I lost our jobs with the zoo. I found a job working in a meat house. The work was difficult and dirty, but it paid the rent. Leonard had been trying unsuccessfully to get a loan from a bank. He wanted to borrow the money to open his shop, but without collateral or someone to sign the note the prospect proved impossible. But he possessed a persistent patience, which when he committed his whole person to something, would produce positive results, and he was finally able to raise the money in February of that year. I assumed he got it from a bank, but he wouldn't tell me how he got it.

We opened our shop on 8th Avenue in Brooklyn, in what had been a tailor's shop. Leonard painted over the sign which read "Goldberg Brothers" and we named our place the "Radio Wave." It was a small place, but it did give us a place to move the radios. Not in the best of neighborhoods, it was still our place and the beginning of our business partnership.

In the first couple of weeks, business wasn't good, but then the word got around that Leonard could fix anything. First came one radio, then two, then four, and before we knew it we had more business than we could handle. Leonard was happy with the success, you could see it in his face, but I was restless again. There have been times in my life when I was confident in my own capacities and other times when I wondered why the heavens didn't strike me from the earth. For some unknown reason, I felt the latter. Leonard seemed to know what he wanted from his life, and I envied him for that. But my goals were ambiguous and less clear. Sometimes I wanted to talk about it, but I did not have the vocabulary to give it speech. Because so much of what I was thinking and feeling sounded ridiculous to me, I began to keep a journal. I lacked the discipline to keep it everyday, but whenever the moment seemed right, I would scribble down my thoughts, impressions and observations.

For example, "April 17, 1941, today I read in the paper that the Nazis have moved into Greece. I remember what Demo had read to me and the dreams. When I showed the article to Leonard he laughed, saying, 'Don't you have enough problems, Nigel, without taking on those of the whole world.' I feel so alone sometimes. Am I the only one who feels this way?"

I would sit sometimes on the steps of the shop and stare at the buildings. There was a newsstand on the corner and a Jewish delicatessen across the street, and shoe shop and a dressmaker a few doors down.

Leonard came out and said to me, "You look like a gargoyle perched on the cathedral."

"I feel like a gargoyle."

"Come inside, you'll scare all the customers away."

"Have you ever wondered about why we're here? If there is any point or meaning to life?"

"No, not really. I know what I want and I know how to get it."

"I wish I could be so sure. I thought this was what I wanted. But it's not enough for me."

"I don't think you know what you want," he said. I didn't think he meant it to sound as harsh as it did. But he was right about me. I did not know what I wanted.

"When I was on the farm, I thought it was the farm that made me restless. Now that I'm here, I think it's something else."

"You have to have concrete goals. Otherwise, you'll never accomplish anything." He went back inside, while I continued to sit on the steps. I knew he was right. But I didn't know what to want. Then

an idea occurred to me that maybe I should read again. But I had no idea what to read.

I must have seemed ridiculous when I came into the booksellers the next day and asked in all seriousness, "Could you recommend a good book about the meaning of life?"

This older man had the most perplexed look on his face, and it moved through what seemed seven different expressions before he responded, "What do you mean about the meaning of life?"

"I mean something that talks about the purpose of life, what our goals should be, you know what I mean."

"Do you mean a philosophy book?"

"I'm not sure what I mean. Just something not so long, I don't have a lot of time."

He laughed a little, and then stroked his forehead. I guess my question was so absurd or so utterly stupid that it took him completely by surprise.

"Now let me see," he began. "We have Plato and Aristotle and Seneca, the philosophers." He pointed to a shelf. "We have religion and theology." He pointed to another shelf.

"No, I'm not interested in religion or theology. I just want something about life. You see I'm a little confused."

"Perhaps you might like some Confucius." He responded. In retrospect I realize he was making fun of me.

"Whatever you pick will be fine."

He stared at a shelf for a minute, and then handed me a copy of a thin book.

"This is one which you might like. The teachings of Lao Tzu." I could sense he was getting a perverse satisfaction out of giving me this book. But I paid for it anyway and went back to the shop. There I sat on the steps with the book in my hand and I began to read. I couldn't put it down and for two hours I sat silently and immovably, with this book fixed in space before my eyes. Leonard kept watching me from inside the shop, but he was preoccupied with the radios and did not have the time to bother me. When I had nearly finished with the book, he came outside.

"What is that you're reading out here?"

"The teachings of Lao Tzu."

"The what?"

He grabbed the book out of my hand and looked at it.

"Why are you reading this?"

"The bookseller recommended it."

"Oh, Nige," he sighed. "When are you going to realize people are pulling your leg?"

"It's really quite good," I explained to him. "Would you like to hear some of it?"

"Not really. Just don't turn Chinese on me."

He went back inside and continued to work on his radios. I know he thought I was off-balance, and maybe I was. But the thought of repairing radios the rest of my life had the same appeal to me as farming. I believed I would never be satisfied. Not all that I read in Lao Tzu that day did I find interesting, nor did I understand, but much of it confirmed there were others who felt what I felt and who understood the questions that plagued my heart. At twenty-one, few of us have the perception and the sensitivity to understand the deeper issues or to ask the deeper questions. But I was beginning to ask the questions which would shake me to my very center.

To change the subject a little bit, there was an older man, who ran the newsstand down the block. His name was Mr. Talbot. I knew this only because I overheard someone say to him, "Good morning, Mr. Talbot." I had never actually spoken to him.

Of all the faces that filled that street, his was the most peaceful and angelic. He always had a smile on his face and he always greeted his customers with such sincerity that through that one brief encounter, one felt better the rest of the day.

He would open his stand at six in the morning and close it at six in the evening. I would stop in around eight and pick up a copy of the Times. *I remember that he wore the same gray work clothes everyday and he wore a red beret tilted on his scalp. His hair was silver and it curled around the back of his ears, and he had a thin silver mustache on his upper lip.*

He would smile and tell me, "Good morning, young man," and I would usually respond, "Good morning to you." But one morning I decided to talk to him.

"How long have you been here, Mr. Talbot?"

"Since January of 1930. It must be eleven years. Has it been that long?"

"And what did you do before you sold papers?"

"I was a millionaire. I lost it all in the twenty-nine crash."

"That's terrible," I said, but I didn't know if I should believe him.

"It's not that bad really. I'm a lot happier now that I don't have the money."

I could not understand what he meant, because I had known poverty and it wasn't enjoyable.

"Certainly it must be better to have a little money. It gives you freedom that you don't have without it."

"When I had money, I was owned by my money. Cages come in all shapes and sizes, including those on Park Avenue."

When I left him that morning, I was confused, because although I was not motivated solely by a quest for material wealth, I did believe it was better to be rich.

When I told Leonard about my conversation, he laughed at me, saying, "No one would be as happy as Mr. Talbot, if he lost all his money. He's lying to you."

I never knew if Mr. Talbot was telling the truth, but I'd like to think he was honest with me. Mr. Talbot and I never talked like that again, though he did seem warmer when he greeted me when I picked up the morning paper.

The flight attendant tapped Jim on the shoulder and told him, "Sir, you must take off the earphones. The plane is beginning its landing descent."

Jim turned off the player and removed the earphones from his ears. When he turned his head, he noticed the man in black was still chanting.

Chapter 8

It was raining when Jim arrived at La Guardia airport. He disembarked the plane with the tapes and player inside a small satchel hung on his shoulder. While he waited impatiently at the baggage checkouts, he could see the man in black out of the corner of his eye. He was standing quietly with his hands inside the pockets of his robe. Jim retrieved his suitcase from the belt and carrying his bag, he walked toward the glass doors which opened onto the airport entrance.

At the curb, he saw a man standing in the rain with a cardboard sign. He couldn't make the letters out at first, but then he saw his name.

"Are you looking for James Jacobson from Hadleyburg?"

"Yes, I am."

"Well, I'm Jim Jacobson."

"I'm Constandinos Mozakis from the church."

He kissed Jim on both cheeks which took him completely off guard.

"From what church?"

"St. Nectarios. They didn't tell you?"

"No. No one told me anything."

"I've come to take you to your hotel."

"Thank you, Constandinos."

"Call me Costa."

Costa helped him carry his bag to the car.

"Where's Nigel's funeral being held?"

"At St. Nectarios, tomorrow morning."

"Is it far from here?"

"It's in Astoria. Do you want me to take you to see the church?"

"No, that won't be necessary."

As they drove out of the parking lot, the satchel sat beside him on the front seat. He felt a little apprehensive about taking a ride from a stranger, and he nervously opened and closed the zipper while he sat quietly in his seat. He did not know what else to say.

"There's a room for you at the hotel," Costa began. "But Nigel also left instructions that you can stay in his house."

"That's OK. Just take me to the hotel."

Jim reached into his pocket and retrieved Nigel's note, which he shuffled nervously in his fingers. Then the thought occurred to him to ask.

"Do you read Greek, Mr. Mozakis?"

"Of course."

"I have a note I'd like for you to translate."

He handed Costa the note, which Costa read in a moment and handed back to him.

"Well, what does it say?"

"Are you sure you want to know?"

"Yes."

"It says, 'I see you have gone out from my room and there is still so much I want to say to you. I just wish I had the courage to tell you face to face. I'm your father, Michael.'"

Jim was stunned. For two days he had carried this note in his pocket, without realizing what a bombshell he was holding. "How could he be my father?"

"I don't know."

"Take me to his house, please."

Costa turned the car around and proceeded toward the house. So much of what had happened in the previous days gained immediate clarity. He finally had the answer to many of his questions, but it was the beginning of a whole set of others. How could it be that Nigel was his father? A hundred scenarios played themselves out in his mind while his emotions surged through him like an electric current, causing him to tremble and modulating from fear to confusion, to relief, to anger, to regret, and to guilt.

The house was in Bayside, New York. It was a two-story Tudor style with a well-landscaped yard with a stone walkway which led from the street up to the front entranceway. A six-foot metal security fence circled the perimeter of the property with two metal gates at the front driveway and at the walkway to the house. Costa stopped the car in front of the walkway and both men got out of the car.

"I could go inside with you, Mr. Jacobson."

"No, I'm all right."

Costa helped him take his bag out of the trunk, and then handed him the keys to the front gate and house.

"Here's my business card," Costa told him. "Please call me if you need anything."

"Thank you, Costa."

With a little apprehension, he began to walk toward the house as Costa pulled away from the sidewalk. His gait was cautious and deliberate, because he did not know what to expect. He was still stunned by what he had heard and he found it difficult to accept.

When he opened the front door, he found a red tile entryway with a living room to the left, what looked like a study on the right, and a staircase directly in front of him. Everywhere he looked were religious pictures of various sizes and styles, much like the art that he had seen in Nigel's room. There were also photographs of Nigel, and a woman, whom he presumed to be Beth Fox and of others whom he did not recognize. There were plants of various sizes and types, and an assortment of artifacts. On one wall was hung a Greek Flag. Above the mantle he saw a huge print of what looked like three angels sitting at a table. This he found curious, but the rest seemed uninteresting and foreign to him.

He set his bag on the tile floor and walked into the living room, where he immediately felt like an intruder and he began to fight this implacable impulse to leave, a feeling which only grew stronger the longer he stayed. He considered calling a cab to take him to a hotel, but his curiosity prevented him. He tried to relax on the sofa, but he could only sit uneasily as though awaiting some unforeseen tribulation. When he realized how childish his anxiety was, he decided to take his bag upstairs and find a place to put his things. Upstairs he found three bedrooms and a bathroom connected by a long hallway. There was a closed door at the end of the hall, which whetted his curiosity. When he opened this door, he discovered a TV room with a chess table sitting in the corner. He walked up to the board and noticed a game in progress as if someone had left it and had not had the time to finish it.

He took his bag into one of the smaller bedrooms and laid it on top of the bed. Then he snapped open the latch and the case popped open like a roll of biscuits, and his clothing jumped out. As he turned around to find a place to put his clothing away, an older woman walked into the room. She was immediately startled and dropped some sheets on the floor.

"You frightened me," she told him. "I didn't expect anyone till tomorrow."

"And who are you?"

"I'm Dina, Nigel's housekeeper."

"According to this note here, I'm supposed to be Nigel's son." He handed the note to her for her to read. "But I have to believe this is some sort of mistake."

"So, you know already."

"I don't know anything."

"I'm not sure I'm the one who should tell you this. Father Nick was going to tell you tomorrow."

"Tell me what?"

"You were kidnapped over forty years ago and left in an orphanage."

"And you're sure it was me?"

"Of course, Michael. This is your home. The room where you just put your things was your nursery."

"Please forgive me if I'm a little disturbed by all this. But I don't for a minute believe any of this to be true."

"Nigel struggled for weeks whether or not he should tell you. But he said your life was stolen from you and he wanted to give it back to you."

"Give it back? I have a life." His voice grew louder.

"Calm down," she soothed him. "I've fixed some soup. Come downstairs and eat."

She directed him downstairs to the kitchen, sat him down at the table, and gave him a bowl of soup.

"Who else knows about this?"

"Besides me and Father Nick, no one else. Nigel didn't want the press to find out."

"If I was abandoned at an orphanage and not found, then how did Nigel find me after so many years?"

"So many questions! Stop being a reporter a minute and relax. You can talk to Father Nick tomorrow. He'll answer all your questions."

After finishing the soup, Jim returned to the living room and again sat down on the sofa. The impulse to leave returned, and he fought himself again, much the same way an actor overcomes stage-fright through the sheer force of his will. He could not imagine a more ironic turn of events. He even considered that he might be dreaming, though dreams have a sensation all their own, and he knew he was not dreaming. That morning he had awakened convinced of who he was and where he belonged, but in a few short hours he discovered that all those fundamental assumptions had been called into question. Much like a dam weakened by an earthquake may take hours or even days to collapse from stress, a growing panic was erupting within him, a shift in paradigm which threatened the center of his psyche. Outwardly, he still seemed calm and controlled. He even encouraged himself by saying, "It's not so bad really." But it was much worse than he could even imagine.

Dina came into the living room and found him sitting pensively on the sofa.

"Is something wrong?" she asked him. "You look disturbed."

"I'm OK," he responded. He was lying.

"Maybe you should go out for a while. I'll have dinner ready about six o'clock."

He sat for a while longer and then decided to go upstairs and get Nigel's tapes. When he retrieved the satchel from upstairs, he decided to leave.

"I'm going outside for a little while," he told Dina from the hallway and then he left. After walking around the neighborhood for about an hour, he found himself in front of the train station. There he decided to take a train into the city where he might play tourist for a time. He put the headphones on his ears and began to listen again.

After I talked to Mr. Talbot, I began to read again. The bookseller must have thought I was crazy. One week I would read Kant and the next week I'd read Voltaire. But I had so many questions, and none of what I had read seemed to satisfy me. Business during the months of June and July seemed good, but Leonard seemed worried. He had told me that he had calculated the loan expenses and we were making enough money. But I could sense that he was not entirely honest with me. Then in August when business began to slack off, when fewer customers came in to buy and fewer radios came in for repair, Leonard finally told me the true situation.

On a rainy and windy Thursday morning, I came in late to the shop. I had been up reading till late the night before and had overslept that morning. As soon as I got through the door with my paper, he called me to the back of the shop to the room where he repaired the radios. His face seemed tortured and he was sweating profusely.

"Nige, I have to tell you something. We have to leave New York."

"What are you talking about? I'm not going anywhere."

"I didn't tell you the truth. I couldn't get the money from the bank. I got it from a loan shark. Now I can't make the payments and he's going to kill us."

"You must be kidding me. This is one of your jokes."

"I'm not kidding you. We have till four o'clock today to come up

with five hundred dollars or we're history."

"How could you be so stupid? You don't go to the loan sharks for money," I shouted at him.

"It was the only way I could get the money. I'd been to every bank."
"So what are you going to do now?"

I felt like knocking out his teeth, but restrained myself.

"I don't know."

"What do you mean you don't know?"

I started pushing him and he pushed me back. Before we knew it, we were rolling and punching each other on the floor. It was the most senseless and pathetic fistfight one could ever see, because neither of us knew how to fight. When I finally was able to pin him to the floor and about to swing my right fist into his mouth, I stopped myself.

Then the words just popped out of my mouth, "Let's join the navy. We can be out of New York in just a few days."

So, Leonard and I went down to the recruiter and within a few days we were out of New York. We had abandoned everything at the shop and no one knew where we were going, except Leonard insisted on going back for the robe and turban. Again he said, "It might come in handy."

It's hard for me to explain the strange obsession Leonard had with those things. It seemed much more than idle curiosity. But I could not find words adequate to express what I suspected were his real motives. I did not know at the time, but would discover later that he was related to the great Harry Blackstone and that a number of his relatives had been stage magicians. But this information would not come till years later, and I only had the visible evidence on which to formulate an opinion. I believed something was seriously flawed in his judgment, and though I had spent a number of months with him, I was convinced that he had suppressed some sinister secret, which found its implicit expression in this impulse. But I could no more find words for this than I could speak Russian or French. I also could not understand how he could have put us in such danger and not seem proportionately disturbed about it. But even in the worst of times, Leonard was always an optimist and nothing seemed to disrupt his temperament for very long. So in August 1941, we both enlisted in the Navy just four months before Pearl Harbor, and neither of us considered how dangerously close we were to war.

It is an historical fact, though one often forgotten in our nostalgia for those times, that the vast majority of Americans did not want involvement in the war. The war in Europe was considered a European problem that the Europeans should deal with and as for the Japanese, most of us could not have found Japan on a map until Pearl Harbor. We had all hoped we could somehow ride the war out, and much like our attitude toward the depression, we believed just given enough time, it would solve itself.

Americans find it difficult to believe in evil. People may make mistakes, but they don't commit sins. I, too, found it inconceivable that evil could be organized, that it could have rational goals, and that the systematic attainment of these goals, excluded no atrocity, no matter how barbaric. We believed in the inherent goodness of men. It's part of our national mythology, with Washington and Jefferson, and Lincoln as our national saints. But I'll talk more about this when I get to an appropriate place.

The navy tested both of us and decided to send us to electronics school after basic training. I never realized how much I remembered from Leonard's incessant drills. I became a radio operator and Leonard a technician, and they sent us to London for further training.

Jim remembered the pictures of London he had seen in the scrap book, and another piece of the puzzle fell into place. Then the train arrived at Penn Station and he exited onto the platform. After he came out onto 32nd street, he saw street vendors selling books for a dollar and silk ties for three dollars. Torn newspapers, discarded ticket stubs and smashed drink cups were scattered in small heaps across the street and sidewalks. It was reminiscent of his own apartment where cleanliness finally surrendered.

"Big cities are dirty," he told himself as if to make excuses for the general disarray.

What was London like in 1941? It was a tortured soul, a city in trepidation and it was all because of the blitzkrieg.

Everywhere one looked one could see the evidence of destruction: houses, churches and schools destroyed in an instant from the rockets red glare, and there were the sirens at fever pitch calling us at all hours of the day and night into the shelters.

Leonard's vision of a world transformed by science had inspired me, but I began to understand how destructive knowledge could be. Did those German scientists, when they sat as school boys drilling themselves on Newton and Descartes, hope one day to rain such terror from the skies?

Jim had stepped out on a street and a cab nearly ran over him.

"Get outta the way, mack." the cabby shouted at him, and held his horn down until it broke into Jim's consciousness. He finally moved back onto the sidewalk and the cabby cursed him under his breath as he passed. Jim then put the earphones back on his ears.

At this point, I beg forgiveness for one digression. As I mentioned before, my mother and I were exchanging letters about once a week during this whole period, except when I went into basic training, when I didn't write her until after it was over and I had been given my orders to go to London. She wrote me in mid-December, but the mails being what they were, I did not receive the letter until early March. In it she told me about the farm, she mentioned in passing that my cousin, Michael, had come down with chicken pox. I remembered him as a lanky eight year old who followed me around the farm as I did my chores. He was always asking me, "What are you doing, Nigel?"

I found him most annoying, but I usually tried to humor him and give him honest answers. He was a bright little boy whose mind seemed intent on learning everything he could.

The general content of the letter concerned another one of my mother's dreams. She earnestly warned me to refuse any assignment to London, because she was afraid for my safety, but by the time the letter reached me, the die had been cast, and it seemed anticlimactic to take it seriously. I never understood why she took such interest in her dreams, yet with the bombings and the incessant air raid sirens, I could understand why she might be concerned.

She also wrote about Mary Parker, whom she had persistent hopes I would write, but I had no interest in writing her. I told myself I was too busy to take an interest in girls.

But the truth was that I was lonely, as lonely as I had ever been in my life, and I would have given my eye teeth just to talk to someone candidly, and I missed the farm and wondered if it all had been a mistake.

There was a hiss and the tape snapped off. Jim was standing before a subway station entrance. He decided to take a ride up to the offices of Newsmaker magazine. It was three o'clock and he had hopes of catching Julie in her office.

The subway station had a stench which clogged his sinuses as soon as he entered it. He had forgotten how filthy the subways had become. Clanging loose change in old coffee cups, several homeless men approached him to ask him for spare change. He shooed them away with the rationalization that they would only use it for booze or crack.

When he entered the subway car, within seconds a man began to shout, "I'm a vendor for street news, a paper sold by the homeless to help us get off the street. We're not looking for a handout. One dollar a copy is all I ask."

Several passengers bought a copy of the paper, but most just ignored him and averted their faces in hopes that he would just disappear.

Jim emerged on 59th street across the street from Newsmaker's executive offices. He took a deep breath before he crossed the street and entered into the foyer of the building. Inside he approached the receptionist.

"I'd like to see Julie Jamison. She's in the entertainment division."

"Is she expecting you?"

"No, I don't think so."

"Your name."

"Jim Jacobson."

The woman lifted the phone to her ear and spoke a few minutes. Then she placed it down on the table.

"I'm sorry, Mr. Jacobson, but Ms. Jamison is not here today."

"Are you sure?"

"Of course. You'll have to come back tomorrow, or I can take a message."

"Take a message then. Tell her that I came by to see her."

"Alright, she'll get the message."

He decided not to take a subway back to Penn station, so instead he took a cab. When he returned to the station, he bought a train ticket and boarded the train to Bayside.

Chapter 9

After sitting down in his seat, Jim took the third tape out of its case and put it in the player. He again placed the earphones on his ears.

The plan was for me to complete my training in early April, and then go into the Pacific Theater. But I had one last phase of training before I made the change.

We were testing new radio equipment, and a young lieutenant named Jamison, was scheduled to go out in a patrol boat on the channel. Jamison was one of the first people I met when I arrived at the base. They called him the "Whiz kid", because there was nothing that he did not know about radios. He was barely thirty, but had the respect of every senior officer in the place. I didn't know much about his personal life, or how he came to be in the navy. But someone had told me he was a graduate from MIT, and his father, who manufactured radios, had encouraged him into a military career. The only thing I knew about him of a personal nature was that he had married young at twenty to a girl he had known since childhood. I only knew this because I happened to meet him on the occasion of his anniversary, and he told me that.

Leonard and Jamison hit it off from the start, largely because they spoke the same language, that of capacitors and frequency. His conversation was filled with so much technical jargon that he might as well have been speaking French. Almost everyone else, including myself, found it difficult to talk to him. But I liked him, because he had a good heart, and he never held his rank above me.

The men used to tease him a lot, because at mail call, he received so much mail from home. We figured his wife must be writing him everyday, with the number of letters he received. But the truth was that we were jealous. Except for my mother's letters, I received no mail at all.

On the day of the test everything was set, except no one could find

Jamison. He had received a cable that morning at breakfast and disappeared.

"Where's Lieutenant Jamison?" Captain Hardy asked me.

"I have no idea, sir."

"Go find him, Fox. It's almost time for the test."

"But no one else has found him."

"Did I give an order?"

"Yes, sir."

"Then follow it!"

I must have searched the entire base before I found him in recreation room three. He was slouching in a chair and I could see that he'd been crying, and I could smell the stench of whiskey from across the room. I came closer to him and discovered he had a whiskey bottle in his hand, and he was drunk.

"What's wrong with you? You're supposed to be at the test."

Then he handed me the telegram which I read:

```
We regret to inform you of the untimely
death of your wife and your brother in
an automobile crash this morning.
```

I too began to cry.

"I'm sorry, Richard, I didn't know."

"Here I am off fighting the Gerries, and they die at home. I can't take it any more."

He lifted the bottle and took another swallow.

"You can't solve this problem this way."

I took the bottle from his hand.

"That's easy for you to say. You haven't lost your wife and brother."

He grabbed the bottle back from me. Then he took his wallet from his pocket and he pulled out a picture of his wife.

"Look at her," *he spoke with such tenderness.* "See how beautiful she is." *His eyes filled with tears as he spoke.* "I don't know how I'm going to live without her. And see my kid." *He pulled out his picture.* "Eight years old and so much like his mother I could cry."

I knew the captain could not see him like this. His military career would be over or worse. So, it was then that I made my fateful decision, and I went back to the captain to tell him the news.

When I returned to the docks, the captain asked me, "Where is Jamison? I told you to get him."

"Sir, he got news his wife has been killed stateside. He was going to do the mission. But I asked him if I could do it for him. If it's all right with you, Sir, I'll take the boat out."

He rubbed his forehead and then agreed, "OK, Fox. You can take the boat out."

I sighed in relief. Then I climbed in the boat and started the motor.

"Good luck, Fox," the captain told me.

My task was a simple one. I was to take a small patrol boat out onto the channel at night and test the range of a low-level radio transmitter. They were trying to develop low power FM transmitters for small patrol craft. Everything went well until I was about ten or eleven miles offshore. When I was almost at the stopping point, the radio began to have electrical problems and kept cutting out. I heard a phrase here and there and then only scattered words as though someone was randomly reading the dictionary. For over an hour it was working only sporadically, and then suddenly not at all. I sat for almost four hours while the radio was completely silent.

I wanted to sleep, but I couldn't sleep. I kept myself awake by singing "What can you do with a drunken sailor early in the morning," and then I began to sing the old barroom ballad about bottles of beer on the wall. I was down to twenty-five bottles of beer on the wall, when it finally became too tedious for me, and I stopped. The silence was deafening. I began to count the stars and to pick out the constellations, but I never had a serious interest in the night sky and couldn't remember them all. The ocean with its rhythmic ebb and flow rocked the boat like a cradle, and my eyelids grew heavier as if the ocean mist were singing me a lullaby. I began to have what sailors call, ocean mysticism, when a feeling of trepidation gave way to intense euphoria. I remembered a line from a poem I had read, "All I need is a tall ship and a star to steer her by." The ocean seemed warm and comforting almost like a womb. Yet it was a deceptive gentleness for beneath the softly rocking waves I knew swam chaos. I remembered all the ancient tales of serpents and of dragons, of Leviathan and mermaids, and I thought of Captain Nemo with his submarine. I thought of home, and the lake where Reginald and I used to fish, where sometimes we would sit all night with our fishing lines as silent anchors from a little boat *barely big enough for two. And I thought about how small I was as I stared out in all directions and all I could see was ocean, undulating and shifting H$_2$O, reflecting the night sky like so many fireflies rising aimlessly above the waters. How easily the ocean could swallow me whole. It had swallowed the Titanic without so much as a whimper. Then the radio finally came on again and they ordered me back.*

I turned the boat around, started the motor and began my journey to the shore. Then it happened. I saw what looked like a shooting star dance across that clear dark sky and then I heard a hissing sound, and a missile struck the boat. Then all I can remember is a huge explosion.

What happened between that moment and when I awoke three days later in the hospital, I cannot completely remember, not even now. But I can still picture the plump English nurse hovering over my bed with a thermometer in her hand.

"He's waking, doctor," I heard her say. Then this captain in British uniform approached my bed.

"How long?" I asked him. My eyes were cloudy, but I could see my left leg suspended in a cast, and I was in pain, the worst pain I had ever known.

"Three days," he answered in a deep Scottish accent. "You're a lucky man, Mr. Fox."

"It hurts!" It was difficult for me to speak. The nurse grabbed my hand as I cringed in pain and rivers of tears rushed down both cheeks.

"Do you remember anything about the past three days?" the doctor asked me.

"Not a thing after the explosion."

"You were in the water almost sixteen hours, clinging to a piece of debris."

"I can't remember anything."

"When they found you, you were shouting, 'My God please help me.' and for the last three days, you've been saying that in your sleep."

"That's strange. I don't believe in God."

"Lost at sea," the nurse broke in, "Anyone believes in God."

"Why am I in so much pain?"

"You're leg has been broken very badly. I patched you together as best I can, but I can't work miracles."

"How bad?" I asked him.

He hesitated to say. "We may yet have to take it off."

*"No, no, no!" I shouted. "No one is taking off my leg.
I came into this world with two legs. I'll go out of it with two."*

"I can make no promises. But I'll try to save it."

"How long?" I forced it out. "How long before you know?"

I raised myself up by both arms and this brought even greater pain.

*"Relax," the nurse said as she pushed me back onto the mattress."
Dr. MacGregor will do the best he can."*

*The doctor turned around and left the ward. Around me I saw rows
and rows of beds, and on each of them a soldier. Some had lost an
arm, and others had lost a leg, and still others had lost both arms and
legs, a horrific sight which frightened me.*

*"If you start to feel sorry for yourself," the nurse warned me, "just
look in the bed next to you."*

*To my right was a young boy no more than twelve, who had lost
both legs. He lay there moaning and shouting unceasingly, while a
young woman knelt at his side and prayed. I could hear her speaking
softly in what sounded like Greek. She cried as though her heart had
broken. It was the saddest sight my eyes had ever seen.*

*She sat with him throughout the night, but the boy grew worse, and
I could sense he wouldn't make it. Yet she prayed for what seemed like
hours. Several times in the night, I awoke to see her kneeling, and when
I rose in the morning she was still praying.*

"Have you been up all night?" I asked her.

*"I'm sorry my English is no so good," she answered me in a deep
Greek accent.*

"I asked if you have been up all night," I said more deliberately.

"Yes."

"Aren't you tired?"

"He's my brother. I no get tired."

"Where's your family?"

"They are all dead."

*When she said these words, I looked closely at her face. Her
features were delicate and gentle, framed by long black hair, which she
had tied behind her back, but it was her eyes which captured my
attention. Their quiet intensity intrigued me. She seemed much wiser
than her years, and she carried herself as one with courage, as though
she had survived some tremendous trial. Though in them was a
tenderness I'd never seen before. She dressed modestly, without*

makeup, yet seemed much more attractive in her simplicity than a hundred women well made-up. She was dressed with that beauty which virtue clothes, to paraphrase a proverb I once heard. I didn't realize it at that moment, but I had fallen in love with her. It's odd the way it happened. It wasn't the way I had imagined it at all.

"What's your name?" I asked her.

"My name, Elisavet, Elizabeth Katsanos."

"And your brother?"

"Demetrios." She paused.

I watched her as she wiped his forehead, and changed his dressing, and kissed him on the forehead, and then it hit me. She was the same girl from my dreams. I can't describe the intensity of emotion which rushed through me then, when I realized who she was. If I had told anyone, they would have thought me mad. After she had washed his face and had laid his head down on his pillow, she knelt on the floor and throwing her face down to the floor, she continued to pray. Then a nurse came into the ward and began checking charts from bed to bed.

"How are you feeling this morning, Mr. Fox?" she asked me when she came to my bed. But I didn't answer her, because I felt like hell. She also seemed fascinated by this young Greek woman, prostrated on the floor in front of us.

"I've got good news. They're not taking off your leg."

"Thank God." I said, but I did not believe in God. She continued on with her rounds.

"Good news?" Elizabeth asked me.

"Yes."

"I pray for you too. What is your name?"

"Nigel."

She struggled to pronounce it, but she couldn't pronounce the j sound.

"I'll call you Neilos. He was great saint."

I looked over on the table beside the bed and there I saw, among my other things, the pocket bible. It was a little damp when I picked it up and I handed it to her.

"An English Bible to help your English."

"Efkaristo," she responded. "Thank you!" She smiled at me and took the Bible.

"But, I have nothing to give you."

"You've already given me more than you know," I told her. I don't think she understood me. Shortly after that she left to go off to work, or so I presumed, and by the time she returned that evening, her brother had died. I remember seeing her in the hallway, as the doctors told her the news. I saw her crying as she had cried in my dreams, and I heard her say those very same words which had haunted me. "My God, they are all dead. I lost them all."

The train stopped at the Bayside station and Jim got off on the platform. He turned the player off and placed it back in his satchel. It was only a short flight upstairs and he was standing on Bell Boulevard. There was a bank to his right and a row of stores in front of him. It was approaching six o'clock and he was hungry, so he began the walk back to Nigel's house.

He felt restless and apprehensive and he did not know how to take what he was hearing. He had so many questions and so few answers. 'Could there be a hidden plan behind this random chaos? Is there such a thing as fate? 'These questions plagued him as never before. He had been drilled since childhood that the primary forces are economic, the laws of supply and demand. There are religious and political motives, but each man's decision is motivated by his margin of utility, and then these other motives are rationalized. To believe in dreams and in omens is to abandon reason and ignore reality. He knew that at the ground of his being. But something intrigued him about the dreams. "What if I am wrong?" he thought. He shivered a moment at the thought of it. But he knew he could not be that wrong.

"There are certain things I know are true." He began to construct an argument inside his head. "There are laws of nature and principles of causality, and these cannot be broken. If Nigel had a dream about this woman, and then he saw her, it is simply coincidence." But he could not argue the other side and his argument sounded hollow to him. He decided to rest his mind for a time.

When he knocked on the door at Nigel's house, Dina let him in. "I was afraid you wouldn't make it in time," she told him. "I fixed dolmadas, spanikopita and lamb, and some baklava for dessert. Those were Nigel's favorite foods."

Jim did not respond to her.

"Are you OK?" she asked him.

"Yes, I'm OK." He stared at a picture of Beth hanging on the wall. "What was she like?"

"She had what we call in Greek a *kalo pnevma*, a beautiful spirit. You look much like her in the eyes."

"How did she die?"

"In a car crash four months ago."

"Damn," he said, rubbing his forehead with the palm of his hand, "Just four short months."

He walked into the kitchen, but Dina directed him into the dining room where she had prepared a place for him. He saw two place settings on the table.

"Are you eating with me, Dina?"

"For God's sake, no. Father Nick is coming by. That's all right, isn't it? He called while you were gone."

"That's fine," Jim said. "I could use the company."

He sat down on the sofa in the living room, and quietly waited for the priest to arrive. A short time later the doorbell rang and Dina opened the door.

"Welcome, Father Nick."

A short Greek man in a long black robe entered the room.

"Good evening," he greeted Dina. He kissed her on both cheeks. "And you must be Michael." Jim stood up and likewise he kissed him on both cheeks. Jim felt a little awkward at receiving such affection from a man.

"Go on in, sit down and eat."

They both sat down at the table and Dina brought in the food. Father Nick stood up and Jim awkwardly mimicked him. He chanted, "The poor shall eat and be filled and they that seek the Lord shall praise him. Glory to the Father and the Son and the Holy Spirit, now and forever and unto ages of ages, Amen. O Christ our God, bless the food and drink of Your servants. For You are holy now and forever and unto ages of ages. Amen."

Then he sat down.

"I'm sorry I'm late, but I have so much to do and so little time."

"I'm sure you have a lot of questions," Father Nick said after eating a few bites of lamb. "Ask whatever you like. I'll do my best to answer you."

"How can Nigel be my father?"

Father Nick laughed. "That's an easy one. You were kidnapped forty years ago."

"And Nigel found me six weeks ago," Jim interrupted him. "I've been told that. But I still have no proof. Four days ago, I knew who I was and where I was going, and without one shred of proof, you expect me to erase forty years of my life and embrace this truth. How do you know that this is not some grand delusion of a dying man? He wanted to find his son and he found him."

"I sat across from Nigel, just as we are now, and told him my own misgivings about his telling you. 'It will be too much of a shock for him,' I told him. 'You can't expect him to accept it easily.' But Nigel said in his usually compelling way, 'His life was stolen from him, and I should at least give him the choice to have it back.'"

"You still haven't told me anything that compels me to accept it."

"I've known Nigel for twenty years and I trust him. If he was convinced, that's good enough for me."

"It's not good enough for me."

"He said you'd fight it with every fiber of your being, because you had the same stubborn spirit he had, but that when you came around, you'd see the necessity in why he told you."

"That reminds me of another thing he said to me. He said he was putting me in danger. I thought he was kidding."

"I'm afraid you're not ready to deal with that yet."

"What's with you people? Why is everything some big mystery to you? Why can't you just come out with it?"

"You wouldn't believe it."

"That's a big cop out. You may be able to fill your pews by feeding that desire for mystery, but I wasn't born under a rock, I need facts."

"I've known people like you all my life. They put life in a neat little box, and think they understand everything. Yet they refuse to accept anything which contradicts their opinions, even when it happens right in front of their eyes. They won't see it. They can't admit they're wrong."

Jim was getting agitated and got up from the table.

"I'm sorry, Michael. Please sit down."

"Don't call me Michael."

"Alright, Jim."

Jim sat down and continued to eat his meal.

"I didn't come over here to agitate you," Father Nick continued. "I came over to try and make you feel a little better. I guess I'm failing."

Jim smiled and said, "Can't we talk about something else?"

"Of course."

"Can you tell me about his dreams?"

"There's not much to tell. He had a few dreams. They came true."

"You seem to see no problem with that idea?"

"No, should I? There are over twenty weeping icons in North America. Pieces of painted wood which weep a sweet oil called myrrh. I've heard the testimony of hundreds of people about healing and miracles from anointing with the myrrh. I could dismiss it all as the active imaginations of a few gullible people, actually hundreds of gullible people, or I can accept in humility that I don't know everything about how this world works."

"This all sounds a little too fantastic, weeping icons and prophetic dreams. Why don't these signs ever occur before skeptics like me?"

"They do, but they refuse to accept it. I could take you to see a weeping icon and you would only rationalize that someone was squirting the myrrh in the eyes when no one was looking, and fooling a few extremely gullible people into believing in a sign. I could even let you examine the wood, and you would not believe. There is always an avenue of disbelief for those who want to disbelieve."

"It sounds like you're living in a world of pixies and fairies," Jim responded cynically.

"No. Faith is not built on signs but on conviction." He paused. He could see in Jim's eyes a growing contempt for the topic of conversation, so he acquiesced, "We're not going to resolve this today."

"No."

They did not speak of the subject again that evening. After a half an hour of superficial conversation about New York, Dina brought out the baklava for dessert. Father Nick talked about Greece.

"You should visit Greece sometime," he told Jim. "It is the most beautiful place on earth."

"You can't go visiting many places on my salary except perhaps the food stamp office."

"I guess not."

After finishing dessert, Father Nick excused himself from the table and said, "I hate to eat and run. But I have a lot to do for tomorrow. I have Nigel's funeral in the morning, and two baptisms in the afternoon. We can talk a little more then."

He let himself out of the door and Jim sat quietly at the table.

"Would you like me to fix you some tea?" Dina told him as she cleared the plates from the table. "It's difficult for you."

"That's an understatement."

"I have some ice cream."

"No, I'm not feeling very well. I'd like to lie down for a while."

Jim got up from the table and went upstairs to the bedroom. He closed the door and latched it behind him.

"Damn," he said under his breath. "What have I gotten myself into?"

He noticed that there was a phone on a table in the corner.

He picked it up and dialed. A woman answered it, "Hadleyburg Times."

"Yeah, Patricia. It's Jim. Is Reynolds there?"

"Sure, Jim. I'll get him."

A few moments later, Reynolds came onto the line, "Yeah, Jacobson. How's the story coming?"

"Jack, I want outta here. I'm surrounded by a bunch of Greeks and they got it in their minds that I'm Nigel's long lost son. This priest came over to dinner tonight and was talking about weeping pieces of wood and other weird things, and I can't take it any more."

"I don't think you have much choice," Reynolds answered him.

"What do you mean?"

"I mean you have a story to write, so write it."

"Look I've covered every other story you've asked me to cover in the last five years. Can't you cut me a little slack on this one?"

"In a word, NO. Goodbye."

Reynolds hung up the phone. Jim laid himself down on the bed and he remained as still as a statue as he stared up at the ceiling. He saw the satchel which Dina had brought up from the living room, and he decided to continue with the tape. After a deep soul-wrenching sigh, he placed the earphones back on his ears and listened.

When I saw her walking away after she got the news, I felt an intense sadness for her, but also for myself, because I was certain I would never see her again. I couldn't even get out of bed to catch up with her at the door, and I never felt so helpless.

Leonard came to see me the following afternoon, and I could see the anguish in his face, even before he said, "I'm sorry, Nige. If I hadn't borrowed from that loan shark, we'd still be in New York. If there's anything at all I can do to make it up to you, just ask me."

"There is one thing you can do for me."

"Yes, Nige."

"There was a girl in here yesterday. Elizabeth Katsanos. See if you can find her for me."

"Why?"

"Don't ask me, just try and find her."

"Alright, I'll try."

He handed me a box of candy and a few magazines he had brought with him. We talked a little about radios, and then I asked him, "What happened with Lieutenant Jamison?"

"He's gone back to the states. His father pulled a few strings and got him out of the navy."

Before he left, I reminded him to look for her.

"I'll do what I can."

I really didn't expect him to be able to find her, and when he returned a week later with no success, I was not surprised.

"You can't find a young woman in a city the size of London with just a name."

"I had hopes," I answered him.

"You're not falling for this girl, are you? You're the one who has no time for women."

"No, Leonard. I'm just curious."

It was much more than curiosity. She was all I could think about that whole first week. I kept looking at the foot of the other bed and imagining her praying there. I didn't know what I would say to her if she should show up again, but something in her eyes had haunted me, and I was convinced I had to see her again. Leonard would have thought it a childish obsession, so I kept the thought to myself. But each day she remained away, the more I yearned to see her.

Doctor MacGregor came in every morning about ten o'clock and would ask me how I was doing, and every morning I would give him the same anguished answer, "Terrible."

"Cast will be coming off in a few weeks," he would remind me. "You should begin walking after that."

A plump nurse named Agatha who came in on the day shift would occasionally flirt with me. But for the most part, my days were spent quietly in bed.

I began to read again, at first popular fiction, because that was what I could easily get my hands on, but then I asked the nurses to bring in books for me. One of the younger nurses, whom I had flattered, brought me a copy of Dickens' <u>Oliver Twist</u> which I read almost continuously for three days. I was at the part of the book when Oliver left Fagan, when it happened. I looked up and standing in the *doorway of the ward was Elizabeth Katsanos. She smiled briefly when she noticed that I noticed her. She was wearing a beige and brown dress which loosely fit her slender frame, and she carried a bag in he arms. After seeing her say a few words to one of the nurses, I watched her as she walked toward my bed.*

It deeply surprised me that she had come to see me, and I still find it difficult to understand what she found attractive in me during those years. But she stood nervously before my bed and in the best diction she could master, she told me, "I came to see if you OK. I brought you something to make you feel better."

She reached into the bag and retrieved a small package. "It's baklava," she said and handed it to me.

I opened the package and removed the pastry from the paper. I placed it in my mouth and it was the richest and most delicious pastry that I had ever tasted, much better than the baklava I had eaten in New York. I don't know if it was so good, because she had made it for me, or if it would have tasted the same had I been a total stranger, but the wonderful taste of it still lingers in my mind.

"You like it?" she asked me.

"Yes, it's wonderful."

"Good." she smiled. "I make you more next week."

"Why did you come to see me?" I asked her.

"I like you. My English is no so good. I want to see if you OK," the words slowly struggled to birth from her lips.

"Thank you."

"Efkaristo."

"Efkaristo," I struggled to pronounce.

"I read the book," she said as she pulled the bible from her bag. "My English getting better."

"Yes it is."

She sat beside me and we talked for over an hour. It must have sounded odd, as she struggled to give words to her thoughts and as I struggled to fill in the blanks, but what I discovered about this beautiful young woman brought tears to my eyes.

"How long have you been in London?" I asked her.

"Five months. Maybe six. I live with, how you say, aunt and uncle." Her English was slow and deliberate. "My family is all dead. Killed by Nazis when they march into village."

"And how did you escape?" I asked her.

"We hid in cave outside the village. After three days we escape in small boat out into the Mediterranean." She struggled to pronounce it properly. "We drifted for week, maybe more until Arab fishing boat pick us up and take us to North Africa. Then we walk by foot into French Morocco. From there we take freighter to England."

"How long?" I asked her.

"Pente menas. Five months." She finished. "My English no so good."

"It's fine," I tried to reassure her. As she had struggled to explain what had obviously been a nightmare for her, the images of her ordeal became as vivid to me as though I shared them with her. Afterwards she sat quietly and I couldn't take my eyes off her. I had never known anyone of such courage, and I felt totally unworthy to even be talking to her. I asked her how she could have endured so much, what kept her going, and she answered me simply, "My faith in God." Then I thought of myself and how close to suicide I had come over Mel, and I never felt so foolish in all my life. After we talked a little about the farm, and about my mother, she told me, "I'm sorry, but I must go."

"Thank you for coming, efkaristo," I told her. Then with an awkward smile, she told me goodbye. "Yasou." The time seemed to rush too quickly while we were together, and I was deeply sad that she had gone.

The next few days, I kept replaying the conversation in my head. I had never known anyone like her. I considered telling her about my dreams, but I did not want to dredge up bad memories, so I decided if she should come back to see me, I wouldn't talk about it.

Dr. MacGregor came in the following morning and spent some time explaining to me how he had repaired my leg. I can't remember all that he said, but I remember his telling me, "It hasn't healed as well as I'd like. I'm sending you back to the states to have further surgery."

He also showed concern about bone fragments which had been dislodged in the leg. He showed me a diagram of the leg and where he felt the danger lay. Though I didn't understand all that his concern entailed, I was worried when he said, "They must be removed, if possible."

It was during this week that I wrote home my first letter, describing what had happened and spending several pages alone describing my conversation with Beth. I also began having sporadic yet intense flashbacks about my missing 16 hours in the channel.

The tape clicked off on the first side and Jim flipped it over.

In the first and most vivid of the flashbacks, I remembered clinging to a piece of debris in the shape of a cross, while my leg throbbed in the most agonizing pain I had ever felt. It hurt so much, I couldn't keep my eyes open, and I began to hallucinate from the pain.

I saw a man standing on the debris dressed in what looked like a white painter's uniform. He looked down at me from what seemed a great distance and he said to me in a voice which cut the air, "It looks like you need some help."

"Yes," I said.

The waves rocked his head back and forth, and I had difficulty keeping focused on him.

"I suggest you pray," he told me.

"But I don't believe in God." I started to lose my grip on the wood and began to slide into the water.

"It's not time for philosophical reservations. PRAY!"

"My God, Please help me," I said softly.

"Louder."

"My God, Please help me!" I spoke much louder.

"Louder."

"MY GOD, PLEASE HELP ME!"

I must have been shouting at the top of my lungs, and then my eyes closed. When I opened them, he was gone. I clung to that wood with every sinew of my being and shouted with all the wind my lungs could hold, "My God, please help me," over and over again as though I couldn't stop myself. Psychologists say the human mind in self-protection will suppress the memory of traumas it cannot immediately face. When this memory returned to me, I dismissed the whole incident, and I never spoke about it to anyone for fear of being thought a nut.

Leonard came in to visit me again several days after my visit with Elizabeth. He again brought magazines and candy.

"I see you're looking much better, Nige."

"I feel a little better."

"How's the leg?"

"It hurts like hell. But it's better."

"Is the food here OK?"

"Nothing to write home about."

I could sense he was trying to tell me something, but what it was I couldn't guess. Then he blurted it out in one breath, *"I've got bad news. I'm shipping off to the Pacific tomorrow."*

"It's OK, Leonard," I tried to alleviate the anguish in his face. *"I'll survive."*

"But it isn't fair!"

How many anguished hours had I spent in my life trying to understand its odd injustices? I couldn't even guess.

"Remember that girl I asked you to look for?"

"Yes."

"She came to see me a few days ago."

I don't think he knew what to say about it.

"She may come back in a few days to see me again."

"That's good news."

"Don't worry about me. I'm OK."

We talked for a few minutes longer and then he told me, *"I have to go."* He shook my hand, wished me luck and then he left.

I can't describe all the feelings and thoughts that raced through my mind as I saw him walk out that door. He had been an angel of mercy in one of my most desperate hours, and we had shared so much together. But I had the strangest sense that the path which my life was taking would not be his, and I wasn't sure if I'd ever see him again.

I received a letter from home the following day. My mother was saddened by what I had told her, but the general tone was one of cautious optimism. She mentioned briefly what everyone was doing. Reginald was still seeing Mary Parker's sister. My father had begun planting again, and my cousin Michael had been helping with the small chores around the farm. It was the first letter in which she had not asked me to write Mary Parker. All that she said about Elizabeth was that it was nice that I had someone come to visit me.

On a Saturday afternoon shortly after that, Elizabeth came to see me again. Wearing a green dress with a ruffle at the collar, she smiled again as she was standing in the doorway, and this time she waved her hand in a brief hello. I could see from the distance that she had no *makeup on her face, something I hadn't noticed in her first visit. She had tied her hair back again, but this time had a green elastic headband that cut across her scalp.*

"I brought you some baklava," were her first words to me and she had another package with her which she opened in front of me.

"Dolmadas," she told me. "Stuffed grape leaves."

The thought of it frightened me at first, but she put one in her mouth and then handed me one. It tasted unlike anything I had ever eaten, both bitter and sweet at the same time. But after a few bites, my palate grew accustomed to the taste, and I began to like it. When she handed me another one, I found it quite delicious.

"You like?" she asked me again.

"Yes. They're very good. Did you make these?"

"Yes, but my Aunt Sophia helped me."

"Dolmadas," I pronounced.

I learned more about her living situation during this second conversation. She lived to the west of London with her Aunt Sophia and Uncle Petros Aristides. Her uncle was a medical doctor who had trained in Athens, but who had left Greece shortly after the Great War. Her family had owned a farm north of Salonika, in a village called Arnos. I learned she had five brothers, four older and one younger, the youngest Demetrios being the one who had died in London. She said that Costa and Pavlos and Markos had all been killed when the Nazis marched into her village, but that her oldest brother Nicholas, who was much older than she, had left the farm when she was no more than a child, and she barely remembered him. "He went to holy mountain to become monk," she told me.

Though her culture seemed as far removed from mine, as mine in Wisconsin was from New York, we found we had much in common. We both had raised pigs and we had risen early in the morning to milk cows. When we talked there was an electric charge in the air. We laughed, we cried and in the end, I felt closer to her than to anyone I had ever known.

"You like to read?" She asked me.

"Yes, a little."

"I bring you book next time. What you like?"

"Anything would be fine."

"I ask uncle Petros. He give you something."

When she left at four o'clock that afternoon, again I was deeply saddened. The time rushed so swiftly when she was with me and moved at a snails pace when she was away.

It never occurred to me what an odd romance this was, with me captive to my bed and she like the beautiful butterfly drifting on delicate wings to see me. We came from such different worlds, and sometimes I envied her world which seemed so full of life and hope. Through her, I had begun to realize that it's not so much where I lived that mattered, but how I lived.

She came to see me again on Tuesday night after work, and she brought a copy of Dostoevsky's <u>The Brothers Karamazov</u> *for me to read.*

"My uncle thinks he's best writer," she told me. "It is long, but good."

She didn't say much that evening, but she listened to me as I talked about everything from my trip on the train to the zebras at the zoo. She laughed when I told her about the zebra who ran in circles.

"It was the craziest thing I'd ever seen, Every time I'd spray him with water he'd run in circles."

"He sounds like circus zebra."

"You know that never occurred to me."

I was falling so deeply in love with her that it frightened me. She came to see me often after that, sometimes three to four times a week. We'd talk; I'd help her with her English, but she was learning so much on her own that what I could add seemed inconsequential. I could see the improvement almost every time we talked.

I can't tell you what she saw in me. I don't know. At first I thought it was out of sympathy that she came to see me, or because I had given her the bible, but I began to realize it was much deeper than that. I had never received such undeserved kindness in my life.

Soon the weeks had passed and it was time for the cast to come off. Dr. MacGregor came in one morning as he did every morning, but this time with a nurse, carrying a large pair of scissors.

"The time has come," he greeted in his Scottish brogue.

"The cast comes off today."

"It's here already?"

"I'm sure you'll be glad to get rid of this thing."

"Glad? Jubilant." I think that was the first time I used that word.

"Move your toes," he told me and I wiggled them.

Then the nurse, with delicate fingers, began to cut the cast, beginning at the toes and moving along the right side of the calf. It felt a little like cold water touching the skin. Soon she had reached the end, and the cast popped open. Then she and the doctor spread the cast open and removed it from my leg. It was then that I saw the scar running six or seven inches down the side of my calf.

"How does it feel?" he asked me.

"Better, but it still hurts."

"Let's put some weight on it." he said. The nurse swung my legs to the side of the bed and then both of them helped me to my feet. When I stood up on my leg, an excruciating pain shot up from my leg, up through my back and into my neck. I collapsed a moment later onto the bed.

"Why didn't you tell me it was going to hurt like that?"

"You'll walk, but not without pain," was all that he said.

When Elizabeth came to see me a few days later, she saw the cast was off and became especially elated.

"I pray for you," she told me. "It's so good your leg is healed."

"Well, It's not completely healed," I tried to explain to her, but she wasn't interested in all the technicalities.

"I have good news," she told me. "I get better job tomorrow. No longer I work at sewing machine. I inspect clothing." I think I had forgotten to say she worked in a shirt factory in London's garment district.

"That's wonderful."

"Maybe when your leg better we can see some of London."

"That would be good."

The only things I had seen in nine weeks were the grungy walls of the ward. But I didn't have the heart to tell her that I was likely going back to the States for more surgery before I'd have the chance to see anything of London.

There was a sad irony in our situation. I loved her so much it hurt, but there could be no life for us. I looked into her eyes and then tears began to slide down each cheek.

"Why do you cry, Neilos?"

She wiped my eyes with her handkerchief.

"I'm being sent back to the States soon."

"*No worry. I love you,*" *she said it as tenderly as a kiss.* "*I have dream about you while I in Arnos. I see you standing on platform and all around you faces, so many faces they look like field of flowers, and then you cry.*"

"*Why didn't you tell me this before?*"

"*You would think me silly girl.*"

"*I had dreams about you,*" *I began to explain my dreams to her. She began to cry as I described what I remembered. After I finished, I paused and then said,* "*I love you, too.*"

"*I know.*"

I would have blurted out a marriage proposal then and there, had I had a way of making it possible. But it seemed hopeless, as hopeless as her brothers' coming back to life. There was a sinking feeling in my stomach and every muscle in my body ached. I thought the cosmos morbidly sadistic, toying with lives like a cat with mice, and then she said, "*If God wishes it, we find a way.*" *This one sentence captured her entire outlook on life. If this courageous young woman could find hope, then I wouldn't give it up as a lost cause.*

We saw each other almost everyday for the next few weeks, and then the fateful news arrived. Dr. MacGregor came into the ward one morning and said, "*Tomorrow you're leaving for the States.*" *It was news I awaited with trepidation, and when it finally came it brought such sadness as my heart had never known. The whole day long I awaited Elizabeth's arrival. I was as close to tears as I could be without crying. Any stimulus could have triggered such a torrent that I would have crumbled into nothingness. But I held myself together by force of will, if nothing else, and I was determined to make our last evening together as wonderful as possible.*

Before she arrived, I had the nurses set up a table in the lobby, with candles and wine, and the best food the cafeteria could muster. I even had them use a bed sheet as a white table cloth. Then with painful difficulty I walked from my bed into the lobby, so I could wait there at the table until she arrived.

When she walked into the room and saw what I had prepared, she immediately broke down and I, too, began to cry.

"*You should not,*" *she told me as she sat across from me at the table.* "*You will hurt your leg.*" *Her face seemed more beautiful than I had ever seen it.*

"I'm leaving," I just blurted out. "Tomorrow."

"I know you must go."

We stared at each other in anticipation. The air was thick with silence, and then I said with hesitation, "Will you marry me?" I finally had the courage to speak my heart. Then I said it more forcefully, "Will you marry me?"

She smiled and then she began to cry.

"I'm sorry, I didn't mean to say anything wrong." I felt terrible. But she wiped the tears from her face and blew her nose.

"You say nothing wrong," she said. "Yes. I'll marry you."

Neither of us knew how it would come to pass nor when it would be possible, but that night we promised each other our whole lives. Then I kissed her.

My God, I miss her.

Jim could hear Nigel's voice crack as though he were about to cry. "There's so much more I have to tell you. But for now I have to stop. "Then there came a high-pitched hiss and the tape clicked off. He sat the player down on a table next to the bed, and stared up at a ceiling fan spinning on the ceiling. Within minutes he was sound asleep atop the bed linens. He hadn't even taken off his shoes.

PART II

When Priests are more in word than matter;
When Brewers mar their malt with water;
When Nobles are their tailor's tutors;
No Heretics burn'd, but wenches' suitors;
Then shall the realm of Albion come to great confusion.
When every case in law is right;
No squire in debt, nor no poor knight;
When slanderers do not live in tongues;
Nor cutpurses come not to the throngs;
When usurers tell their gold i' th'field,
and bawds and whores do churches build,
then comes the time, who lives to see't
that going shall be us'd with feet.
(King Lear III:2)

Chapter 10

When the clock chimed eight o'clock, Jim realized he had fallen asleep in his clothes. Dina came into the bed and told him, "You're going to be late, Michael."

With one huge lunge forward, he rose until he was sitting on the edge of the bed.

"I pressed your suit. It's hanging in the closet," Dina continued. "Do you want someone to drive you to the church or do you want to drive the car?"

He was still a little groggy and didn't understand the question, so she repeated it, "Do you want someone to drive you to the church or do you want to drive Nigel's car?"

"I can take a cab."

"Don't be silly. Please take the car."

She picked his shoes up off the floor and placed them on the floor of the closet. Jim moaned as he forced himself up from the bed.

"I've laid out a towel for you in the bathroom. Please tell me if you need anything else."

"Sure. Thank you."

He turned the water on very hot, the way he liked it, and climbed into the shower. Then he moved the shower head so the jets hit his face. "Ohhhh," he moaned as the water hit his skin.

"I hate funerals," he shouted into the stall. He stood in the steam for almost a half an hour, before finally turning off the jets.

He dressed methodically, in a gray pinstriped suit, which he almost never wore, and a white dress shirt and a designer red tie. He knotted the tie several times before he was satisfied with the way it hung.

"I've made you some breakfast," Dina told him when he came into the kitchen. "Some eggs and bacon and toast."

"Thank you."

He sat down at the table, and she poured him a glass of orange juice.

"How do I get to the church from here?"

"Very simple. Take The Grand Central Parkway to Astoria. It's on the corner of 23rd Avenue and 26th Street."

He made a mental note of the directions, while he took a few bites of the egg.

"Is the service long?"

"No, about an hour and then there is a burial service at the cemetery."

"I've never been to a Greek funeral."

In fact he had never been to a Greek church at all. He had been to several different Protestant churches for the weddings of friends, and once he had attended a Catholic mass for the funeral of a co-worker, but he felt himself fortunate to have successfully evaded the excesses of the religious life, until now.

Dina laid the keys to the car down on the table next to him and poured him another glass of juice. After finishing his eggs, he rose from the table, picked up the keys and left the kitchen with keys in hand.

A white wooden two car garage stood at the end of the driveway about twenty yards behind the house. A hedge ran along the whole length of it except for a small space for a walkway which ran from its edge to the back of the house. Jim walked to the end and stood before the double doors. He attempted to open the latch, but the doors were locked. Then he began to try the keys to find one of them which opened the latch. He tried four of five keys before finding the right one, and then he carefully lifted the door up above his head.

Inside, he was surprised to discover not only a blue BMW sedan, but also a Japanese car which had obviously been in a serious wreck. The windshield was shattered on the driver's side and the front end was completely crushed. It collapsed two feet, leaving the wheels turned out from each other. He stood awestruck as his gaze fixed on the mangled piece of machinery.

Dina had come outside a moment to empty trash from a wastebasket into a large trash can, and she approached Jim when she saw him staring at the car.

"I'm sorry. I should have told you about the car."

He struggled to phrase a question concerning what he was seeing.

"What would possess a man to keep something like this?"

"I don't know."

"It's horrible. Is this how she died?"

"Yes."

"The thought of it just gives me chills."

Examining every fold and wrinkle of the once smooth finish, he walked around the front of the car and knelt down to look beneath it. The violence that the wreckage betrayed convulsed him, yet he could not take his eyes off it.

"Did she die instantly?"

"No. She lingered for several hours till they found her."

He sighed and shuddered and shook his head in disbelief. He could not see the photographers snapping his picture as he examined the car. No longer was he a reluctant observer, but now he had become a major part of the story. After a few more moments of anxious contemplation, he turned to Dina and said, "I guess I'd better be going."

He opened the driver's door of the BMW and climbed inside. Lying next to him on the seat was a tape recorder and several unopened cassettes. He surmised that Nigel had been taping himself in the car. After a little hesitation, he placed the key in the ignition and turned the engine over. His forehead began to sweat from tension as he put the transmission in gear. At the front gate he stopped the car and got out to open the gate. It was there that the reporters confronted him.

"Did Nigel tell you anything about his powers?" one young blonde woman accosted him in staccato English. "We heard that he denounced his powers."

Another man interrupted her, "What were his last words?"

Soon, four or five others also shouted questions, but he said nothing in response. He simply climbed back into the car and pulled out of the driveway. Cameras were clicking and pens were putting ink to paper as he disappeared down the block.

When he arrived at the church, he found no place to park. He had to drive through several different streets before he found a space on 22nd Avenue two blocks south of the church. Then with deliberate precision he paced 26th Street across Crescent Street until he was within yards of the church. He was surprised when no press representatives accosted him on the way.

The building was a huge brown brick edifice with a brown dome on the top. From the outside, it looked simple and unimpressive, more like a Protestant church than what he expected. To the right of the church was a Greek day school named after its patron. He could see Greek lettering in the windows. He entered the church through two well-polished brass double doors and immediately realized that the exterior of the church betrayed its true character. Inside the church was impressively ornate with white marble and the finest woods and four large frescos painted on four of the walls, each depicting various bible scenes, from Adam and Eve, to the life of Jesus, with a number of scenes he did not recognize. To the left of the altar stood a baptismal font and another smaller altar, overshadowed by a Madonna and Child in Byzantine style, which he recognized from having seen it in an art magazine he had perused in college. Then to the right of the altar was what looked like a reliquary which apparently held relics of St. Nectarios.

His immediate impression was one of disdain. He surmised that the church had been built by wealthy Greeks as an opulent homage to their homeland, and he found such excesses morally inexcusable. He wondered if they were as generous with the poor or if their coffers were suddenly empty when the truly needy would come calling. He remembered what he had read about Catholic churches in South America whose altars and chalices were of the finest gold with precious stones, while the peasants who ignorantly worshiped in them were starving. 'Perhaps Marx was right,' he pondered. 'Religion is an opiate to pacify the masses.' But he dismissed this thought when Nigel's casket was suddenly wheeled through the door.

A thousand thoughts came rushing through his mind, too many for him to take hold of even one. He remembered every casket he had ever seen, including his mother's, as two men in black pushed the casket through the center aisle until it came to rest at the front of the church. His mother's funeral over twenty years before was as fresh in his mind like yesterday, and he remembered why he hated funerals. He remembered he could not shed a tear until months had passed, and what a difficult time his father had endured. Though the thoughts of her grew more infrequent with each passing year, her death had cast a darkening shadow over his entire life.

'I'm such a fool,' he told himself, 'to worry over forgotten feelings.' But he could not put the thought of her out of his mind.

He watched them as they lifted the casket off its carrier and placed it on a stand in front of the altar doors in the center of what seemed like a wall of flowers. Even in death, Nigel was surrounded by flowers. Then the men did something he had never seen at any funeral he could recall. They opened the lid to reveal Nigel's corpse, though from where he was standing he couldn't see a thing.

'How can they do this?' he asked himself. 'How can they look at death at a time like this?'

Then one by one, the church began to fill, first with elderly Greek women with their heads reverently covered and with gray dresses whose skirts almost reached their ankles, and then with families with young children who were skipping and laughing, barely understanding what was happening that day. Jim stood and watched them all as though he were a camera panning across the hall and recording everything he saw. He felt awkwardly out of place as he heard them speaking softly in Greek among themselves. When his gaze reached the left side of the church, he saw five men wearing black armbands and talking quietly among themselves. One of them was Costa Mozakis, who had picked him up at the airport, and another was Jim Jamison, Julie's father, who despite his seventy-two years looked quite youthful. Several of the men kept staring at him and he averted his eyes to keep from noticing.

"Mr. Jacobson," said one of the funeral directors. "It's our understanding you're the sixth pallbearer."

"And who said that?"

He did not know what else to say. He wanted to shout out his objections, but he remembered he had refused to carry his mother's casket, so he stopped himself and said, "I guess I am."

"Well, here's a black band to put on your arm. And you need to sit on the first aisle."

Jim placed the band on his arm.

"What can it hurt to carry the casket?" he tried to reassure himself. But he had nagging doubts about his deepening involvement.

He stood at the back of the church and waited like an expectant bridegroom. Yet he had no clue of what to expect next. Then he saw Michael Wilson, smiling and shaking hands in the narthex of the church.

Wilson was the quintessential politician, both erudite and articulate, with a pleasant charm that made him immediately likeable. People were naturally attracted to him and when he smiled he was strikingly attractive despite his age. Like Dorian Gray, he seemed ageless and as fine wine he seemed to grow richer and more ebullient with each passing year. Jim reflected on his own impressions of Wilson. He had been a political maverick, building a following among the young and upwardly mobile. Having opposed the Viet-Nam war and having marched during the sixties for civil rights, he inspired in those of Jim's generation both admiration and esteem. He seemed to embody the values of a whole generation who had been raised in the age of television.

While Jim reverently watched him through the glass of the sanctuary, he could not see Nigel's man of great evil, but a personal hero. It was a strange irony that these events would throw him together with a man he had only admired at a distance. He began to believe that Nigel had been hopelessly deluded and that he should dismiss everything that Nigel had said, including Nigel's claims to be his father.

A few minutes passed and then he saw Julie enter through the doorway.

She immediately greeted Wilson with a hug and kiss on the cheek. Then both of them entered the sanctuary.

"Jim," she greeted. She reached up to hug him, but stopped herself. "I got your message that you came to see me at the magazine. Is everything OK?"

"Yes. I was in the vicinity and just decided to drop by."

"It's a pity we have to see each other again under these circumstances."

"Yes it is," he said with all the ambiguity his heart felt about the situation.

"Have you met Michael?"

"No, not really."

"He's known me since I was this tall." She held her hand out at waist level. Oddly, in the four years they had spent together, she had never once mentioned how close she had been to Michael Wilson.

Wilson reached out and firmly shook Jim's hand.

"Maybe after this is all over, we can all have dinner."

"That would be nice," Julie said.

"Sure," Jim agreed.

"We'll talk about it," Wilson ended and began to walk with Julie toward a seat in the front of the church. Jim wondered what other secrets she was concealing.

The church began to fill with the aroma of incense, so much in fact that Jim's eyes began to water and his nose began to run. Then Father Nick stood at the center of the church and began to chant in Greek. Jim had no idea at all what he was saying. Then an usher encouraged Jim to go to his seat and a cantor began to chant in English, "Whoso dwelleth under the defense of the most high, shall abide under the shadow of the almighty."

Jim's mind began to wander from thought to thought and from impression to impression, as though his focus of attention floated like a balloon carried to and fro by the winds. When the priest chanted in English, he caught only a few phrases, and when he chanted in Greek, the words hypnotized him as though it were a lullaby, and his mind drifted erratically like in a dream. He remembered the day in college in 1974 when his father called him, and in two short words, "She's dead," totally turned his life inside out. Some say it's easier when one knows a loved one is dying, but he would have wanted it quick and painless rather than the long lingering suffering she endured.

"Damn it," he told himself as he looked at the ceiling. "I can't let it do this to me."

He stood at a sufficient distance so as to avoid looking directly into the casket. He preferred to remember Nigel alive. But his attention was redirected as though by some hidden force, and he found himself turning his head in the direction of the casket. Twice he forced his gaze back up at the ceiling where a huge portrait of Jesus looked down on the crowd.

Then he started to cry—at first only a trickle down each of his cheeks, but then his eyes filled with tears, and like overripe olives they fell down his face. Yet, he did not understand why he was crying. Then he pulled a handkerchief from his pocket and wiped both his eyes.

The service was more beautiful and moving than he expected, though he found the incessant talk of resurrection unnerving. 'Knowing what we've learned about biology and DNA,' he pondered. 'How can they believe in resurrection?' Though he didn't want to get into another religious discussion, he was curious to ask some simple questions. But he decided to restrain himself for fear of hearing about weeping pieces of wood again, and he realized that funerals are for the benefit of the living and not for the dead.

Soon the prayers were over and the incense extinguished. Then Father Nick got up in the pulpit to speak. "Oh death where is thy sting! Oh Hades, where is thy victory," he began. "We say these words every Pascha as a hymn of joy for the resurrection. But what is our faith if when faced with life's most horrible tragedy, we shrink from belief. It's easy to say I believe in the resurrection as some abstract concept, like goodness, or mercy. But when we look into death's horrible face, then tell me, do we believe? Nigel lies here dead. I've lost a friend. We sing and we pray about future glory, yet we hurt so much we can barely move. 'Lord have mercy,' we sing, but we ask where is His mercy? But our church teaches that this is not the end. We were not made for death, but for life. As Saint Paul says, 'If there is no resurrection from the dead, we are the most foolish of people.'"

Jim stopped concentrating on the sermon, and his mind began to wander. Again, he found himself staring toward the casket. Then his eyes caught those of Julie, and she smiled at him.

It was seven years before that he had met her on a train. He was heading from New York to Chicago, and she was going to visit the University of Chicago. They rode twenty hours sitting across from each other, ten of which they said nothing. He was much bolder then, and had asked her, "What's your name?"

At first she didn't respond. So he asked her again, "What's your name?"

"Julie Jamison."

"I'm Jim Jacobson. Where are you heading?"

"Chicago."

"So am I. I work at a small weekly in the suburbs. But I'm not always going to work there. Someday, I'll be a commentator."

He talked about his father, about where he had gone to school and about his dreams. But she was reluctant to talk to him and would not respond. But he kept talking and finally wore her down.

"I'm a reporter too," she finally told him.

"You are?"

"Yes. I'm going to visit the University of Chicago to see about graduate school."

Then they talked about reporting, about Chicago, and about each other. By the time they left the train, they agreed to see each other again. The five years that had passed since he had seen her seemed like a century, and he felt much older, but she looked no different from how he remembered her.

Finally, he grew tired of fighting the impulse to look. He turned his head and he stared into the casket. When he saw Nigel's lifeless remains, something snapped inside of him and he began to cry intensely. Costa, who was sitting next to him, grabbed his hand and held it firmly, but Jim continued to cry. When Costa put his arm around him, Jim felt uncomfortable receiving such affection from a man and pushed Costa's arm away.

"God, what a mess I've made of my life."

After Father Nick finished his sermon and came down from the pulpit, the funeral director closed the lid of the coffin and locked it shut with a small handle. Then he instructed the pallbearers to approach the casket and lift it from its stand. With machinelike precision, they lifted the wooden box and carried it out the double doors and into a hearse parked at the curb. With the slam of the doors, Nigel was on his way.

"I hate funerals," Jim told himself again.

Julie came up behind him and waited patiently for him to notice her. When he turned around, she asked him, "Are you OK, Jim? You've been crying."

"I don't know why I'm crying." He paused. "You know I've had deep regrets about the way I ended things with you. I'm sorry."

"It's OK."

"It's not OK. I don't think there is a relationship I've handled right in the last eighteen years."

Then a man, not wearing a suit, but jeans and a tee shirt, came up and stood behind him. He leaned over and whispered in Jim's ear, "I'm sorry to interrupt you. But I'm here for a friend. Have you finished the tapes?"

Jim immediately became afraid and shook his head "no".

"I'm going to hand you a business card in a minute. On the back is a phone number. Call me when you've finished them. But please don't tell anyone about the tapes."

"Who are you?" Jim asked him.

The man handed him a card and disappeared without an answer. "What was that all about?" Julie asked him.

"Someone trying to sell me something." He did not know why he lied. But the warning given by Reynolds pierced his consciousness like a dagger. He read the card which said 'Flushing Floral Supply' and then put it in his pocket. 'They're all a bunch of nuts,' he thought to himself.

The funeral director, looking tired, signaled it was time to depart and people who had been engaging in random conversation began to move in quiet rhythm toward their cars. Wilson and Jamison climbed into a limousine parked at the curb and Julie soon joined them.

"You're welcome to come along with us," she invited him as she climbed into the car.

But he answered, "No, I'd rather drive myself."

Jim walked back to 22nd Avenue with his head bowed and his eyes focused on the sidewalk beneath his feet. He noticed how the concrete slabs had shifted and what at first looked level was as uneven as the surface of the ocean. After surveying its whole length and breadth, he threw the door of the car open, and he soon joined the caravan on the way to the cemetery. At Flushing Cemetery, there was a short grave-side service, and then they lowered Nigel's casket into a hole in the ground. Jim watched the whole procedure with the intensity of a painter.

"Would you like to eat dinner with me tonight?" Julie asked him.

"Sure."

"Where are you staying?"

He felt hesitant to answer, but replied, "I'm staying at Nigel's house."

"Then I'll be around about seven, if that's OK."

"That's fine," he replied, but his mind seemed preoccupied.

"Are you coming, Jim?"

"No. I'd like to stay for a while."

"Alright," she said as she leaned over to him and kissed him on the cheek. Then she climbed into the limousine and departed.

He lingered at the grave side long after all the other spectators had gone. For nearly an hour he sat quietly and watched the workers as they slowly filled the hole with dirt.

"It's an amazing thing," a voice broke the silence and startled him. "We don't see the sheer absurdity of it all. We take a body, shove it into a box and then stick it in the ground as though it were as perfectly natural as rainwater."

Jim turned his head and discovered a bearded man with glasses standing behind him. He was about fifty, and he puffed a pipe with such ferocity that the plumes of smoke rose as a cloud above his head.

"Who are you?" he asked the man.

"The better question to ask is *who are you?*"

"Look, I'm not in the mood to play games. Just tell me who you are or go away."

Jim turned his head back and continued looking at the grave.

"I'm the *deus ex machina* in this little drama."

"What is it you want?"

"I want to talk to you about Nigel."

"Then talk."

He continued to puff on the pipe and began to blow rings after every inspiration.

"I came to warn you. You have no idea what you've stepped into."

"Why can't any of you come straight with me? From you to Father Nick to Nigel, it's like you're all tongue-tied. What is it you want from me?"

"I can't say more. We're being watched. From the moment you stepped off the plane until now, you've been followed."

"It seems to me you've been reading too many Tom Clancy novels."

"Doesn't it strike you funny that Jamison and Wilson should be involved with Nigel?"

"Of course."

"Then think it out. What reasons could they have for being involved with him?"

"I'm not going to play guessing games."

"Alright, I'll give you a clue. You'll never read about it in the papers."

"I don't believe the papers." he paused.

"You've heard of the Knights Templar?"

"I don't believe in conspiracy theories."

"Good," the man responded as he puffed several times on the pipe. "Neither do I." He paused. "There is a wellspring of people longing for spirituality. Not everyone is happy with this grab for the gusto lifestyle our society promotes. But like everyone else, even these people must be controlled. A little spirituality makes for a pliant submissive proletariat. But too much can lead to revolution."

"So what you're saying is that Nigel was being used."

"Think about it a while." He paused. "I have something for you." He reached into his pocket and pulled out a photograph. "This is the man who's been following you."

Jim looked closely at the photograph and noticed a man in a red beret, but did not recognize him.

"Keep an eye out for him."

Jim wanted to speak, but he said nothing, because he did not know whom to trust.

The man continued, "Nigel came to me because I had written a book about secret societies. But unfortunately, this is all I can tell you."

"But you haven't told me anything."

"Again, I offer you a word of warning. Go back to where you came from before you can't go back."

Then he turned around and began to walk away.

"That's all you're going to tell me. You come here and scare the hell out of me and then walk away as though nothing has happened."

The man kept walking.

"Damn you people," he began to shout. "I should give you all what you deserve. I should stick around here and become a thorn in all your sides."

Chapter 11

The image of Nigel's lifeless face kept impinging upon his consciousness, and as hard as he tried to think about other things, he could not push the thought from his mind. He remembered how unlike himself Nigel looked in death and he also remembered his mother's face with its death mask painted on her wax-like flesh. Then he turned on the radio of the car in hopes to distract his attention, but when the radio began to play a love song, he could not help himself, he began to cry. Each chord of the chorus brought more tears, and as he sang along, he nearly shouted the lyrics with tears streaming as fountains down each of his cheeks. Then he turned the radio off to stop himself from crying.

His grief had been like sudden blindness, as though a huge partition of pain had been placed in front of his eyes, and what was translucent had become opaque. They told him it would get better with time, but as a blind man out of necessity learns to cope with his blindness, he had learned to acknowledge the death of his mother, but he had never come to terms with it.

He remembered all the shallow condolences, and the "I know what you're going through" speeches that people felt obligated to make. But he knew that his pain was uniquely personal and something he could not share with anyone else. 'One can lose his favorite motor car,' he proposed to himself, 'and despite the loss regain some equilibrium. But how can someone replace his mother or father?' The thought occurred to him how totally alone he had become, that he had pushed everyone, including his father, out of his life, and had embraced his grief with a self-indulgent masochism. He wanted to talk to someone, but he had no one whom he completely trusted.

Then he began to realize that he was lost, somewhere in the south of Queens. In the midst of all his emotion he had made a wrong turn somewhere. So, he stopped the car and he found himself staring into the Atlantic Ocean. 'I must go out to the sea again, to the lonely sea and sky, and all I ask is a tall ship and a star to steer her by,' He recited in his mind. He could hear the calls of seagulls and the roar of the waves against the sand, and above him he heard the roar of a jet engine as a 727 cut across the sky.

Then he remembered a poem he had written in college about the sea and something at the funeral came to mind. 'Whoso dwelleth under the defense of the most high, shall abide under the shadow of the Almighty.' He thought to himself, 'God, what a fool I am, crying over forgotten feelings.' He was beginning to stop fighting what was happening to him.

When Jim returned to Nigel's house, it was about three o'clock. He had been lost twice on his way back home. First he found himself on Hillside Avenue in Jamaica and then in Great Neck. With the assistance of two gas station attendants, he was able to find his way back to Northern Boulevard and from there back to Nigel's house. When he pulled into the driveway, he was again accosted by reporters, but he acted as though they weren't there, and put the car away in the garage without speaking so much as a grunt. When he entered the front door, Dina was vacuuming the living room carpet and stopped the vacuum to talk to him.

"How was the grave-side service?" she asked.

He wanted to say, "It was terrible," but he stopped himself and responded with a casual and acceptable, "It was OK."

"I'm making a turkey for you for supper."

"Thank you, but I'm going out to dinner tonight."

"Then have you eaten lunch?"

"No."

"I made some sandwiches. They're on the kitchen table. Please help yourself."

He walked into the kitchen and found neatly arranged on a platter, a stack of sandwiches with the crusts cut off the way caterers prepare them for wedding receptions. Beside the sandwiches was a plate of fried potatoes, cut into ridges. He grabbed a couple of sandwiches and popped them into his mouth like popcorn and he finished them in four huge swallows. Then he grabbed a pitcher of what looked like lemonade and poured himself a glass. He downed this in three huge gulps. He could not remember the last time he had tasted lemonade. But this was so good that he decided he might actually like it again.

Dina turned off the vacuum again and shouted to him, "You have some messages. I put them by the phone."

He found four messages sitting next to the phone. On each he saw a name and a phone number with a short message written with such exactitude that it resembled calligraphy. He lifted the messages to read them. The first message was from the Associated Press, which he wadded up and tossed into a waste can near the back door. The second was from Marshall Hebert, a name he did not recognize, with a Manhattan phone number. He set this one aside. The third was from Michael Wilson's Office, asking him to call for an appointment. This message he set atop the message from Marshall Hebert. The fourth message was from his father in Chicago, though how his father had found him at Nigel's he could only speculate.

He recognized his father's number as his University number, so he dialed this number first. It rang a few seconds and then a woman answered.

"Economics department."

"Is Doctor Jacobson there?"

"No, he's stepped out for a few minutes."

"Tell him his son called him from New York, and he can reach me at the number he called earlier."

"I'm sure he'll be back in a few minutes. You can wait."

"That's fine. Goodbye."

He hung up the phone. He knew his father as a man of exacting efficiency who would never call solely to make idle conversation. If his father had gone to the trouble to track him down, it must be over something truly important. He decided he would keep the line open and not return the other two messages until after his father called. He folded the messages in half and put them in his pocket. Then he went upstairs to change his clothes.

Upstairs he found that the room was meticulously clean, more like a museum than a bedroom, and Dina had laid out a change of clothes for him. Both the slacks and shirt she had pressed with creases better than a dry-cleaner would make them. Such attention to detail seemed neurotic to him. Then a compelling question occurred to him. *Why is this woman still here?* Though, he did not have a desire to investigate the issue any further.

What he wanted to do was go back to Hadleyburg, but he knew that if he returned without a story, Reynolds would fire him, and with his bank balance at eighty-five dollars, he'd find survival impossible. It was a perplexing dilemma. He could remain in New York and face deeper involvement in ever increasing intrigue, or he could return home to face certain poverty. For the first time he began to realize that, like it or not, he could never go back to the life he had lived. Nigel's arrival had forever changed his circumstances.

He was almost completely dressed when Dina called from downstairs, "Your father is on the phone."

He picked up the receiver in the bedroom.

"Yes, Dad. I'm here, what do you want?"

"Jim, what's going on?"

"What do you mean?"

"I got a letter this morning from Nigel with a certified check for $100,000. All the note says is, 'thanks.'"

"Oh, my God, he didn't."

Jim seemed to find humor in the situation.

"What's going on?"

"Why, he was a nut, dad."

"That may well be, but it doesn't answer my question."

There was an edge of volatility in his voice.

"Why are you so angry about this? Just cash the check."

"I have a reputation to uphold. I can't afford to be receiving checks from someone like him. He mailed it to the University, and Paula opened it. Now I'm certain it's the talk of the department. You owe me an explanation."

Jim struggled with whether or not he should tell him the truth and after a few moments, he finally acquiesced.

"He thought he was my father. I guess the check was sort of a payment for services rendered."

There was a distressed tone in his father's voice as he answered, "How does he figure that? I'm your father."

Then Jim, again fighting his own reservations, told him, "Look Dad, I know about the adoption."

The news dropped like an overripe apple as over twenty years of muteness gave way to the truth. A hesitant silence lingered for several minutes before his father answered, "How long have you known?"

"Since Mom's death, I found the adoption papers among her things."

"It's been a long twenty years. I'm sorry. I promised her I wouldn't tell you. She believed it would hurt you to discover the true circumstances."

"I know that too."

"We never intended to hurt you. We both wanted you. Why should it matter what your real mother wanted?"

"You lied to me. For all these years you lied to me."

"I'm sorry. I know there is no excuse for it. But times were different then. It was a tremendous scandal to be illegitimate. We thought, why should you carry the anger of having been abandoned by your mother, if you didn't have to?" He paused. "I guess we should talk about it."

"That would be great."

"Then I'll cancel my classes till the end of the week and see if I can fly to

New York tomorrow."

"I could use an ear right now."

"I'll call you when I get to New York."

"Sure, Dad. I'll see you tomorrow. Goodbye."

As he hung up the phone, he looked at the clock sitting by the bed, and he saw the time was four o'clock. *Three hours,* he thought. *What can I do for the next three hours?* His eyes danced erratically across the room and when he saw the satchel, they hesitated a moment. He was reluctant to hear more for fear that some even more disturbing revelation awaited him. But after a short moment of timidity, he gave in to his impulses. Grabbing the satchel again, he removed the player and slid the tape labeled 'number four' into it.

He could not bear to hear Nigel's voice, so soon after he had been buried in the earth. He wanted to rip the headphones off his ears and toss the player against the wall, but for the sake of his story he forced himself to listen anyway.

When Elizabeth left me on that our last evening in London, I was devastated. I did not know whether I would ever see her again or if our words would be like those of so many other lovers whom fate dictated must be parted. Soon there would be an ocean between us and that ocean seemed as formidable a barrier as death.

I wrote my mother the morning I left London and told her what had happened. I would often imagine her sitting across from me and I would write as though I were speaking to her. Sometimes if I imagined hard enough, I could see her as vividly as the day I had last seen her at the station. I told her that I had come to love this beautiful young woman, although it seemed impossible. Yet I didn't hear my mother's voice, but my father's.

"A man should stick to his own kind," I could hear him. "It's a hopeless endeavor to love someone you cannot have."

He had always been sensible about such things, or so I thought at the time. Although as I mentioned earlier, he turned out to be more complex than I ever imagined. But then I could only remember what I had often heard him say.

I remembered what a scandal it had been when this Catholic woman married a preacher's son, and it had our whole church in an uproar. "He should have known not to marry an outsider," my father had said, when the church ostracized the man and revoked his preaching certificate. For he, like most of them, considered a Catholic worse than a murderer. It was for this reason among others that I found religion unattractive and religious people undesirable.

"If he loved the girl," I remember arguing with him, "What difference does it make what her religion was? It seems to me in a world where so many people hate each other, we should be happy when people love each other."

"Since when do you know about such things," he had lectured me, and I knew if he had been in the room then, he would be telling me all the reasons that my relationship with Elizabeth was another lost cause. I didn't think he ever got over the fact that I didn't marry Florence Scrapper.

On the other side, my mother was always so hopeful and tolerant. I didn't think she confronted him openly about her own opinions, but I could sense she was able to persuade him when she felt the cause was a just one.

When I finished my letter, I set it down beside me on the bed, and I asked a nurse for a cup of water. When the nurse returned, she also brought my mail, and among several letters from home was the one and only letter Leonard ever wrote me.

It was a strange letter, I remember because he talked more about himself than in any previous conversation we had shared. Perhaps because he was facing death and he felt he had to tell someone his thoughts. And I remember him telling me, and I paraphrase from memory, that he had never been a religious man, but after having come face to face with death, he had begun to realize that without a deity nothing made any sense, and he was beginning to rethink his positions on a number of issues. He didn't give any particulars about what had happened to him, but I could sense something had happened to him which deeply disturbed him. He also wrote the most curious thing. He told me he had figured out how the Great Bartholomew had done his act and he was hoping to have the opportunity to test his theory. Then he promised me once the war was over, he would do everything he could to get me back on my feet. At the time I believed them to be empty promises.

When I left London, it had been ten weeks to the day since I first awakened in the ward. It's hard to explain, but it seemed like both the longest and the shortest ten weeks in my life.

They sent me by ship to a naval hospital in Bethesda, Maryland, where I had the second of what would later be five operations on the leg.

About this time of my life, so much is a blur, because I spent so much time in bed and the remainder in a wheelchair. If suffering purifies the soul, I believed mine had been through the heavy duty cycle, and if it were not for letters from Beth and from my mother, I don't think I would have survived it at all.

I read a lot during those months, because I had little else to do. One particular book which sticks out in my mind was Thomas Mann's The Magic Mountain, *which I found comfort in reading, though the circumstances were different from my own. It seemed odd to me that a country which produced the Nazis could also produce someone like Mann. He wrote about suffering with such insight that I've often reread the book throughout the years. Though I probably would have been the last to admit it, I also began to read the Bible. What I found of particular poignancy were the Psalms, especially Psalm 90, which begins, "Whoso dwelleth under the defense of the Most High, shall abide under the shadow of the Almighty," though I had yet to come to terms with God or to have anything faintly resembling religious belief.*

From the summer of 1942 until the end of November, I remained in the hospital, recuperating from five operations to correct the problem in my leg. After the fifth and what would be final operation, I was confined to a wheelchair and wasn't sure if I'd ever walk again.

I remember how angry I had become at fate and how unfair life seemed for causing me such great pain as the result of an act of kindness when I saved the lieutenant's naval career. I had neither the maturity nor the experience to realize then that wisdom comes only through suffering and without pain there is no birth. In a real sense, I was both being born and giving birth. The boy whom I had been was dying and the man I was to become was being born.

My twenty-fourth birthday came and went with a whimper that October, and I spent the day alone.

Dina came into the room and gathered up Jim's clothes from the bed and left the room with them. Her preoccupation with cleanliness and order deeply annoyed him, and had he not been focused on what Nigel had been saying on the tapes, he would have gone after her and taken back his suit. Yet, what

Nigel was saying was beginning to touch him, because he too had spent so much of his last five years alone.

My loneliness was in its own way more agonizing than the physical pain I had suffered. For my physical pain there was morphine, yet for my loneliness only a kind voice could have soothed me, and kindness seemed as rare a commodity as rubber during the war.

I talked superficially to a couple of the other patients, but most of the others seemed cold and indifferent to me. Even Dr. Massengill who operated on my leg had little bedside manner. I vividly remembered how after the third and most painful of the operations, he came into the ward where I was resting and in typical temperament grunted out, "How do you feel?"

"Terrible." My leg was throbbing in so much pain that the slightest quiver caused my teeth to chatter.

"Your leg looks good. Two more minor procedures and you'll be ready to go back to work."

"Then why am I in such pain?"

"No problem. The leg is healing fine."

"No problem." I felt like strangling him, because he wasn't the one feeling the pain.

"We're going to reduce the dosage of morphine until we take you completely off. Find something to take your mind off the pain."

"What am I supposed to do to take my mind off it? I'm in pain"

"Try meditation. It can't hurt."

Then he went on with his rounds. I told Beth in one of my letters about the pain and she wrote back to me about a simple prayer which she thought might help me, though I didn't feel like praying. "Whenever the pain becomes unbearable," she wrote me, "just say to yourself 'Lord Jesus Christ have mercy on me' until the pain goes away."

I thought it silly when she wrote about it. But one day when I was in such agony I could barely move, I tried it and to my surprise with each successive repetition the pain lessened until I hardly felt it at all. Sometimes I spent up to half an hour at a time, reciting the phrase until the pain subsided. I'm certain the other patients thought me nuts for doing it, but it worked, though why it worked I couldn't even guess.

From letter to letter, Beth's English showed marked improvement.

At first she only communicated in simple sentences with words common to the McGuffin reading books I had as a child, but as her vocabulary expanded, she seemed ever more facile and articulate. I had never known anyone who had struggled so hard to find apt words to express herself. One letter she wrote me contained five words I had never seen before, and I had to go to a dictionary to look them up.

"I've never known anyone to get as much mail as you get," the nurse told me one morning as she handed me a stack of letters. It seemed as if my mother wrote me almost everyday and Beth every three to four days.

"What do they have to say to you in such abundance?"

"Let me read you one."

She seemed reluctant to listen, yet I opened one of my mother's letters and began to read it anyway.

"Dear Nigel. I'm sorry to hear you are still in so much pain. Your father and Reginald bought a used tractor today from the Willets. It was that ugly green one that sat outside their barn. The county told them they had to move it inside, because it was such an eyesore. I told your father that if he wanted the tractor, he had to get it painted. So he, Reginald and Michael spent the entire day in the shed painting it bright red. Michael suggested in honor of her new look, we christen her with a name. So the tractor is now affectionately called 'Bertha' after your father's maiden aunt. You never knew her, but up into her sixties she always dyed her hair a bright red, and she would show up at the house periodically, uninvited and she always brought the most awful apple pie, which we felt obligated to eat."

I stopped when the nurse seemed bored with what I was saying.

"Well, you get the idea," I said.

Then to my surprise she told me, "I grew up on a farm."

"Where?"

"In Nebraska. I hated it."

I thought she was going to say more but she stopped herself and continued down the ward.

My mother's letters were always vivid and full of details. I think she knew how important it was for me to feel connected to something and I could almost picture what was going on at home as though I were there watching it. When she talked about the tractor, I could see him standing before and examining every inch of its metal

*physique. When she talked about the harvest, I could see them
sweating beneath a hot August sun and cutting corn with skin as red as
newly harvested radishes. When she talked about the snow, I could see
the rolling hills covered with white linen as though asleep. I could see
Reginald and my father feeding the cows and washing pens as though I
were there beside them. My father enjoyed farming as much as any
painter enjoyed putting brush to canvas, and when he worked, he
committed his whole person to the task as though anything less was
unworthy of himself. Yet, I could never understand what he saw in
farming.*

*When I neared the end of the letter about the tractor, my mother
mentioned in passing that Michael had tested for the university. He
apparently passed an entrance exam, and his score was so good that
chances looked promising he could start University the next term on
scholarship. At fourteen he had a clearer vision of who he was and
where he was going than I had at twenty-four, yet he had always been
studious and I remembered him as incredibly bright. I should have
been happy for him, but I felt a little jealousy. Anything Michael
applied himself to, he seemed to master with ease, while I seemed to be
carried to and fro by whatever wind was blowing. I set the letter aside
and looked across the room. The ward consisted of twelve beds, six on
each side. I was in the second bed on the north side. On my left was a
seaman named McIntosh who had injured his back and was in traction.
He said very little save when he wanted his pain medication. To my
right was Alex Ohotin, a son of Russian immigrants, who had grown
up in a Russian neighborhood in Harlem. He and I had the most
cordial of relations though our interaction consisted largely in
discussions about baseball, because he was a Brooklyn Dodgers fan.
Sometimes to agitate him, I said I loved the Yankees and we'd argue a
little about who had the best pitcher or catcher, though at the time my
interest in baseball was nominal. Occasionally we'd play a hand of gin
rummy, but he beat me so badly I usually wouldn't ask him to play
again.*

*Alex had been at the hospital three months longer than me. He had
injured his leg at Pearl Harbor when the Japanese attacked. He used
to joke, "I'm the luckiest man alive," because he had left the Arizona
just minutes before it was destroyed.*

In the other beds in the ward, so many patients came and went, many staying for only a few days and I had little time to get to know any of them.

Two days before Christmas 1942, when Dr. Massingill came in to read my chart, he smiled and said, "Nigel, I have good news." I was almost certain they would give me a medical discharge, but he continued, "Your orders came through today. You're being sent to a naval air station in New York City after the first of the year. You're going back to work."

The news gave him great satisfaction as though I had been one of his professional successes. Yet, I was unsure of my stamina or if I'd be able to endure my ever-present pain.

During those seemingly endless months while I was captive to my bed, I had often thought about what I would do when they finally released me. I had even considered going home to Wisconsin, though I still had great misgivings about the farm. When I pondered the prospect of going back to New York, it appealed to me, yet I was frightened. It had been two years since Leonard and I fled the loan shark, but I was still afraid he might somehow find me.

I remember the day I left the hospital in Bethesda that it was snowing, and my leg throbbed in a dull pain as I walked out of the ward into the courtyard of the hospital complex. I had a brown wooden cane which the navy supplied to me. It was not very attractive, but was sufficient to the task. I left with no fond goodbyes, no handshakes, no well-wishes from friends. After a short walk to a waiting car, I climbed inside, and a navy driver took me to the train station. He left me at the gate and wished me a small, "Good luck," before he departed.

I had no idea which direction my life was going or what would await me in New York. Yet, like a song returns to a familiar chorus, I again found myself going to New York by train. From Bethesda to Penn Station was four and a half hours. It would have been enough time to read half of a short book, or to write several letters to my mother and Beth, but I didn't feel like reading or writing. I spent my time watching snow blow against the train window, and it seemed like a carpet of white stretched out in all directions. It resembled a comforter, hastily tossed from bed with hundreds of random folds and creases as it lay on the floor. We stopped in Wilmington and Philadelphia and Newark.

The thoughts that kept running through my head were not about New York or Wisconsin or even London for that matter. I kept thinking about my cane. I stared at it with an intense fascination. Lifting it and spinning it between my fingers, I thought of all the people I had seen with canes, like men in top hats with tuxedos and old men with balding heads and mohair sweaters, and old women with their hand-knit shawls who shuffled across the busy city streets. I thought of schoolmasters and of barristers, of gentlemen with gout, and of all the crippled and lame whom life seemed to have forgotten. It was like a badge of honor or a statement of position and rank. Yet, I held it tentatively, afraid to accept what it meant. Later it would become for me a tangible symbol of my suffering.

It was nearly midnight when we pulled into Penn Station, and I emerged from its bowels like a war-weary Ulysses returning home from Troy. As I stood at the corner at Harold Square and breathed in the cold New York air, I was worried about what would become of me. Every human life has guideposts, which stand as gates separating what came before from what comes after. I sensed I stood at one of these points.

The tape clicked off on the first side, and Jim took the headphones off his ears for a moment. He reached into the satchel and found a yellow pad and pen. Then he began writing down notes, mostly names and places and dates, as though by association he would tie them all together. Then in bold letters he wrote across the page, 'WHO IS THE LOAN SHARK?' He was finally beginning to think like a reporter. He flipped the tape over and again heard Nigel's haunting voice.

When I reported to my duty station the next morning, it was not the kind of work which I expected. A chief warrant officer named Rusk greeted me and directed me to the lieutenant's office. I sat in a chair in the outer office for what seemed like an hour before I was called back to talk to him. When I entered the office, I saluted him and he told me, "Sit down." I read the name plate on his desk, Lieutenant Capelli, and sat down.

"Welcome, Mr. Fox. Do you have any idea what kind of work we do here?"

"No. Not really."

"We're a Special Services unit. You're one of the fortunate few to get such an assignment."

"What exactly is Special Services?" I asked him.

"We engage in electronic surveillance of the enemy."

"Do you mean you're spies?"

"We don't like to use that word. We are information gatherers."

He talked a little more about the nature of the work without going into detail, and then he gave me a tour of the base. It was a place unlike any place I have ever seen, filled with gadgets and gizmos of the latest technological enterprise. It was a wonderland of scientific endeavor, and I, like Alice, would discover some of its secrets. Had Leonard been assigned here, it would have been heaven for him, but he was somewhere in the Pacific on a destroyer, though I didn't know where. For the next two and a half years until the end of the war, I would spend my time by testing equipment and by learning as much as I could about electronics.

Chapter 12

Dina came into the room and tapped Jim on the shoulder.

"I'm sorry to interrupt you, Michael. But you have a phone call."

He stopped the tape and asked her, "Who is it?"

"It's that man who called you earlier, Marshall Hebert."

He rose from his chair and moved toward the telephone on the other side of the room. After taking the earphones off his ears, he answered it.

"Yeah. This is Jim Jacobson. What can I do for you?"

"I'm Marshall Hebert. I called earlier."

"Yes."

"I know you're writing a story about Nigel, and I have some information which might be of interest to you."

"Alright, what is it?"

"I can't tell you over the phone. Can't we meet somewhere?"

"I'm very busy right now. You're sure you can't tell me over the phone?"

"Someone might be listening. It should only take a few minutes."

Jim could sense the paranoia in the man's voice, yet unlike the others the man seemed more interested in his own protection than in intrigue.

"OK. Where would you like to meet?" He wasn't sure why he acquiesced.

"There's a diner at the corner of Northern Boulevard and the Clearview Expressway. Do you know where that is?"

"Yeah, I think I can find it."

"I'll meet you there in thirty minutes. Goodbye."

Jim hung up the phone and then grabbed the satchel from the table. After placing the player and headphones back inside, he zipped it shut and placed the bag on a shelf in the closet. Then he rushed out the door, down the hallway and to the front door of the house.

"I'll be back in a little while," he shouted to Dina as he left through the front doorway.

He was determined to escape the house undetected by the press. He went to the back of the house to a spot where he was certain they could not see him, and he scaled the security fence with the stealth of a cat. He dropped himself into the backyard of an adjoining house. Then with a gait more like a crawl than a walk, he dashed to the front of the house and onto the sidewalk, running south toward Northern Boulevard. It was a longer walk than what he anticipated, and he had some difficulty breathing the humid air. His heart raced in his chest and he could almost hear each successive heartbeat.

Soon, he was on Northern Boulevard. He waited about ten minutes until a bus stopped to pick him up and twenty minutes later it dropped him off within a few blocks of the diner. He jogged the last few hundred feet. In front of the Diner, pacing nervously, like an expectant father, was a man close to Jim's age with short brown hair and glasses. He was wearing a style of clothes more popular in Europe than America, and he carried himself humbly with his head bowed to the ground.

Jim approached him and said, "Are you Marshall Hebert? I'm Jim Jacobson."

"I didn't think you were coming. I'm sorry for the deception. But I'm David Fox. Please, let's go inside."

When Jim heard the man's name, his mind began to search through all that he had learned about Nigel. Yet he could not remember a David Fox. He did not know if he should accept at face value what the man told him or if he should view even this with the same skepticism he had viewed everything else. He decided that to satisfy his curiosity, he would hear the man out. But he would not be the first to speak his mind.

After the hostess showed them to a table in the corner of the restaurant, the young man sat down across from Jim and he began to talk.

"I'm Nigel's nephew. I've been in Europe doing some postgraduate work, when I got this telegram from Nigel. It was about a week ago."

David reached into his shirt pocket and retrieved a folded piece of paper, which he handed to Jim to read.

"David, please stay in Europe. My life is in danger. May not be safe for you here either. Nigel," Jim read.

"I was supposed to come home last week. But then I got this telegram. I'm sorry I didn't go to the funeral, but I was afraid."

A waitress came by and took their orders.

"I'll take an orange soda."

"Do you have cheesecake?" David asked her.

"Yes."

"Then give me a slice and a glass of tea."

Looking a little annoyed that they had not ordered more, she left the table with their orders.

"I don't think your life is in danger," Jim assured him. "I think Nigel was suffering from an overactive imagination."

"Then you don't think someone killed him."

Jim began to chuckle softly at what seemed to him the most preposterous of proposals.

"No, Nigel was not murdered. My own conjecture is that he had a stroke."

The waitress brought their drinks. "Is there anything else?" she asked them.

"Yeah," Jim said. "I'll have a turkey sandwich."

"Sure. And you, sir?"

"Nothing else. Thank you."

She again left the table.

"You're sure I have no reason to worry?" David continued.

"I was with him. He died of natural causes. I'm certain this whole threat was something concocted by his imagination."

The waitress brought out the cheese cake and Jim's turkey sandwich which they both ate quietly. As he was eating, Jim felt calm for the first time in days. He had constructed a plausible explanation for all that was happening and through the soundness of his argument, he had convinced himself, though from the expression on David's face he could see that David was not convinced.

What could he say to alleviate the fear and how was it that Nigel could infect so many others with his own hysteria? These and other questions filled his mind, though he held his tongue, refusing to let one pregnant word escape his lips.

Then he asked, "Where were you studying?"

"In Wiesbaden. My doctorate is in German Philosophy. Nietzsche. Kant. Hegel. Heidegger. I'm particularly interested in the early period and in Goethe."

Jim's knowledge of German philosophy was limited, and he felt reluctant to betray his ignorance.

"I thought Goethe was a poet," he hesitated.

"He was. But he dealt with the deepest issues in his poetry. I remember Faust's opening monologue. '*Haben nun auch Philosophie, Juristerei und Medizin and leider auch Theologie durchaus studiert mit heissem bemuhn.*'" He spoke German without a trace of accent. "'*Da steh' ich nun, ich armer tor, und bin so klug als wie zuvor;*' He says he studied philosophy, law, medicine and theology and he stands no smarter than he was before." He paused. "That's the whole study of philosophy. The quest for the unknowable."

"That's what this story feels like," Jim interrupted him.

"What do you need to know?" David asked him. "Maybe I can help you."

Jim seemed distracted a moment. "What time is it?"

"It's a quarter to six," David said after he looked at his watch.

"I'm sorry, but I've gotta go. Could you give me a lift back to Nigel's house?"

"Sure."

They paid the check and left the diner. While Jim was climbing into the rented car which David was driving, he asked David, "Where are you staying?"

"At a hotel not far from here."

"Maybe we can eat lunch tomorrow. Give me a call."

"Please, don't tell anyone you talked to me. I know I'm being silly. But I don't want anyone to know."

"OK," he reluctantly agreed.

Neither of them said a word during the five minute trip back to Nigel's house. When Jim opened the door to disembark the car, David turned to him and told him, "Maybe we can talk tomorrow and clear the air about some things."

"Sure, just give me a call in the morning, and we'll go to lunch somewhere."

After Jim closed the door, he watched the car pull away and disappear down the block. The whole encounter felt dreamlike and unreal. Yet he was curious to talk to David again when they both had more time. When he opened the front gate leading to the steps, he was surprised that the press had not confronted him at the sidewalk, though he knew they were fickle and their attention span infinitesimal.

When Jim walked through the front doorway and into the hallway of the house, Dina stopped him as he was climbing upstairs.

"There were several phone calls for you while you were gone," she began. "Michael Wilson's office called. They're sending a car for you tomorrow at six, so you can eat dinner with the governor." She paused. "Your father called from Chicago. His flight arrives at Kennedy airport at four o'clock tomorrow. And someone named Reynolds called asking about your story. I wrote down his number by the phone."

"I'll call him in a little while," he muttered in an uneven cadence as he continued up the steps.

'Why is it so hard to write this story?' the thought provoked him as though spoken by an inquisitor. He had covered difficult stories before and somehow found the discipline to write about them, yet he could not find a context within which to place what he was learning about Nigel. He pondered what he had told David, and the logic of it so appealed to him that he was ready to attribute all that was happening to the delusions of senility, except for one nagging fact. He remembered the statue-like sentinel, standing near the door of Nigel's hospital room, who he had first seen when he entered the hallway, and he remembered how odd he felt when the sentinel had disappeared. 'Could there be some truth to all this threat of danger?' he wondered. Once upstairs, Jim resolved to push these thoughts out of his mind.

Then he opened the closet door and retrieved the satchel from the top shelf. Again, he went through the ritual to prepare the player and headphones, so that he might finish the tape which he had earlier begun. 'With these constant interruptions,' he thought. 'I'll never get through them all.'

He placed the headphones on his ears and again pressed the play button.

When I decided to make these tapes, I struggled with what periods of my life I could most easily skip over and it not affect the continuity of what I had to tell you. So many things had happened after the war after I left the Navy that I seriously struggled with whether I should tell you about these years at all. But then I remembered something which happened during these months which had bearing on much of what was to follow.

It's hard for me to describe how strange it felt to be at the base. I felt like a ghost, somehow there, but not connected to anything that was going on around me. I worked in the midst of the most sophisticated electronics of the age, yet I felt like a visitor from another time. I was given a brief glimpse of a world yet to come and this glimpse terrified me, not so much because I was afraid of science, but because I saw the ease with which we could eavesdrop on anyone. With enemies as clearly villainous as the Nazis, it seemed morally justified to use whatever means necessary to defeat them. 'But what about when they are finally defeated?' I often pondered. 'On whom then would we eavesdrop?'

I usually tried to push such questions from my mind, by reminding myself of the seriousness of our mission. But there were days I felt intense uneasiness about my work, though I really couldn't explain why.

My letters to Beth and my mother were filled with my thoughts about the war, but with nothing specific about what I was doing, though my duties primarily consisted in mundane tasks such as running errands for the officers, which would hardly be considered secret.

Beth wrote about many things, from describing her work to telling me about the bombs. One constant theme throughout her letters was the difficulties she faced because her English was not so good.

"People think me stupid, because I can't use right words," she once wrote me, and I responded that ignorance is often a more powerful destructive force than bombs.

Because they kept me so busy during those first few months, I was only able to write about once a week, though letters from my mother and from Beth kept coming at the same frequency, and without them the loneliness would have killed me.

My direct supervisor was a lieutenant commander named Ogilvy. He was nearly forty at the time with a thick head of red hair, which stood straight on the top of his head like a pencil eraser. Though he never smiled when we spoke, he was always courteous to me. He had a reputation for being a hard nose, but I never felt him unfair.

"Good morning, Mr. Fox," he would tell me every morning. He carried a clip board in his hands with a list of my duties for the morning. "This morning you test circuits on the M7 model." I would spend the morning completing the tests, then after lunch, he would assign me a new set of tasks. Everyday for nearly two and a half years proceeded in precisely the same fashion. I rarely had any idea what the devices actually did. I did not have a secret clearance, nor was I privy to the private conversations among the officers, but I had a sinking suspicion that many of them were more malevolent than what they appeared.

"Michael, you have another call," Dina again interrupted him. He was beginning to become annoyed by what seemed incessant interruptions.

"Who is it?"

"It's Mr. Reynolds from your paper."

"Alright, I'll take it here."

He moved to the phone and placed the receiver to his ear.

"Yes, Mr. Reynolds."

"Jim, how's the story coming?"

"It's coming, sir." Jim couldn't tell him that he hadn't written a single line.

"I want something on my desk in two days, and I'm sending Kingman down there to take some pictures."

"You're sending Burgess here?"

The thought of it unnerved him.

"When is he coming?"

"Tomorrow night." He paused. "I reiterate, a story must be on my desk in two days. Understand?"

"Yes, sir."

"Then, good luck." He hung up the phone.

"Yeah, good luck. I'll need it."

The last thing Jim wanted in the midst of all the other confusion was Burgess trailing him around like a bloodhound and sticking his impertinent nose where it did not belong. He knew the real reason Burgess was coming was to baby-sit him until he wrote the story. He was beginning to regret he had ever gone into the newspaper business in the first place. Then he turned the tape back on.

Among the enlisted personnel at the base, there were few whom I had any real interaction with. But there was a young man named Carlson, whom I talked with from time to time. He was incredibly tall. Standing nearly six foot six, he towered over me like a giant sequoia. I remember the first time I talked to him. Someone told me he had played college basketball before he was drafted, and he had fingers long enough to hold a basketball with one hand. One day he was working at a desk across from me and I asked him, "Where did you play basketball?"

"The University of Texas," he spoke with a distinctive southern drawl and I could almost hear five separate vowel sounds pushed into the first syllable of 'Texas'. "That was before they drafted me."

"Are you from Texas?" (Though my question seems a stupid one now, I was only vaguely familiar with the differences in southern dialect.)

"I'm from Mount Vernon. Ever been there?"

"No, I haven't. Where is it?"

"It's in east Texas, on the way from Dallas to Texarkana."

All these names meant nothing to me, though I had seen western pictures and had an image of Texas as a land of cowboys and Indians.

"What's it like?"

When he began to describe it, it was enough like Wisconsin to be my home.

"We have a county fair every June, with a livestock show and rodeo."

From him I learned about sombreros and tortillas and tamales and a host of Spanish words which had come into his language as a result of contact with Mexican culture, though from the way he talked about their culture, I could sense he felt contaminated by it.

"Why can't these Mescins learn English," he complained. "They sit and chatter like a bunch of birds. This is America, not Mexico."

"It's hard to learn another language." I told him. "It would be hard if you were suddenly thrown into Mexico." As we spoke, I thought of the difficulties Beth was having in London.

"You're not a Catholic-lover, are you?" he asked me, and I realized that he was becoming agitated with me. There was in his heart the same bitterness against Catholics that had turned me from religion in Wisconsin. So, I decided to drop the subject altogether.

I have never been able to understand why people are threatened by other cultures, because my understanding had been enriched and my vision expanded as a result of contact with them. But he seemed to be frightened by the Mexican people. We would talk again about other subjects, but never again did I speak of Texas or Mexico.

There were others whom I talked to during those months, but never about anything more serious than a baseball game or deeper than the latest issue of the sports magazines.

When time for leave came, the enlisted personnel would rush to the city, usually for wine, women and song, and not always honorably, and yet I remained at the barracks with a book or two and my pad and pencil.

Though I was as pliable a patriot as anyone and could easily be excited by a call to arms, I longed for something deeper and more resilient. I didn't understand it then, but I yearned for spirituality, and not the kind of religious life I had experienced in Wisconsin.

Even then, a certain virtue was attached to a quiet renunciation of the religious life, glorifying a kind of epicurean individualism. 'Eat, drink and be merry for tomorrow we die,' was as much our battle cry as our call to arms against the Nazis. 'Was it not religion that had been the great harbinger of war?' I thought, 'and was it not a Christian world which produced an Adolph Hitler?' I could not see the contradiction between my unquenchable love for Beth and my denial of religious values.

Much of what I read during this period lent support to my positions. The intellectual environment of the age was hostile to traditional religion, and a host of writers from W. Somerset Maugham to James Joyce gave voice to the new hero, who had thrown off his religious prejudice in favor of his individual enlightenment.

I must have read a dozen novels during that time, but none of which inspired me, or satisfied my longing to know more. I wrote Beth about the restlessness which had become my ever-present companion and in the best English she could master, she responded to me, "Neilos, Pray! Ask God for peace of mind, and go to the Greek Church." I envied her conviction, because I had so little. The only thing I was certain about was my own dissatisfaction.

I struggled with my conscience over whether or not to heed her advice and go to the church until the early summer of 1944. Then on one of my leaves after finding an address in the phone book, I rode a train into Manhattan to a small Greek Church on Seventeenth Street. I kept telling myself it was just idle curiosity which brought me there.

The outside of the church reminded me of my dreams. It was small and unimpressive with a dome much like the one I remembered. I stood outside the doors for almost ten minutes before I had the courage to go inside.

I remember how awkward I felt the first few moments when I walked in. The service was already going on, and the smell of incense nearly clogged my nostrils. They were chanting in Greek. I stood at the back of the church behind a pillar in hopes not to appear out of place, and after a few minutes of anxiety I felt a little more relaxed.

If I had heeded any of my religious training, I would have immediately rushed out the door for fear of damnation. Every evil I had heard the preacher condemn was manifestly present there, the incense, the vestments, the rituals. There were processions and exhortations and prostrations, and though I hadn't the foggiest clue about what was going on, I knew something was going on. When it was over, the priest moved to the center of the church with a basket of bread which he was handing out to those in line. People kept staring at *me as I stood in my navy uniform, and I felt a little awkward. I was captivated by the paintings in the church and soon found myself standing in line with the rest of the people. When I reached the priest he said something to me in Greek and I answered him, "I'm sorry. I don't speak Greek."*

"God be with you," he spoke in English with a strong Greek accent, and he handed me a piece of bread. Then I left the church. I found myself reflecting upon the experience for most of the day. The melodies kept playing in my head and the smell of incense followed me like a cloud of sweet perfume. It's hard for me to put into words the breadth and depth of the impressions I had during my first experience with Beth's church. But I could not recall ever experiencing anything like it in my life. I had a sense I was encountering something very old, older than I could yet imagine.

It would be several weeks before I had another opportunity to visit the church, and during those weeks, I felt a greater restlessness than before. I was not ready for a religious life and all the dos and don'ts it entailed. I recognized that to become part of Beth's life demanded a complete transformation of my lifestyle, and I did not feel comfortable with that kind of change. But I loved Beth and was determined to find the strength to become part of her life.

There was silence again as the tape ran on for a minute before reaching the end. When Jim took the headphones off his ears and set them down on the table, he felt a nostalgic melancholy, though he didn't know why. Images of the four murals at the church faded in and out of his mind's eye. He remembered Hell with its flames and the strange figures he could not recognize. But he pushed this all from his mind when he saw that the clock radio read 6:56. He knew he had only a few minutes to prepare himself. Julie, he remembered, had always been punctual.

Chapter 13

When the doorbell rang downstairs, the clock in Nigel's living room was on its fifth resonant chime. Jim had come down the stairs and was standing in the entranceway when Dina opened the front door and let Julie inside. Once he saw her, he couldn't help but remember the affection they had once shared and a deep sense of regret overcame him.

Five years had passed since he had last seen her, when he had told her how hopeless it all seemed, and nothing had changed in the ensuing years which compelled him to think otherwise. "After all," he would argue in those moments of regret, "Julie had been raised in a world of affluence, of privilege and of power, a world antithetical to every value that I hold." He had convinced himself it was impossible from the outset that the chasm of difference which separated them in temperament, in lifestyle, and in financial circumstances, had been as wide and impassible as death and in the end these differences had doomed their relationship to failure. He never imagined, once he told her goodbye, any circumstance arising which could bring them back together.

As he was standing on the stairs and watching her as she entered the foyer, a panoply of impressions rushed through his awareness—feelings, memories, some localized, most unconnected, passed simultaneously as before his mind's eye, all competing as restless children for his attention. One moment it was their first meeting, the next their last, all experiences blurred as soft pastels upon a painter's pallet and then shifted like a canvas rippling in the wind. He felt uncertainty and incompleteness, as though all the warring impulses that had separated them in a moment of possibility now embraced each other and on their edges had become one. It left him speechless, unsure of what to say.

He stood for a moment and stared at her before coming downstairs. He had often rehearsed, like a boy in school, what he might say if life had given second chances, but even these impressions seemed like distant phantoms only whispering inaudibly in the background.

He heard her say, "Hello," to him, but it was as though through cotton and he heard himself respond in kind. But his mind was uninvolved as though observing everything at a distance. She asked how he'd been, and he nodded in acknowledgment, not connecting to what was being said. Then she proposed, "I've been thinking where we might eat. I know a good seafood place." And even though he hated seafood he heard himself say, "Yes. That's fine."

It felt dreamlike as though light were dancing through the room.

"Are you all right?" she asked him.

"Yes, I'm fine."

And when he forced himself to focus more, he could see that she'd been crying, and after a moment of awkward anticipation, he acknowledged it.

"I see you've been crying," he didn't know why he told her that.

"It's terrible. I've cried all afternoon. I keep pinching myself to see if it's all some terrible dream." She paused. "I thought I could hold it together. I hadn't cried at all till I got back to my apartment. But then I put on the radio to soothe me, and this silly song made me cry, and I couldn't stop myself."

As soon as she stopped talking, his mind began to dance again. He could see that some subtle metamorphosis had transformed her, as though a shifted universe had opened up between them and the well-heeled woman he remembered phased into the simpler one who now stood before him. No longer was she wearing the most expensive designer fashions with her hair in a meticulous coiffure. Instead, she dressed simply, no make-up on her face, with her hair pinned back behind her ears. He could not explain the nature of this transformation, but it was obvious that it had occurred.

"So you knew Nigel well?" He asked her as he opened the front door for her and they began to walk toward her car.

"In the past few months, he's been like my grandfather."

Jim realized he could not speak freely about Nigel.

"Is your job OK?"

"I don't want to talk about work. What about you, Jim?"

"What about me?"

"Burgess told me all about the paper."

"What else did Burge tell you?"

"He said you've been unhappy."

"I've not been unhappy."

She opened the car door for him and let him inside.

"It's all right to be unhappy. Father Michael says the world's curse is happiness."

He wondered who Father Michael was and how anyone could believe happiness was a curse. He could count on his hands the number of days he felt genuinely happy and he had come to know intimately the curse of sorrow.

Several times, as he sat quietly beside her in the car, he contemplated revealing himself, but despite his anguished desire to unburden himself, he lacked the fortitude to breach his own defenses.

When the waitress led them to their table and sat them down across from each other, Jim looked at her closely for the first time, and he could see something different in her eyes.

"I never expected to see you again," she broke the anxious silence. "So much has happened these past five years."

"Neither did I," he responded.

"You've lost some weight."

"A few pounds."

"But you haven't changed really."

"You look very different," he observed.

"Yes, I do."

As her demeanor became more serious, she was interrupted by a waitress who handed them both menus. She glanced at the menu a moment and then set it aside.

"I think you should know something about me," she continued. "I'm not the same person I was five years ago. I'm studying to become Russian Orthodox."

Jim was stunned.

"I know," she continued. "I know how you feel about the religious life. But it's really been wonderful."

Jim grew anxious and began to slide nervously on his chair.

"Relax. I'm not going to proselytize you. But there are some things you should know." Her voice grew softer. "Nigel was not anything like you must be imagining him. He did so much good, things you could never know." She paused. "Did you know he spent three days a week working in a soup kitchen feeding homeless people?"

The thought of Nigel serenely distributing bowls of soup to vagrants amused him.

"Once, when I was with him," she continued, "he told me how doing good was both intoxicating and humbling. (She paused.) I know you're surprised at all this, especially coming from me. But as I said, I'm not the same person I was five years ago."

The waitress came to take their orders.

"I'll have the fried clams," Julie acknowledged, while Jim ordered shrimp, the only thing on the menu he could tolerate.

"How often have you been to this homeless shelter?" he asked her. He still found the idea unsettling.

"I used to go more. But now I go about once a week, usually at night when they take soup to the homeless around the city."

Jim had once read of this syndrome, where the super-rich, largely out of pangs of conscience for their overabundance, would suddenly become obsessed with a philanthropic spirit. But somehow in Julie's case, he sensed there was more to it than this.

"Why don't I take you there after dinner and let you see first-hand?"

"No, I don't think so."

"I'm sure it would move you."

"I think it would overwhelm me. I'm just not in the mood to see homeless people."

She bit her lip as though she wanted to say more.

"How did you get involved with Nigel and this homeless shelter thing?"

In fact, he was profoundly perplexed how the woman he remembered could have become the one who was now speaking. Any explanation she could offer might provide some insight into this enigma.

"It's a rather long story."

"Then tell me."

"I'm not sure you'll want to hear it all."

"As long as we can avoid a religious discussion, I'm interested."

"You must remember my mother," Julie began.

"Of course."

"She died a year ago."

He remembered how close she had been to her mother.

"It was terrible. One minute we were talking as you and I are now, the next she was collapsing and dying in my arms. It was a massive stroke. There was nothing I could have done."

"And this prompted you to become philanthropic?"

"No, I became despondent. It devastated me."

Jim remembered his mother's death, though he tried to push the recollection from his mind.

"I couldn't deal with it," she went on. "Everything, the house, the clothes, my friends, they all seemed so trivial. So pointless. And I began to drink. First only a little to numb the pain, then I could hardly get up in the morning without a drink."

Jim was not surprised that alcohol had been her drug of choice. He remembered how much she had liked fine wines, even when they were seeing each other. But that she could so easily fall off the wagon surprised him.

"I was not your polite and quiet drunk. I was rude and loud and self-destructive. After one particularly obnoxious episode, when I told my family to go to hell, I ended up living in the streets of Harlem, drinking cheap wine and sleeping most of the time. It was there that Father Michael found me."

Jim tried to picture in his mind everything she was telling him, but he found the images incongruous with both his recollection of her and her present appearance. Then their waitress brought them both their plates and set them down in front of them.

"And I suppose Father Michael is Russian," Jim interrupted her.

"He showed compassion for me," she continued. "And he listened to me. And No. He is not Russian. He's American."

Jim wondered what ideology she might be espousing had some other more esoteric group had shown kindness to her, and he found it difficult to understand what appeal some old world religiosity would have on an educated urbanite of Julie's background. But this was only the newest in a string of dilemmas which confounded him.

"He helped me to see how the person I was to become was trapped inside the person who I had been. He taught me my old self had to die in order for my new self to be born."

"I don't buy this old-self new-self stuff. People remain pretty much the same throughout their lives."

"Most people," she responded. "But not because that's the way it's supposed to be. Sometimes it's easier to be static, to be locked in one place and time. "

"It is better to be locked in one place than tossed about by any wind that blows. An oak tree is more durable in a hurricane than a dandelion."

"You don't fool me with these cynical one-liners. You once wrote that it was in our dreams we become truly alive."

"I wrote a lot of silly things when I was younger. But time comes and you have to grow up." He paused. "Why are you doing this? Why are you talking to me like this? Our relationship was over. And from my side of the table nothing has changed."

"I just wanted to tell you how sorry I am for all the mistakes I made. I never wanted you to suffer."

"It's not my place to grant you absolution for past sins."

"No, but you can forgive me."

"For what? We did what we did. Nothing can change that."

"I understand your frustration."

"You understand nothing about me. You can't. You think because you live on the streets for a month that you understand homelessness. You have a safety net that most will never have."

"What kind of safety net?"

"Your rich family." He paused. "I have no one. I am in this world alone, and if I fail, it's for keeps."

"Being rich is no end all and be all. Believe me on that."

"It has its advantages. You name me any other drunk who could walk into a job at a major magazine."

The harshness of his words upset her.

"Is this what you've become in the past five years, a bitter spiteful man?"

"No, I'm sorry. I just can't do this." He tossed his napkin on the table and raised himself to leave.

"Please sit down, Jim. Talk to me."

"Talk to you? About what? About my life, if you could call it that." He paused. "Nothing has turned out as I expected it."

"Alright, then go. Push me away, like you push everyone away."

But even though he wanted to leave, his feet felt frozen in place as though some invisible force restrained them there, and finally after a few moments of hesitation, he returned to his seat.

"Jim, what's wrong?"

"I'd rather not talk about it."

He could sense she understood his reluctance and she acquiesced.

"I'm sorry for being such a jerk," he continued. "I just can't seem to write this story."

"Have you decided on a length? That usually helps me get started."

"I haven't decided on anything."

He began to rub is eyes, at first from nervous energy and then more deliberately.

"I can't be objective about this. I'm too involved."

He could sense she didn't understand the full import of his remark, but he was not prepared to talk about it.

"You start out with certain presuppositions about the world, certain fixed points of reference, which give your life coherence, and suddenly without warning, you find it all yanked out from under you."

"Yes, I know exactly what you mean. You can tell me what is bothering you."

At times he wished to break through the barrier he had so painstakingly constructed to protect himself, to allow his deepest feelings to find release, but he found the vulnerability of trust unbearable.

"I'm sorry. Not yet."

She respected his wishes and did not press him.

"These past days seem unreal to me, almost dreamlike."

Julie interrupted him, "Sometimes things happen to get our attention. It's a way for God to get through to us."

"I don't believe in God. At least not in a God who gives a damn what we say or do. (He paused.) What really irks me about religious people is their unsurpassed narcissistic belief that God is involved in every detail of their lives. He allows whole peoples to be slaughtered in genocide, children to be tortured and murdered all over the world, but he somehow takes the time to help them shop for pajamas."

"I don't think you're being fair in your characterization. Not all religious people are so narcissistic."

"What is the chief motivation of the religious person? What question does he constantly ask himself? How can I be saved? In his solipsistic view the whole universe exists solely to save him."

"The alternative is nihilism," she interrupted him, "where we're nothing more than an accident, the end-product of random chance. And nothing that we do or say or think ultimately matters."

"Given what I know about the world, that seems much more reasonable."

"What proof do we have that our thoughts bear any relationship to reality?" she asserted. "It takes as much faith to believe in reason as it does to believe in God."

He was startled by her tenacity.

"Can't we talk about something else?"

"Sure. Whatever you want to talk about."

Jim sat quietly, pensively, unsure of what subject to broach without inciting controversy. He had not anticipated a philosophical debate, nor was he emotionally prepared to deal with the issues which such a discussion might engender.

Julie finally broke the pregnant silence.

"How is your father doing?"

"I talked to him last night. He seems to be all right."

He wasn't prepared to go more into greater detail.

"Tell him I read his book, *Pragmatic Utility*. It was interesting."

"It was a bore. Nine hundred pages of utopian economic theory about what the world would be like if it wasn't the world."

"You sound a little jealous, Jim."

"I'm over forty years old and I work for a small town paper, making probably a third of what you're making at the magazine. Long ago, I learned to accept my limitations."

"What do you want to do?"

It was the same question she had asked him five years before, and he remembered how confident he had answered her. He gave the same answer, "I once wanted to be a serious journalist."

"A good journalist seizes a story and pursues it until he has found the truth."

"You're telling me I should continue with this story."

"I don't believe anything happens by chance. There's a reason for everything."

He didn't know how to respond to her remark, because he was convinced so much of life was unredeemed chaos. Then they sat staring at each other for a few anxious minutes.

"I have a confession to make. I sort of knew you were in Hadleyburg." Her voice betrayed her vulnerability. "I know I can't turn the clock back to redo everything I've done wrong. But I had to make peace with myself. When I was at the bottom, when I lost all hope, I couldn't forget my betrayals. I just had to tell you I'm sorry." She paused. "Father Michael told me I had to stop listening to all the voices inside my head, telling me who I was and how I was to behave. I had to find a single voice, and allow myself to blossom like a flower. I've done this thing and these past few weeks have been wonderful."

She spoke with such earnestness that it unsettled him.

"I don't know what to say," he responded.

"I don't know if we will ever see each other again. But I just wanted to tell you this. I know it must sound strange to you."

"A little," though he was confused over what point she was making.

"I guess I'm trying to say we should allow ourselves to become who we truly are."

For Jim, this statement engendered a bitter irony, because the past few days had caused him to question every assumption by which he defined himself. Then their waitress approached the table and interrupted them.

"Is there anything else I can get for you? Dessert?"
She reached over the table to take their plates.

"No, I'm fine," Julie answered and she noticed Jim had barely touched his food.

"Please take it," he responded.

"You could have eaten more. You barely touched your food."

But Jim was unresponsive, lost in his own thoughts.

"Why didn't you tell me how close you were to Michael Wilson?"

"It was a long time ago when I was a little girl, before the call of politics had seized him, I was upset. I was upset with him, because I thought he took my father away."

"I don't even know who I am anymore. It's like I'm through the looking glass." He paused. "Four days ago, I had a life, a set of fixed conditions. Now everything is upside down."

"Jim, what are you talking about?"

"It seems as if Nigel thought he was my father."

He hoped by giving voice to this assertion that its absurdity would become self-evident. But Julie did not seem disturbed by it. Instead, she sat quietly, staring intensely at his face.

"You're not shocked by this?"

She removed her glasses from her bag and placed them on her eyes, then leaned forward until their faces were only a few inches apart.

"Why should I be?" she paused. "You look like Beth in the eyes."

"There's no way I'm that man's son."

"You make it sound so terrible. I think it's wonderful. A couple of times I came into the office, and Nigel and Father Michael were talking about something, and then they suddenly stopped. It was unlike them to be secretive about anything. I wonder if that was it."

"I don't know what's gotten into you people. But there is no way I'm Nigel's son. I was abandoned by my mother on the doorstep of an orphanage."

"You are the right age, you were adopted and there is a resemblance. It seems logical to me."

"There are thousands of other possibilities. I see no compelling evidence to convince me otherwise."

"Nigel wouldn't have put you through this if he wasn't certain." She seemed convinced of this.

"Let's say for the sake of argument that Nigel was my father. What difference does it make? He's dead now."

This argument appealed to him over all the others because even if he was forced to accept Nigel as his father, it required no radical change in thinking.

"All knowledge changes us," she countered. "Only in ignorance can we remain the same."

He remembered her intelligence and her tenacious will. Though he could see that much had changed about her, the core of her personality remained intact.

"How do others at the magazine feel about your views?"

"I don't talk about them much. I find I live in such a different world from those around me that to describe the way I see things, might make them think I'm crazy."

He still found it inconceivable that the woman he remembered would be so easily converted to some esoteric religious doctrine. He could more easily accept Nigel's prescient powers than this. That many who had struggled with drug and alcohol dependencies had followed a pattern of religious conversion was not news to him. He was aware of the high-profile rock artists, politicians, and movie stars, who had found in religious fundamentalism an escape from their dependencies. But that someone like Julie, whose intelligence and independence he had admired, could embrace what he saw as an old world mysticism, deeply confounded him. It shouted out for explication; but he was not prepared to enter into a religious discussion, because he found religious arguments unpersuasive, and he believed they ultimately were rationalizations of other more deeply-rooted psychological motivations.

"Is everything OK?" she asked him. His mind had wandered away from the conversation and he sat zombie-like in a trance.

"Yes, I'm OK." He regained himself.

"I hope you don't think I'm crazy."

It surprised him that his opinion mattered.

"No. I don't think you're crazy. We do what we have to do to make it in this world."

For Jim, this seemed a good time to end things, so he gestured to the waitress to bring them their check, and when she returned, Jim opened his wallet to reveal his last forty dollars, which he carefully laid out on the table.

"I'll pay for mine," Julie acknowledged. "Please. I insist."

She returned a twenty-dollar bill to him and he begrudgingly accepted it. Then they both walked quietly to the car.

"Perhaps I can see you Saturday. That is if you plan on staying in New York," she proposed.

"Sure."

Then she drove him back to Nigel's house and stopped the car at the curb in front of Nigel's gate.

"Good luck with the story," she told him and kissed him on the cheek. "My number is 555-8731. Call me if I can be of help."

He returned her kiss and climbed out of the car. Then he stood at the curb and watched her as she disappeared down the block.

Chapter 14

When Jim entered the house, Dina returned to the kitchen after opening the door for him. He could see the door for Nigel's study was left open, and rather than go back upstairs, which was his first impulse, he decided to investigate the room. Several times previously he had passed the door and had fought the impulse to go inside. After all, the room was private and he would not have wanted an intruder inside his own private space, though Jim didn't know why this moral imperative inhibited him.

When he opened the door, he found a simple paneled room with a large oak desk and swivel chair. Covering two walls were shelves of books, and several photographs were hung in prominent positions on the two remaining walls. He noticed several small wooden religious paintings, resembling the others that were scattered throughout the house, and a picture of Beth, looking much younger, with a baby in her arms. To this picture he was immediately attracted, and he moved toward it for a closer look. His eyes scanned across the shelves, past religious books, and books about electronics and a number of books of popular fiction. 'Somewhere inside this room,' he thought, 'must be the secret to all the intrigue;' though he did not have a single clue to make his search meaningful.

After making a cursory examination of the room, he rested a moment in Nigel's chair. He began to look more judiciously with his eyes dancing around the room, like a bee in flight. But nothing he saw caught his interest. Then he began to search the desk. First opening drawers, staring briefly inside, then closing them, he found only pen and paper, a ruler, and some personalized stationery. A larger drawer seemed more interesting, with a shoe box full of letters, some bills and a calculator. But these gave him only impressions, nothing concrete. He was about to give up and go back upstairs, when his eyes finally fixed on a book jutting out from the shelf. "*Secret Societies,*" he read the title, by Dr. William Harvey. He returned with the book to his chair. He held it in his hands a moment, before laying it down in front of him on the desk. It was then he discovered the photograph on the back of the book jacket. It was the same man who had confronted him at the cemetery. He opened the jacket and read the biographical blurb inside. There he discovered that Dr. Harvey taught history at Columbia. Then he resolved to take the book upstairs with him, to skim its contents, so that he might glean some information from its pages.

From an initial glance, Dr. Harvey had written in the same scientific prose which characterized his father's work. On the first page, he counted fifteen footnotes. He found such reading difficult and would often ignore the footnotes altogether, because they broke the rhythm of the prose. He sensed that somehow the key was here, but he didn't know where to look. Jumping from page to page, he scanned a sentence here and there, but there was so much specialized vocabulary, he found it difficult to understand anything he read. There were names and places and dates, and at the end of each chapter was an extensive bibliography. There was a chapter on the Knights Templar, with photographs and drawings of various sites throughout France. He rifled the pages several times, and then noticed that one of them had the corner folded over. On page 237 was a photograph of an ink engraving of Jacques De Molay, with a caption reading "The last Grand Master of the Templars before the Pope banned the organization and confiscated all their property."

"Why did I neglect my history studies?" he chided himself. "Maybe then, I could make some sense out of this." He set the book down a moment to gather his wits. It was at this moment that he resolved to seek out Dr. Harvey the following morning in order to ask him more specific questions. He was uncertain which questions to ask, but he was determined to get some answers. Lingering in the wingback chair a few more minutes, he took a quick inventory in his mind of all that had happened the previous days. He felt as though several weeks had been compressed into the last four days. Then he rose up and retrieved his satchel from the closet.

After removing the yellow tablet, the tape player and a pen, he placed the tape labeled *#5* into the player and laid the tape and player beside him in the chair. Then he began to write his thoughts on paper. "Nigel became obsessed with the idea of secret societies. His paranoia became so intense that he sought out an expert on the subject." He stopped a moment and then he wrote in bold letters, "SECRET SOCIETIES. HAVE TO KNOW MORE."

Dina was shouting from downstairs, "Michael, you have another phone call."

He picked up the phone and placed it to his ear.

"Jim," he heard Julie's voice. "I almost forgot to tell you something. Nigel only mentioned it in passing. But I think he kept a journal. Maybe he wrote something there that might help you."

"Thank you. But I haven't a clue where to look for it."

"How's the story coming?"

"I've got some notes. Maybe I'll start writing tonight."

He didn't want to tell her how hopeless it all seemed, because he didn't know where to begin to write. There were just too many isolated bits of information. Without a coherent context to thread them all together, any story he'd put to paper would seem schizophrenic. He sensed it was beginning to come together, but he only perceived the edges as though he were looking at it askew. All that he had learned in journalism school seemed useless against so impenetrable an adversary.

"Perhaps there is something you can do for me."

"Just name it, Jim."

"Find out what you can about Dr. William Harvey. He teaches at Columbia. What are his political leanings? Find out his religion."

"Sure, Jim. But why?"

"I'll tell you when I have a clearer picture of things."

"Jim, what's going on? You can trust me."

"I'm not ready to talk about it."

"Alright, I'll call you as soon as I have something."

"Thank you, Julie."

After he hung up the phone, he wondered if he had done the right thing in involving her in this intrigue, but he knew he had limited time and any help he could find would make his task an easier one.

Of all the theories that were knocking around in his head, Jim still found preference for those which centered the source of the intrigue in Nigel himself. He was reluctant to consider even one of a number of conspiracy scenarios that his imagination had constructed, because whenever possible, he preferred the simplest of explanations. He picked up Dr. Harvey's book again and stared at its front cover. There were Greek letters and ancient symbols, scattered randomly across its face. Yet, he did not know what any of them meant. After rifling though the book as one might a deck of cards, he set it aside. He picked up the tape player and placed the tablet in his lap. He decided to take notes as he went along.

In December 1944, my mother wrote me concerning the farm and for the first time in almost two years she mentioned Mary Parker. Reginald, she related, had really taken a liking to Mary's sister,

Martha, and the talk around the county concerned their impending engagement. I think the whole county knew before they did. She told me that my father had bought two new milk cows, and that in honor of the war he named them Eisenhower and MacArthur. The papers were filled with news of the war, from victories in North Africa to the liberation of Italy. She asked me if I regretted not being in the midst of things when victory seemed just months away. I couldn't tell her the little I knew of how our work had hastened the end of the war. My mother also mentioned in passing that Michael had finished his third term at the university. I felt a little envy when I read this, because I felt my choices had been limited when he had his whole life before him. I wrote back to my mother about the depth of my loneliness, and how I had been having trouble sleeping. I had recurring nightmares about the explosion and about the war, though I was as far removed from combat as any civilian at home.

I could hear my father's voice in those moments of intense loneliness, "I could have told you that the farm was a better life. I've never been lonely." And perhaps he was right. I had begun to consider whether the whole thing had been a tremendous mistake. But then the thought of Beth and the image of her face pushed his voice from my recollection.

The days before Christmas were filled with what the Germans call 'angst,' a restlessness of spirit which I could not put into words. I read very little during this time, finding it difficult to concentrate for more than a few minutes at a time, and I thought often of the farm. I felt as though somehow I didn't belong, that I had been living a life other than the one which had been scripted for me.

"After all," I would tell myself. "I know all about hogs and chickens, and corn. But what did I know of radios and the like?" I had an image of myself inconsistent with what I was doing. It seemed as if my life had no direction and the chasm which separated me from those whom I loved was as wide as death.

Beth wrote me a letter that December in which she told me that her heart longed for Greece, and I wrote back that I understood her desire to go home again. It had turned out to be a very different world from what I had expected.

On Christmas Eve, 1944, I came into Manhattan and wandered the streets from Macy's on 34th street to 42nd street and beyond. I gazed into store windows and watched the crowds, and then with resolve, I decided to return to the Greek church on 17th Street.

What drew me there, I couldn't have vocalized, except that I longed to see Beth, and I believed that by going there in some inexplicable way I might have contact with her. I didn't understand the metaphysics of it all, but I was beginning to believe in realities beyond that which I could see. I'm certain if I had tried to explain it to anyone, they would have thought me crazy. I went to the back of the church as I had done before, and I stood quietly and watched. The choir was singing a hymn, quite beautiful, though without instruments, and the odor of the incense was sweeter than I remembered it.

Then I remembered Brother Woodrow standing at his pulpit with his bible opened and balanced precariously in his left hand.

"Your incense is an abomination to me," he had shouted, his voice quavering as he spoke. "God does not delight in the ritual of the ungodly. We must shed the ungodly idolatry of the pagans and worship God in spirit and truth." His voice cracked as he emphasized truth. *"Let us praise Jesus. Let us praise him."*

Then the congregation would shout, "Amen, Brother Woodrow. Amen."

I snickered a moment when I thought of him. He was so convinced of what God did and did not want.

When the service was over, I remained at the back of the church and watched the people leaving, one by one. The old women, the children with their mothers, all disappeared out the front door of the church until I was left alone. Then after a few moments of quiet reflection, I too left the church. Outside, I was overcome with sadness, and though I tried to fight the tears, I cried a little, because I felt totally unconnected to anything, almost invisible.

The war had been so costly in lives, especially since D-day. There was no family which had not been touched, even ours. My cousin Richard had been killed on Omaha Beach along with thousands of others, and my mother had written me in September of the news. Of twelve men from the county who left to war, only six returned when it was over.

The remaining months of the war seemed to linger, like winters in Wisconsin sometimes lingered into May. Then in June came VE day. Yet after the initial celebrations and elation of a long ordeal finally over, few of us could feel truly joyful reading about the horrors of the death camps which filled the papers and stunned the world. Beth wrote me that she was not surprised at what atrocities the Nazis had committed. She had seen in microcosm what they were capable of doing. But nonetheless, 'We should pray for them.' I thought the suggestion absurd.

When Japan's surrender came a few months later, I was both relieved and confused. The war had been such a tremendous travail that I don't think any of us thought about what we would do when it was finally over, that is anyone except Leonard.

Two weeks before my discharge from the Navy, I received a telegram from Seattle, Washington. The lieutenant brought it out to me as I was working on the line. I opened it expecting some terrible news. It simply read, "Stay in New York. I have a plan to bring Beth to States. Leonard."

It was the first word I heard from Leonard since the letter he had written me over two years before. I had not really thought about where I would go after my discharge, though I was beginning to reconsider returning to the farm. I don't know how he found me in New York, or why I even heeded his request, but when I was discharged in November, I did not go back to Wisconsin as my mother had wanted. Instead, I let a small apartment in Bensonhurst Brooklyn. I was determined to make a new life for myself, and somehow raise enough money to bring Beth to the states.

For some people, their lives follow predictable patterns. They roll toward an expected conclusion as though gliding dependably as a train on its rails. But for me, life seemed more erratic, like a river overflowing its banks and seeking a path of least resistance. I felt I had lost control of my destiny, and the things I most wanted, I seemed powerless to attain. In many ways, I was still the same frightened young man who stood in the rain and thought about death. It was a feeling which would haunt me throughout my life, no matter how successful I later became. I could never forget how frightened I had been and yet still remain. God help me.

A few days after my discharge, I received another telegram, forwarded from the base. Leonard asked me to meet him on January 20th at three o'clock at a restaurant in Manhattan.

I can't remember the name of the restaurant where I met him, but it was Italian, and the aroma of garlic, oregano, and sweet basil hung in the air like a cloud of incense. Leonard was sitting alone at a small round table in an alcove, and above his table hung a map of Italy with his head blocking Sicily from my view. He looked haggard and fatigued. Yet in his eyes, I saw the same controlled intensity which had always characterized his countenance. Despite the fact that his appearance seemed to have changed little from how I remembered him, he seemed subtly different, as though he had lived through some tremendous ordeal and lived to tell about it.

He was holding a glass of wine and taking small deliberate sips. When he saw me from the corner of the room, his eyes, as though they could see into the very marrow of my bones, followed me until I sat down across from him at the table. He had the same aura of otherworldliness which I remembered from before.

"You look like you've been to hell and back," I told him. I don't know why I opened with that remark.

"I have," he bluntly answered me, and then set his glass down on the table. I remember he was wearing a worn leather jacket, and his hair was cut much shorter than before.

"We have a lot to talk about," he told me. I didn't know what he was getting at, but I was anxious to hear his plan.

He lit a cigarette and began puffing on it ferociously.

"How long have you been smoking?" I asked him.

"On and off, two years."

He crushed the cigarette in an ashtray on the table.

"Things change."

"You said you had a plan to bring Beth to the States."

"I'll get to that." He took a small notebook out of his pocket, and began to write in it. Then after a few moments, he put it back. "Did you get the letter I wrote you?"

"Yes."

"It pretty much sums up where I've been."

"And where is that?" I wasn't toying with him. I had a very difficult time understanding his letter.

"I've been mistaken about so many things. Something happened to me out at sea. I've had to rethink everything."

He took a huge gulp of wine and continued, "I was on a battle cruiser, and we were hit pretty bad. I was supposed to stand watch one night." He paused to puff on a cigarette, and his hand shuttered slightly as he took it out of his mouth. "And there was another Matthews on board. He stood my watch by mistake and died. I'm alive because of a clerical error. It seems so pointless, doesn't it?"

He smashed the cigarette out in the ashtray.

"I've tried to make sense out of it. But I can't. Then the thought occurred to me that there's something I'm supposed to do. That's why it happened."

I had never before heard him speak like this and it startled me.

'Was this the Leonard I remembered?' I recall thinking at the time. He had always been so confident. But what I found that day was someone very much like myself. He was nervous, almost anxious. He seemed unsure of the future. There was a tentativeness to his personality, which made him seem both younger and older than when I knew him last.

As the conversation grew much deeper, he seemed more at ease, though he kept puffing on his cigarettes as though he drew his life from them.

"What about your radios?" I asked him in an attempt to focus him on his expertise. But he seemed uninterested in this line of questioning, like a man obsessed with something beyond himself, he came back again to the accident as though he couldn't push it from his mind.

"Do you believe in a life after death?" I recall him asking me.

"I'm not sure," I responded.

"There has to be something more than this, or it's all so pointless, and I still don't think it's pointless." He paused again. "Because of a typing error, I'm alive, and another man is dead. Don't you see the senselessness in that?"

I understood death is a fickle suitor, who gives his affections unpredictably, but I never felt obliged to dwell on the subject, and in the vast panoply of injustice in the world, this small enigma seemed insignificant. But Leonard seemed practically intoxicated by these thoughts. "I've got to make some sense of this," he kept saying as though returning to the chorus in an aria. No matter which direction the conversation turned, I found myself again discussing his accident. I wanted to hear about his plan, but he didn't seem ready to speak about it.

Finally, more out of frustration than malice, I interrupted him,

"What about your plan to bring Beth here?"

"Alright, I'll tell you what I've thought about."

Then his voice changed timbre and tone, and he began to speak more calmly.

"The oddest thing happened out there on ship. Remember that turban from the Great Bartholomew. I had it in my locker on the ship. I was sleeping one day on my cot, when I heard a voice coming out of the locker. I thought I was having a schizophrenic episode, then it happened again. I jumped up from the cot, opened the locker, and there I discovered the voice was coming from inside the turban. It was then, Nigel, that I began to realize how our friend Bartholomew did it. The turban is a radio receiver." He paused. *"I took the turban down with me to the radio room and there I began testing various frequencies until I found the one that worked. To my surprise it was an FM signal not normally used for ship-to-ship communications. Apparently, someone stood off at the distance and broadcast instructions to him. That's how he did it."*

"But who," I interjected.

"That's the intriguing part. It could have been almost anyone."

I tried to remember who was present at every performance, who might have been his compatriot. But I could think of no one.

"So what does this have to do with your plan?" I asked him. I had trouble understanding where he was going.

"We're going to do his act, Nige. I'll send. You'll receive."

"No way. I'm not getting on a stage and making an ass of myself."

"Come on, it's all a matter of electronics."

"Electronics? It's a confidence game."

"You want to bring Beth to the States, don't you?"

"Sure, but I'm no performer. I can't pull it off."

I could sense he was finding pleasure in my maneuvering, but he seemed unmoved. To every objection I raised, he mounted an effective counter-argument, and in the end he prevailed, and I agreed to do the act, with a compromise, that once we had the money for her ticket, we would retire Bartholomew's turban forever.

I didn't realize it then, but I had set in motion a series of events which, had I known their consequence, I would never had agreed. I say this not so much because of regret. I do not believe I could have acted otherwise, but because there was a certain inevitability in what was to *follow, as though I set a huge clock in motion, and its hands moved toward their appointed hours. I've often pondered what a tremendous blessing that it was that I could not sense the future then.*

The tape clicked off on the first side, and Jim seeing that it was almost eleven, set the player aside and stood up from the chair. He stretched his arms into the air. Then he returned to the chair and flipped the tape over to the second side.

The summer of 1946 began with a warm summer breeze. I was twenty seven years old with most of my life still before me, and yet so much had happened to me in but a few years. When I had moved to the apartment in Brooklyn, I had accumulated so many letters that I had to carry them in two large boxes. I had purchased a Greek book, and was drilling myself in the mornings and evenings, and during the day I delivered flowers for a florist.

I would ride a bicycle all over Brooklyn, carrying flowers to lovers and mourners, for all the occasions when flowers became appropriate. The times seemed much simpler then, and the horrors of the war had begun to recede like a distant mirage on the horizon. In the evenings, Leonard and I occasionally met to experiment with the turban, but he was still awaiting the parts for a competent transmitter. I remember how silly I felt the first time I put on the setup. I was standing in front of a long mirror, and Leonard, trying to control a laugh, stood behind me. I looked ridiculous, even more so than Bartholomew, and my Midwestern voice did not fit the costume.

"We have to do something about your voice, Nige. It ruins the effect. Can't you speak with a foreign accent or something?"

I tried to change my voice several times and say, "I'm Nigel the Magnificent." But each attempt proved more ludicrous than the last, and Leonard, chuckling inaudibly, shook his head at each attempt.

"I can't do this. I sound ridiculous."

"Alright. We'll leave the voice alone for now. Straighten your back a little and move your shoulders back. You need more poise."

"Perhaps I should go to finishing school," my voice was pregnant with sarcasm.

"Let me look at you a minute," he continued, then walking around me as though I were a dressmaker's dummy, he examined me.

"A beard. That's it. You'll need to grow a beard."

"I don't want to grow a beard."

"Come on, Nige. It'll heighten the effect."

And as with everything else, his will prevailed and I began to grow a beard.

During the weeks to come, I'd meet him several evenings, and we'd rehearse. He'd chide me for being unconvincing and, I'd voice my misgivings about the whole enterprise. But we'd continue, often practicing late into the night. I thought about writing Beth and telling her all about our plan, but after I began several letters, I couldn't bring myself to finish them. I was too afraid what she might think of me. I sensed, almost unconsciously, that there was something deeply foreboding in what we were about to begin, but Leonard's ebullient confidence silenced all my misgivings.

He even had some playbills printed up, which showed me standing in the robe and turban, with the words, "Nigel the Magnificent," printed in bold letters beneath my photograph. I can't help but laugh when I remember it.

The phone began to ring upstairs, and Jim turned off the player as soon as the ring invaded his consciousness.

"Hello," he answered it.

Julie spoke in earnestness, "Jim, I have the information you wanted."

"Thank you."

"I called a couple of my friends at the *Post*. From what they tell me, Dr. Harvey is a real wacko, one of those conspiracy nuts, who advocates every conspiracy theory from the Kennedy assassination to the October Surprise. He writes regularly for a magazine called *Conspiracy* and he often gives speeches to various left wing political organizations about how the coming New World Order will lead to the deaths of millions." She paused. "Why would Nigel talk to someone like him?"

"I don't know."

"There's something else. He apparently believes in some super-secret group called 'The Brotherhood,' that he believes is the power behind the power, pulling all the strings."

"It sounds a little nuts to me. If things are screwed up, it's not because of some organization called 'the Brotherhood'. It's because of the collective incompetence of us all."

Jim rarely spoke as forcefully about an issue as this one. But he was not prepared to take seriously anyone like Dr. Harvey. He was even surprised that Columbia would have kept someone on staff whose ideas seemed as far out on the fringe as this man's. Yet beneath his skepticism, he sensed a nagging fear of its possibilities.

"That's about all I could find out tonight, Jim. I hope it helps."

"Thank you, Julie. You've been more than helpful."

"Please call me if you need anything else."

"Sure. Goodbye." Then he hung up the phone.

When he returned the headphones to his ears to continue listening, the time on his clock read 12:00 a.m.

When Leonard was taking me through the motions about how the turban worked and how we would imitate Bartholomew, I had little thought of what the future consequence might be. In those years, I made so many decisions without thinking about them.

I've changed so much. Sometimes I take out a worn copy of the playbill and look at it. I wonder what's become of the young man who dispassionately set out to deceive. I had convinced myself that the ends justified the means and that we would make the money to bring Beth to the states and that would be the end of it.

Nigel paused.

There was a maple tree outside the window of my walk-up, which in my quiet hours, after I had finished my deliveries, I'd meditate upon. It reminded me of a tree near our farmhouse, where I had spent many a summer day as a boy. I looked down the block to the butcher shop, passed the tailor shop, and I'd imagine the footpath from the back door of our house to the pond where I used to sit and fish on lazy August afternoons. There seemed a world of difference between Wisconsin and New York.

In the evenings I would walk with my cane, tapping a gentle rat-a-tat on the pavement. Once I walked as far as our old neighborhood, and I stood before the window where our radio shop had been. Now a woman's dress shop filled the small space with femininity. I've often been surprised by how little has remained constant in the ensuing years.

Though I had Beth's letters and my mother's to occupy my quiet hours, I felt alone, and when Leonard was there, it felt as though we were strangers. He seemed lost in a world of his own making, of frequencies and cathode ray tubes, and of Bartholomew.

When he finally got his electronics components, he created a small radio transmitter which he could hide on his person. Then he set out to create an elaborate code, composed of sighs and whistles, and nondescript words so that he might appear a restless spectator when giving me clues. He even scripted a patter of vocal criticisms and derision, all pregnant with information. If anything else, he was resourceful. But I had grave misgivings about the enterprise. But not for the reasons which would later prove important.

Jim paused the tape a moment to reflect on his first impressions of Nigel's hospital room. He remembered the playbill in Beth's old scrapbook, and the flowers. Then his thoughts began to dance from impression to impression as though torn free from logical connections. Image after image flashed before his mind's eye, so many that his inner voice broke in like a refrain, trying to give it meaning. 'God, I wished I had paid more attention,' he kept telling himself, until he silenced his mind again with the player.

It was in the autumn of 1946, nearly nine months after my discharge from the Navy, when Leonard and I embarked on what he called, our first 'mind experiment.' We had rehearsed for what seemed like decades, and though I felt as anxious as ever about the implausibility of the endeavor, I wanted the restless anticipation which had lingered over so many months to abate, and I was ready for the games to begin.

I can't put into words how foolish I felt when I wore the robe and turban. Bartholomew had been several inches taller than me, and when I wore the robe, it hung only two inches from the floor.

When I walked, I was constantly afraid of tripping over the hemline. The same was true of the turban. It fit so loosely on my head that I would wear a woman's garter around my temples to keep it from slipping over my ears.

I shall never forget the day, September 20, 1946. It was hotter than the fires of damnation. Summer had lingered too long. Inside the robe it felt like a sauna, as I was bathed in perspiration. Jim was driving us from Brooklyn to Riverhead, New York in a 1936 Ford truck that he had borrowed from his landlord. It barely ran, making a racket like a bailing machine, and it kept dropping out of gear whenever we hit a bump in the road. Leonard had to stop periodically and force it back into gear before we could go on.

I didn't know what to expect because he said very little during the drive eastward. All I knew with any degree of certainty was that were going to a small burlesque theater and that we were opening for another act. Leonard was sketchy about the details.

I remember asking him, "Leonard, I hate to ruin the surprise. But what kind of act are we opening?"

A sly smile spread across his face.

"You'll see. Just have some patience."

"I hope it's not some kind of striptease show. I'm really not in the mood for that."

"Relax, Nige. It's all above board."

"I agreed to do this for Beth, but I'm not going to make an ass out of myself."

"No one's asking you to make an ass of yourself. I'm sure you'll be pleasantly surprised."

"I already look like an idiot."

"You look fine."

"Why don't you wear this silly costume then, if it looks so good?"

"No, Nige. It suits you more than it suits me."

"I thought so. It's OK for me to look like a jack ass."

"You'll do fine."

"I don't know why I agreed to do this in the first place."

"You agreed to do this because it's a way to bring Beth here."

We had departed Brooklyn about seven o'clock in the morning, and by eleven o'clock we were a few miles outside of Riverhead, when we blew a tire. Then we spent nearly an hour struggling with a rusty jack before we got the tire changed. I never felt as self-conscious as when a car drove passed us, and I caught the faces of two laughing children. I was convinced that the rest of the visible world was laughing at me, that Cervantes could not have envisioned a more ridiculous quest than the one we were making.

I can't adequately describe what a humbling experience it is to look ridiculous. Yet, in an inexplicable way it was invigorating, even liberating. Throughout most of my life I had been self-conscious about my appearance. I had either wanted to be taller or my nose to be smaller. I thought my eyes were set too far apart. I even wanted a little more curl in my hair. But at that moment, these concerns were the farthest thing from my mind, and the robe, like a suit of armor, allowed me to face down these insecurities, and slowly, almost imperceptibly, I began to grow more comfortable with my appearance.

"Sure, I look ridiculous," I began to tell myself, "but it's my own unique ridiculousness." I even began to believe the whole venture was possible.

In every human life there come points of nexus, where one feels connected to the vast flow of events. This seemed one of those moments. I felt euphoric for the few idle minutes I sat on the running board. But then as abruptly as we had stopped, we both climbed back into the truck and continued on our way.

"Why are we doing this?" I asked Leonard.

"I've told you that," he answered me.

"No really. Beneath it all."

"I'm curious," he seemed ready to say something else, but stopped himself.

"Curious about what?"

"About the capacity for people to believe the impossible, about the malleability of human perception, about the principle of objectivity. I want to know about illusion. About the power of suggestibility. About the psychology of human belief structures."

He stopped himself again.

"By pulsing a series of electronic impulses across a plate of phosphorescent glass, you can create an illusion of motion, of objects, of humanity. The human mind organizes these impulses into pictures and images. I want to know how that's possible."

Like so much of what Leonard would talk about, I didn't quite understand what he was getting at, and I knew if I asked him to explain himself, I would only become more confused.

About noon, we pulled into Riverhead, and Leonard circumnavigated the town square several times before he finally parked the truck in front of the municipal building. It was one of those allpurpose Romanesque structures reminiscent of our county courthouse in Wisconsin. Across the square was an old vaudeville theater and next to it was the brick edifice of a Methodist church. That the church was so close to a burlesque house seemed perplexing to me, but our preacher at home had always derided the Methodists for being "liberal-minded", a term I found an ironic compliment, because I admired the "liberal-minded" for their spirit of tolerance.

As I climbed out of the truck and stood at the corner of the square, a rush of emotions swept through me like a severe summer storm. I felt both fear and expectation, anger and euphoria. It was reminiscent of my first time swimming, when at eight years old I stood motionless on a diving board, when my father in his ever stringent desire to force manhood upon me, pushed me out into the water and I crashed into the water with a such a splash it knocked the wind out of me. I don't think he knew how close I came to drowning in those first few moments of panic. And here I was again, standing before the abyss, and Leonard was about to push me.

"God, I must be crazy," I rebuked myself. "I've no idea what I'm doing."

But I struggled in silence, while Leonard ever-distracted in his own thoughts, walked behind me.

"Your performance begins at two o'clock," he began to give me details. "It's almost one now. Let's get a bite to eat."

The last thing I desired was to parade around in costume. But I steeled myself like a seasoned trooper and followed him into a coffee shop. I was undaunted by my ridiculousness.

Of course, people stared at me and some even laughed, usually attempting to disguise the fact. I began to contemplate what sort of revenge I might take if it all turned out to be a joke. But Leonard behaved with all seriousness.

We ate quietly without incident, with Leonard betraying none of his thoughts, until I broke the silence.

"What exactly are we going to do?"

"What we've rehearsed."

"What if it doesn't work?"

"Why are you such a pessimist? Of course it will work."

"I just think people are too sophisticated for all this."

"They want to believe the ridiculous. Of that fact, I'm certain."

He lit a cigarette and began to puff on it.

"You'd think that as far as we've advanced technologically, people would stop believing in all this superstition. But the more we are able

to understand and control our environment, it seems the harder it is to eradicate the irrational. It wouldn't surprise me if fifty years from now people are back to worshiping trees."

He smashed his cigarette out in the ashtray.

"They'll believe it, because they want to believe it."

Then he stood up a moment from his chair.

"Nige, you give a good show, and their minds will do the rest."

I couldn't understand his confidence when the whole prospect of going before an audience terrified me.

After lunch, Leonard and I separated and he disappeared. I went to the back of the theater to find the rear entrance. I was supposed to find a man named Jake to take me to my dressing room.

"Are you Jake?" I asked several people, until one directed me over to a hulking brute nearly seven feet tall. He towered over me like Kong, yet when he greeted me, his voice was rather timid and reserved, "So you must be this psychic act."

"Yes, I'm Nigel Fox. I need to know where I go."

"I figured that. Follow me."

He led me to a small room at the back, barely larger than a broom closet.

"Someone will be here to get you when it's time."

I found a small table near the back of the room, and there I waited. It seemed forever. And I kept my mind occupied by reading old playbills tossed in various piles around the floor. It was like a record house of vaudeville's glory days, when each act would have its heyday, and then be forgotten. There were ads for acrobats and animal acts and comedians. There must have been a hundred of them stacked around the room. I wondered if we too would be forgotten and tossed into the pile.

Finally, some one came and retrieved me and led me out on stage. Even though we had rehearsed for every contingency, I still fought a sense of panic, which was welling up inside of me. I had never faced an audience, yet something about the situation seemed familiar, almost too familiar.

When the curtain finally opened, I was sitting alone on stage with a small table in front of me. I felt alone, more so than I had ever felt. Though I could see clusters of people scattered across the theater seats, I could not see Leonard anywhere. I wondered if he had abandoned me. *The noise of my own heartbeat seemed to fill the quiet room.*

Then I began, *"The human mind has capacities not imagined."*
I spoke with a feigned British accent. "Today we shall explore one of the deepest mysteries of the human mind. Communication in the absence of words and pictures. Communication with the mind alone."
I paused a moment. "I shall demonstrate the power of the human mind in a few simple experiments of telepathy."

I kept waiting for Leonard to acknowledge me, but the turban was silent.

"I shall blindfold myself and ask anyone in the audience to hold up an object and I will through the power of my mind alone determine what it is and what significance it has."

I wrapped the blindfold over my eyes and turned my back to the audience, and then I said, "Someone, please stand up."

At that moment, an unquenchable panic consumed me and I began to sweat profusely. It was impossible for me to know if anyone had in fact stood up, and I became convinced that Leonard had abandoned me.

"How can he do this to me?" I agonized. Rage was springing from inside of me.

Then I heard, "I'm sorry, Nige. The batteries went dead. I've been all over town looking for new ones. Ask someone to stand up again."

I repeated my request.

"OK, we have one," Leonard continued. "He's forty or so and he's holding up a fountain pen."

Then with the firmest resolve I could muster, I responded, "Though this is not an exact science. I would say you have a writing instrument of some kind. Perhaps a fountain pen."

Someone else shouted, "What am I holding?"

And Leonard in his special code told me it was a pocket watch.

"A pocket watch," I announced. "You have to be more original."

Several more stood up and one by one, I overcame them all. With each newly conquered challenger, my confidence improved.

"You're doing fine," Leonard encouraged me. "Bartholomew couldn't have done it better."

I played my part with dispassionate self-constraint and I was everything Leonard had wanted me to be. But all I wanted was my ordeal to end, so that I could leave the stage.

With each new revelation, I became more adept, and with uncharacteristic wit I filled the hour with banter and observation, and with as much showmanship as I could master. I was even surprised at how well I was doing. But I still felt uncomfortable with this deceit, and I kept rationalizing how it was necessary to bring Beth to the States. Finally, at three o'clock, the ordeal was over, and I stood silently as the curtain was closed.

"That went all right, for the first time," Leonard greeted me as he met me back stage. "They want us back for five more Saturdays. We're gonna make it."

But I had a lump in my throat from the whole experience and didn't relish five more episodes.

"Do you think these people really believed this nonsense?" I asked him.

"Some of them did."

"And that doesn't bother you?"

"Why should it? It's not my fault if they're gullible."

The five weeks passed quickly and with each successive performance, my showmanship improved. Then the presence I commanded on stage began to take on a life of his own, and I began to speak of him in the third person, as I though I was an actor, and he was a character I was playing. I even began to make fun of him as though he were separate and distinct from me. It was a device I used to assuage my conscience.

After Riverhead, we began to travel into the counties north of the city, into Westchester, and Rockland and Putnam counties. Leonard had us performing in school auditoriums and gyms, anyplace where people could gather. He once proposed the closer the audience was to me the more impressive my powers would appear, though I found his proposal ridiculous. I couldn't believe that anyone could be so gullible. Yet when I saw many of their faces afterwards among the skeptics, there were always a handful of believing souls, and this bothered me.

I often thought of writing Beth and telling her what we were doing, but I was certain she wouldn't approve of me.

'I had been raised for better things,' I would tell myself, and because of my ever-vigilant inner voice, it became more difficult to attend each successive performance.

'Leonard,' I wanted to tell him. 'Let's put a stop to this.' But I

didn't have the heart to disappoint him, nor could I find a way to stop.

After one particularly powerful performance, when it seemed as if each word I spoke was faith-inspired, a young boy of no more than eight or nine, stood up to heckle me.

"You're no psychic," he began to yell. "My mamma tells me better."

"Of course I am," I answered him and stood my ground. "I'm Nigel the magnificent."

Then Leonard ever mindful of his clues, began to tell me what he knew about the boy. He had overheard him speaking about his puppy dog, and without a thought of consequence, I revealed this clue. "I know about your dog," I told him. "His name is Max. You play with him in your back yard and he likes to bury things." I relayed what Leonard was telling me, piece by piece, in ever more elaborate detail, until he too was silenced, until spontaneous applause, softly at first, then rising in pitch and timbre, began to pulsate across the hall.

When Leonard came backstage to congratulate me, he said, "That was wonderful Nigel. I've never seen you in better form."

I lashed out at him, "I guess now we're in the business of deceiving children."

"What's wrong with you? I have wonderful news. We've been booked for the city two nights next month."

"What's wrong with me?" I repeated, my voice quavering from anger. "What's wrong with me? I don't want to do this any more."

"It's just an act," he tried to diffuse my rage.

"An act, you say," I pulled a stack of letters from the dresser drawer.

"This woman wants me to find her son, and this one to speak to her dead husband." I tossed each letter at him. "And this one wants me to give him the winning horses. Need I go on? This one wants to find a jilted lover. This one wants me to find a lost dog. The list goes on and on. They leave them here for me so I might be their savior. It's tearing me up inside."

"I didn't know about the letters. But it's not our fault they're so gullible."

"It's not our fault."

Tossing the remaining stack at him, I left the room, slamming the door as I went out.

What I didn't tell him, what disturbed me most, was that I wanted to help them.

That evening when we returned to Brooklyn, while sitting at my bedroom window which overlooked the harbor, I resolved somehow to end it all, and it was then I wrote to Beth and told her about our plan. I can't remember the exact wording of the letter. But in it I put to paper all my anguish and uncertainty about the whole endeavor. I had to get my feelings out, whatever she might have thought of me. It was the one and only time I made mention of our work. Then I mailed the letter the next morning as I went to work at the florist shop.

During the course of the next week, as I was going about my daily duties, I tried to imagine what was happening across the ocean. I imagined the letter as it made its way by plane, by truck, by letter-carrier, to the East London flat where she lived with her aunt and uncle. I tried to picture her face as she opened it and began to read my anguished words.

"How would she react? What would she think? Would I ever hear from her again?" An ocean of silence lay between us and it was as deep and as inexplicable as the ocean I contemplated through my window.

Each day when I returned from work, I made the last steps to the mailbox with the same nervous lump in my throat. "Would this be the day?" I anticipated. But when I found the box empty again, I feared the worst, that I had lost her.

The days blur into a vague memory now, but I remember a couple, or maybe three more performances, between when I mailed the letter and when I finally received a response from Beth. I didn't know how much money we had raised by then, but the continued indulgence in this deceit left a bitter taste in my palate. When her letter finally reached me, I felt certain that a century had passed, and I held it in my hands with ambivalent reluctance before I finally gained the strength to open it.

I expected the worst, perhaps because as Raskolnikov was tortured by his conscience for killing the pawnbroker, I desired to purge myself, by confession and penitence, though at the time I had no exact vocabulary to describe what I was feeling. I wanted someone else to acknowledge my guilt.

Instead, her letter began like all the others. In firm and flowing cursive she wrote, "Dear Neilos, I have often read your bible in English to help me find good words to speak. In Greek we say, pistevo, vetheis apistis mou. *I believe, help my unbelief. We are fragile and temporary people." She crossed out the word 'temporary' and wrote 'mortal.' "I cannot judge you or condemn you when my own* amartias, *sins are so many. I pray that you look into your heart and pray for guidance." She continued. "I have good news. I have made enough money now to purchase a ticket to America. I shall be arriving by boat on May 16th. I will write later when I have more details."*

I started crying and my tears soaked the letter.

The tape clicked off and Jim, too fatigued to continue, set the player aside on the table. Reclining his head on the pillow, he had only wanted to rest for a few minutes before going on, but as soon as he stretched out on the bed, he was fast asleep, still wearing his clothes and shoes.

Chapter 15

Jim was completely incognizant of how much time had passed, when a loud thunderclap startled him from his sleep. He could hear a hard rain beating on the roof above him and at the window behind him. The noise resembled a hundred typewriters all moving at once. After rubbing his eyes, he sat up on his bed with the heels of his shoes balanced precariously on its edge. He remained like this a few uneasy minutes before an intense thirst compelled him to stand up and begin a trek downstairs to find himself something to drink.

As he began his descent down the staircase, the same irrational impulse to flee seized him again. Though he attempted to push these thoughts from his mind, he could not. He knew he had lost his greatest asset as a journalist, his objectivity, but he felt compelled to finish his investigation. The prospect of the next morning hung over him like a guillotine. Both Burgess and his father were soon to arrive and he was unprepared for either of them.

When he reached the kitchen, he poured himself a glass of orange juice, and sitting stoically at the table, he reflected on the past few days. So much had happened in such a short time that he felt as though he had lived a lifetime in but a moment. Feeling both anxiety and humor, he even suppressed a chuckle when he thought about how preposterous it had all become.

He noticed some of the religious paintings hanging randomly around the kitchen, and he rose up from the table in order to get a closer look at them. From picture to picture, he moved in a semicircle around the room until he had examined all of them. Staring intensely at one painting of a Madonna and Child, he struggled to understand what he was seeing, but the writing on the piece of artwork was in Greek and with his limited knowledge, he could only decipher a few letters. Before him was a culture, a history, and traditions, as foreign to his as the Chinese to Marco Polo, and he knew in order to make sense out of the quandary, he had to come to understand some of that vast difference.

He returned to the table, and after finding a pad and pencil, he began to draft a checklist of all that he had learned, and what still seemed confusing.

He resolved that later that morning, he would seek out Dr. Harvey and confront him with many of his questions. He was so wired up he could not return to bed. So, he decided to listen to as much of the next tape as time permitted before beginning his trip to the city.

Once upstairs, he found the tape labeled #7 and following a routine which had become second nature to him, he prepared to listen to the next tape. He sensed it must have been four or five in the morning and he turned on the player again.

I resolved that the Saturday after I received Beth's letter would be my last performance as Nigel the Magnificent. I didn't tell Leonard about my decision, because I was certain there would be a tremendous argument. He seemed obsessed with the prospect of taking our deceit before larger and more opulent audiences. But I had resolved to purge myself of the guilt of the experience by giving my share of the revenues to Leonard as a sort of peace offering for ending the partnership.

As I waited to be called the final time, I had the same uneasy lump in my stomach, and my hands tingled from restless anxiety. I remembered how nervous I was the minutes before they had announced Milly as the winner of the livestock contest, and I remembered the moments before I asked Beth to marry me, when it seemed as if my tongue had fallen out. I felt divided from myself, as though out-of-body, watching it all, until finally someone knocked on the door, and in a young voice told me, "It's time to go on."

When I arrived on stage and stood in the dark, I was terrified, but I forced myself to carry on. A single spotlight flashed on above me and the intensity of the light almost blinded me. All I could see in front of me were formless shapes, the mere silhouettes of human faces. And in front of me, barely visible, stood a sword-like microphone, my only defense from the crowd beyond. I approached it slowly with a ghostlike glide, and then slowly began.

"There is much in the world that the human mind cannot explain, that the human heart senses to be true despite what reason tells us. There are many who scoff at the powers of the human imagination. But tonight, Ladies and Gentlemen, I shall take you into the realm of the impossible. We shall push the very limits of human capacity. I will not hear, yet hear. I will not see, yet see. Tonight we shall have a

glimpse of eternity." I paused. "The ground rules are simple. Anyone, in order to test my powers, must stand up. An usher will find you and take from you a simple object, something which has significance to you, and I, blindfolded, shall discern the object and attempt to ascertain its significance."

A stage hand brought onto the stage a large black blindfold, which I wrapped around my eyes and then continued. "To further compound the difficulty, I shall turn around and face the back. You can begin any time."

There had been previous performances when Leonard took nearly ten minutes to talk to me, and I stood in abject horror believing he had abandoned me. On this final night, when what seemed like twenty minutes had passed and he did not give me my first set of clues, I imagined the worst. Then, in that strange code of his own devising, mostly sighs and grunts, he told me there was a lady's handkerchief.

I had become astute at intuitive guesses learning largely through trial and error. People offered objects for various reasons, but handkerchiefs were fairly common, and unless it was a particularly expensive one, it had little sentimental value. I acknowledged it and quickly moved on.

Next there came a pocket watch, an umbrella, a cigarette case, a deck of playing cards. Each I announced with little commentary. A woman tried to stump me with a music box, but Leonard sitting in the balcony with his opera glasses in hand, could easily pick out its unusual shape.

I remember a man's overcoat, a nutcracker, and a young couple who provided a copy of their marriage license, which gave me the occasion to get the biggest laugh of the evening, when I teased them about it. It was a totally effective ruse.

When I finally took my last bow, and the curtain closed in front of me, I was even more convicted in my decision to set it all aside.

*"Nigel, you were fabulous," Leonard greeted me back stage.
"I'm certain we'll get booked on Broadway next, and I've even been thinking about a whole new set of clues."*

Like a child obsessed, he seemed intoxicated with the idea of ever more complicated ruses. But I wanted nothing less than a complete separation from it all. It was the same feeling I had about farming when I made my decision to leave Wisconsin.

I cannot recall exactly what he proposed. I found it difficult to concentrate on his words. When he finally finished his ten minute soliloquy, I firmly responded. "I don't want to do this anymore."

His mind did not seem to register what I was saying, and he continued to explain his ruminations.

"I said I don't want to do this anymore."

"You're kidding me. We're so close to making it perfect."

"I can see this is intoxicating for you. But I can't do it. I'm out."

"Come on, you're kidding me. I've got us booked for two more weekends."

I could see that there was no talking to him, and I wasn't in the mood to argue about it. So I walked out on him, and I tossed the robe and turban into a trash can as I left the theater.

Rushing out after me, Leonard fished out the robe and turban from the trash can, and kept insisting to me, "Look, Nige. Let's talk about it."

"There's nothing to talk about. I just don't want to deceive people anymore."

"People want to be deceived," he pleaded earnestly. "It makes reality tolerable." He paused. "Let's have dinner and talk it over."

But there was nothing he could say to change my mind.

The tape clicked off on one side and Jim turned it over.

Over dinner, Leonard and I discussed our plans and prospects. I remember him saying at one point in the conversation, "I want to get into the television business. I see great potential for it. Much more than you or I can imagine now. I'm sure just as radio made the world smaller, television with its immediacy will only make it more so."

But in 1946, television seemed as odd a preoccupation as UFOs today.

"Nobody takes it seriously," I tried to engage him. "They see it as a passing fad like spats and the Charleston."

"Nige, think a minute about the possibilities. It will change the face of everything we know. No longer will we have to wait to see something happen. The world will be right in front of our eyes. It will come into our homes instantaneously, from sports events, to famines, to wars."

"It sounds frightening to me." And it did.

"There's a power beyond anything you and I can imagine."

"And what will entice all the world to stare into your little box?" It was difficult for me to imagine it.

"The same impulse that brings them to see Nigel the Magnificent. It's magic."

His vision of a world dominated by television seemed almost diabolical, what we would later call Orwellian. Yet he meant it in the most beneficent way. I don't think he could have envisioned the full consequence of his projection, nor could he realize the power television would eventually attain as a technology of psychological persuasion, and as a means of distorting reality, rather than illuminating it.

When there came a lull in the conversation, I told him, "I have good news. I got a letter from Beth and she is coming to the States in May."

"That's wonderful." He seemed genuinely pleased. "How did she pay for the ticket?"

"I'm not sure."

"We'll have to have a party for her." Then in uncharacteristic candor, he explained, "I've never been any good with women. They're too little like machines, unpredictable. Like religious institutions they demand constant commitment and are intolerant of weakness."

I sensed his words betrayed some past experience, but he was a very private man and wouldn't go deeper than what he had already revealed.

"I'm sorry."

"Nothing to be sorry about."

He lit a cigarette and began to puff on it nervously.

"I really should be going," he continued. "I'll give you a call in a couple of weeks." After he left me alone at the table, I sat for a few minutes thinking about all that had happened that evening. I couldn't put any of it out of my mind. Then I paid the bill and began my hour trek back to Brooklyn.

On the train, I thought about Beth and about my mother and I remembered the long train ride from Cleveland when I first met Leonard and how he stared at his hands. I had the sinking feeling I'd never see him again.

During the next several weeks, I fought a nagging depression which seemed to sap all my energy. It was difficult for me to concentrate on my work and felt a dull misapprehension about the future. Beth wrote me several times during those weeks. Her letters always began with a brief prayer and ended with "chronia polla", which I came to understand as a wish for long life and happiness. But despite her best wishes, I couldn't shake the feeling that when she finally arrived, I would have nothing to offer her, save the few dollars a week I earned at the florist shop.

Then she wrote me about the one issue I had been dreading all along.

"Nigel," she wrote, "If you and I are to be married, you must be baptized by the priest. It is our way."

This would have been only a small concession on my part had I not had such contempt for the religious life with all its inherent hypocrisy. But I would even endure this humiliation, because I loved her so much.

I remember when I was eleven or twelve, Brother Woodrow, the bombastic preacher at my mother's church, had approached my father about the issue of my baptism. My father, believing religious instruction to be a woman's affair, deferred the question to my mother. There transpired between them some long-winded discussion about the sinful condition of my soul and about my desperate need for repentance. But my mother, not wanting to force the decision upon me, but wishing for me to choose it willingly, asked me in the presence of the preacher, "Nigel, it's your decision. Do you want to be baptized or not?"

When I answered, "No, Mom. I don't think so," Brother Woodrow's eyes pierced through me like knives.

Even though I could sense she was disappointed by my decision, and even though Brother Woodrow was fit to be tied, she did not coerce me. I think because she believed I would eventually come around. It had been my only brush with the religious life, and I felt fortunate to have had the courage to refuse it. But here nearly twenty years later, I was faced with an even more drastic conversion and like a fattened pig led to the slaughter-house, I went willingly without so much as a whimper.

It was in mid-April while on a delivery in Brooklyn that I finally gained enough courage to stop at a Greek church and talk to the priest. I had little idea of what to expect, nor could I find the best words in which to phrase my request, but I resolved to go through with it, wherever it led.

I rang the bell at the parsonage, and a silver-haired woman, about sixty, opened the door partway and asked in an obvious Greek accent, "What do you want?"

"I want to talk to the priest. Is he home?"

"Why do you want him for? You're not Greek, are you?"

"No, but I want to be baptized."

She opened the door and escorted me into a parlor area where I sat down in a Victorian chair. I could hear her speaking in Greek to someone else in the other room, and then the priest, wearing a long black robe and with a full and flowing gray beard, entered the parlor and took a seat across from me.

His accent was not as deep as hers when he asked me, "You want to be baptized?"

"Yes."

"Why?" His tone of voice betrayed complete bewilderment as to why I would be asking this. So I began to explain myself.

"When I was in a hospital in London during the war, I met a young Greek woman whom I wish to marry, and she has told me I must be baptized in order to marry in her church."

He stared at me with stoic passivity.

"I'm not sure what all this entails," I continued. "But I'm willing to do what is necessary." I hoped the earnestness of my request would sway him.

"What do you know about our church?"

"I've been to many of your services."

"Do you know Greek?"

"No."

"You cannot understand. It is good you desire to know more. But I cannot baptize you."

His demeanor was immovable.

"Why can't you baptize me? Is it because I am not Greek?"

He laughed.

"It is because you are insincere. The religious life is a great responsibility. You must understand what it requires before you can be baptized."

"I will take whatever lessons you demand."

He was unimpressed.

"What do you know about our church?" But before I could answer

him, he went on. "The Christian life is one of martyrdom, the death of self. Our church traces itself through unbroken history to the time of the martyrs, to the early Christian Fathers, to the apostles and to Christ Himself. You must believe this with your whole heart before I can baptize you."

Every church makes an exclusive claim to truth and I understood this claim. But I did not believe in such a church as he described, and if those were the conditions he was setting for my baptism, it was most certainly a lost cause. I could never in sincerity agree to those conditions.

When I left the parsonage after an awkward goodbye, I was overwrought. It appeared I had reached an impenetrable obstacle and Beth and I would never be married, and when I had a chance to reflect on it the rest of the day, it angered me. For Brother Woodrow, it would have been as simple as a 'yes.' For this man it seemed impossible. I resolved later that evening that I would make an earnest try to learn more about the Greek Orthodox Church, but I felt pessimistic about the prospects.

Chapter 16

Jim hadn't realized he had fallen asleep with the headphones still in his ears until Dina came into the room in the morning and found him asleep in the chair. She shook him gently, but he was unresponsive.

"Michael," she prodded him. "It's nine o'clock."

Jim began to show signs of animation.

"It's nine o'clock, and I have breakfast for you downstairs."

"Alright, I'm getting up."

He took the headphones out of his ears and set the player aside on the dressing table. When he tried to calculate how long he had slept, he was unable to concentrate because of his fatigue. He couldn't remember if he had finished the tape, but he remembered Nigel saying something about the Greek Church, but he was uninterested in continuing any detailed religious discussion.

He came downstairs to the kitchen and found a plate of food prepared for him.

"You shouldn't be sleeping in a chair, Michael," Dina greeted him. "It's not good for the back."

He ate his eggs with indifference, and he consumed his coffee in several gulps without cream or sugar. He pushed his plate away and stood up from the table.

"I'll be gone most of the day," he told her. "So you needn't fix me any lunch."

"That's all right. I will have your supper ready about six."

She seemed as willing to serve him as though he were paying her salary. Then he wondered who was paying her now that Nigel had died.

Much about the situation made him uncomfortable. Though he knew much more than when he had arrived, there were still disturbing questions, and it seemed the deeper he probed into things, the more perplexing the questions became. He thought about skipping ahead in the tapes, listening to the last tape in the sequence next, but after weighing the pros and cons, he decided that once he had the time, he would continue where he had finished. He remembered what he had been taught in journalism school, that reporting is often slow tedious work, much like sifting through trash cans, and that a good reporter could learn a library from what another person throws away. Yet, he found himself repelled by the thought of digging deeper, as though he were afraid of what he might find.

After breakfast, he packed a notebook, his tape player and the tapes into a canvas bag, and he began to prepare himself psychologically for his trip to Columbia. He wasn't sure what he would ask Dr. Harvey once he found him, nor was he certain Dr. Harvey would speak to him, but he was convinced his first attempts at investigation must begin with him.

He stood for what seemed an eternity on the railway platform as he waited for the Long Island Railroad. He knew little about the New York subway system but that he hated them, and he was certain he could navigate once he got into Manhattan. At Penn Station, he studied the subway map for over ten minutes before embarking on the One Line uptown toward Columbia.

While standing nervously in the crowded car, pressed awkwardly between a half dozen commuters, he remembered what he had hated most about Chicago, and how in Hadleyburg he had grown to cherish space. When the doors finally opened at the appropriate stop, he took a deep breath and then fought his way up through the crowded stairway. When he reached street level, he felt an odd paranoia as if someone was following him, but then chided himself for his foolishness.

His search through Columbia began at the administration building. He asked a receptionist, "Can you tell me what building Dr. William Harvey works in?"

"He's in the History department."

"Where's the History department?"

"It's in that building there?" She pointed out the window.

Jim thanked her, and in a hurried pace ran down the steps and toward a gray four-story building across the courtyard. He read the sign outside, and then rode the elevator to the third floor. Once upstairs, he made an office-to-office search, reading names on the doors until he found an open door for the chairman's office. Then he walked inside.

"I'm sorry to bother you. But I'm looking for Dr. William Harvey. Can you tell me where his office is located?"

"It's the third door on the left. But I don't think he's there now," a young woman answered him. "I can take a message for him."

"No, I'll check for myself."

Jim found the office locked, but a schedule of his classes was posted on the door. He read it. Dr. Harvey was teaching a seminar at ten o'clock in room

202. He looked at a clock on the wall and noticed it was nearly eleven.

He asked the woman in the office, "Where is room 202?"

"It's in the library on the second floor."

He rushed down three flights of stairs and out of the building. Then practically in a sprint, he dashed across the courtyard into the library. He would have continued running had security not stopped him to check his bag. When he rushed upstairs to the second floor, he could see Dr. Harvey descending a flight of stairs at the other end of the hall.

"Dr. Harvey," he shouted.

The professor turned to look at him. Jim dashed down the hall with the bag making a thumping noise as it hit him on the hip.

"Dr. Harvey, please stop."

"I don't know why you've come to talk to me. I've told you all I'm going to tell you."

"I must talk to you, please."

"I'm a busy man. I don't have time to talk to you. You should have taken my advice and gone home."

Jim was breathing hard and tried to catch his breath.

"I want to talk about the Brotherhood."

"Please keep your voice down. I can't talk to you here."

"I'll go anywhere you like. I'll meet you any time you like. You can blindfold me. I have to talk to you."

"I'm sorry. I can't."

"I'm begging you." Jim found such groveling extremely disarming.

"Alright, I'll give you five minutes. But only five minutes. Just come to my office."

Jim followed him across the courtyard and back into the history building. Dr. Harvey said nothing until he reached the front of his office and unlocked the door.

"Alright. Come inside."

Jim found a chair across from him and removed a stack of congressional documents which was precariously balanced on its edge. He scanned the room with his eyes dancing from artifact to artifact. He noticed several books about freemasonry, others written in German and one book title, *The Illuminati*, as well as thousands of pages of congressional testimonies and committee reports. Then he picked up a book called *Tragedy and Hope* which was lying on the corner of the desk.

"What's all this stuff?" Jim asked him as he laid the book back where he found it.

"Just wait a moment before you say anything."

After opening a cabinet filled with electronics equipment, Dr. Harvey threw on a few switches and then responded, "You can talk now. It blocks out any listening devices."

After this extravagant display, Jim became convinced that he had made a mistake, because Dr. Harvey was a bigger nut than he had previously surmised, and any discussion with him would send them both into a paranoid fantasy of Dr. Harvey's own creation. Dr. Harvey closed the cabinet and sat down at his desk.

"So talk, Mr. Jacobson. Your clock is running."

"I need to know what Nigel told you."

"Why didn't you take my advice and go home?"

Dr. Harvey opened a drawer and removed his pipe and tobacco. After filling the pipe, he lit it and began to feverishly puff on it as he had done at the cemetery.

"Dorothy, you're not in Kansas anymore."

"I'm not here to play games. I want some answers."

"Are you sure about that? Sometimes the questions are more intriguing than any answers you might find."

"What did Nigel tell you?" Jim repeated.

"You don't have the faintest clue as to what's about to happen to you. I don't usually involve myself in someone else's folly. But in your case, I hate to see a sitting duck."

He blew several smoke rings into the air and they floated as miniature halos above his head.

"Nigel came to me two weeks ago and sat across from me where you are sitting. He went on and on about some super-secret group called 'The Brotherhood' and asked me if I could help him fight them. He said, 'My life is in danger. I'm an old man. I don't care about myself. They can kill me. I just don't want to see my work destroyed.' Having studied and written about these groups most of my adult life, I'm more receptive to it than most. I told him, 'If someone has threatened your life, that's a police matter. You should go to the police.' and he said, 'I can't trust the police will protect me.' I thought he was a little crazy and I told him what I'll tell you, I make it a personal policy not to get involved. Then he reached into his pocket and handed me a ring."

Harvey opened his desk drawer and retrieved a gold signet ring with a single rectangular stone. Atop the stone, a gold triangle with a five pointed star in the center was mounted. He handed the ring to Jim.

"This ring he told me is the Brotherhood's ring."

Dr. Harvey cracked a half smile as though to betray his disingenuousness.

"That's all I know about Nigel's brotherhood."

He sat the pipe down on the table and began to stroke his beard.

"And there's one other thing that he said, 'I'm sure they are going to destroy my work and blame it on someone else.'"

"And you believe him?"

"Why not?"

"And I suppose you think I'm their patsy."

"Makes a certain sense, doesn't it? You never liked him anyway."

"I don't believe any of it. Secret brotherhoods! Special rings! It's a little nuts if you ask me."

"Why? Because it sounds too paranoid? And I suppose you think this isn't the way things get done." He laughed. "The top one percent of the population controls 80 percent of the wealth in this country. They control over half of the top Fortune Five Hundred companies, and those they don't control directly, they control indirectly through interlocking boards of directors. In Europe, the situation is more centralized. Many of the same families have controlled the wealth since the time of Clovis. (He paused.) Don't tell me you don't know who Clovis was. The first of the Merovingian Kings. There are a number of ruling families in Europe that trace themselves as direct descendants of the Merovingian Kings. And then we have the Knights Templar."

Jim stared at him with incredulity.

"I don"t believe any of it."

"Whether you believe it or not, every institution in this country whether it is economic, religious or political, serves one purpose only, to legitimize the ruling class. All these words about democracy, self-rule, civil rights, and economic opportunity, are so much smoke and mirrors to mystify the masses. Do you really think these decisions are made in Congress? In the White House? They're made in corporate boardrooms, on golf courses, in private meeting houses of their various brotherhoods. Today this industry lives. This industry dies. These people have jobs. These people lose theirs. You and I mean nothing to them."

Jim was surprised by the depth of his cynicism.

"I'm not ready to adopt your fatalist viewpoint."

"You will. It's impossible to fight them, when you don't know who they are." He paused a moment and looked again at his clock. "I've given you more than five minutes. I'm sorry, but I have work to do."

"May I have the ring?"

"Sure."

Jim took it from him.

"I've done as much as I can do for you. I'm sorry."

Jim remained in his seat a few restless minutes more, pondering if he should press Dr. Harvey further. But he resigned himself to the fact that he had learned from Dr. Harvey all that he was going to learn, and he stood up to leave the office.

"Thank you for your time, Doctor."

"Take my advice, Mr. Jacobson. Go home."

As Jim closed the door behind him, he was certain he had reached an impasse. He stared a moment at the ring and then slipped it into his pocket. His mind was both agitated and distracted, tossed from notion to notion, like wind inside a letter box.

After boarding the train at Penn Station, he began to think again about Nigel's death, about everything that had happened that evening from the moment he entered the room until he was told about it in the hallway. For the first time, he pondered the possibility that Nigel had been murdered, though he found the idea preposterous. Then he removed the ring from his pocket and held it out a few inches in front of his eyes, examining it as child might observe a butterfly. He pondered what secrets it might conceal. Secret cabals, rituals, these were the projections of paranoid delusions. For all he knew, the ring had come as a prize inside a cereal box, yet beneath his skepticism percolated a grievous doubt. He placed the ring back in his pocket and resolved to put this out of his mind.

He unzipped the bag and removed the player and the headset. After skipping ahead on the tape, he finally stopped it at the last point he remembered before falling asleep. Nigel had said, "I would try to learn more about the Greek Orthodox Church."

Jim had experienced an idle curiosity in religion as an undergraduate and had even taken a comparative religions course to fill out an elective. But even then he viewed religious beliefs as the superstitions of pre-technological ignorance, when the world was perceived as a vast array of unseen and misunderstood forces. Nigel's forays into religious investigation didn't interest him, but he realized he couldn't just skip over it. For the sake of a complete picture of the circumstances, he resolved to hear it all.

And I would try to learn more about the Greek Orthodox Church. But I felt pessimistic about the prospects.

That evening after I returned to the room where I was staying, I found the letter in which Beth had told me about her plans, and I reread it several times. She had once tried to explain to me her religious beliefs, but like so many other occasions, I only focused on the items which most interested me.

I remembered a conversation we had shared so many months ago in London. As always, she had struggled incessantly with her English, and I learned to understand her despite her obvious grammatical mistakes.

She had told me she had a brother who had gone to the Holy Mountain, "*O Agios Oros*," as she called it and I asked her to tell me what that was. Then she told me as best that she could explain that "*Panagia*" had decreed a certain tract of land to be set aside for the sanctification of the world, a place devoted to prayer and fasting. I later learned that "*Panagia*" referred to the Virgin Mary, and that a peninsula in Greece called Athos, meaning the high place, has been dedicated to her. Beth's brother had gone there to be a monk, when Beth was a small child.

"Have you gone there to see him?" I innocently asked her, and she laughed. "Oh. No. Women are not allowed on the Holy Mountain."

I then realized that I understood nothing about her religion, and when I reflected on that conversation so many months later, I felt no more informed. Being a product of the American experiment, I wondered how I could come to understand a culture as foreign as hers.

After work the next day, I decided to stop by the Brooklyn Public Library and see what I could discover among the books. I understood that book knowledge had its limitations, but I had to begin somewhere.

There were only a limited number of books available, and I debated whether I should read about Liturgy in the Greek Orthodox Church, or another book about the Monastic Tradition of the Eastern Church. I decided I would read about liturgy, though I didn't know exactly what the word meant.

I had some difficulty finding the book, and I had to ask the librarian for help. Now so many years later, it seems a little comical, these two men from Brooklyn searching through stacks to find a book neither of *us could understand. When we found the book, its cover was almost new, though the book had obviously been sitting there for years, and it had only one date stamp in the back and that was for April 1931, the only date it had been borrowed. When I got the book home, I began to read it on my bed, but so many words were unrecognizable to me that I had a difficult time making sense out of what I was reading. Even an old Miriam Webster dictionary which I kept near my bed proved useless in discerning their meaning. But I struggled to understand, writing the words I did not know on a pad of paper. By the end of the third chapter, it had grown to over two dozen words.*

It rained almost every day that April, and I would make my deliveries for the florist shop with the book pressed between my yellow raincoat and my chest. Once the book slipped and fell to the pavement, and I jumped off the bicycle to snatch it just before it bounced into a puddle. Then the bicycle fell with a resounding clang, and I found myself lying in the puddle with a dozen roses scattered around me. But I had saved the book from drowning.

I learned a lot from that little book. It explained to me how the early Christians worshiped, and about the persecutions they suffered under the Romans, then the Muslims. But when I finished the book, I was no more convinced of religious belief than when I started.

After I finished the book and returned it to the library, I borrowed the second one about monasticism, which I read in the evenings. I found it more difficult to understand, because so much of the book dwelt on the utter emptiness of life in this world. The monastic movement appeared to be a rejection of human life, a type of willing submission to death, and I found this viewpoint unacceptable. I agreed that much in this world is superficial and insincere, but I had come to believe that significance came not in the rejection of the world, but in the power of individual achievement. My life had meaning, I surmised, because a unique life lived with intensity made a difference in this world. It was a belief in this principle which had brought me to New York in the first place.

Yet, despite my reticence about the religious sensibilities presented, I found something strangely appealing about what I was reading. I had the same feeling of Déjà Vu which I experienced on my first train ride into New York, and as much as I tried to shake this feeling, it persisted, and it became most acute on the day I returned the book to the library.

I was distracted trying to fit in the trip between deliveries, when I bumped into someone in the line in front of me. I looked up and noticed it was Leonard. I had not heard from him or seen him since our last night together as an act, and I'm convinced if we hadn't bumped into each other there, we would likely have never seen each other again. Leonard had been deeply disappointed at the breakup of our partnership, and knowing his temperament, I had believed any rapprochement from my side would be met with sarcastic resistance. He had never been an easy man to know and during the weeks which passed, I had become accustomed to being alone, unwilling to become entangled in difficult relationships. But to my surprise, Leonard seemed genuinely pleased to see me.

After a perfunctory greeting he asked me how I had been doing.

"Alright, I guess."

"Is Beth still coming to New York?"

"Yeah, in late May or early June, I think." I paused and asked, "What have you been doing?"

"I've been trying to get into the television business," he spoke with a tinge of despondency in his voice. "But no one seems to be interested. They believe it's not a profitable enterprise."

I was a little amused that he was still obsessed with this dream.

"What is the problem?" I asked.

"Money. I even offered to franchise it. I take the risk and suffer the loss. But no one wants to lay out the initial investment in capital for production. I've spoken to every radio manufacturer who'll listen to me, and no one wants to take the risk."

"It's an unknown," I responded.

"It's not an unknown. No more than the Wright brothers were an unknown. They're just short-sighted."

"Perhaps you're trying the wrong approach. I would approach it from a more pragmatic direction. Explain the long term benefits. Give them an idea of the whole picture."

"That gives me an idea, Nige. I've got an appointment with Bigelow Radio next week. Why don't you come along and talk with them?"

I was reluctant to get involved with another of Leonard's enterprises, but as a way of making amends to him, I agreed to go along.

"Sure. Just give me the details."

"I'll come by this weekend, and we can make our plans."

Leonard then said goodbye and departed. I didn't even realize what I had set in motion. When Leonard came that weekend, we laughed as deeply as we had ever laughed, yet despite what seemed to be an easing in our conversation, he still seemed distant.

When he spoke about cathode tubes and resistance with his usual fervor, I found my mind drifting away. At one point in his explanation, my thoughts blanked out, and only when Leonard asked me, "Are you listening to me?" did my mind refocus again.

"Oh, yes."

"I was explaining about phosphorescence," he reiterated.

Without thinking about it, I blurted out, "The glow worm."

"Yes, the glow worm." He paused. "When electrons of a certain frequency strike the phosphorescent panel, it glows."

I wasn't interested in a technical discussion about the theory of television signal production, and I sensed that the radio executives were like-minded.

"Have you thought about using an economic argument?"

"Like what?"

"Like how much money they can make in advertising revenue, selling time as they do in radio."

It was with a tinge of sarcasm that I made my recommendation, because I never liked radio commercials and the prospect of transferring radios format to a new technology I found unappealing. Even then, I had the sense that Leonard's technological wonder would soon become yet another avenue for selling soap.

Yet, he was interested in all those nobler aspects, much the same as when he first told me about his plans in 1937.

"You want them to show an interest in television," I told him. "Tell them it's just a radio with pictures."

But for Leonard these words were heresy, and I could see that he was becoming irritated by my remarks.

"I'm not going to reduce my vision to peddling products. Television has much more potential than that."

"Leonard, I'm joking. Relax."

I didn't believe for a moment we would ever be part of the television business, if such a business ever took off. But I did not have the heart to tell him what I really felt.

The tape clicked off.

Chapter 17

Jim realized that in his preoccupation with the tape, he had missed his stop at Bayside and the train had stopped at Port Washington several stops away. After rushing off the train, he soon discovered that the time was nearly half past two and he had missed his father's flight. He found a payphone and then dialed.

"Hello," Dina answered.

"Yes, Dina. Has my father called?"

"Is that you, Michael?"

"Yes. Has he called?"

"He's here."

"Damn. Can I talk to him?"

A few moments later, Jim's father came to the phone.

"Jim, where are you?"

"I'm sorry. It took a little longer than I expected. I missed my stop, and I'm in Port Washington, NY."

"Do you need a ride back?"

"No. I'll take the train back. Are you all right?"

"I'm fine."

"I guess you made it to the house in one piece."

"Physically. What's going on here?"

"I'll tell you all about it as soon as I'm there."

He hung up the phone and then crossed under the tracks to the platform on the other side. His gait was nervous and arrhythmic, and, almost sprinting, he scaled the final steps. But he did not realize how far apart the trains ran, and after making his frantic dash, he stood on the platform nearly twenty minutes before the next train arrived.

As he stood there, waiting anxiously, balancing from one foot to the other, his mind began to rush again. First, he thought about his father, whom he was eager to query about his adoption and about the circumstances of Nigel's letter; then secondly, concerning the contents of the tapes, which became more of an enigma the closer he came to finishing them; and then about "the

Brotherhood," whose existence he could not help but doubt. As much as he tried to be completely objective about the issues, he could not escape the emotional baggage attached to every category.

He arrived at Nigel's house at nearly three o'clock, and with some trepidation he rang the front bell.

"I'm back," he shouted into the intercom.

Someone inside buzzed open the front gate, and he began to walk up to the house, but before he could enter inside, Jim's father opened the front door and met him on the sidewalk. His father extended his hand to Jim, who awkwardly shook it.

"We have a lot to talk about," his father told him.

Jim could sense the urgency in his voice, but did not understand the full import of his remark. Then he followed his father back inside and both of them sat down in the living room.

"You're looking good, Jim," his father began.

"Looks can deceive."

"You've lost some weight."

"A few pounds."

"It's been a long time since we talked like this."

"Ages."

"I know you must have a lot of questions."

Then came a period of awkward silence. Jim often thought of what he might say at just such a moment, but now all premeditation abandoned him.

"What have you discovered about this Nigel person?"

He didn't know how to answer this question, because he knew many specific details about Nigel's life, but as to the larger questions of character, he seemed hopelessly confused.

"Not a lot," he finally answered.

"I heard he sold televisions."

"Yeah, I heard that."

"It's a little odd then there isn't a set in this house." Jim hadn't seriously reflected upon it. But there wasn't a single set anywhere in the house, not in the living room, not in the kitchen, not even in Nigel's private study. This was yet another one of the perplexing enigmas which had already characterized his investigation.

His father continued, "I can't quite put my finger on it. But there is something very strange about this house. It doesn't look lived in. Over the years, people accumulate things, mostly junk, which tell a visual story about what's happened to them.   This house looks like it has been consciously picked over."

"I think you're being a little paranoid." He paused. "I'd like to talk.   But let's go somewhere else."

"Sure, but let me put my suitcase away."

Jim's Father went into the hallway and grabbed his suitcase, then a few minutes later returned downstairs.

"There's a strip of stores and restaurants a few blocks away. Let's get something there."

When they both left the house, Jim felt relief, though he did not know why, and he could sense that his father was holding back something.

"It's not what I expected," his father began to explain. It's much more residential."

"You mean Queens?"

"Yes."

"Don't let it deceive you. It's still a big city."

"You sound like a veteran."

"It's been an eventful few days."

Jim wanted to tell someone all that had happened, but he held back, afraid to dump it on him all at once, and he still found it difficult to trust his father, because of all that had happened between them before.   Even before his mother's death, their worlds had been as distinct and separate as those of different religious faiths, and afterwards, they had drifted even farther apart until they hardly spoke at all, keeping the relationship more out of obligation than affection. And when they had ventured to speak about more serious issues, it inevitably deteriorated into an argument.   Though this afternoon, Jim didn't want to argue and he spoke with a candor unlike himself.

"I'm afraid," he began. "I'm scared to death."

This remark surprised his father, who broke his stride to listen to him.

"I'm waiting for the next shoe to drop," he continued.

"That's part of why I came."

"I remember reading Oedipus the King in high school. How a plague was besetting the city of Thebes. He went to the oracle of Apollo to ask what he should do, and he was told to find the previous king's assassin and bring him to justice."

"I know the play."

"But he was the assassin, and his own curse came down upon his head. I wonder if I should want to know the truth."

His father did not immediately respond to the remark, but they kept walking silently the remaining four blocks. When they finally reached Northern Boulevard, Jim suggested an Italian Restaurant and they went in.

After a hostess escorted them to a table and handed them both menus, Jim sat down. But, unable to relax, he balanced himself on the edge of his chair. To his surprise, his father seemed totally calm.

"These prices are a little too steep for my budget," Jim said once he read the menu.

"Don't worry. I'll take care of it."

"You can't afford these prices either. I know what they pay college professors these days."

"But you forget. I have one hundred thousand dollars."

His father reached into a pocket and removed Nigel's letter, which he set down in the middle of the table.

A waiter approached the table.

"Could I interest you in something from the bar?" he asked them.

"I'll take a glass of red wine," his father responded.

"No, I don't think so. I have to keep my wits about me."

A few minutes later the waiter returned with a glass of red wine which he carefully set down in front of Jim's father.

Jim shifted anxiously in his chair, then turned to his father and asked him, "Can I look at it?"

"Go ahead."

He opened it and discovered the short letter with a check folded inside.

"It's a cashier's check."

"Yeah. I can see that. He really must have convinced himself he was my father."

"Well, that's why I'm here." His father took a huge sip from the glass.

"If I were you, I'd take the money and run."

"I promised your mother I'd never talk about these things. But it's been eating at me all these years. It will be a relief to finally get it out."

"To get what out, dad," he spoke with more affection in his voice. "I'm not so sure I like the sound of this."

"There is much that isn't what it appears to be," said his father. He bit his lip a moment as though to steel himself for what was to follow and continued, "Your mother and I really wanted a child, and she couldn't have any."

"I know."

"We tried the usual routes, adoption agencies and the like, but it seemed to take too long. She didn't want to wait. So we went to, I guess you would call them baby brokers, who promised to bypass all the rigmarole. They'd get us a baby nobody wanted for a fee."

"You're trying to tell me you bought a baby." Jim's voice began to rise in pitch and timbre. "You pontificated to me my whole damn life about ethics and economic responsibility, and you buy a baby. What a hypocrite."

He was beginning to draw attention to himself and the waiter approached the table.

"Is everything all right here?"

"No, everything is not all right here."

"If you can't control your temper, we will have to ask you to leave," the waiter chastised him.

Jim had pushed himself up from his seat and was balanced precariously on his fingertips. "I'm all right," he softened his voice and lowered himself to his seat. "So you're trying to tell me there is a chance this man is my father."

"I don't know that. But he could be. We didn't know for sure where you came from. We believed what we were told, that your mother had abandoned you."

Jim pushed his hand across his forehead and scalp.

"In all the things that matter, I am your father. I changed your diapers. I taught you to ride a bicycle. I'm the one who picked you up when you fell, who educated you when you were ignorant, who bailed you out of jail when you were protesting the war. I just don't want you to lose sight of who we raised you to be."

"I can't accept it."

"I can understand your anger with me. What do you want me to tell you? We made a mistake. I'm sorry."

"You've lied to me my entire life."

"You haven't exactly been a fountain of truth. How long have you known about this?"

"Since shortly after the funeral."

"And you never told me anything."

"How could I?"

"You should have told me."

"And what would it have accomplished?"

"We might have had this conversation eighteen years ago and avoided all these years of anguish. I'm not going to make an apology to you for my life. I always tried to do right by you, to be the best father I could be." He spoke these words with anguish. "My father and I never got along. All he cared about was the almighty dollar, and I've spent my entire life as a repudiation of everything he stood for. When he died in 1964, I wouldn't even go into the hospital room to see him. My mother told me he kept calling, 'Where's Tommy? Where's Tommy?' He must have died thinking that I hated him. I don't want you to make the same mistakes I've made."

Jim was surprised by the frankness with which his father spoke. He could not recall another time he had been as candid. But Jim was still unable to open up. In these past few days, he had felt so many profound emotions that he was unsure of how to respond to any new situation. When he finally did speak, it was not in response to his father's remark, but as an aside.

"Shouldn't we order something to eat?"

"Yes, that would be a good idea."

His father gestured for the waiter to approach them, and they both ordered from the cheapest section of the menu.

"I saw you have a new book out."

"Since when have you taken an interest in my books? But yes, I have a new book on steady-state economies."

"Do you think anyone will listen to you?"

"They haven't yet. But there is always hope someone in power will see the light."

For the first time some of the tension between them was dissipating.

"You can't violate every principle of economics and not eventually pay the penalty," he began to speak in a professorial tone. "It's no accident that when an industry is deregulated, the average wage of its employees declines, then worker morale declines, then productivity declines. It's a natural pattern. Human nature being what it is, people always take advantage of a vacuum."

Jim had always been surprised that his father took these issues so seriously. Over the years, he had learned to accept his own impotence. He knew he could never change the world. But his father seemed forever trapped in the throes of some adolescent rebellion, always fighting onward in quixotic fervor.

Then the tone of their conversation grew lighter. His father asked him about the paper and Hadleyburg, and with the fondness one usually reserves to describe a good friend, he began to detail his duties at the paper. He described the town square, the shops, the parks, the movie theater, each in delicate detail as if he had personally designed and built them all. His father listened quietly with little comment.

"You know it's not Chicago," he mentioned at one point. "But I'm getting used to it." But there was an edge of sadness in his voice, because he sensed that he might never return. He remembered how often he had bitterly complained to his father about how boring it all was, and now how he longed for such boredom again.

"Are you still writing poetry?" his father asked him.

"It's been a long time. But I do remember one of the last ones I wrote." He began to recite. "The human heart seeks its peace in dreams, as a tender shoot strains for the sky, nothing can muffle despair's anguished screams, when heartfelt dreams are allowed to die. There's much more but I can't remember it all."

Jim took a sip of his drink and continued.

"As mother so often told me, poetry doesn't put food on your table or gasoline in your car."

"Your mother was wrong about many things."

Jim looked at a clock on the other side of the room, and he noticed it was nearly five thirty.

"We really should be getting back. I have a story to finish."

"Sure. Let me get the check."

Chapter 18

Sitting two tables away from them and watching them the whole time they were eating, a bearded man, wearing a red beret, sat shuffling a deck of cards. Jim had seen him briefly out of the corner of his right eye, but otherwise took little notice of him. Yet, the stranger watched with the intensity with which a surgeon studies the movement of his own hands. Once or twice during the course of the meal, Jim had made eye contact with him, but there was nothing to set this man apart from any of the other customers, and Jim's attention immediately returned to his father. Jim never noticed that the stranger was wearing a small insignia on his lapel which resembled the triangle emblem on the ring in Jim's pocket.

He hadn't a clue about the danger which quietly surrounded him. Nor did he anticipate the whirlwind which was about to disrupt his life. It is often difficult for the innocent to recognize evil, even when it stares them in the face, and Jim, despite the cynicism he projected outwardly, inwardly possessed an innocent heart.

Their walk back to Nigel's house was pleasant, though a slight chill was in the air as the edge of a cold front blew into the city. Jim said very little to his father as they walked, but finally broke his silence.

"How long are you planning on staying?"

"Several days. I might drop by my publisher a while and rattle some of the cages."

Neither of them noticed that the man in the beret was trailing them and moving inconspicuously in the shadows.

Jim wanted to unburden himself, to tell his father about all that had happened in the past few days, but when he tried to speak of "the Brotherhood", or Nigel's tapes, he was unable to express himself, and he couldn't understand his self-constraint. When they reached the house, Jim rang the bell on the gate and someone buzzed them inside.

"My God. I forgot all about Burgess. I was supposed to meet him at Kennedy airport."

"What time was his flight in?"

"I don't remember."

"Who is this Burgess?"

"He's the photographer at the newspaper. The guy I went to journalism school with."

Jim reached to open the front door, and he could feel someone's hand on the other side of the knob.

"Where in the hell have you been, Jim?" Burgess greeted him at the door.

"Burg, this is my father."

The two men shook hands.

"How long have you been here? And how did you find the place?"

"Over an hour, give or take a few minutes."

They all came inside and Jim's father closed the door behind them. Jim could see Burgess' suitcase on the living room carpet and his camera case balanced on the edge of the sofa.

"Is Dina here?" Jim asked.

"No, she left. Said she had some errands to run and wouldn't be back till the weekend. I've taken the opportunity to do a little snooping."

Burgess had always had more of a reporter's instinct, and neither conscience nor scruples ever prevented him from sticking his nose where it didn't belong. Jim's father seemed entertained by the prospect of further enlightenment and fixed his eyes on Burgess as he began to explain.

"Something isn't right about this house."

"I had the same feeling," Jim's father interrupted him.

"I've been over every inch of this house in this past hour and I went down into the basement to see what was down there. It's empty. Come on. I'll show you."

He led them both down a small flight of stairs and into the basement, then turned the light on. Except for a couple of old bicycles and an old radio, it was empty. He showed them places on the floor where the outlines of squares indicated where boxes once sat.

"You should see my parent's basement. It's got so much junk in it you can hardly move."

Jim seemed confused why this issue was so important to him.

"Somebody has come in here and taken all this stuff out."

"So what? Why couldn't Nigel have done it?"

Burgess pulled a notebook from his pocket and began to turn the pages.

"It's not only that. I have looked in every drawer, every cabinet, every shelf, for a letter, a bill anything that might reveal something about this man, and I've come up empty." He paused. "Except for this." He pulled a three by five photograph from his shirt pocket and handed it to Jim. "This was stuck underneath the bottom of a drawer, and I found it quite by accident."

The photograph pictured a younger Nigel with another man Jim could not recognize. Jim stared at it intensely.

"Do you know who this is?" Burgess asked him.

"How could I?"

Jim noticed the man with Nigel was wearing a ring just like the ring that Dr. Harvey had given him.

"Maybe it's Leonard Matthews, his business partner."

"Who's Leonard Matthews?" Burgess pulled a newspaper clipping from his pocket and began reading it aloud.

"Nigel Fox, who with his business partner, David Atkinson, was one of the early pioneers in television, is survived by a nephew and two cousins."

"What is that?"

"It is an obituary."

"They were in the Navy together. They had a radio business. The obituary must be mistaken."

"I made a few phone calls. David Atkinson was his business partner."

Jim was experiencing the same feeling of cognitive dissonance which had haunted him his whole stay in New York.

"I'm sure there's an explanation," Jim posited. "We just haven't discovered it yet." He was reluctant to reveal what he had learned from the tapes.

"Maybe this Leonard Matthews changed his name," Jim's father proposed. "My grandfather changed his name after he immigrated here."

"I don't think so," Burgess interjected. "You're sure his name was Leonard Matthews?"

"That's what he said."

Burgess began to write something in his notebook.

"What do you have in that book?" Jim interrupted him.

"Just ideas, just ideas." He folded it up and placed it back in his pocket.

"You seem to be enjoying this. Playing amateur sleuth."

"Don't you like a good mystery, Jim. Nothing this intriguing ever happens in Hadleyburg."

"Thank God. I'm sick to death of mysteries."

Jim rose up from the sofa and began to leave the room.

"Where are you going?" Burgess asked him.

"I'm going upstairs to take a nap."

Jim's father asked him, "Is everything all right?"

"Not really," his voice betrayed a deeper anxiety. All he really desired was distance from the whole situation, or so he kept telling himself, and he was completely unmotivated to finish his assignment.

Once upstairs, he closed the bedroom door and stretched out on the mattress, but his mind was racing too quickly to rest. He could hear his father and Burgess talking downstairs, but their voices were muffled. For a few restless minutes he stared at the satchel on the dresser, then after a courageous attempt at resisting the impulse, he snatched the satchel from the dresser, opened it, placed the next tape in the player, and then put the headphones in his ears.

Chapter 19

On May 14, 1946, just two days before Leonard and I were scheduled to go to the radio company, it was unseasonably hot. So hot, I was trying to cool myself by sitting outside on the fire escape with my legs dangling over the edge. About eight o'clock, I heard a loud knock from inside the apartment and immediately turned around. I noticed two uniformed police officers standing in my open doorway and immediately sensed that something was wrong.

"Mr. Nigel Fox," one shouted. "Are you home?"

"Yes. I'm here," I shouted back at them. "What can I do for you, officers?"

I climbed back into the apartment and met them in the living room.

"I'm Officer MacGregor and this is Officer Grasso."

"Do you know a man named Leonard Matthews?" the other officer asked me.

"Of course. Is something wrong?"

"I'm afraid we have a bit of bad news. Mr. Matthews was found stabbed in Chelsea. He's been taken to Mt. Sinai hospital. We found your name and address in one of his pockets."

The officers escorted me out of the apartment to a squad car parked on the street. As they drove me from Brooklyn to the hospital to see him, I kept thinking about all our plans, about the television business, all subsumed by thoughts about the fragility of life. One could be vibrant and alive one moment and left for dead the next. Then after a while the hum of the motor and the sound of the tires on the pavement seemed to lull me into a trance. It felt dreamlike, though I knew I wasn't dreaming.

When we arrived at the hospital, the officers led me to a ward on the second floor. They kept asking me questions about how well I knew him, but my mind was too clouded to respond to them. I found Leonard unconscious and fighting for his life after six hours of horrific surgery to repair a hole in his left lung.

"Are you a relative?" a young nurse asked me as I held his bed rail firmly with my right hand.

"No, just a friend. His family is all in Cleveland."

"Have you known him long?"

"Seven years I think." Though at that moment, it felt more like seventy.

I watched him, and listened to the uneven rhythm of his breathing as he struggled to inhale, and I sensed in my heart of hearts he wasn't going to make it, though I tried to push these thoughts from my mind.

At one point a police detective named Horowitz stepped in to look at him. He asked me if Leonard had said anything at all, and I responded, "No," and then he left.

That night I stood vigil like an honor guard, standing, waiting, watching, as the night marched its slow cadence to the dawn.

At one point a nurse came in to give him blood, and I would have given my own blood if I thought it would have helped. By early morning, he was struggling even more strenuously. Then at eight o'clock, he breathed his last anguished breath and died. I had always counted myself fortunate that I had not seen a human death up close and that its horror for most of my life had remained a distant mirage. But this day my friend had died, and it devastated me.

Burgess was standing a few feet away from Jim and watching him with a self-obsessed intensity. Several minutes passed before Jim finally noticed him.

"How long have you been here?"

"I came up here to see what you're up to."

Jim stopped the tape.

"I'm listening."

"I hate to give you a lesson in courtesy, but we're guests, and a host doesn't go off to hide in his room."

"I'm sorry, but I have a story to finish."

"What is he saying?"

"He said his friend, Leonard, died."

"Another piece in the puzzle."

"This isn't some puzzle to put together. It's a man's life."

"Don't tell me you're getting sentimental." He paused. "Didn't you once tell me sentiment was for the weak and neurotic."

"Yes, I said that."

"Then what's going on with you? Sooner or later, you'll have to level with me."

"Nothing's going on. I'm just confused."

"There's something else I found when I was searching the house. I haven't a clue what it is."

Burgess reached into his shirt pocket and removed a medallion. On it were letters in Greek and a small picture of some religious scene. Jim looked at it a moment then handed it back.

"Why don't you come downstairs and share your tape with the rest of us. There's a tape player in a drawer in the dining room."

"Alright, I'll bring the tapes downstairs."

He grabbed his satchel and tape player, then left the room.

"The hermit returns from his cave," Burgess announced sarcastically as they both descended the stairs. Jim felt relief that he could finally share this experience with others, but he was still afraid. Burgess found the player and prepared the tape to play.

"He's explaining how his friend, Leonard, died and how he got into the television business," Jim offered as a few words of explanation.

I sat in the room for over an hour, waiting for the morgue to come for him. I felt like crying, but I knew if I allowed myself, I couldn't stop. I kept thinking about the farm and all the animals we had raised from birth and then sent to the slaughterhouse. My parents had tried to teach me to accept death as the natural and fitting outcome of life. As the days have beginnings and endings, every life had its season, but I desired to escape the constant reminders of mortality.

I waited what seemed an eternity for the orderlies to come and to take Leonard away. A nurse even came in to show me out, but I refused to leave him. Finally, at ten o'clock they came for him, and when they took him away, I felt an inexplicable emptiness, as if someone had ripped my heart right out from my chest.

I didn't feel like going to work that morning. So, I went home and went to sleep. At about four o'clock that afternoon, I awakened and resolved to go to Leonard's place and gather up his things. I decided I would ship them back to Cleveland for his family. While sorting through his desk, I discovered a set of sketches and circuit diagrams outlining his designs for televisions, and I remembered how long he had worked for his dream.

Though reluctant to pursue the task on my own, I felt a strong obligation to complete what he had started. I packed everything up in boxes, but set the diagrams aside and took them home with me to study them that night. I must have been up to three in the morning, poring over them the way an architect studies a blueprint. I sat at my desk, staring at the ocean while I tried to make sense out of what he had written. I could hear his voice as though he were still alive, explaining to me every subtle nuance of his plans as he sat in front of his open circuit books with a pencil on his left ear.

"Television is the technology of the future," he once told me. "I envision a day when people have not one television, but several in every room in their houses."

At the time, I couldn't see the fascination with the little box, when the movie theater was readily accessible and, for those of our generation, larger than life. But Leonard argued that its immanent presence in the home would make television much more powerful.

The next morning, I put on the best clothes in my limited wardrobe and despite my misgivings I left early in the morning for the station to take the train to Tarrytown, where the radio factory was located. I took the subway from Brooklyn to Grand Central station, and then a passenger train. The whole time I continued to study Leonard's diagrams, and to rehearse what I would say.

Once at the factory, I waited nervously in a lobby until a secretary to one of the vice-presidents advised me it was time to go inside. She led me through a long corridor of doors to a room at the end of the hall. I had expected someone staid and middle-aged, but instead I found a young man, about thirty, wearing a grey vest and matching trousers. He had round eyeglasses about the size of silver dollars. When he saw me, he smiled.

"I'm not what you expected, am I?"

"No, not quite."

"I'm David Atkinson." He reached his hand out and we shook. "I have a bachelor's degree in Physics from MIT and an MBA from Harvard business school, and I know the radio business inside out." He paused. "Please take a seat."

I awkwardly sat down in a bulky captain's chair across from him.

"So, where's Mr. Matthews? I expected both of you today."

"Leonard is dead. He was stabbed to death two days ago."

"I'm sorry. If you'd like to make this some other time, I can have my secretary reschedule you."

"It's alright."

"I can see you have some drawings for me."

I handed him the stack of sketches which Leonard had made, and he took them back with him to his desk. Nodding his head and making a nervous hum, he studied them a few minutes and then set them aside on his desk.

"Did you do these?"

"No. Leonard drew them. He was always more electronically inclined."

He lit a cigarette and began to puff on it passionately as he paced across the room.

"You must know corporations are remarkably conservative. They don't like to take unnecessary risks. They feel a certain obligation to their stockholders to protect their investments. Television. Now that's a big gamble. No proven track record. I don't think it's likely you're going to get the directors here interested in taking the risk. Let someone else test the waters before we venture in."

"I wonder if that's what they said about the wheel," I found myself saying. I had heard Leonard snap back at me with just those words. "You're right. They probably did."

He returned to his desk and sat down across from me. Then he picked up one of the drawings and examined it again. Rubbing his hand across his forehead, he continued, "I don't mean this as any diminution of your character. But you must realize you have no proven track record. You have no education, no credentials, nothing to make any investment in you a plausible success."

"I know I lack credentials, and I lack the expertise, but I promised my friend I would give the dream a chance. What I say, I say for him, not for myself. I'm no philosopher, but the little I gleaned from Leonard's vision has shown me that it is inevitable, this technology will prevail. If you won't take the risk, someone will, and if no one here will, maybe the Japanese or Germans will, someone with nothing to lose and everything to gain by trying. I came to New York with only a few dollars in my pocket, and I've survived. I'm sorry to have wasted your time."

I reached out for the diagrams and he stopped me.

"No, just wait a minute. I'm going to make a few phone calls and see what a prototype would entail."

"So you are interested?"

"A little curious." He paused. "I'll get a prototype together and call you. We'll see what we can do."

I knew what he said was a brush off, that I would likely never hear from him again. But I had followed through on Leonard's plan, and I felt I had repaid whatever obligation I owed him. When I left the factory I felt an odd mix of disappointment and relief, disappointment because I had been unable to follow through on the one thing Leonard desired, and relief, because I hadn't liked the television idea anyway. I found most popular entertainment banal and trivial, and I had my suspicions that even this new device would succumb to the same mediocrity. But despite these misgivings, I still felt an almost childlike awe at the prospect of it. I had long ago lost any sense of awe at life. I saw no mystery or magic. But when Leonard had talked in his childlike fervor about the wonders of television, for those brief moments I could remember my childhood and I shared his sense of wonder.

As for David Atkinson, convinced at that moment he didn't care, I went home to Brooklyn to resume my life.

The next day and those that followed were routine. I arose early and went to work at the flower shop. In the evening, I came home and ate a light dinner. After dinner, I would usually spend an hour writing letters to my mother and Beth, and I would read any letters I received.

This day I had much to tell both of them, but the most difficult news of all was Leonard's death.

Because Leonard's family had his remains shipped back to Cleveland for his funeral, and I didn't have the money for the train fare there, I couldn't attend, but my heart was there in absentia.

I remember reading that evening a letter Beth wrote me with more details concerning her arrival in New York, and I was surprised how cogent her English had become. I remembered how once she struggled for every word, but now she seemed more articulate, more erudite.

A listless depression settled over me during the next few days. I found it difficult to get up in the morning and my nights were restless with bouts of insomnia. On those nights when I could sleep, largely from exhaustion, I began to have vivid nightmares again, filled with images of death and destruction, of such horror and deprivation, that I still shudder at the thought of them. Even then, I sensed that there was something wrong; that no one else had dreams like these. But I resolved to endure them as I had done before in hopes that these too would pass.

There came wars and famines and pestilence, massacres and atrocities, rolled out like a hideous tapestry every night before my mind's eye; and I as an unwilling spectator observed every bitter twist of yarn, powerless to provide assistance. I thought I was going mad, and I think I would have if after a couple of weeks they hadn't stopped. But like a violent summer thunderstorm, as suddenly as they had come, they were gone, and as I hoped, for good.

On June 16, 1946, Beth finally arrived in New York, and I went down to the docks to meet her. When I first saw her face among the field of faces before me, amidst the joy I was feeling at seeing her was a gnawing sense of apprehension. This beautiful young woman, whom I had come to love more than my own mother, was as awesome a mystery to me as the cosmos, and I couldn't understand what she saw in me. When she first noticed me standing on the docks, she smiled. She had pinned her hair back behind her ears and was wearing a modest olive green dress which hung loosely on her torso.

"Neilos," I heard her shout at me. "Neilos."

She looked both frightened and expectant, and as she moved closer her physiognomy seemed lit up as though a spotlight shone upon her face, and her eyes were like two powerful lamps, which, like a lighthouse, drew me toward her.

I must have rehearsed in my mind a thousand times what I'd say to her when we were finally reunited. Every phrase and nuance was on the tip of my tongue, but then she hugged me, and all I could manage were a few unintelligible sounds like an infant first testing the sound of his own voice.

"We must get my bags," she told me. Though she still spoke English with a deep Greek accent, her diction had remarkably improved. As we walked, I stood awestruck, remembering all the conversations we had once shared as though the years which separated us were just a moment. She smiled again and told me, "I have things for you in my bags. Books and Icons, other things." Once we retrieved her baggage, together we carried them to the subway station and rode

the train into Astoria. There she planned to stay with her cousin until we were able to marry. As she sat quietly beside me, I couldn't take my eyes off her. I kept pondering what she saw in me and why she would travel so far from home just to be with me. When we arrived in Astoria, we walked four blocks from the Ditmars station to Crescent Street, where in a red brick row house, maybe a hundred yards south of Ditmars Boulevard, I met her cousin Evgenia Petrides. They hugged immediately when Evgenia opened the door, and she invited us both into the parlor, a modest room with a small sofa, a table and four chairs. There we talked for over an hour, mostly about Greece and about Greek cooking. Both struggled to speak in English though I could see the effort frustrated them. Later, they moved to the sofa and began to speak in Greek while I watched them both from the table. I was reluctant to leave. After so many years of separation and then an awkward meeting, I felt unsatisfied. But I had work in the morning and a long train ride back to Brooklyn. At ten o'clock, I acknowledged I had to depart. Then, with a hug and a gentle goodbye, I left them both and started home to Brooklyn.

There seemed a peculiar inevitability to what was happening, as though the fates had laid out my path, and like Odysseus I had set sail from Troy. Each step along the way, my feet seemed guided as though I were a playing-piece in an elaborate game.

'Where will the gods send me now?' I pondered with a chuckle. On the way home, I kept thinking about the Greek priest who wouldn't baptize me because I lacked sincerity, and I knew before Beth would marry me, I had to be baptized and I also knew that I was not ready for the religious life.

The arguments against it had always seemed persuasive to me. Most of the religious people I had encountered were hypocritical, self-righteous, lacking in tolerance and compassion. But Beth embodied none of these characteristics. Instead, I had admired her humility, longsuffering, patience, perseverance, her willingness to believe. She had once explained to me in her awkward English how the Christian life consisted in forbearance, in looking inward to one's own sins and not to the sins of one's neighbors. Until I met her, these traits seemed only abstract ideals, but she lived them. And having endured untold hardship, she felt no bitterness toward anyone. I had once written her about my own sense of worthlessness, and in her elegant simplicity she responded, "God knows that we are but dust, yet has compassion on us." For her the Christian scriptures were a living book and she breathed them. But on that humid June evening on my way home from Astoria, as the train beat its heart-like rhythm, I was not persuaded. And I pondered what it would take to convince myself.

Over the next two weeks, Beth, in her zeal to persuade me, gave me a number of books to read—several about Greek monasticism and one about the prayer of the heart. Though I found most of them interesting reading, the fascination the Greeks had with austerity and self-denial completely baffled me. I had grown up in close connection to the land in rhythm with its ceaseless cycles, yet I never attained spiritual euphoria from cultivating a field, or feeding a pig. When the endless monotony of farm work became unbearable for me, I felt compelled to leave the farm.

So much of her religion seemed to involve the repetition of mundane tasks, and I lacked the discipline to find it palatable. During those first few weeks, I tried in earnest to believe, but despite all my best efforts to understand it, I could not. It all felt so impossible. But love has a way of making the improbable probable, of softening the most inflexible heart, and she had such love for me that in my unworthiness, I felt compelled to try.

"Neilos," she would say. "We must work with God. Our 'synergia' transforms us."

"This religious stuff is getting a little too much for me," Jim interrupted. "I don't care what rationale he had for joining her Greek religion."

"Let's hear the rest of the tape," Burgess responded. "I'd like to hear what he has to say."

"Don't tell me you're being taken in by this guy."

Jim's father sat quietly amused as he watched the verbal swordplay between them both. A faint smile curled on the edges of his mouth. Then Jim turned the tape back on.

I often thought as I listened to her speak that her voice had a natural cadence, very soothing, like a lullaby, and when she spoke Greek it seemed like singing.

The tape clicked off as it reached the end of the first side.

"How many of these tapes are there?" Jim's father asked.

"A number of them."

"And how far are you into them?"

"About halfway."

"And he just talks about his life on all of them?"

"Yeah, basically it's an oral autobiography."

"Turn the thing back on." Burgess interrupted them.

Jim, startled by Burgess's remark, flipped the tape over and turned it back on.

During the course of the next few weeks from late June through the end of July, I spent my days in Brooklyn delivering flowers and my evenings in Astoria. Arriving home sometimes close to one o'clock, I slept only four to five hours a night, and the stress was taking its toll on me. I considered moving to Astoria, but I had grown comfortable with my apartment, and I knew I would miss the sight of the ocean every night before I went to sleep. The sine-like rhythm of the waves relaxed me. Often in the long train ride back to Brooklyn, I thought about the ocean, how vast and deep and full of hidden life it was, and how I stood at its edge, afraid to step inside.

In Astoria, I felt adrift. My evenings were spent first with Beth and Evgenia. We'd share a simple meal, usually salad and mixed vegetables, and then we would sit outside with others in the Greek community. And though Beth made every effort to make me feel more comfortable, there were awkward moments when hours would pass without a word of English, and I would sit quietly contemplating how I could ever be part of her world when it seemed so alien and unconnected to me. But I was determined to persevere, because I could see in her expectant expression that she wanted it so.

"Neilos," she once told me at a time when I must have looked totally perplexed, "I know this is difficult for you. But God wants us to be strong."

"I don't understand a word."

"In time you will," she responded. And gradually, I began to learn a few words here and there.

One evening, I arrived in Astoria to find a note on Beth's and Evgenia's door that they had gone to hear this monk from one of the monasteries on the Holy Mountain. I walked eleven or twelve blocks to the address on Steinway Street which Beth had written on the note. There I found a small group of around thirty people, mostly women, huddled together in this small living room while this Father Nicodemos, sitting on a chair in the midst of them, was speaking in a soft almost inaudible voice.

I approached Beth to sit down next to her, but before I could speak, she placed her finger in front of her mouth to caution me to silence.

"He's talking about the prayer of the heart," she slid closer to me and whispered. "It is a way of seeing." And she repeated the Greek word "Theoria."

"There is within all of us" she translated for me as she spoke, "this organ within our souls which the Fathers have called the 'nous.'"

The first thought which popped into my head was the image of a hangman's noose, which immediately I tried to push from my mind.

"The nous *is more than the mind," she continued. "It is the center of the spiritual part of a man we call the soul. A* nous *which has been cleansed by prayer and fasting, by the therapeia tis ekklisia, the therapy of the church, is able to see the uncreated rule of God." She struggled with her English.*

"The world itself is a frightening place to look at," I suddenly blurted out. "It seems to me if this uncreated rule of God exists, it would be terrible to perceive."

I don't know why I said it, but I could see from the expressions on everyone's faces that they were shocked by my outburst, especially in English.

He stopped a moment and asked Beth a question in Greek and she responded in several sentences. The only word I recognized was "Ameriki." Then he turned and looked directly at me with eyes that seemed to pierce through me.

"Alithos," he began. "Alithos foveros."

"Truly frightening." Beth translated.

They continued. "If we were to perceive even for a second the Uncreated Glory, the Uncreated Energies of God in our fallen sinful condition, it would be truly hell for us. (I recognized the word 'Gehenna' from Brother Woodrow's ranting sermons.) God in His mercy allowed us to lose the ability so that in this life we can prepare. It will not always be this way. One day we all shall see Him as he is, some of us for paradise, some of us for hell. Pray to be prepared."

After the meeting, they all walked up to kiss his hand, but I, unaccustomed to such rituals, stood off at a distance.

"I'm sorry for blurting out like that and interrupting him," I apologized to Beth after she rejoined me at the back of the room.

"It's no problem." She smiled. "It was God's will."

She reached into her blouse and removed a small postcard. "Father Nicodemos gave this as a blessing for you."

It was a photograph of a religious painting of Jesus with some words written in Greek beneath it.

"What does it say?" I asked her as she handed it to me.

"It says, 'Blessed are the pure in heart for they shall see God.'"

I placed the card in my shirt pocket and when I returned home that evening, I found a place above my writing desk and mounted it there. As I sat there a moment before beginning a letter to my mother, I thought about how alien it was to me, and how in a very real way I was seeing another world right in the midst of New York.

I remembered something Leonard once told me about how every great achievement of man began first as an embrace of the totally alien, and encountering this alien culture accomplished one great achievement, it had pushed Leonard's death from my mind, and for a time I had forgotten about the death of his dream. That is, until that August when it hit me in the face again.

It was sometime in early August, I didn't know exactly when because I had stopped regularly checking my mail, when I discovered a small postcard in my mailbox stuck among a number of advertisements. And I would have tossed it out had I not glanced at it a moment.

All it said was, "Please come and see Mr. Atkinson on Wednesday afternoon, September 26." I put the card in my pocket and when I got inside, I marked a note on my calendar. I hadn't the faintest clue why he wanted to talk to me.

When I told Beth about the postcard, her first reaction was cautious. "You must be very careful," she told me. "The devil is like a hungry lion seeking someone to eat." But I didn't believe in the devil, and I loved her too much to argue about it.

I remember sitting quietly in the waiting room in Tarrytown and thinking that all I really wanted was to regain Leonard's drawings. From twelve o'clock to four o'clock I waited, and I wondered if I'd ever be called inside. At four thirty, David Atkinson briefly came outside, handed his secretary a memo, then without so much as a glance in my direction, he disappeared behind closed doors. I considered if it had all been some huge mistake, and I fought an impulse to get up and leave.

"You may go inside now, Mr. Fox," his secretary finally told me. Then with measured and deliberate steps, I marched into his office and took a seat across from him.

"Relax," he smiled. "I have good news." He paused. "I gave one of our engineers your friend's drawings to review and we were impressed."

"Leonard spent a lot of time on these drawings."

"He did more than that. He outlined a whole program for the development and transmission of images. It's years ahead of anything we've worked on. Some of the technologies he describes don't even exist yet."

"He always was a visionary."

"Were you aware that he applied for patents to a number of key components in television construction?"

"I vaguely remember him mentioning it."

"And were you also aware that he applied for the patents in both your names?"

Leonard had once given me some papers to sign, explaining that he was giving me credit for something because some of his ideas arose from our discussions. But at the time I disregarded it because of the sheer improbability of it coming to fruition.

"Yeah, I signed some papers."

"To put it simply, we wish to manufacture a television of Leonard's design, and because of Leonard's death, you are now the sole owner of these patents. I'm prepared to offer a substantial amount to license these processes."

For some reason the magnitude of what he was describing didn't register in my mind.

"I've had our lawyers draft a licensing contract," he continued. "I'm prepared to pay up to $200,000.00 initially and five percent for each unit sold."

"That's $200,000.00?" I asked. I thought I heard it wrong.

"Yes. I'd offer you more, but I'm going out on a limb on this, and a good chunk of it is my own money." It was at that moment that I

realized that Leonard had made me a wealthy man.

I sat in silence for what seemed an hour before I could find any words to respond.

"Well, what do you think?" David asked me.

"I'm overwhelmed. I came up here to ask for the drawings back."

"Is it yes or no? I'm prepared to begin production in six months or so."

"Pardon my indecisiveness, but could I have someone look over this?"

I reached for the contract, which he graciously handed me.

"Sure, but we'd like to get started on this as soon as possible."

I took the contract back with me to my seat and then began to skim it, clause by clause. Though I had difficulty understanding all the technical language, I could see that it was reasonable and nothing seemed unusual.

"I still would like a closer look at this," I told him.

"Alright. Take it home and study it."

When I left, I knew my life had changed. And everything that followed after that seemed a natural cause and effect of that meeting in his office.

The tape clicked off.

Chapter 20

Outside the house with its motor still running sat Governor Wilson's limousine. His chauffeur was ringing the bell on the front gate of Nigel's house at the moment Jim snapped open the tape player and placed the tape back in his housing. Burgess went into the kitchen, and as though he had become accustomed to doing so, he answered through the intercom, "Who is it?"

"The governor is here to pick up Mr. Jacobson."

"Well, tell the former governor, he'll be out in a few minutes," he answered with a tinge of sarcasm in his voice. "What's with these people still calling him governor? He hasn't been governor for ten years now."

"Who is it?" Jim asked him when he reentered the room.

"The governor is outside, and he wishes to see you," Burgess spoke with affection.

"Damn, I forgot all about him."

"What does he want?" Jim's father interrupted.

"Who knows? I'll be back in a few minutes."

Jim went upstairs and retrieved a jacket from his suitcase which he put on as he descended the stairs. A grimace had spread across his face. He opened the front door with some reluctance and then made his way down the walkway leading to the car. At the curb, he struggled a moment with the gate's locking mechanism which seemed reluctant to open, and then he shuffled nervously while he waited for the chauffeur to open the door for him to climb inside.

Across from him sat Michael Wilson, dressed in a blue silk business suit, and beside him was the man in the red beret who had followed Jim from the restaurant.

"Could I offer you something to drink?" Wilson spoke in a voice exuding charm. The limousine began to pull from the curb.

"No, that's all right."

"I think I'll have a touch of vodka."

He poured himself a drink from a small bar beside him while the other man stared.

"Don't let Marcus bother you." He continued. "He's harmless."   He paused. "My people tell me you worked on my first gubernatorial campaign."

"Yes, I did."

"In fact they've told me a lot about you.   Your father is an economics professor at the University of Chicago. Your mother has been dead a number of years, and since graduating from journalism school in 1976, you've drifted through a series of small-time reporting jobs, until now, where you work at the *Hadleyburg Times* earning maybe $23,000.00 a year. I could go on."

"I get the drift. What do you want?"

"Direct. I like that." He paused a moment. "Marcus, hand me the magazine."

Marcus reached into a satchel sitting beside him and removed an issue of Newsmaker magazine. On the front cover was a picture of Nigel in his robe and turban and the words in bold letters, "He's a fraud!"

"I'm prepared to pay you $25,000.00 for the right to use your name on this story."

Marcus opened the satchel to reveal a stack of bills.

"Go ahead, read it. I'm sure you'll find it fascinating."

Inside, he found further photographs and excerpts from Nigel's personal letters. One page contained a full page reproduction of an undated letter in which Nigel explicitly confessed his guilt. Jim realized this was the letter which Nigel had spoken about.

"As you can see, it's all there in black and white."

"And what if I refuse?"

"You don't seem to understand; you can't refuse."

"You're going to use me to crucify this man. Why me? Couldn't anyone write this story?"

"You're the best candidate we can find. And as you yourself once wrote, 'Someone should do an exposé and stop this nonsense.' And someone has." Wilson smiled. "Don't look surprised. This is the natural order of things. Take the money. No one will fault you for this."

"How can you do this to him after what you said about him earlier?"

"The wind blows where it will."

"*I don't want your money.* And I'm not going to let you put my by-line on this story I didn't write."

"I don't think you understand."

He nodded to Marcus who removed from his vest pocket a stack of photographs which he spread across his lap. They were photographs of Jim at every place he had been in the past few days. Then Marcus removed an automatic pistol with a silencer from the satchel and also laid this atop his lap.

"Marcus could as easily have shot you as take your photograph."

Jim had finally come to realize the gravity of his situation and he began to perspire profusely.

"I don't wish to frighten you, but to give you food for thought."

Jim could sense that the car was coming to a stop. Then Wilson looked at his watch and smiled.

"You can go now, Mr. Jacobson."

Jim opened the door and climbed outside. He realized he was somewhere near Times Square, but he didn't know exactly where.

"I'm sorry that you have to learn this the hard way."

Marcus closed the door behind him, and Jim stood anxiously on the corner of Broadway and Fifty-Second Street watching the limousine pull away and disappear down Broadway. No words seemed adequate to describe the sense of devastation which had overcome him. A powerful feeling of paranoia, which through his own force of will he had previously sublimated, now erupted violently inside him. It left him impotent and mute. He lacked the comfort of a religious zealot who could face such adversity in the sanctuary of his god. This had been his folly alone, born from within and nurtured to maturity, and he knew with increasing clarity that he faced an adversary more cunning than himself whose pernicious potency exceeded all expectation.

How can I fight such an enemy?" his mind kept positing. "With what weapons can I hope to deter him? And should I fight at all?" He kept repeating to himself, "I was warned. What kept me from listening?"

He had never envisioned himself in heroic terms, and he had neither the will nor the desire to be part of an epic conflict. Yet the memory of Nigel's words kept dancing through his mind. Nigel had told him that he would come to fight this battle, taking the mantle willingly and courageously. But he could not even silence the cacophony in his head.

His first thought was to call his father, but he could not remember Nigel's phone number. He found a pay phone at the corner and searched his pockets for a coin. Then he nervously dropped it in the slot.

"Yeah, I'd like the number for a Nigel Fox, in Bayside, New York."

"I'm sorry but that number has been unpublished at the customer's request," a recorded message informed him.

"Damn." He slammed down the phone.

He remembered speeches that Wilson had delivered twenty years before.

Filled with the passion of conviction to a just cause, Wilson had extolled the virtues of tolerance and forbearance when violence and prejudice seemed to run unchecked. He had captured the heart of a whole generation with his calls for social justice and the peaceful resolution of differences.

This was the man who for one brief summer captured the idealism of Jim's youthful yearnings before the pervasive cynicism of his later years had stolen from him his lust for life. Though in the aftermath of this encounter, he was genuinely afraid for himself, he was more disturbed by his grave misjudgment.

"How could such a man be turned? What hideous secret did this change conceal?"

He remembered a rally in Baltimore when Wilson, speaking extemporaneously, called the crowds to virtue.

"We have but one cause," he had entreated them, "the cause of justice and its vindication. We live for but one truth, the power of the one good against the multitude of impiety. Ours is a cause inspired by conciliation, nurtured by self-sacrifice and bearing fruit in all that is honorable." Such words had once moved Jim to action, yet they had become, upon reflection, a bitter mockery.

Jim's journey back to Bayside was surfeit with such self-reflection. Every image, impression and impulse that had touched his consciousness in those past few days, he held before his imagination and reexamined them. Much of what Nigel had told him at the hospital, he had immediately dismissed. Still, he struggled to remember what he so willingly had forgotten. He had come to doubt his own capacity to judge reality, and wondered if he had been as mistaken in all of his opinions.

He hung anxiously to the hand bar of the number seven train as it careened and pitched its way from Times Square to Flushing Main Street. When it rose above ground at Hunters Point like a red snake sliding out its hole, he was hypnotized by the *clack, clack, clack* of the wheels against the rails and the roar of the electric motors. The train rocked rhythmically like a cradle while those sitting with heads bowed caught a few moments of cautious sleep. At one point a homeless veteran in Army green began singing off-key and passing a cup from face to face. Like most of the others, Jim ignored him. Jim's mind was not in the train at all. It danced as though suspended in the air by nervous energy, and when a sudden jolt would yank him back to consciousness, he would immediately fade out.

Jim took notice that the clientele was of a different order than those who rode the railroad. Here were the immigrants and the foreign-born. From all points of the globe, they had come to seek a better life, and in a cacophony of distinct and different dialects, their voices blurred. When the train pulled into Main Street Station, after a few false stops, it screeched and clanged to a halt. Then the doors slid open with a puff of air as though they had held their breath.

Jim remembered how utterly powerless he felt in the face of his mother's death. The same sense of insignificance which tugged at him then, submerged him now. He stood quietly, studying a worn bus map mounted to the wall until his mind could focus on which bus to take.

Chapter 21

Over an hour and a half had passed between the time Jim left the house and returned there again. When he rang the bell on the front gate, he didn't know what he would tell his father, and he was sure Burgess would only use the information to ridicule him. Yet despite his overwhelming misgivings about divulging these secrets, he felt compelled to speak to someone about them.

"Who is it?" Burgess almost bellowed through the box.

"I'm back."

"So, MacArthur has returned."

The gate buzzed open, and he began to take slow and diffident steps toward the front door. As before, Burgess met him at the doorway.

"So what happened? You've been gone long enough."

"I'll tell you everything once we're inside."

Burgess was never one to be put off easily and continued, "Well what did his eminence say?"

"Where's my father?"

"He's upstairs taking a rest."

Jim could see his satchel sitting on the table and several of the cassettes stacked beside it.

"I can see you've been busy going through my things again." But Jim was too disturbed to let this invasion further agitate him.

"Just skimming through them. I've made a few notes." He pulled out from his pocket the tablet which was nearly filled with his scribbling.

"So have you learned anything from all this?"

"I need more time with them."

"I'm in trouble, Burg. Serious trouble."

"I can see that."

"We're way out of our league here. Wilson intends to publish an exposé on Nigel in Newsmaker magazine, and whether I approve it or not he's going to put my name on it."

Burgess began to chuckle.

"I'm glad you find it amusing. He scared the hell out of me."

"Do you remember a conversation we had a little over a week ago? And I quote you, 'Someone should publish an article on this Nigel Nut and put an end to all this nonsense.' "

"Yes, I said it."

"It's a little ironic, isn't it?"

"I'm glad you're so amused by all this. At least someone is getting some pleasure out of it."

"I'm not trying to make light of the situation. But it is all very ironic." He paused. "I've sat here for over an hour skimming these tapes. What possesses a man to invest this much time in something? I've got this strange impulse, I've got to get behind the question, to find out the reason for the reason."

Burgess opened the tablet and began to look at his notes.

"I get the sense that he knew he was going to die and leave something undone, and that it was important for whoever listened to these tapes to get a sense of the whole picture, whatever that is, and that's why he has been so meticulous about it. There is just so much we don't know."

"The philosophers say the first step to wisdom is the acceptance of one's ignorance," Jim's father interrupted.

"How long have you been there?" Jim asked him.

"Long enough." He paused. "You can't beat the devil by fighting according to his rules. If forty years of fighting lost causes has taught me anything, it's this."

"I can't just roll over and play dead."

"Sometimes in the natural order that's the only way you can survive."

His father's advice left a bitter taste in his palate, but Jim was beginning to come to the same conclusion on his own.

"A foolish man will dig a ditch and fall in it himself," his father quoted another proverb.

"So what do you want to do?" Burgess interrupted them. "I suggest we hear the rest of what he has to say, and then decide."

"Then we're in for a long night," Jim responded. "Burg, maybe you can order a pizza for us, while I try to figure out where we left off."

Jim began to search through the tapes. He had lost count of where he was and he placed several in the player only to eject them once he realized he had heard them before. Finally, he tried the tape labeled number nine, and he recognized he had not heard this one before. Then, he turned up the volume.

On the train ride back from Tarrytown, I must have reread the contract a dozen times, trying to pull the meaning out of every unfamiliar phrase. Yet, I was still in a state of shock. 200,000 was more money than I could imagine, and I was overwhelmed by what I considered good fortune. When my sense of disbelief wore off, I was convinced I had to seize the opportunity before it forever passed me by. Now, these fifty odd years later, I wish I had had the foresight to refuse the cup because the money couldn't compensate for what was to follow. But at that moment my mind was filled with promise, and I didn't think of consequences. In some strange, inexplicable way, I had inherited Leonard's vision.

By the time the train pulled into Grand Central Station, I had resolved to sign the contract and mail it back before anyone had the opportunity to dissuade me. And once I reached the platform, I scribbled my name at the bottom, put it into an envelope, and dropped it into a mailbox near an exit. Then in my own irreligious way, I mumbled to the heavens that it would all turn out well.

When I arrived home to my apartment, I was so full of nervous energy that I couldn't bring myself to do even the most mundane of tasks. I thought of writing my mother because an unopened letter of hers sat on my desktop patiently awaiting a reply, but I couldn't write a word. I considered going into Astoria to tell Beth what had happened, but it was all so new to me that I couldn't bring myself to go outside again.

I sat for a while at my desk, staring at my mother's letter, but not ready to open it. Then I slit it open with a letter opener and unfolded it to read.

"Dear Nigel," she began. "I was so happy to hear that Beth has finally arrived." (I could hear her gentle voice as though she read these words to me.) "Your father often asks about you and hopes to see you soon." (It had been over seven years since I had seen the farm and I wondered if he really cared to see me.) "We hope that circumstances allow you the money to visit us next summer. All is well with the farm. We milk. We harvest. We plant our gardens. Reginald has bought a used tractor from the Morrisons, and your cousin Michael has been admitted to law school starting in September. We hope that God somehow provides the money for his tuition. I hope that you are healthy and dressing warm. I'll write you again soon. Your

loving mom."

I sat the letter aside and laid myself down to take a nap. But before I could drift into a restless sleep, I remembered Michael with a dreamlike vividness. As always, he was hovering near me as hummingbird might, asking questions about everything I did. For a moment I pondered into what kind of young man he had grown.

The next morning, I went to work as usual. I greeted Mr. Wiggins, the manager, and Beverly who worked the counter, and Isaac in the back. It was almost as though the previous day were just a dream. I picked up my bicycle and my first delivery and with a couple of "good mornings" and "good days," I was sailing down the block with the wind blowing in my hair. It still hadn't dawned on me what a drastic change in course my life would take.

I stopped at a fruit stand at the corner to buy myself a banana, which with consummate skill I peeled and ate while the bike cruised on. Then suddenly a few blocks down, almost as though a rock had hit me in the chest, I realized what I had done and stopped the bicycle. I stood motionless as though frozen in place for fifteen minutes before I climbed back on again and finished my task.

The rest of the day felt like a dream. My mind was detached as though part of me was watching myself at a distance. I couldn't concentrate and a couple of times I was nearly hit when I pulled out in front of passing cars.

"Watch where you're going you stupid idiot." one man shouted as he passed me by. After my last delivery at four o'clock, I resolved to go into Astoria to tell Beth what had happened the previous day. I didn't know how she would react. I suspected she would be disappointed in me, because in her simple way she had once denounced the quest for material things. 'But was this really a quest for material things?' In my mind I constructed an elaborate defense, resting primarily in carrying to completion Leonard's plans. I was finishing what he had started, bringing to fruition a dream which had I not continued would have died with him. There seemed something almost noble in what I was doing. But despite the strength of my argument, I couldn't convince myself of its merit. I even considered not telling Beth, but I had kept no secrets from her and I knew her capacity to see through any ruse I might attempt. I resolved to be completely candid.

A light rain was falling when I boarded the train that evening, and *when the Astoria line rose onto the elevated tracks, I could hear the rain like pebbles thrown against a wall beating out its irregular rhythm on the window glass.* Rat a tat tat ping *each successive wave of rain expressed. Though there was something quite familiar about it, I couldn't connect to any memory. When I arrived in Astoria, the light rain had turned into a steady downpour, and without an umbrella, I raced down the platform stairs toward street level, then five blocks to the row house where Beth was staying. The rainwater cemented my shirt against my skin. I rang the bell and Evgenia came to the doorway.*

"Oh, Neilos," she greeted me. "Elizabeth is resting."

"I hate to bother her, but I have some news."

Beth came into the corridor. "It's all right. Come inside."

After she opened the front door, I sat down on a chair in the entranceway.

"Is something wrong?" she asked me.

"No, not really."

I was struggling to find just the right words.

"I have some good news."

She smiled.

"They want to make Leonard's television."

"Who are 'they'?" she asked me.

I didn't know the answer to that question and for some odd reason I didn't think to ask.

"It's a consortium," I answered. "A group of investors and they agreed to pay me $200,000 for the rights to Leonard's patents."

I could sense she didn't understand much of what I was talking about, but I resolved to clarify.

"So much money," she said. "What would you need with so much money?"

"I don't need the money. It's not about the money."

"I don't know. With such money comes great responsibility. You must think about it."

"It's already done. I signed the agreement yesterday."

She seemed a little disturbed with me.

"Then we must do good with the blessing," she told me. "We must bless others with our blessing."

I had a whole checklist of things I would have liked to have done with the money, but Beth had other ideas, and I loved her too much to compel her to do otherwise.

"Perhaps an opportunity will come to help someone," she explained herself. "With so much money, much good can come from it."

She kissed me on the cheek.

"Thank you for telling me the news. It is good news. Thoxa to Theo." Then she crossed herself right to left.

That had always been like her, to see an opportunity for goodness even in my most selfish decisions. She always had a way of inspiring the best in me, and what she proposed I rarely dismissed. I just couldn't bring myself to disappoint her. That evening we talked about many things, and when I left for home I felt better for having talked to her.

And before I forget, she also told me that evening that she had found a priest to baptize me, Father Athanasios, a monk from a monastery in Crete. He had come to America for surgery, and he was recuperating in a house not far from her. She wanted me to meet with him to discuss all of the arrangements, and as always, I agreed to talk to him.

The next few days were filled with anxious expectation for some response from David Atkinson. In my naïveté, I expected an immediate response. When nearly a week had passed and I heard nothing, I wondered if it had all been some hoax and were David and his cohorts chortling a hearty laugh at having duped me. Each day I went to my mailbox after work, and each day I found only bills or letters from my mother.

She again wrote me concerning the struggles her brother was having in raising the tuition for my cousin Michael's tuition. My Uncle David had even tried to mortgage the farm to raise the money, but times were tough, and the bankers were reluctant to lend.

Nearly two weeks had passed without a response from David Atkinson, when on a Friday afternoon in mid-October, I found a curious note in my mailbox. It was a small postcard, on the front was an etching of the Statue of Liberty, the kind tourists pick up when they visit her. On the back was one sentence, "Come and see your new baby. David Atkinson."

When I approached Mr. Wiggins the following Monday morning to

*ask him for Tuesday off, he snarled at me, "Who do you think you are?
Some Wall Street executive who can take time off whenever he wants?
I have a business to run here, and you've taken off three days in the
last three months."*

*"I'm not trying to create problems for you. I just need to take the
day off."*

*"Who's going to cover for you this time? You're not going to see
me out riding a bicycle."*

"I'll find someone to cover for me."

*I hadn't a clue who I might ask, but I knew how important it was for
me to return to Tarrytown as quickly as possible.*

*When I got home after work, I went around the neighborhood,
asking anyone with whom I had a passing acquaintance if they might
work for me the next day. Everyone without exception had prior
commitments, and after over an hour of inquiries without success I
finally succumbed to the pressure of despondence and surrendered. I
resolved to go into Astoria to see if Beth could find me someone.*

The tape clicked off on one side and Jim flipped it over to the other side.

*At that point in my life, I was genuinely afraid of losing my job, so I
didn't want to upset Mr. Wiggins. I remember how tenaciously I had
struggled from payday to payday, often eating only rice and vegetables
because I didn't have money to do otherwise. 'It is no disgrace to be
poor,' I would encourage myself whenever my mood would dampen. A
letter from home or a kind word from Beth would usually lift my spirits.*

*I didn't take that Tuesday off, or Wednesday, or the following
Tuesday after that because I couldn't find someone to cover for me.
Three weeks had passed without an opportunity, and I was tortured by
a sinking feeling that I was letting my one great opportunity slip
through my fingers as sand. I was coming to realize I had to make a
choice between the uncertain potentiality of television, and the secure
and comfortable mediocrity of the florist shop. In mid-November, I
finally decided that I had to take the risk, so, I arose early and drafted
a simple note saying how much I enjoyed working at the shop, but that
opportunities called me elsewhere, and I slid the note under the front
door. I knew in my gut it was a coward's way out, and that I should
have resigned in person, but I couldn't bring myself to face Mr.*

Wiggins directly. I was afraid that he'd talk me out of it. I returned home and then prepared myself to go to Tarrytown. It was for me a monumental act of faith.

It's difficult to describe the full palette of emotions which, like bright and effervescent pigments, rushed through my senses. I felt an intense apprehensiveness, as though great danger awaited me. Yet simultaneously, I experienced an unfettered sense of freedom. It had been as risky a decision as my coming to New York, and it possessed the same religious intensity as that first trip from Wisconsin.

"You may go in now," the secretary told me after a short wait in David's office.

"I nearly thought you were never coming," were David's first words.

"I had some difficulties."

His face was animated as he walked to the other side of the room.

"The first prototype of Leonard's design."

He lifted the cloth cover off of the television.

"Well, what do you think?"

"It's a television," was all I could think to say.

The rectangular box measuring about two feet by two and a half feet by two feet, set atop a pedestal like a religious artifact, and David treated it with the same pious reverence a Catholic might treat a statue of the Madonna and Child.

"We have a camera set up in the factory," he began to explain. He turned on a switch, and a white light filled the box, gaining clarity and contrast until an image could be recognized.

"It's truly a marvelous thing." he acknowledged.

Our eyes fixed on this wooden box as though hypnotized by its aura. We watched in childlike wonder the panorama of activity on the factory floor. I could see everything, from workers assembling radios, to those at the end of the line putting them in boxes. There was something almost Godlike about it.

"I have a check here for you," he continued. "It's just a small down payment on my promise."

He handed me a cashier's check for $25,000.00, which I folded in half and stuck in my pocket. I was so enraptured by the television that it didn't even register how much money he was giving me.

The rest of the afternoon was spent in touring the factory while

David showed me every stage of the operation, and he began to explain to me the process by which the television would be mass-produced.

"Once we create a demand for them, I'm sure we'll be able to sell a thousand units a month," he told me.

"But, they have to have something to watch on those televisions."

"We're working on that too."

He then began to explain to me how the radio networks were planning to go into television in a big way, how first they were reluctant because television seemed just a novelty item. But now they saw a tremendous opportunity to expand their audiences and thereby increase their advertising revenues.

"We will be at the forefront of a new technology," he explained. "The sky's the limit."

I couldn't quite believe what had happened that day, and when I got back home, I sat at my desk for the longest time, staring at the cashier's check. In those days twenty-five thousand was an unbelievably large amount of money, and I didn't quite know what to do with it.

I kept thinking about Mr. Talbot with his newsstand. He had once told me that money was a cage from which the unfortunate, once trapped, can never escape.

When I told Beth the next day, she began immediately to figure where the money would do the most good.

"We must give five thousand to your cousin Michael," she said. "He must finish his school. And the rest we must give to help the poor."

I took the check to the bank the next day and deposited it in a savings account. I bought myself a new pair of shoes, a warm winter coat, and a typewriter. The rest of it I left untouched until Beth and I decided what charities deserved it best.

I wrote my mother a letter explaining what had happened, and I enclosed a cashier's check for five thousand dollars to help pay for my cousin Michael's law school. And for the next two weeks, I went about distributing money to various charities with the generosity of a philanthropist. It was one of the most exhilarating experiences I had ever encountered. After everything was said and done, we had two thousand dollars left for ourselves, which we set aside to setup our household once we were married. But, I would have even given that away if Beth has asked me to do so. I loved her that much.

Sometime in early December when my mind was still preoccupied with televisions, Beth took me over to meet Father Athanasios. For weeks she had been telling me what a pious and holy man he was, and with what wisdom he spoke concerning the Christian life. In Greek, she called him "yeronda" which meant "old man", but also has a reverential aspect. I remember walking into a small living room and seeing perhaps thirty to forty people huddled together to listen to this frail little man, much as they had done when the monk from the Holy Mountain had visited weeks before.

He appeared about sixty, with a long gray beard and flowing gray hair, which he had tied into a kind of a pony tail behind his back. He was thin as a toothpick and wore a long black robe which folded in creases on his lap. When he spoke, his voice seemed as gentle as a small child's, and his phrasing was deliberate as though great thought went into each word, though I couldn't understand but a few words in every other sentence.

His listeners seemed as captivated by his words as children at story time. When one would ask a question in Greek, he would answer it in a few short words. I had no idea what he was talking about.

"Could you translate for me?" I asked Beth.

"Shhh," she answered. "Let me hear him."

I sat for fifteen, maybe twenty minutes, staring at my fingernails, before I finally noticed he was looking straight at me. His eyes seemed to pierce through me like physician's instruments, and I felt awkward and uncomfortable.

"I speak some English," he spoke to me directly. "Do you have a question?"

"No, not really."

"God understands our questions." Then he must have repeated the same thing in Greek.

Actually, I had a hundred questions, from simple ones like, 'Why did he wear the long black robes?' to more complicated ones about the nature of God. But I couldn't bring myself to ask them.

After the meeting broke up at eleven P.M., the men went off to one room to drink coffee together, and the women congregated in another room like servants consigned to the kitchen. Only Beth had the boldness to enter the room to speak to him, and I followed her.

"Yeronda," she began to speak to him in Greek, and he rose from the table to meet me.

"So you wish to be baptized," he spoke to me in a heavy accent. Then he spoke a few words to her in Greek.

"We will speak tomorrow at three o'clock."

"Efcharisto," she thanked him, and then in customary Greek fashion, she bowed down to get his blessing. I found the whole experience a little unnerving.

Then I followed her back into the kitchen where she greeted several of the women, kissed each of them on the cheek, and then bid them farewell. When we left the house I was completely confounded as to what had happened to me.

"What was going on in there?"

She smiled.

"Oh, Neilos, he talked about metanoia." She paused. "I think you say 'repentance.'"

"Yes, but what did he say?"

"You ask him tomorrow."

Then she kissed me on the cheek, and told me in Greek, "I love you."

At that moment when she kissed me, I had come to realize that aside from Beth and her acquaintances, I was close to no one else. That in fact, her world had become my world.

The next day, Beth took me to meet with Father Athanasios in private. After she bowed down again and received his blessing, we entered a parlor where we all sat down. He was holding a long beaded rope that he appeared to be counting which at first I thought were rosary beads. Beth would later explain to me its significance. He smiled briefly and she told him something in Greek.

"Elizabeth asked me to explain 'metanoia.'" He paused. "'Renew your minds,' St. Paul says. Metanoia means a renewal of the mind. (His English was deliberate, though colored by a rich Greek accent.) Sin clouds our minds and we become as the blind, unable to see the world as it truly is. The greater the sin, the greater our blindness."

His talk of sin disturbed me. Having rejected my own religious upbringing, I had renounced such ideas as sin and guilt. But he spoke in a gentle cadence, more compassionate than Brother Woodrow, and I could sense from his inflection that he meant something different from what I supposed.

"What do you mean by 'sin'?" I asked him. I wanted to make his words more palatable.

"Amartia," he explained, "means missing the target. As an arrow pulled with insufficient force falls to the ground before it strikes, we, too, fall short of the target God has set before us. The Christian life is a struggle to reach this target."

Then he explained himself in Greek. Afterwards, Beth began to ask him questions in Greek and for what seemed an hour, he answered her slowly and methodically like a teacher with a textbook in hand. I didn't understand a word, but I sat quietly, patiently, waiting for a chance to speak. Finally, Beth looked at me and smiled. "I'm so sorry, Neilos. I forgot you don't understand." She paused. "I was talking about your baptism."

Jim clicked off the cassette player.

"Is it absolutely necessary we listen to this religious nonsense?"

"Come on, Jim. Turn the tape back on," Burgess retorted. "I want to hear what he has to say."

Jim's father was amused by the whole interchange.

"I don't see what relevance this has. I don't want to waste any time."

In fact the religious discussion made him feel uncomfortable, though he didn't know why.

"Let's hear what he has to say, Jim," his father interjected. "It can't hurt us."

Jim begrudgingly restarted the tape.

My Baptism. That had, after all, been my reason for coming.

"He says it would be good at Epiphany in January. I think it is a wonderful time."

I nodded my head in passive assent.

"I know it will be difficult," Father Athanasios continued. "But we must find you books in English to read."

Beth smiled as though she had been pleased by the outcome.

"Whatever you want, Beth."

Her conquest of my will was finally complete. I left that afternoon realizing I had committed myself to conversion to her religion. But I only vaguely understood what that entailed and what might be expected of me once I made the commitment. An understanding of this would come much later. For that moment it was enough.

The tape clicked off.

PART III

Though I walk through the valley of the shadow of death...
  (Psalm 23:4)

Chapter 22

As the tape clicked off, there were a few shrill moments of silence like the haunting stillness of a hurricane's eye, then, as though he couldn't stop himself from speaking, Jim blasted out, "You know, they must have killed him. I wouldn't have believed it at first, but it's the only thing that makes sense to me now. That must have been why he had a guard posted." (He spoke as if not directing his words to anyone.) "And they must have taken his things away."

"What are you talking about," Burgess interrupted him. "Who are they?"

"The Brotherhood," he answered. It was his first mention of the name. He continued, "You know, I didn't want to believe it."

"You seem to think we know what you're talking about, but I haven't a clue." Burgess answered him.

"Nigel said Wilson and the others were part of some super-secret group called 'The Brotherhood'. They are behind the scenes pulling all the strings."

"I'm a little skeptical about conspiracy theories," Burgess reacted. "We can't organize something as single-minded as the post office and make it work efficiently. You're talking about some massive conspiracy involving thousands of people. It's impossible."

Until the events of the past few days, Jim would have found this argument persuasive.

"Perhaps they're not as large as we suppose. It is only necessary to occupy a few key seats of power and thereby exert influence over a wide range of institutions."

"Much like the underground was organized in France during the war," Jim's father interrupted. "It could be organized in cells, with each person only knowing a few other contacts, with only the upper echelon seeing the full picture."

"Then Wilson may not even know who his handlers are," Jim continued the argument. "You could have thousands of people organized in such a way, and not one of them could betray the whole organization."

Burgess quivered a moment, "It's damn scary."

"Of course this is all hypothetical," Jim's father continued. "I'd have to see strong evidence to convince me of it."

The bell for the front gate rang in the kitchen, and Jim peered out the window to see who it might be. He was worried that Wilson might return. At the curb a pizza truck was stopped.

"It appears our dinner has arrived."

"I'll get it," Burgess volunteered, and he went out the front door. Jim watched him as he made his way down the walkway, paid the driver and retrieved the pizza box. Within a minute he was back in the house.

"I say let's move this conference to the kitchen," Burgess proposed.

Jim snatched the player and tapes and carried them with him into the kitchen. Jim's father retrieved three plates from the cupboard and set them on the table.

"What would you consider compelling evidence?" Jim asked them.

"I'd like some sort of document which could be directly verified," Burgess responded. "Some physical evidence which could be followed to conclusion."

Jim's father nodded in acknowledgment.

"And you, dad?"

"I don't know. Sometimes it's a little thing which pushes the balance one way or the other."

"I read this book *Born in Blood* all about the supposed link between the Templars and freemasonry and how they want to take over the world," Burgess interjected. "I just didn't find it very compelling."

"It's like all that stuff about the Illuminati and Adam Weishaupt," Jim responded. "You know the arguments. How the great seal of the United States is filled with occult symbolism from the Masonic all-seeing eye to the thirteen steps in the pyramid, the thirteen stars in the shape of the Star of David."

"The thirteen arrows and the thirteen leaves on the olive branches," Jim's father added. "How the number thirteen represents the perfect number in witchcraft, all this Friday-the-thirteenth paranoia."

"And the fact that very few buildings have a thirteenth floor," Jim completed the analogy.

"Yes," Burgess acknowledged. "And the whole New Order of the Ages. It seems we've all read from the same play book."

"Yes, Burg, but what if we're wrong?"

"Do you really want to join the militia types and start taking these conspiracy theories seriously?"

"Of course not."

"Then let's keep our heads about us and not rush into any hasty decisions. I've seen it happen. You start down a trail of coincidences, and before you know it you're believing the most outrageous conspiracy theories."

They sat down at the table with the cassettes and tapes between them, then, as though they hadn't eaten in days, they began to devour the pizza.

"Put another tape on," Jim's father encouraged. Jim placed the next tape in the sequence into the player and turned it on.

I sometimes find it hard to believe how captivated we were with television is those early days. We had no real idea what to expect from it and were enchanted by its mysterious potentiality. Even I had been bewitched by Leonard's muse. But my first dose of reality came with the first cold northeaster of the season during the third week of December.

I contacted the radio factory in Tarrytown to find out what was going on with the televisions, and largely to find out if more money would be forthcoming because without steady employment my money was getting tight. I discovered to my surprise that David was no longer working there and no one at the factory had heard anything about the television deal. Some vice-president of marketing got on the phone and told me bluntly, "Mr. Atkinson no longer works here. You'll have to contact him at his residence."

Of course I had no idea where he lived, nor could I hope to find him with just his name. It was the first clue that something was seriously amiss in our arrangement, but I was too blinded by my own ambitions to see the full consequences. I had convinced myself that what seemed on the surface a major problem was instead just miscommunication and I would hear from David shortly. It was just a test of my resolve, and eventually all would work itself out. It was this pernicious optimism which had enabled me to give away so much money, because I heartily believed our arrangement would produce an abundance of income, and I could well afford to be generous. But October surrendered to a conquering November and each day of silence brought only greater despair.

As my private cash reserves began to evaporate like a puddle in the August sun, I began to realize I had to find another job, and stop living the life of a drifter. By mid-November when it appeared I would not be able to make the rent without dipping into our final two thousand, I began in earnest to look for work. After many days of disappointment, it became apparent to me I would have to lower my expectations and take whatever I could find. And within several days, I was again working, this time in a grocery store.

It was a truly humbling experience to sell cans of peas and corn and peanut butter after I had tasted the life of affluence which television had promised me. In my mind, I had created this image of myself as pioneer and entrepreneur of a new technology, and I could hardly swallow the lump in my throat whenever I rang the cash register.

And I'm sad to say, I never thought about Leonard whose fervent work had made my brief taste of affluence possible. It never occurred to me that I had ridden to success on another man's stallion.

The store where I worked was called "Barnies", named after its owner and proprietor, Barnard Lowenstein, who, having immigrated to this country in 1915, was quick to praise and slow to judge his adopted home. His English was deliberate though colored by a deep accent, and being of a shorter stature than myself, he was the first person in New York in whose presence I actually felt tall.

He was always very serious and profoundly disciplined. He kept his store as meticulously ordered as a well-stocked warehouse.

"I expect an honest day's work from you at an honest day's pay," he told me when he hired me. "If you do well you will be rewarded. If poorly, you will be punished." I was grateful to have the job and acceded to all his conditions.

The remaining days of November seemed to rush like the wind. I spent my days at the grocery and my evenings poring over books which Beth insisted I read. I must have read five books in the course of three weeks, ranging from the lives of various saints to a book about inner prayer. It all seemed completely alien to me, as though I were reading about Napoleon or some Roman histories. I still found it difficult to picture myself in this world, though I could see something powerfully enticing about its promise.

Every time I saw Beth, she would speak about my baptism. She had the same excitement as though planning a wedding, though I viewed it as a rite of passage, an ordeal one endures to attain the benefits of another life. It would be like my basic training in the Navy—once over the new life begins. I had no capacity then to understand what an apt analogy it was.

"Neilos," she once told me, "baptism is the door through which we enter into the life of Christ." But I saw it in more personal terms. It was my entrance into her life and the blessings that entailed. During this time, I often pondered what a different course my life would have taken had I never met Leonard, or Beth, or had I stayed on the farm like my brother Reginald. It was a feeling which often recurred as each new experience brought both regret and expectation. And then of course, there was television.

By mid-December, we had seen our first snow storm, and I had come to accept that my television career, as short-lived as it had been, had come to end. I felt both regret and relief at this realization because I had attained completion. I could finally silence the chorus of doubt inside my head with the firm conviction that I had completed Leonard's work and could now move on. "After all," the argument kept playing in my mind, "I had been ill-suited for the life of an entrepreneur, and I should go about building my life with Beth." But as with so many of my opinions and judgments at the time, I was totally mistaken in my perception of the circumstances.

On the twenty first or twenty second of December, I had completed my work for the day and was on my way home. It was one of those winter days when the chill reaches the bone. I stopped by a newsstand to pick up a copy of the Times. As I was crossing the street, a taxi moving erratically from one side of the road to the other swerved right into my path. Almost instinctively I jumped to avoid being hit, but the car swerved the same direction and struck me. I remember falling to the ground and my head hitting the pavement. But what happened after that is now a complete blank. My next memory was waking up in the hospital.

It would be the second time in my youthful life that I had come face to face with my own mortality.

There was a doctor named McCracken who chanted in a monotone hum, "You're a lucky man Mr. Fox. You only have a mild concussion. It could have been much worse."

"What happened to me?"

"You were struck by a taxi cab. The driver had a heart attack and lost control of the car."

"And how did I end up here?"

"So many questions."

"How long have I been out?"

"A day," he paused and then continued. "A young lady was here to see you earlier. But she had to leave."

"Will I be all right?"

"You'll be released tomorrow."

Then with as much dispatch as when he had arrived, he was gone.

Then there came the dreams. Of course, I had experienced dreams before, but none like these. The first was filled with the wildest imagery, as though every story I had read as a child were tossed together as one might throw together a load of laundry to be washed.

There were sled rides, and tractors, and huge talking corn stalks, not so much frightening as amusing and bizarre. They all kept telling me in a wide assortment of voices, "Be kind, Be gentle. Let the voice of your better self prevail," and in juxtaposition there was the huge screen of Leonard's television, flashing before my eyes every trauma I had experienced as a child, from bicycle accidents, to arguments, to the sickness which nearly killed me. I was forced to watch it all while the screen rocked back and forth like a baby in a cradle. "You must modulate your frequencies," a huge voice kept interrupting it all, until finally in a shrill voice an oboe played this haunting melody while the corn stalks cried.

When I awoke, I was overcome by the dream's intensity, and I lay motionless, afraid to move while the sound of my own heart seemed like thunder to my ears. Later, I could rationalize that it had all been the product of the concussion, but at that moment it felt like hell itself.

The second dream was more vivid than the first, but filled with the same haunting imagery. The crying corn stalks, the rocking television, the eerie music, except a child's voice kept repeating as though in a nursery rhyme, "Nothing you can do or say will make your bad dreams go away." I awakened from this dream in a cold sweat, and the rest of the day I couldn't put these images out of my mind.

When Beth came to visit me that evening, I remember how anxious she seemed, though she kept crossing herself and saying, "Thoxa to Theo," because I had come out of it generally unscathed. "We should always be grateful when God spares us," she explained. "It is a good time to make amends for our lives." Though for some reason, I was afraid to tell her about the dreams, perhaps afraid she would make too much of them.

"*I brought you Baklava,*" *she told me. In addition she had baked me these white almond cookies whose Greek name I could never pronounce. "And here is a book to read.*"

She handed me a pamphlet on the Jesus prayer. I remembered her earnest pleas on its behalf when I had first met her in the London hospital.

"*Do you feel all right?*" *she asked me.*

"*Yes, I'm OK.*" *I could see such love for me in her eyes that I found it difficult not to cry.*

"*I have good news,*" *she told me. "This came yesterday for you in the mail.*"

She handed me a postcard which at first I thought came from my mother, but instead it read, "I'm sorry for all the confusion about our situation. But all is arranged again. Please come by our offices to discuss plans. Sincerely, David Atkinson," *and beneath it was an address and phone number in the Empire State Building and in the top left corner was a circle with a triangle inside, which at the time, I didn't take notice of, and beneath this emblem, in script were the words, "Jamison Electronics.*"

"*Is it about the televisions?*" *she asked me.*

"*Yes.*"

"*I shall pray.*" *Then she kissed me on the cheek, though even then I sensed her trepidation about the whole enterprise. The following morning they released me from the hospital, and I went back to work at the grocery store. Mr. Lowenstein was reluctant to take me back because I had missed two days of work, though I begged him for forgiveness and promised to make up the time.*

The tape clicked off on the first side and Jim flipped it over.

It was nearly New Year's Eve before I ventured to ask for time off from work. I took the occasion of a follow-up doctor's appointment, a checkup after my car accident, to also schedule an appointment with David Atkinson.

The doctor's appointment was fairly routine. He checked my eyes, my reflexes. He had me perform a few neurological tests, and with his characteristic abruptness, he concluded, "Everything seems to be in order."

"I don't know if I should be concerned about it, doctor. But ever since the accident, I've been having these recurrent wild dreams, vivid dreams unlike any I've ever had."

"Have there been headaches, dizziness, any other symptoms?"

"No just the dreams."

"I wouldn't be concerned about it. It's not unusual for a mild head trauma, followed by a consequent concussion to be accompanied by vivid dreams. They should gradually diminish over the next few months."

What I didn't tell him for fear of being thought a lunatic was that I was beginning to believe the dreams really meant something.

When I left the doctor's office to begin my trek to the Empire State Building, I didn't feel the same sense of excitement as when I went to see the prototype. Instead, I sensed something foreboding about it, though I couldn't have explained just why. I remember the sudden tremor which pulsed through my body as I entered the front doorway of the building, but I dismissed it as nervous energy. As the elevator lifted me upwards to the 47th floor, a lump developed in my throat which seemed to slide down into my stomach as if by gravity, and when the doors opened up, my eyes were overcome by the huge corporate symbol, that triangle and circle, which was more than four feet square. It dominated the wall in front of me. When I opened the office doors, a rush of cold air swept over me, and my body stiffened to meet the cold.

"I'm here to see David Atkinson," I told a receptionist at the center of the room.

"And who may I say is here?"

"Nigel Fox."

I paced a few minutes in front of the counter, hoping to warm up a bit while she spoke on the phone to someone in the inner office.

"Take a seat. He'll be out to see you in a few minutes."

I found a place on a small leather sofa and sat down awkwardly on its edge. Ten maybe fifteen minutes passed while I kept myself busy reading a magazine on a table. Finally, David, wearing a blue blazer and gray slacks, entered the waiting area and approached me. He seemed different from when I last saw him, though I couldn't pinpoint why.

"It's good to see you again, Nigel." He reached out and shook my

hand. "Come into my office. We'll talk."

I followed him through the ornate oak doors into the large office overlooking Central Park.

"Please sit down."

I sat down.

"I'm sorry about the confusion these past few weeks. But our television deal fell through. Short-sighted fools."

This confirmed what had been my greatest fear.

"But I'm not concerned about that," he continued. "We've worked out an even better arrangement. It's not what I offered you before, but it has its advantages."

"Exactly what is it then?"

I was concerned he would ask me to return the twenty-five thousand dollars. But he handed me another contract to sign and this time I was determined to read it all.

But the language was even more difficult than the first, filled with clauses whose twisted grammar seemed more like German than English, and whose wherefores and therebys seem to mimic the Elizabethan English of Shakespeare and the Bible, much more than any contract I had read before.

One clause concerned re-licensing agreements and listed percentages and standards of depreciation. Half the words I had never seen before and I could never have understood its meaning.

"Is everything all right, Nigel?" he asked me.

"Yes." I didn't want to tell him I couldn't understand a word.

"It's a standard licensing agreement. You're free to have your attorney look it over."

I reached the section concerning compensation, which concerned my payment for each set sold. In the previous contract it had been five percent, but in this one it was seven percent. In that respect it appeared to be a better agreement. There was a clause about reassignment of apportionment, and another about buyback provisions, which I did not understand.

"I'm sorry I can't offer you the same lump sum payment which you were previously offered. We had to buy out of the previous agreement, and the most we can offer you is another ten thousand dollars. It's on page three of the agreement." He turned the page and pointed out the clause to me.

"It's a graduated compensation scale. When we reach a threshold of a certain number of units sold, you will receive lump sum cash payments in these amounts."

I read the figure, *"One hundred thousand dollars."*

"Of course that's if we sell that many units." He paused. *"But I'm reasonably confident we will."*

"These patents are worth that much?"

"Potentially more. We are on the threshold of a new technology, a new industry which has the capacity to reshape the world as we know it."

"Alright. I'll sign it."

"You're sure you don't want your lawyer to go over it."

"No, I trust you."

I signed my copy of the contract and his copy of the contract. *"I feel like I'm signing away my firstborn,"* I joked a little and he chuckled.

He reached into his desk and handed me a certified check for ten thousand dollars, which I folded in half and placed in my coat pocket. I could see from his face that he was pleased with the outcome.

"I'm sure you'll not regret this partnership," he told me as we shook hands. *"Thank you."*

I folded up my copy of the contract and placed it into my pocket; and so began my career in the television business.

I wish I could say there was some hidden agenda or dark hook which lay hidden in the contract. Something intangible about David had always allowed me to trust him, and the contract, if anything, was fair. In fact, it was not a standard licensing agreement at all, but much more generous, and for reasons which would become clearer to me later, it had a grateful hand behind it.

When I left the office that day with the check in my coat pocket and the contract neatly folded next to it, I hadn't made the mental connection which would have made it all make sense.

There was much about that period in my life that was ill-thought-out and ill-prepared. I lived as though sleepwalking, as though drugged by my own naïveté. For so long I had let others make my decisions that when faced with a series of sudden opportunities, I felt ill-suited for the task.

As the subway train kept rolling incessantly toward Brooklyn, I kept *thinking about the money. I resolved this time I would not give it all away. I was determined to have something tangible to show for it. I kept thinking about Leonard. After all, it had been his dream coming to fruition, not mine, and he had once dreamed of owning a small shop where we could sell and repair radios. I decided I would do just that, but I would also sell televisions. I resolved to begin looking for a place as soon as possible.*

The tape clicked off.

Chapter 23

"What time is it?" Jim asked.

"It's about nine o'clock," Burgess answered.

"And how many more tapes are there?"

Burgess counted them. "Six," He answered.

"We're talking about roughly six more hours of this before we get to the point."

Jim's father joined in, "Why are you so agitated by this? If you don't want to listen, let's stop."

"I'm not agitated. I just wish he would get to his point."

Jim wouldn't talk about it, but what really disturbed him was the incessant replay in his imagination of everything that had happened while he was with Michael Wilson. He knew the governor was trying to intimidate him, and to a large degree it had been successful, but he wouldn't allow himself to take the death threat seriously. He tried to distract himself by talking about something else.

"What do you know about Clovis and the Merovingians?" he queried.

"Why do you want to know?" Burgess answered him.

"It's something this nut, Dr. Harvey, said a couple of days ago when I went to see him at Columbia."

"He was a medieval Frankish King."

"He said there is a whole group of European nobility who believe themselves descendants of this king."

"They also believe that Jesus survived the crucifixion and went on to marry Mary Magdalene, and that their children were the ancestors of these Merovingian kings."

"For someone who doesn't believe in conspiracy theories you seem to know a lot about them."

"I read a lot. And of course there's the internet."

"The internet. The seed bed of every wacko fantasy ever perpetrated on mankind."

"You're the one who brought this up in the first place," Burgess snapped back at him.

"Come on, both of you. Do you fight like this all the time?" Jim's father interrupted them.

"What else is there to do in the bustling metropolis of Hadleyburg?" Jim answered back. "That and watch the paint peel off the walls."

It was becoming more difficult for Jim to sustain this caustic temperament while the strain of the past few days was continually depleting his defenses.

"OK, Let's hear the next one."

Burgess placed the next tape in the player and turned it on. Then Nigel's voice, a little hoarse, continued with his story.

> *In each human life, we set aside special rituals for times of passage, like lines of demarcation between one life and another. And even if they have no religious foundations, there is often something religious about them.*
>
> *My high school graduation was one such event. Filled with ritual and formality, it moved from moment to moment in a fixed dance as though imitating some ancient tradition whose foundations had been long forgotten. It was the memory of this event which haunted me as I prepared for my baptism that cold January evening.*
>
> *It is difficult for me to describe with anything approaching clarity what happened during this ritual. One has to experience it to truly understand it, and any words I use to describe it seem inadequate to convey either the splendor or the simplicity. It was one of the oddest paradoxes that it could be complex and simple at the same time.*
>
> *It began with a series of prayers chanted first in Greek and then in English, I was asked to renounce the works of Satan, the works of the world, and literally to spit to the west as though cursing my former life. Then I turned and faced the east.*
>
> *I was anointed and more prayers even more beautiful were read. Then I was led to a large baptismal tank where I was baptized— three immersions for each name in the Trinity. Afterwards, a lock of my hair was cut, and I was anointed again, on my forehead, ears, hands and feet, each time with a recitation of a verse from the Bible.*
>
> *In its structure it was so simple, almost like a children's game. But there was something mythic and otherworldly about it. And despite my sincere effort to understand what was happening to me, I could not.*
>
> *Beth had told me once, "It is a great mystery." She used the Greek*

word, mysterion, *but I hadn't understood how literally she meant it. I just knew I had to go through it even if I didn't understand it. A seed was planted in me that day which took nearly fifty years to bear its fruit.*

There was much about the ritual which I had been carefully indoctrinated against as a child. The incense, the chanting, the religious art; all these things had been meticulously condemned by Brother Woodrow in sermons too numerous to recall. His disdain for anything which resembled Catholicism was so profound that I am certain if he knew, he would have insisted I'd taken leave of my senses and have locked me in the storm cellar to keep me from going through with it. I can still see him beating his fist on the lectern and shouting, "God has no mercy on the ungodly heathen. We must keep ourselves clean of idolatry and things of this world."

Yet here, I stood surrounded by Beth, her roommate, and a host of well-wishers, and I accepted their congratulations as though I had won a tournament or something. It was the oddest thing in the world. After all the prayers, the hugs and embraces, we sat down to eat a meal and share a few words about the day.

After the meal, Father Athanasios began to speak in Greek. And as before, they all gathered around to listen, but I couldn't understand a word. Beth sat next to me and translated in my ear everything he was saying.

"In baptism, we pass from death to life, we are no longer citizens of the world, but citizens of the Kingdom. Our allegiance should be to the Kingdom where our inheritance is. As our Lord has said, 'Do not lay up for yourselves treasures on earth, where moth and rust consume and where thieves break in and steal, but lay up for yourselves treasures in heaven.'"

He spoke deliberately as though carefully choosing his words. Then he began to speak in English.

"It is a tremendous blessing, a cause for rejoicing, that Neilos has been called to us. It is a challenge for us to live deeper, to be fervent in our struggle against the passions, to love God more zealously, and to be strong against the temptations of the world."

Then he spoke again in Greek the same words. For some odd reason I felt as though I had done something extraordinary. Later, I would come to understand that I had only taken the first step in what was to become a lifelong search for answers.

For the next several weeks which followed my baptism, I felt this intense euphoria and I began to integrate myself into her community. I must admit that I was a bit naive in thinking how easy it would be for me to overcome twenty years of my conditioning in Wisconsin and fully acculturate to Beth's way of life. After the initial excitement of it all, I began to realize that I had entered into a world I had little experience to comprehend and that I had become essentially unmoored, adrift without any familiar points of reference.

It would be easy to blame the people around Beth when they seemed confused about how to deal with me. But they accepted me in as much as they could accept me. Language differences are often a battleground for suspicions, and without a pressing motivation to assimilate, people often gravitate to the like-minded, especially when faced with an alien and potentially hostile environment.

These were arguments I'd tell myself whenever I felt uncomfortable in the presence of Beth's community. But despite my best efforts to rationalize, I still felt out of synch with everything around me.

The months of February and March were bitterly cold, more reminiscent of winters back in Wisconsin where for weeks we would become virtual prisoners in our farmhouse. Because of the awful weather, I found it difficult to make the trip to see Beth, and when the weather was too treacherous to travel, we'd arrange to make periodic phone calls to each other though neither of us owned a telephone.

There was a payphone in the back of the grocery store, and I'd call her twice a week at a candy store near her apartment. She would encourage me to pray and to read my bible. She had given me a small prayer book and had asked me to recite the morning and the evening prayers inside it, though I lacked the discipline to do it every day. I never had the temperament for such religious discipline and perhaps for this reason as much as any other, I found it difficult to pray them. Yet, she would remind me in a firm and gentle voice, "You must pray everyday. There are so many demons to overcome." And she prayed, often with prostrations, and as fervently as I had seen her pray the night her brother died. Oftentimes, I had forgotten this was the same woman who had walked across North Africa.

After my baptism, the only thought which seemed foremost in my mind was completing all the necessary preparations for our wedding.

It had been my overriding goal for so long that its impending attainment left me completely disoriented.

The tape clicked off. Burgess had been furiously writing in his black notebook, and when Jim tried to look over his friend's shoulder to see what he was writing, Burgess closed the notebook and returned it to his pocket. Then, he flipped over the tape to play its second side.

Like everything else in Beth's religion, the wedding ceremony also had its own peculiarities. Later, I would come to understand the separate histories of the Eastern and Western churches, but then I was constantly surprised by its novelty or, as Beth would tactfully remind me, its antiquity.

Now, I could provide a host of lengthy explanations about the differences and similarities, but at the time I couldn't articulate any of this. I saw the wedding ceremony in the same way I saw my baptism, as something I had to pass through in order to obtain something else which I desired. And more than anything else, I desired to marry Beth. I would have passed through fire if that was what it required.

I must say something else about this period, because in my haste to tell you everything I have forgotten to mention the radio shop.

Across the street and down the block at the opposite corner from the grocery store, there was a radio store. It reminded me a little of Leonard's store which we had abandoned to enter the Navy. I passed by it everyday, and never took much notice of it. Until one day, I noticed a small sign in the window which read, "For Sale."

Passing by it six or seven days, seeing the sign, and always fighting the impulse to go inside, I finally succumbed to the desire one morning. When I pushed the door open, a small bell rang above my head, and an older man in his sixties with snow white hair and a huge bulbous nose came out from the back room.

"May I help you?" he spoke in a deep Slavic accent.

"I saw your 'For sale' sign in the window. I was wondering how much you want for the store."

He seemed amused as though I were teasing him and turned around to go back into his office.

"I'm serious."

"You don't have enough."

"How much is enough?"

"Six thousand. Seven thousand."

In my imagination, where he had stacked radios, I could see televisions, lined in rows, each showing a different picture.

"I'll give you five thousand."

"You don't have fifty dollars." He waved me out.

I could understand his incredulity. I was dressed in my work pants, and a red flannel jacket and couldn't have looked more impoverished, but it was as serious an offer as I could make.

"I'll be here tomorrow with five thousand in cash. You have the papers ready to sign, and the cash is yours."

He looked at me as though I were mad. But I had every intention of going to the bank the next morning and withdrawing the money. It would be an inside joke, something which Leonard would have done, and I felt an arrogant self-indignation in the thought of showing this radio shop owner wrong. It seems ironic now that what would become my life's work, selling televisions, began as an act of vanity to show up a radio salesman, but that's precisely how it all began.

The next morning I went to the bank and withdrew the money, and I showed up at his counter with my money in hand.

"So you've come back to bother me," he told me.

"I have the money we talked about."

He smiled incredulously.

I opened an envelope holding fifty one-hundred-dollar bills, which I counted out on the table in front of him.

"Where did you get this kind of money?" He pushed it away from me. "I don't want any illegal money."

"I withdrew it from the bank. Televisions, you've heard of televisions? That's where I got the money."

It was obvious that he didn't believe me. So I began to explain to him how it was that I came to be in the television business, about Leonard and the patents, about my experience with radios. I spent twenty minutes talking to him before he finally started coming around.

"Radios have been my business for twenty years. Now, I wish to retire and go to Florida."

"I know what you mean. Sometimes we need a change."

We talked a little more about radios then he finally acquiesced.

"OK. You can have the store. I'll have the papers drawn up, and

you come back tomorrow."

I slid the money back into the envelope and after a quick handshake, I went on my way. The next day, I returned with the money and I signed all the necessary papers. As uneventfully as one drinks a morning cup of coffee, I had entered the retail business.

I didn't know anything about running a business, and though I had a rudimentary knowledge of radios, I was way out of my league when it came to the intricacies of television. I knew I would have to learn that as well.

Leonard had often tried to explain to me what was unique about his designs, but I was not really interested. Of course, I understood the basics about electron guns and phosphorescence. I understood the design of a cathode ray tube, and from my radio training I understood frequency and amplitude modulation. The basic design of a television was not unknown to me. But what made Leonard's television unique over all the others was a complete mystery, until of course it became necessary for me to understand it.

I realize of course in my haste to paint the broad outlines of this picture that I forget to mention certain details. The name of the store was "Max's" from the owner, Max Belikovsky, and my first decision once I purchased the store was what to do about the sign out front. Shakespeare had once said, "A rose by any other name would smell as sweet," to diminish the power of names. But I remembered the Bible-story my mother read me as a child, where Adam was shown all the animals in the world and told to name them, as if in naming them he gained dominion over them. I felt this same sense of dominion as I struggled for a name. I thought of naming it after myself, but my modesty dissuaded me. Then, I thought of naming it after Leonard, for after all it was the fulfillment of his dream and not mine. But this seemed confusing. I struggled for days, writing down names, then crossing them out. I couldn't seize upon the perfect phrase. I felt like a new father struggling to name a first born son, who just couldn't settle for a suitable compromise. There were trite names like, "Radio Shoppe" and "Radios Galore," and the humorous ones like "Electroland" and "The Frequency Factory." I even contemplated naming it "Milly's" after the cow that had made it all possible, but even this seemed a pointless exercise. Finally, I decided to leave it as "Max's". After all, I reasoned I didn't have to bear the expense of changing the sign. It would be under Max's name that I would build my success, and from 1947 when I opened the first store until 1970 when I sold all forty-eight of them, Max's name was written across the marquis. But I'll talk more about this later.

The night after I bought the store, I went into Astoria to tell Beth what I had done. I could predict that she would not be completely pleased by my decision because she had previously told me her misgivings about television. But I had prepared myself with a legion of arguments should she voice any serious objections. I rang the front bell.

Chapter 24

Burgess could hear the buzz of the front gate bell as it rang in the kitchen. Rising up from his chair, he moved quickly to one of the windows overlooking the street. Jim and his father hardly took notice of his movements because both were completely engrossed in Nigel's narrative. Then, Burgess got their attention.

"Jim, we've got visitors."

Jim turned off the player and immediately joined him at the window. They could see two men standing at the gate. One looked Asian, Chinese or Korean, and the other Mediterranean. Both were dressed in the off-the-rack blue suits with dark blue ties.

"They look like cops," Burgess surmised.

"I wonder what they want."

"I'm sure we'll soon find out. I'll go open the gate."

Burgess disappeared into the kitchen and buzzed open the gate, and Jim watched the men from the window as they began their careful trek toward the front door. Jim could see the Asian man was carrying a large manila envelope beneath his arm. When he could see that the men were within three feet of the door, he opened it with hesitation.

"What can I do for you?" he asked them.

"I'm detective Huang," the man introduced himself, flipping open his detective's badge so that Jim could see it.

"This is detective Georgikakis." The second man nodded.

"We're looking for someone named Jim Jacobson."

Jim hesitated a moment, but then replied, "I'm Jim Jacobson."

"Can we talk somewhere privately?" Detective Georgikakis continued.

"Sure, I'll take you into the kitchen."

The two men followed him as he led them through the front foyer and into the kitchen. Burgess stood off at a distance and watched.

"I think you should take the tapes back up stairs," Jim's father proposed.

"Good idea."

Burgess gathered up the tape player and the tapes, and as inconspicuously as possible, disappeared with them upstairs. In the kitchen, Jim sat down with the detectives. There was a pregnant moment of silence before anyone spoke. Jim didn't know what they wanted, but he was certain it had something to do with Michael Wilson.

"We're from the 109th precinct, homicide division," Detective Georgikakis began.

The lump in Jim's throat seemed twice its size.

"I suppose there's been a murder then."

He was reluctant to volunteer any other information until he discovered why they had come.

"Yes," Detective Huang answered. Jim could see that they were as closed-mouth as himself.

"Who was killed?"

Detective Huang opened the manila envelope and removed a stack of photographs. He spread them out in front of him. They were apparently autopsy photographs, which Jim deduced from the official markings on the borders. Immediately, he recognized the victim as the man he had met as David Fox.

"Do you recognize him?" Detective Georgikakis asked him.
They could see that the photographs disturbed him, but Jim didn't know what to say. He faltered a moment and finally answered, "Yes, I know him. But I only met him once, three, maybe four days ago. We had lunch at a diner on Northern Boulevard. He told me his name was David Fox, and he was the nephew of Nigel Fox."

The detectives did not react to what he was saying.

Jim continued, "He didn't show me ID. I really can't be sure who he is."

"Anything else?" Detective Huang responded.

"No, not really."

"Think about it."

Jim had difficulty remembering the full content of their conversation, but he could remember that David seemed anxious, even afraid. He remembered what David had said about Michael Wilson.

"When was he killed?" Jim asked. But the detectives didn't answer him. "How did you come to me?"

They continued to stare at him with the same cold detachment.
Jim felt agitated, yet, he knew he had to keep his head.

"You don't think I had anything to do with this? I didn't know him."

"We don't know what to think," Detective Georgikakis responded. "But we have to start somewhere. Show him the paper."

Huang removed a plastic sandwich bag from his inside jacket pocket and laid it out beside the photographs. Inside was a crumpled piece of paper with Jim's full name and a telephone number scribbled on it.

"Are there any photographs of Mr. Fox inside the house?"

"I don't think you understand. This is not my house. I don't even have a key to the front door. I came up here a few days ago to cover a story. I'm a newspaper reporter from Hadleyburg. This guy calls me, tells me he wants to talk to me. I meet him at a diner. We eat a meal, he talks and then he drops me off at the house. One hour tops is all I spent with him."

"This is not your house," Huang interrupted him. "Who are the others?"

"The older man is my father, Thomas Jacobson, and the other man is Burgess Kingman, a photographer from the same paper where I work."

"Do you have any ID?" Georgikakis asked him.

"Sure, I have a driver's license."

Jim reached into his wallet and removed it. Each of the detectives took a cursory glance at it, and then Georgikakis handed it back to him.

"What did you talk about with Mr. Fox?" Huang interrogated.

"Nothing important. Really."

"I think that will be all for now," Huang said as he slid the photographs back into the envelope.

"That's it?"

"For now," Huang responded. "But we'll be back. I promise you."

The two detectives arose and left the kitchen. Jim followed them to the front door.

"Stay close to the house," Detective Georgikakis told him. "We'll be back to talk with you."

Jim slowly closed the door behind them.

"It's never wise to withhold information from the police." Jim's father advised him.

"What am I going to tell them? Some super-secret society called 'The Brotherhood' had him killed. They'll think I'm a psycho case."

Jim was beginning to realize the seriousness of his situation. "Jim's right," Burgess chimed in. "We have to have some evidence."

"What evidence?" Jim lamented. "Maybe, it's just a mugging and we're building this whole thing up in our minds." He nevertheless did not believe this theory himself.

Jim nourished the thought of Hadleyburg, of the sedate life he had once lived without The Brotherhood, before Nigel had swept it all away. He was growing to realize that the life he had once lived was forever gone, as though he had entered another dimension, and the doorway into it had dissolved behind him. "I've lived too long," he told himself. He was beginning to accept that everything Nigel had said that night in Hadleyburg might be true, and he struggled to remember the details of the conversation.

"How could I have been so stupid?" he turned to his father and said. "I worked for Michael Wilson's gubernatorial campaign."

"I remember."

"I think I heard every speech that man made. It was all a damn lie."

"Evil people often use the goodness of people against them," Jim's father explained. "We can't blame ourselves for wanting to believe in the good."

"I never trust anyone," Burgess interrupted. "Especially the politically righteous. It's damn easy to say all the right things."

"I'm sorry, I didn't want to involve you in this," Jim told his father.

"I'm already involved."

"I'd like to hear the rest of the tapes," Burgess interrupted them.

"Then get them," Jim asserted.

Burgess disappeared up the stairs.

Chapter 25

Burgess returned with the tapes and player, which he set down once again on the dining room table. After searching for the next tape in the sequence, he placed it in the player and turned it on.

Beth and I were married on May 19, 1947 in the customary Greek fashion. There were no wedding vows or wedding march. It was a solemn ceremony filled with ritual and symbolism, chanting, singing and incense—everything I had come to expect from her religion. I stood silently and expectantly in a white tuxedo while Beth, never looking more beautiful, stood beside me.

"Wait a minute," Jim interrupted. "Wasn't he about to ring the doorbell when we last left off?"

"Yeah, that was the end of the previous tape."

Burgess removed the tape from the player and inserted the previous one. He rewound it a few moments and then turned it on.

But I had prepared myself with a legion of arguments should she voice any serious objections. I rang the front bell, and after a minute or two of silence, I could hear the sound of footsteps coming down the long staircase, which led to their second floor apartment, and the sound of the door latch being unlocked. Evgenia opened the door for me.

"Kali espera," she greeted me. Then she shouted up the stairs in Greek, "Elli, Neilos is here to see you." I learned to recognize the Greek because she had said it a number of times before. From inside the apartment, I could hear the voices of several people engaged in intense discussion, though my understanding of Greek was too poor to comprehend what they were talking about. Then Beth emerged and stood a moment at the top of the stairs. Lifting the corners of her mouth in a quick smile, she began descending the staircase.

"Efcharisto, Evgenia," she told her cousin in Greek and Evgenia returned upstairs.

"Ti kaneis?" she asked me.

"Kala," I answered. (This was almost the full extent of my knowledge of Greek.)

"If I've come at a bad time, I can come back."

"No, they were just talking," she paused. *"Georgos and Thanasi, and Themi."* I could sense the urgency in their voices as we ascended the stairs.

"What are they talking about?"

"The war."

"Thanasi has come from Greece last night, and he's telling us about the war."

I walked into the room, and each one greeted me, *"Good Evening,"* and I responded likewise, and then they went on with their conversation as though I hadn't come. Themi began to speak in staccato phrases punctuating his sentences, a swing of his right hand as though he were swatting the air.

"Thanasi was talking about the communists," Beth explained to me. *"How they had come into a village and killed every man, including the village priest who was seventy years old."*

Thanasi held his right hand in the air, and with his fingers extended he demonstrated how they had cut off the first three fingers of their right hands to keep them from making an Orthodox sign of the cross with the fingertips pressed together. I found the discussion brutal and uncomfortable.

Themi, speaking too quickly for me to even catch a word, answered him. I could tell from the inflection in his voice it was a question of some kind.

"Themi asked him if the atrocities were as bad as those under Turkish rule," Beth translated.

"Ne," Thanasi answered and I knew that he meant *"Yes."*

Beth had once explained to me the deprivations the Greeks had suffered under the Ottoman Empire, how they were not allowed to speak their language, or to wear Greek clothing, how their young men were kidnapped and forcibly converted to Islam. One thing I came to understand about the Greeks was their intense nationalism born from four hundred years of cultural suppression.

I sat there for a half hour listening to Thanasi describe the horrors he had witnessed with his own eyes, and I realized I had no frame of reference from which to understand it. My life had been too pastoral, even in New York. And I still didn't have the capacity to believe in an organized and coherent evil. I postulated that people must somehow be like me, somewhat rational and motivated by the same impulses which moved me. Beth would attempt to persuade me that this was not the case, that within the hearts of all of us was the potential for great evil, but despite her best arguments, I refused to listen.

As Thanasi went on to explain in excruciating detail every moral outrage which the communists had inflicted, I grew weary in listening. I had not come over for this reason, but any discussion of my purchase of the radio shop seemed trivial and anticlimactic, and I couldn't bring myself to broach the subject. I decided to listen patiently and find some other time to tell Beth the good news.

The tape hissed a few moments and then clicked off.

"After Greece was liberated from the Nazis, there was a bitter civil war there," Jim's father began to explain in a professorial tone. "With American assistance, the Greek government was able finally to put it down. But not without significant bloodshed."

"And they really cut off people's fingers?" Jim spoke with incredulity.

"I don't doubt it," Jim's father continued. "As Americans we've been extremely fortunate, we haven't known the horrors of war on our own soil— not since the Civil War."

"I disagree," Burgess interjected. "With twenty-two thousand deaths by handguns each year, we just don't call it war."

"We're a naïve people, still enthralled with the false humanism of the goodness in human nature," Jim's father added.

"Put on the next tape, Burg," Jim encouraged. "I'm getting tired."

Burgess put the next tape in the player.

Beth and I were married on May 19, 1947 in the customary Greek fashion. There were no wedding vows, or wedding march. It was a solemn ceremony filled with ritual and symbolism, with chanting and singing and incense, everything I had come to expect from her religion. I stood silently, expectantly in a white tuxedo, while Beth, never looking more beautiful stood beside me.

We wore two white wreaths of flowers on our heads, joined together by a long white ribbon, as was the custom from her village, and behind her stood Evgenia as her matron of honor, and behind me stood Demetrios, a friend of Evgenia's whom I had chosen as best man, though both their roles only approximated the western model.

The service was beautiful from the first evlogia to the last amen. A three voice choir sang the familiar Greek melodies and a cantor chanted all the readings and responses. Though much of it was still in Greek, the Gospel and Epistle readings and other more important prayers were sung first in Greek and then in English.

In the half a dozen weddings I could remember I attended, none had been more beautiful or more absorbing. In a special way, it was even more meaningful to me than my baptism. My only regret was that my family was not there to experience it.

The service began with an exchanging of rings, then we drank from a common cup, and we walked in circle to symbolize our common life together, and in the end, we embraced. Afterwards, we had a small reception in the basement of the church.

The phone was ringing in the kitchen and Jim rose from his seat and left the room.

"Hello," he answered it.

"I've been in meetings at the magazine all day," Julie began. "Why didn't you tell me about it?"

"Tell you what?"

"Louise in layout says you sold a story about Nigel to the magazine."

"Louise doesn't know what she's talking about."

"It's all over the magazine that you really trashed him. How could you?"

"You can't believe everything you hear. I haven't written anything about Nigel."

"Major news magazines don't publish bylines without approval. Nigel could be your father."

"Things are not what they seem."

"Don't be glib with me. Tell me what's going on."

"Michael Wilson is not the man you think he is."

"I don't believe you. Michael would never do such a thing. He liked Nigel."

"Then you know a different Michael from the one I met. This one is a ruthless killer."

"Who put these crazy ideas into your head? I've known Michael for most of my life and he's never had an unkind word for anyone."

"Look, I really don't have time to argue with you about this. I'm in the middle of something."

"I don't know what's going on over there. But I'm coming over the first thing tomorrow to talk to you."

"I don't think you want to get involved in this."

"I'll be the judge of that."

She hung up the phone.

"What was that all about?" Jim's father asked as Jim reentered the room.

"She doesn't believe me about Michael Wilson."

"It is a little crazy," Burgess interrupted him.

"Well. What happened while I was gone?"

"Nothing much," Burgess answered. "He was just talking about the wedding reception."

"I wish he'd get to the point. This is taking forever."

Burgess turned the volume up on the player.

In my haste to get through the events, I've forgotten to tell the one odd thing about the reception. Beth and I had invited a few people to the reception, not more than twenty or thirty, and I was surprised how many of them came. But I didn't think to invite David Atkinson. Needless to say, I was startled when I saw David standing alone at the back of the hall. I don't even know how he found out about the wedding, but he stood quietly, unobtrusively observing the whole affair from a distance. I left Beth a moment to find out what he wanted.

"David," I greeted him. "How did you find out?"

We shook hands.

"You should have told me about your wedding."

"I'm sorry. In my haste to make preparations, I must have forgotten." I paused. "So what are you doing here? Come sit down and eat something. Half the things here I can't pronounce, but they're all very good."

"I came to tell you that Mr. Jamison wants to see you as soon as you're back from your honeymoon."

"Couldn't this have waited? I don't want to discuss business on my

wedding day."

He seemed preoccupied and he wouldn't look me straight in the eye.

"No, I'm leaving for Japan tomorrow. It will be months before I get back."

Reaching into his pocket he removed a small gift box, which he handed to me.

"It's a small wedding gift."

"Thank you."

"But don't open it here."

"Sure." I paused. "You're sure you won't sit down and eat something."

"No, I have to go."

He shook my hand, and as quietly as he had arrived, he was gone. I stuck the box on the top of the table with the other gifts.

"Is everything OK?" Beth asked me when I returned.

"It's fine," I responded and kissed her on the cheek. Though, what I didn't tell her was my own anxiety about his arrival. There seemed something tremendously portentous about him. It seems odd to me now that I asked so few questions about the people with whom I created this business relationship, but I was so blinded by my own ambition that I didn't question what their motives were, or why they wanted to manufacture televisions in the first place.

After the reception, all the well-wishes and congratulations, Beth and I gathered together the wedding gifts and placed them all into two large cardboard boxes. Their opening would have to wait until after our honeymoon. Among the other gifts, I tossed David's small gift box.

I remember sitting beside Beth on the train to Vermont where we would spend our honeymoon. Holding her hand tightly in mine and hearing the faithful clack of the wheels against the rails, I couldn't push the image of David out of my mind.

"Are you OK?" Beth asked me and startled me from my trance.

"I'm fine."

She laid her head against my left shoulder.

"Agapo se," she told me. "I love you."

Ours was a relationship born in adversity from a war half a world away. It was the most unlikely set of circumstances which had brought us together, and by most standards we had nothing in common, neither language, nor culture, nor religion. But I felt closer to her than my own mother, as though we shared a world confined to only us.

As we sat quietly side by side in the railway cab, I couldn't help but think about my first trip to New York and I remembered I had stuck a letter from home in my pocket.

"I got a letter from my mother this morning," I told her. "Do you mind if I read it?"

"Of course not."

I opened it and folded it out.

"Dear Nigel," I began to read it aloud. "We got your letter concerning the trip you plan to make to us. We are all looking forward to seeing you again and seeing Elizabeth. Things are going well for us. We finished the planting two weeks ago."

I could hear her gentle voice as though she were sitting in the seats across from us.

"Thank you again for what you did for your cousin Michael. We hope someday to repay you."

"A good deed is like a pebble thrown into the water," Beth interrupted me. "There are effects we can never see."

I folded the letter up and placed it into my pocket.

"There was a fishing hole back home," I began to explain to her. "Not far from my house. It wasn't large, maybe a hundred yards across and five feet deep at its deepest point. Reginald and I could spend hours there, fishing or swimming, and sometimes we'd skip stones across the water. It was like a sanctuary."

"I had such a place," she told me. "It was a hill near my village. I would go there and pray. You could see our whole village from there."

I sensed how much she missed her home.

"But we must find our peace here," she pointed to her heart. "Then, no one can take it away from us."

Several times during the course of the trip, leaning over to the window, she stared with childlike wonder as the panorama of trees passed before us like a movie screen.

"Thank you, Neilos," she told me. "It will be good to get away from the city."

I had chosen Vermont because it was pastoral, and in some way I hoped it reminded her of home.

I kept thinking, as I sat beside her, how terribly ordinary it felt, how our two separate lives had become one life through the few prayers and an exchange of rings. Yet despite all the time I had spent with her, what a total stranger she was to me, and that I knew her only at the surface as one could say they knew a face. The hidden yearnings of her heart remained a perplexing mystery to me, as I speculated mine must have been to her. And I was afraid, as afraid as I had been that first day when I left for New York. Though, I wasn't a man who pondered life in profoundly philosophical terms, I understood at one level that what I had embarked on was a radical departure from everything that had come before, and there was a part of me which wanted to bolt from the train and run away as fast as my legs could carry me. But I fought myself knowing that what I really wanted was Beth. If you had asked me to explain why, I couldn't have, because I didn't understand what drew me to her. I only knew I needed her as much as I needed a breath.

When we arrived at the hotel, the very first thing that Beth did upon entering the room was to remove two religious paintings from her bag and place them on a table in the corner of the room, and beside these she laid her prayer book.

"Do you remember our last evening together in London?" she asked me.

"How could I forget?"

"I asked for these."

She removed two metal hospital plates on which we had eaten that last meal together, and she set them on the table in front of me. I started to cry.

"I love you, Nigel. More than you can ever know."

She placed a candle on the table and lit it just as I had done before.

"In a time when I was afraid, when the world seemed hopeless, you were kind to me. I will never forget that."

Of the love and adoration in her eyes, I felt totally unworthy, and I never understood what she saw in me.

I remember thinking she never looked more beautiful with the candlelight dancing delicately across her face and her eyes almost shining as when she first stepped off the ship to greet me in New York.

"What are you thinking about, Neilos?" she asked me.

"How utterly random it all seems, that we should have ever met."

"To us it seems that way. But I believe nothing comes by chance."

She paused. "Are you happy, Neilos?"

"Yes."

She smiled.

"I want you to be happy. God knows there is enough sadness in this world."

I poured each of us a glass of red wine, which we sipped intermittently, neither of us being avid drinkers.

"May we never know sadness," I toasted and she lifted her glass in acknowledgment. But it was a lover's boast, a promise I could never fulfill.

From the moment I met her to the last breath she breathed, she wanted nothing but the best for me, and it was with deep regret that I brought such anguish into her life. Yet, if I had ventured to voice a smidgeon of my regrets, she would have told me in her characteristic way that it is through suffering our hearts and souls find redemption, aptly quoting a scripture to support her position. I never knew any one else like her, and any goodness that bore fruit in my life, she had planted in me.

Most of that trip is a blur to me now, and the memory plays its tricks. Upon reflection, it now seems the most blissful week of my life. But then, it was filled with uneasiness and the sense of danger which comes with vulnerability.

While Beth and I were in Vermont, Evgenia and Demetrios had been diligently working to prepare our apartment for our arrival home. For their wedding gift to us, they wanted to make our transition to married life an easier one. When we arrived home, the dishes were all put away, our bed was meticulously set and our wedding gifts were carefully placed on a table in the corner of our parlor.

"There's an old American custom," I explained to Beth before we entered the apartment. "The groom is supposed to pick up his bride and carry her across the threshold."

"You'll hurt your back."

"Let me give it a try."

I struggled a few moments and finally managed to lift her into my arms, and then with two awkward steps, almost waddling like a penguin, I carried her into the apartment.

"It seems a little silly to me," she told me as I set her back down on her feet.

"It probably goes back to some prehistoric ritual whose purpose we have long forgotten," I tried to be philosophical about it.

Then she said something in Greek.

"What was that?"

"A proverb," she explained. "With great foolishness he made me wise."

I returned to the hallway and carried our bags into the apartment. This is where we would begin our common life together, where we would try to create one heart out of two.

"Let's open the wedding gifts," she proposed.

"Now? Can't we unpack first?"

"We have the rest of our lives to unpack."

I could sense she didn't mean to say it in that way, but I conceded.

"Alright, we can unwrap them. But let me get a pen and paper so we can keep track of who gave what."

I went into the kitchen to search for a pen and paper, but I could not find anything there. So I went into our bedroom, and after looking in drawers a few minutes, I only managed to find an envelope and a pencil, which I carried back into the parlor.

"This will have to do."

Then much like a child at Christmastide, she began to unwrap every gift, tossing the torn wrappings into a small pile in the middle of the floor.

On the envelope, I wrote in two columns the name of the giver and the gift. She opened candle stands and cake plates, an electric toaster and a set of knives, and several crystal flower vases. Then she lifted the small box which David had given me.

"Who is from? There's no card."

"David Atkinson."

She opened the box with the same energy and discovered a small religious medallion on a gold chain, which she dangled in front of my eyes.

"It's beautiful," she told me. "Where did David get this?"

"I don't know."

She kissed the medallion and crossed herself. Then she set the medallion aside on the table. I remember picking it up and staring at it a moment. It had the most delicately painted religious miniature of some Bible scene I could not recognize, and I remember wondering how anyone could paint that small. Then I set it aside and moved onto the other gifts.

Demetrios and Evgenia gave us two religious paintings, as was the Greek custom, one of the Madonna and Child and one of Jesus. These Beth carried to a counter in the kitchen and placed them there in permanent view. These would be the first items she would carry into every new place we lived. When we finally bought the house in Bayside, I built a special rack to hold them on the eastern wall.

Burgess interrupted, "Turn the tape back to where he was talking about the medallions."

Jim reluctantly rewound it and played the section again.

"That sounds like your medallion, Jim."

"You can't be serious."

"Yeah, the one you keep locked in that walnut chest of yours."

"There must be a thousand like it."

"It would be a rather odd coincidence."

Though Jim was reluctant to admit it, the evidence was mounting that Nigel's assertion was true. But before he could accept this devastating conclusion, he had to have irrefutable evidence.

"Nothing which I have heard or seen so far compels me to believe I'm Nigel's son any more than a thousand other adoptees my same age could be."

"Why are you so reluctant to consider the possibilities?" Burgess questioned him. "What would you consider compelling evidence?"

"The man was a nut. Despite whatever more personable qualities he may have had, he was traveling around the country as a kind of vaudevillian flim-flam man, claiming to predict future events. I can't say I've not been moved by what he's said. But he was still a nut."

Jim's father finally spoke, "When your mother and I picked you up from the brokers, we found among your things the religious medallion. We asked about it and were told that your birth mother wanted you to keep it as a link with her."

"It hardly makes sense that kidnappers would leave such obvious evidence on a victim," Jim interrupted him.

"Unless they were confident no questions would be asked," Burgess elaborated. "And they felt the risk necessary in order to lend credibility to their cover story."

"I don't believe you. I suppose you believe he could see the future too."

Burgess laughed. "Can't you see I'm pulling your chain? I haven't made up my mind yet." He paused. "As for seeing the future, it is theoretically possible. It has to do with Einstein and the nature of the space-time continuum."

Jim returned to his seat at the table. "I'm waiting," He told Burgess.

"Waiting for what?"

"Waiting for you to explain how it's possible."

"Alright, I'll give it a whirl."

Burgess sat down across from him, while Jim's father, genuinely amused by the conversation, listened.

"You've heard of Euclid?"

"Vaguely."

"The Greek mathematician who laid out the principles of geometry. Squares, circles, parallel lines."

"Yeah, I remember now."

"He proved two parallel lines never converge, and he laid the groundwork for what would become the classical theory about space and time. His ideas were built upon by Pythagoras and were refined in the 1700's by Newton and Descartes into classical mechanics."

"I really didn't want a science lecture."

"You asked me to explain. Then listen. (He paused.) Descartes postulated that space consisted of three physical dimensions, existing at ninety degree angles to each other. Any object could be plotted on these coordinates and its motion could be written as a relationship of its initial coordinates and its final coordinates. Time was considered absolute. As an object moved from point A to Point B, you could plot its motion in fixed units of time and thereby determine its absolute velocity. Then, Einstein demonstrated that all these rules were incomplete, that within the realm of our physical senses these laws hold true, but as we developed the ability to get more accurate measurements, we began to learn that these laws only approximate the real world, that such things as straight lines and perfect squares only really exist within our minds. The world is far more complex and perplexing than we ever realized, that in fact time itself exists as a physical dimension, and past present and future exist simultaneously. So, just as it's possible for us using radio or television to communicate from opposite sides of the world, it could be possible for the future to communicate with the present, for in some inexplicable way it already exists."

"And you believe Nigel was receiving messages from this already existing future as a kind of psychic radio receiver?"

"No, personally I think it's hogwash. I was just acknowledging the possibility."

Jim seemed a little annoyed by his friend's arrogance.

"Come on, Jim. Loosen up a little. You'll go crazy if you take it all too seriously."

But it was the terrible seriousness of his situation which overwhelmed him. Outwardly, he had made every effort to mask the inward turmoil of his psyche. But the stress was proving a difficult and debilitating adversary.

"Let's hear the rest of the tape," Jim almost pleaded.

"Sure," Burgess responded and turned the player back on.

Chapter 26

After we finished opening our wedding gifts, I gathered up the pieces of torn wrapping paper and tossed them into a waste container in the kitchen. Beth had bound together all the cards with a rubber band so that she might later send out "thank you" notes. Then, we began the difficult task of unpacking and putting our house in order.

During the first few days, it was a difficult adjustment from the warmth and intimacy of our honeymoon to the routine and banality of cohabitation. There was much about our different lifestyles which did not coincide. Beth was accustomed to rising very early to begin her morning prayers, and I found this difficult. I was accustomed to staying up very late at night, and she wanted to sleep by nine or ten o'clock. As I struggled to keep awake those first few mornings while we prayed, she struggled to keep awake at night when I wanted to discuss more serious matters. One of the first compromises we were forced to make concerned a common schedule. Of course, there would be other more serious differences, but these would not come to the surface until later.

I think in my haste to talk about the wedding, I have forgotten to relate how I told Beth about the radio shop. Just a few weeks before our wedding, it was the evening after the discussion of the war, and I had spent a frustrating afternoon in the shop. After taking a thorough inventory of the stock, I had come to realize the abysmal quality of most of the merchandise. Apart from a handful of new radios still in their packages, the rest of what lay before me in scattered bins and boxes was junk, mostly obsolete and non-working vacuum tubes, capacitors and switches whose contacts had rusted from years of neglect. That I spent five thousand dollars to purchase it all seemed the pinnacle of folly. I kept considering the blatant ineptitude of the venture and wondered what I could tell Beth to make it more palatable.

"After all," I would argue to reassure myself. "Both Edison and Bell had the most inauspicious of beginnings." But I did not have their overblown dreams of changing the world. Leonard had been the

mystic. My ambitions were small, I only wanted to eke out a modest subsistence selling my radios and, later, televisions.

When I met Beth at the door of her apartment, instead of following her upstairs to her parlor, I proposed, "let's go get something to eat. I have something to talk about."

"Is everything OK, Neilos?"

"Everything's fine."

We walked to the coffee shop at the corner, and I opened the door for her to go inside. I could sense from the expression on her face that she was worried. She had always possessed an uncanny ability of sensing when I was disturbed about something.

"Is something wrong?" she again asked as we took our seats in a booth.

"Must something be wrong? I just wanted to get something to eat."

"I know something is wrong."

"I have news. Do you remember that radio shop near where I live. It's called Max's. Well, I bought it." I paused but she didn't respond. "I'm sorry I didn't talk to you first."

"You don't have to ask my permission. I trust you. Whatever business you go into, we'll find some good to do with it."

"But I'm afraid it wasn't the most prudent of purchases."

"All things work together for good for those who love God," she quoted a scripture. Then she smiled and I sensed somehow it would all work itself out. But of course, I was always the optimist, believing in the most improbable of outcomes and like Don Quixote, I could never see something for what it was, but for what it could become.

It had been my curse since I was a boy that I could never accept my modest place in the scheme of creation that I looked to the stars and longed for a life different from my inheritance. And this yearning drove me to commit myself to decisions often imprudent and ill-conceived. But I couldn't have done otherwise.

On the third, maybe the fourth, day after we had come home, (I remember it because of the intense rainstorm which began the day.) I finally got around to calling Jamison Electronics, as David had asked me to do at the reception. I had been putting it off because I was apprehensive about what they wanted with me.

As I stood at a phone booth in the midst of the pouring rain, the receptionist scheduled an appointment for me the following afternoon.

*I arrived at the offices a half hour before time and sat nervously in the
reception area trying to occupy myself with a news magazine. The
sound of my own heartbeat was amplified as though a stethoscope
hung precariously in my ears.*

*When the receptionist called me into the offices, at first I was
unable to move, my joints locked in place as though in traumatic
paralysis. Then with the full force of my will, I threw myself to my feet.
She escorted me down a long paneled corridor toward two ornate oak
doors which pivoted on spindles at the corners. When I opened the
doors, I found an office even larger and more luxuriant than David's.*

*"Welcome, Mr. Fox," a confident voice greeted me, and the speaker
pivoted on a large leather chair. I vaguely recognized his face and
searched frantically through my memory to recall where I had seen him
before. Then he stood up from his chair, and with almost manic
gestures began to walk across the floor.*

"You don't recognize me, do you?"

I looked intensely at his face and he had this wild look in his eyes.

"I was Lieutenant Jamison, whose life you saved."

*I could recognize the common features of their faces. Yes, there was
a passing resemblance to the man I remembered, but this man was
different as though he had undergone some inexplicable
metamorphosis.*

"I'm not the same as you remember me."

"Not really."

Then he laughed like a chicken cackling, and returned to his seat.

*"I've been watching you, Nigel. Your comings and goings have not
gone unnoticed."*

I didn't know how to respond to him.

*He continued. "I haven't forgotten what you did for me, and I'm a
man who remembers his debts."*

"You don't owe me anything."

"A life for a life."

"So, this is what the patents are about."

*"Nigel, we stand at the forefront of a radical change in technology.
Television will transform the world into something completely different,
much like a caterpillar becomes a butterfly. We want to be at the
forefront of that change, guiding it, forming it, seeing that it becomes
an instrument of positive change. I don't consider myself in the*

business of selling television sets but of selling ideas. The television is just the instrument on which those ideas are played."

He sounded like Leonard, who in his most manic moments seemed quite mad.

"There is a group of us who wish to seize this new technology and use it for positive good. We'd like you to join us, as our way of repaying our debt to you."

"What kind of changes do you wish to make?"

"A more tolerant society, open to diversity, and less dependent on the dead formalisms of the past."

He appeared to believe what he was saying, but the thought of it frightened me. Not that I was opposed to a more tolerant society, but that a secret cabal should decide what would be tolerated. He was perplexed by my silence.

"I'm offering you a chance to become part of history."

"I'm flattered by your offer. But I'm not so sure I want to be part of history. It's too much responsibility."

"Then what do you want, Nigel?"

"I'd be happy just to sell my televisions, to carve out a niche for myself there."

"Alright, I can do that for you. I'll have the papers drawn up and you can distribute our televisions." He paused. "You're certain about this?"

"Yes."

Then, he reached his hand out and shook mine.

"You're making a tremendous mistake. You should join us."

When I left his office, I was certain my contact with this group had ended. I had no reason to believe otherwise.

As I began to ponder the implications of his commitment, of what it meant to distribute televisions, I became elated. I was one step closer to attaining my modest dream. I didn't have a clear idea of when the sets would be ready, or what their distribution actually entailed, but these details seemed trivial in comparison to the attainment of the larger goal.

When I returned to Brooklyn, I didn't tell Beth much about what had happened at the meeting except that I had been offered the opportunity to join some group and I refused, and I told her I would be selling televisions, which was what I wanted to do.

We spent the first two weeks of June cleaning up the radio store. We repainted the walls, and Beth cleaned the bins and shelves with cleanser and a large steel brush. I spent a good part of each day testing electrical components to see which ones were still working and which ones were not. The defective ones I tossed into a box which Beth would empty into the trash each day. Slowly, though perceptibly, the store improved. At Beth's suggestion we invested a thousand dollars in inventory, which filled the empty shelves with the newest and best radios on the market. And finally in the third week of June, we reopened the store.

Business was very slow at first. A few people came inside the store to look around, but no one seemed interested in buying anything. I seriously wondered during those first few days whether we had made a tremendous mistake. On one particularly melancholy morning, when Beth saw me standing solemnly in the back of the store, she encouraged me, "God will help us, Neilos. We must be patient." But patience was the one virtue which I found impossible to achieve.

It had been my impatience which had forced me from the farm, and which had prompted my most impulsive decisions, for better or worse. I kept making comparisons between my experiences with Leonard before the war and the present. Though rationally I knew the circumstances were radically different, I was still afraid of repeating the failure. Yet, it was our failure before which had made this new experience possible.

Beth worked diligently, faithfully, and I could see in her eyes how much she wanted me to succeed. When we sold our first radio to an elderly woman whose radio had broken, she was genuinely ecstatic, though I knew one radio was not necessarily a harbinger of success. But, as a summer rainstorm begins with only a few drops, or a migrating flock of birds arrives first as one looking for a place to roost, the customers came, as much to talk with her as to purchase radios. I tried to understand their movements, much like bees alighting from flower to flower return again and again to the same tree. I think it's because they saw the goodness in her as I had seen it. And in a world so often filled with sadness, she had a pleasant smile and a reassuring disposition.

I brought a table up from the basement and set four chairs around it, and customers would stop to chat. Beth even began making coffee for them. They'd bring their broken radios and their problems, and as best I could I would send them home, radios working, while Beth would make them smile.

Sometimes, standing in the doorway of the stockroom, I'd watch her as she waited on customers, and I was awestruck at the way she had with people. But if I ventured a compliment, she would have gently dismissed it in her self-deprecating way. She genuinely saw herself as the most wretched of sinners in need of continual repentance. I had trouble understanding how someone who could demonstrate such compassionate kindness to others would find none for herself. Though I'm certain she would have said, "Because I see myself as lower in station than anyone I encounter, all are worthy of my respect." There always seemed an odd logic to it all.

By mid July business was steadily improving, though we were still a long way from showing a profit. And our forthcoming trip to Wisconsin began to occupy a large part of Beth's attention. I seriously considered postponing the trip because I didn't think it wise business acumen to close a store so soon after opening it, but Beth wanted to meet my family, and though I was reluctant to admit it, I had missed the farm.

I went to the printers across the street and had them make up a sign that announced our closing for three weeks in August and simultaneously heralded, "THE TELEVISIONS ARE COMING!" I posted the sign in the front window of the store. Of course, for all I knew the televisions could be two years away. As we completed the preparations for our trip last week in July, I wondered how much had changed at home in the last eight years. I could only remember my family as they had been, and I wondered if the years had been kind to them. And Beth seemed more excited about the trip than I was because I had a host of unresolved conflicts with which to contend.

In the eight years since I bid my mother farewell at the station, I had written her countless letters, yet not one time had I lifted a pen to write my father. I rationalized that my mother read my letters to him as I'm certain she must have, but I couldn't bring myself to tell him anything. I just couldn't forgive him for not seeing me off at the train.

He had always been a stubborn man, convinced that outside the fence which bounded our five-hundred acres stood a world filled with darkness. For him, the farm was his Eden, undisturbed and uncorrupted. And outside was the abyss. Yet for as long as I could remember, I longed to escape his Eden and make a place for myself in the world.

To every decision I had made, I was certain he would object, arguing for the wisdom of his years. But rather than struggle against his ever-present voice, I had simply decided not to listen to it. I would make my own decisions with my own resources. Yet I knew upon my return to the farm that I would be asked to give an accounting for my life, and more than anything else the prospect of this disturbed me.

It was a three-day trip by train from Penn Station to Green Bay Wisconsin where Beth and I would take a bus into the county. As always, she insisted we ride coach, and forgo the cost of the sleeper car. And reluctantly I agreed. We sat quietly beside each other in double seats, uncomfortable, but together. Wrapped twice around her wrist she wore her prayer rope with which she counted prayers, one after the other as though it were a Catholic rosary. Beside her on the seat she placed a canvas bag in which she had taken religious books, five or six of them. And when not praying, she was reading one of them, in Greek of course, because she still struggled with her English.

She had given me several books to read, but my mind was too distracted to concentrate on them. I was anxious about what impression she'd make. Would they think her odd? Would Brother Woodrow take occasion to demonize her? I had explained my family situation in excruciating detail, and she had nodded in assent, but I wondered if she really understood.

"These are Protestants," I had told her. "They hate the Catholic Church."

She had smiled and kissed me on the cheek.

I turned and told her on the train, "I should explain something to you. Brother Woodrow may try to save your soul."

"Then I shall try to save his."

"He'll quote a lot of Bible verses to justify his position."

"And I'll quote several to justify the Church."

She seemed more confident than I.

"Don't worry so much," she consoled me. "God will help us."

Of course, I couldn't help but worry, and in my imagination I concocted a hundred different scenarios, all of which ended in my family condemning her to hell. Religious tolerance was not a virtue easily cultivated at home.

I don't want to give the impression that my county was filled with religious bigotry. They were good people, but suffered from the same ethnic exclusivity and xenophobia endemic to any homogeneous community. And educational standards being what they were had kept us ignorant of the outside world. Most of my impressions about the world had been created by what I had seen on the movie screen, with all of its biases and generalizations. The movies had been the popular educator of my generation, much the way television would become a generation later.

The tape clicked off on one side and Burgess flipped it over.

When we arrived in Green Bay, I had never been more grateful for a trip to be completed. Since early in the second day a throbbing pain had been traveling up my back and into my neck and then downwards into my pelvic bone. Yet Beth seemed relaxed and not fatigued. I was bewildered by her stamina.

As I struggled to carry our bags from the train station to the bus station, Beth strolled serenely beside me.

"So this is Wisconsin," I told her. "This is definitely not New York."

She smiled.

"It's pleasant," she told me, though I wondered if she'd have the same impression a week from then.

For two hours we waited for the bus to arrive and Beth sat quietly praying. And she opened her Greek psalterion, a small book of the psalms, and began to read from it, while I sat quietly, pensively, reflecting on everything which had happened to me since I had left home. I examined every event like an historian, pulling meaning from the random dance of time, from my early days in New York, through my tenure in the Navy, through the months I played the vaudeville act. Nothing escaped my calling to remembrance, and despite my best efforts to organize it, it all seemed unconnected and patternless, as though a whirlwind had displaced it all, and I felt unconnected to this place and as helpless as when I drifted alone at sea. Then our bus arrived and I placed our bags inside and tried to forget it all.

My Mother and Reginald met us at the bus stop. She looked no older than I last remembered her, but Reginald had grown from a gangly boy into a stocky man. My mother hugged me and then Beth, and Reginald shook our hands.

"It's so good to see you again. Your father will be so happy."

Reginald placed our bags into the back of an old truck, which very much resembled the Wainwright's truck that I had borrowed on a couple of occasions to drive into Green Bay.

"Is this the Wainwright truck?" I asked him.

"Yeah. But we bought it from them two years ago."

"I'm surprised it's still running."

"Your brother's become quite an automobile mechanic," my mother explained.

Reginald, my mother and Beth climbed into the cab of the truck and I jumped into the bed to ride back to the house. As we were traversing the rough gravel road and I was bouncing like a ping pong ball from side to side, I remembered the time nearly ten years before when Mr. Wainwright had driven Florence and me to the movie theater in town so that we could see Gone with the Wind, *and how I had ridden in the bed. By the time we had arrived, I was covered with bumps and bruises from the ride and could barely stand. Florence thought it the funniest thing in the world as I limped into the movie theater.*

When we pulled into the gates that led up to the barn, I could see that little had changed. The barn had been repainted red from the brown that I remembered, and a new stone walkway and flower garden led from the gate to our front door. I stood up and scanned from the barn to the fields behind our house to find my father, but I couldn't see him anywhere. And my gaze fixed finally on Beth and my mother. They were both engaged in ardent conversation, but I couldn't hear what they talked about. I remember hoping my mother liked her.

"Where is this bride of yours?" I asked my brother as we removed the bags from inside the truck.

"She's inside the house," he answered. I could sense from the tone of his voice he was uncomfortable, though I didn't know why.

As I entered the front door of the house, this strange sensation of otherworldliness seized me, and the doorway I could remember passing through a thousand times before, seemed like a careful but ultimately faulty reproduction, lacking the aura of transcendence that I remembered. Though everything was in its proper place, I felt unconnected to it all, like a butterfly returning to his cocoon might recognize it as his own, but not understand his previous form.

Beth followed my mother into the house, and I could hear them talking in the kitchen. Reggie's bride, Martha Parker, was sitting in the parlor and cross-stitching a table cloth with small red flowers on the edges. She smiled an awkward smile. I could see the same expressions I remembered in her sister's face.

"Hello, Martha," I greeted her. "How are Mary and your brother Lazarus?"

"They're all right."

"And your father?"

"He's fine." She paused. "You look well, Nigel."

I could sense the tentativeness in her replies, because she didn't want to commit herself emotionally.

"It's been a long time," I told her. "Much too long."

"Mary would like to see you."

"Sure, I'd like her to meet Beth."

Then my brother and I carried the bags into the bedroom where I used to sleep. I pondered all the years I had spent with these people, without a clue to their inner feelings. I had often wondered what dark secrets they masked with their muted replies.

As I set the bags down in my bedroom, I could see through the large window which overlooked the fields a tractor crawling insect-like at the edge of our property. Though it was too far to recognize the driver, I surmised that it must be my father, and as though hypnotized, my gaze was transfixed outside the window, I watched him and I didn't even notice when Reginald left the room. I remember coming out of it only when I heard Beth's voice.

"Neilos, Please, come be with us."

"Oh, sure," I responded and followed her back into the kitchen.

"I've been talking to Elizabeth about England," my mother began to explain to me. "I didn't know about the bombings." Though my attention was too unfocused to engage in serious discussion, Beth pulled me to the table and I sat down with them.

"Would you like something to eat, Nigel?" my mother asked me. "I've made some apple pie."

"Sure," I responded and she set a slice in front of me.

"Go on, Elizabeth."

"The sound of the rockets was frightening and when one exploded, I knew someone had died. And I prayed everyday that the bombs would stop falling. Once it happened two houses away, and three people died."

In her later years Beth attributed the nervous shaking in her hands to those anxious years in London, a by-product of the ever-present thunder of the bombs.

As they talked, I nibbled on the pie, but my mind was too distracted to concentrate on them. Though I knew it would be proper to go out and greet my father, I hesitated. I didn't know what I would say to him or how I could make up for eight years of silence. But finally, my conscience won the better of me, and I got up to leave the house.

As I was walking the path which ran from our back door to the fields behind the house, I could see the corn wrinkling like a carpet caught by the wind, and the stench of manure flared my nostrils. All the reasons I had left the farm rushed into my awareness, and I remembered the countless times that I had walked this path, sometimes carrying seed, or milk pails, or hay for the cows, or often to call my father in for the evening meal when he was working and had ignored my mother's meal bell.

As I approached him on the tractor, I kept thinking about what I might say to him, but the words couldn't come together into anything that made sense to me. When I first saw him, he seemed thinner and his hair was almost completely gray. He looked weary, almost worn-out, and I wondered a moment how I could have let him intimidate me. But then I saw the same firm jaw line and I remembered.

"So, like the prodigal son, you've come home, Nigel," he told me as he turned off the tractor. "You look healthy."

He reached out his hand for me to help him off the tractor, and he squeezed my hand as tightly as he could. When he could see that he was hurting me a little, he let go.

"You're getting soft. Too long away from the plow."

I can't recall him ever grinning. When he smiled, he slightly curled the corners of his mouth, though he did seem pleased to see me. I could see it in his eyes.

"Your mother reads me your letters," he told me.

"I knew as much."

"You should come back to the farm."

I didn't want to argue with him so soon after arriving, so I nodded in acknowledgment, though I had no intention of ever returning to live on the farm.

"Have you met Martha?"

"Yes, I have."

"We were pleased that your brother married her."

His silence about Beth disturbed me.

"It's been a good crop this year and we have sold our share of milk."

"I assumed as much."

"We have a good life here."

We didn't say much more to each other as we walked back toward the house, but before he pushed the door open, he started to say something but stopped himself. Then we went inside. Beth and my mother were still sitting at table and engaged in the same discussion as when I left. I introduced Beth to him, and in his self-willed manner, he answered, "Pleasure," and shook her hand. Then he asked my mother, "What can I eat?"

"There's chicken soup on the stove," *she answered him.* "I'll get it for you."

"No. I can get a bowl and spoon."

He reached for a spoon and bowl, then served himself, though his hands seemed unsteady as he set them down on the table.

"Are you all right?" *my mother asked him.*

"A little tired. But rest should help."

Then he sat down across from Beth.

"So you're a foreigner?" *he asked her.*

"Yes, I'm Greek," *she answered him.*

"I've never been away from Wisconsin. Would never want to go anywhere else."

I don't think she knew what to say.

"Beth has been all over the world," *I told him.* "Maybe, she'll talk about it."

"There is not much to talk about," *Beth explained.* "Please tell me about the farm. How many milk cows? How much corn?"

"You know about farms?" *my father asked her skeptically.*

"In my village we had goats and sheep. But I know about farms."

"Can you milk a cow?" *he asked her.*

"I've milked goats. I'm sure I can milk a cow."

"Then grab a bucket and come with me."

"Eat, John," my mother interrupted him, *"we can wait on the milking."*

My father slurped several spoonfuls of soup and then lifted the bowl to sip it as though it were a cup.

"I can go milking with you in the morning," Beth proposed.

"I'm up a five o'clock."

"That' fine."

I knew Beth would be up earlier than that to begin her morning prayers.

My father sat down the bowl and leaned back in his chair.

"Tell me something in Greek."

"Makari i pra'is, oti avto kleronomisi'sin ton gin." Then she translated. *"Blessed are the meek, for they shall inherit the earth."*

"Is that your Greek translation?"

"No. That's the original Greek."

From my father's expression, I could see that this surprised him. He had probably assumed that the Bible was written in English. Then, he rose from the table, bid us goodbye, and returned to his work in the fields. Standing in the doorway, my mother nervously watched him as he walked back to the tractor. When she could see that he was safely back on top of it, she closed the door and then began to fill two bowls with soup.

"I have some bread in the oven," she told us. *"It should be out in a half hour or so."* There was an anxious edge in her voice. Then as my father had done, she began to tell me something but stopped herself.

"Is something wrong?" I asked her.

"You should ask Reginald and Martha to come in for some soup."

So, I went into the parlor to ask them both to come to the kitchen and eat. Then, we sat quietly, no one saying much of anything until Martha asked Beth a question.

"What is a Greek wedding like? My father married me and Reginald. It was a traditional ceremony."

"It was very beautiful," Beth answered her.

"What were the wedding vows like?"

"We have no vows."

"I also see that you're wearing your wedding rings on the right

hand. Why is that?"

I could sense Beth was a little perplexed by the questions.

"Whenever the Bible mentions rings they are always placed on the right hand," Beth answered her.

"Which version of the Bible do you have in Greece? We have the King James version."

I had hoped the issue of religion would remain untouched, because I feared it would end in hostility, but Beth seemed prepared to answer any question.

"For those of us who can read it, there is one in the original Greek, and there is a translation in modern Greek."

"I think the Bible was written first in English, and then translated into other languages. Your Greek Bible must be a translation."

Martha seemed self-satisfied, and Beth looked at me as if to ask whether she should pursue the conversation. I shook my head in dissent.

"Do you have any photographs of your wedding?" Beth asked her.

"Yes, my brother, Lazarus, took some pictures. Would you like to see them?"

"Of course."

Then Martha left the kitchen and returned a few minutes later with a photo album, which he opened on the table in front of us. She began to point out various scenes and to name the people captured in the photographs.

"This is my sister, Mary. This is Bobby Franklin," she pointed to each picture. Because Beth showed genuine interest in learning about them, Martha began to explain every detail about the wedding. As the tone of their conversation grew warmer and I could see a growing rapport between them, I took the occasion to excuse myself so that I might look around the farm. I wanted to discover what had changed, if anything, since I had gone.

As I closed the back door and began to walk toward the barn, a light rain had begun to fall, and the twin conduits which the tractor had carved in the soft earth, from the double doors on the barn to the fields half a mile away, began to fill with water. I thought immediately about the pond where Reginald and I had played as boys. We would run from the barn and over the ridge a mile away to where the pond, hidden by a crest of trees, sat expectantly, as though yearning for our arrival. I wondered if it had remained as peaceful as I remembered it, but I fought the impulse to rush over there. Instead, I decided to enter the barn.

Except for new milking machines which I immediately noticed, everything else was much the same as I remembered it. I counted twenty-four milk cows, twelve on each side of the barn, and in a stall at the far corner, I could heard the neighing of a horse.

My father had done well for himself in eight years, I told myself, as I stood surveying it all. But I found the prospect of returning to this enterprise unappealing, though I knew this was what my father wanted.

I left the barn by the same two doors and began a strident stroll around its perimeter. Behind the rear doors twenty yards from the eastern corner stood my father's workshop where as a boy I had sought seclusion when often the house seemed too confined and prison-like. I would carry a book or writing tablet to the workshop and there close myself off in my own private world.

Now the workshop looked small and inconsequential, with doors awkwardly hanging on tarnished brass hinges. For curiosity's sake, I decided to enter it, to look around and see what memories it evoked. Inside, I found the black wood stove where I had warmed myself on late October afternoons. There were tools and a worktable and spare tractor parts. On the shelf near the ceiling, I could see a peeling plywood box which I carefully lowered to the worktable to explore its contents. Inside, I found a half dozen or so old books, most of which I could remember bringing to the workshop to read. There was a copy of Robinson Crusoe, *and Jules Verne's* Journey to the Center of the Earth, *and* The Wizard of Oz, *and* The Call of the Wild. *Each book I had treasured as a friendship long nurtured, and I remembered how earnestly I had yearned for such adventure. As I rifled the pages of each book, I considered how far I had come from those days, and how unlike my expectations my journey had actually been.*

After returning the box to its shelf, I began to explore the rest of the workshop. Examining tools and parts like a warehouseman cataloguing inventory, I felt determined to find meaning in everything I saw, and because I was so enraptured in the memories of it all, I don't remember leaving the shed, or walking the mile to the pond. But suddenly I realized I was there, and it all seemed much smaller than I remembered it. The oak tree, which had spread a majestic canopy over our heads, now seemed puny and more a twig than a tree. 'Had my memory played tricks on me?' I pondered. I couldn't explain it to myself. Then I sat down on the steep bank and began tossing stones into the water as I watched my reflection quiver nervously.

"Are you OK, Neilos?" I heard Beth's voice, and she startled me.

"I'm fine."

"Your mother told me that you might be here."

She sat down beside me on the bank.

"It's smaller than I remembered it."

I tossed another stone into the water.

"It's because you're bigger inside."

"I keep thinking how I don't fit anymore. It's like waking up from a dream."

She smiled as though she somehow understood it all.

"You can't expect them to see the change or even to understand it. They look at you and see the son who left here eight years ago."

"What happened up there? What did you talk about?"

"The Church," she answered.

"Don't talk about the Church. They'll condemn you to hell before it's over. They're convinced they're right."

Then she grabbed my hand and squeezed it.

"You're much too hard with them." She had always been more generous than I. Yet I sensed she understood their prejudices and accepted them.

"You can't blame them for what they're taught," she continued. "It's the teachers who are responsible."

Then she pulled me up to my feet and gestured for us to leave. I acquiesced.

"What did you tell them about the Church?" I asked her as we began the walk back to the house.

"I talked about the Scriptures. How they were written, and how the names became attached to them."

"And what did they say?"

"They listened to me."

I was certain that anything Beth had told Martha would be repeated back to her father, and he would be quick to refute her testimony, in person if possible.

"They won't listen and they don't understand," I told her, but I didn't think she believed me.

As we approached the back door, I could hear voices from inside the house, and I was a little reluctant to go inside, but Beth opened the door and gave me a gentle push. Inside, we discovered Brother Woodrow engaged in a lively discussion with my mother, and Mary Parker standing by his side. Mary smiled when she saw me, and I could see from her expression that she still had feelings for me. And Brother Woodrow still carried himself with the same arrogance that I remembered in him. I introduced Beth to both of them.

Sitting alone in the parlor and looking as out of place as I felt, my cousin Michael was reading a magazine. He was as aloof and disinterested as my mother had described him. The town had always called him an "odd-fellow," because he kept to himself with only an occasional misplaced remark. But I remembered him as the inquisitive boy always present with his long litany of questions.

Michael rose from his seat and came into the room to greet us, and though he lacked a naturally gregarious personality, he possessed a special charm which would later benefit him in politics.

"Thank you for the tuition," he immediately told me. "I intend to repay you every penny."

"Don't worry about it," I replied.

"A man must repay his debts."

Beth asked him, "How is your school going?"

"Well," he answered. "I was top of my class."

Then he shook our hands.

"I just came over to thank you both. I'll be back later to talk."

Then he left the house as swiftly as a hurricane. From the other side of the room, Brother Woodrow excused himself, and approached to talk to us. I knew the spiritual contest was beginning.

"So you're from the Greek Church," he began. "They're an offshoot from the Catholic Church."

"Not at all. We trace our roots back to the Apostles."

"Do you worship Mary and pray to statues?"

"We worship Jesus Christ."

"I believe in interpreting the Bible literally," he continued. "No man-made traditions." Then he began to explain in excruciating detail

his opinions about justification, sanctification, mortification of the flesh, the verification of the truth of the scriptures. He quoted one verse after another in a barrage as potent as a viper's bite, while Beth listened attentively waiting to speak her mind.

"Salvation comes by justification through faith alone," he expounded. He explained about the rapture, the last days and I grew weary from his time worn speeches, while my mother and Mary nodded in agreement to every point he made. Finally, in what seemed a last gasp before expiring, he quoted the verse, "for all have fallen short of the glory of God."

Beth sat quietly; she smiled awkwardly at me, then shook her head.

"I don't know what to say," she told him. "I can see how earnestly you've studied the Scriptures."

"Well, are you ready to repent of your sins and accept Christ as your savior?"

The question seemed so absurd. I couldn't help but laugh.

"The Christian life demands constant repentance and vigilance," she said. "St. Paul says to pray without ceasing."

I didn't think he was listening to her, just pausing a while until his next volley of verses. But he responded, "You cannot pray, if you are not saved. God doesn't hear the prayers of a sinner."

She was beginning to realize the magnitude of their differences.

"We are all sinners," she answered him. "From the least of us to the greatest, and we remain sinners until the day we die. St. John says in his epistle, 'if we say we have no sin, the truth is not in us.'"

For Brother Woodrow, who was accustomed to uncontested dominance, such a challenge to his authority was usually unacceptable. In other instances, I would have heard him yell. But he spoke calmly and deliberately, "I am a new creature in Christ. It is not I who live, but Christ who lives in me. And Christ cannot sin."

It was futile to talk to him. His world was divided into the saved and the damned, the elect and the non-elect, and once saved one could never lose it. But for Beth, there was the constant vigilance, the prayer and fasting, the almsgiving, a struggle for discipline which continues from baptism to death. "What one can lose easily," she once told me, "one fights to retain." The chasm of difference between these two worlds was as wide and as deep as the ocean, and I knew she could not bridge it. She stood quietly for a minute or two, apparently considering carefully how she might respond.

"I understand what you're saying and I will think about it."

He smiled as though in victory, then Beth excused herself to her room.

"We really should begin unpacking," I told my mother and I also left the room.

"Are you OK?" I asked Beth once I closed the door.

And I remember the anguish in her words.

"That man is crazy."

"I know," I interrupted.

"It's as if he cannot think at all." She paused. "Are they all like him?"

"They're all like parrots, repeating the same thing. The best thing you can do with any of them is not to discuss religion."

She wasn't satisfied with this advice.

"I shall have to be a better example."

Many years of anguish I had spent in heated discusses with Brother Woodrow, always ending with him shouting scripture verses at me. Nothing she could do or say could have any perceptible effect on him.

I sat quietly unpacking our clothing while Beth, praying fervently, placed her religious artifacts atop a table in the room. Kissing each piece before she set them down, she stood the religious paintings on their edges, and laid her prayer book, her Greek Bible, and a wooden cross between them. Then she crossed herself and made a brief prostration. If Brother Woodrow had seen her demonstration, he would have called her a demon, and I felt grateful that the door was closed. Then she did something which truly frightened me. She picked up her Greek bible and began to leave the room.

"You can't do this," I told her as I blocked her at the door.

"He has to hear the truth."

"He'll only yell at you."

"Let him yell. He will listen to me."

Then she pushed me aside and proceeded out of the room. I followed her into the kitchen where Brother Woodrow was sitting quietly at the table, with his King James Bible lying open in front of him.

"I have to talk to you about the Bible," she told him. "Show me where it talks about being saved."

He flipped the pages to a passage and began reading it aloud, "Whosoever shall call on the Name of the Lord shall be saved. Acts two, twenty one."

She turned to her Greek bible and read the same passage in Greek.

"In Greek we say so-zo. I save. It is a continuing process not just one time."

"That is in your Greek translation."

"No, the original Greek. The Bible was written in Greek."

"What do you take me for, a fool? I know the Bible was written in Greek."

"But your daughter said two hours ago she believed it was written in English. Why don't you tell her the truth?"

"It would only cause spiritual confusion. They know as much as they need to know for salvation."

She was beginning to understand the depth of his hypocrisy.

"You willfully hold information from them?"

"You know it was written in Greek, and look how far it has gotten you. Worshiping angels and following the traditions of men."

The callousness of his remarks surprised her. But he had once preached for boldness in proclaiming the faith, and he interpreted boldness as this type of callousness.

Beth rose from the table and said, "God bless you." Then she quietly left the kitchen. Brother Woodrow smiled as though he had easily defeated an adversary, and I became angry at his pompousness. But I restrained my tongue for fear of unleashing all the wrath inside of me. For years, I had endured his vituperative tongue for my mother's sake.

As I walked back into the bedroom, I kept thinking about how much he had intimidated me as a child. Now he seemed only a caricature of himself.

"The Fathers say you should avoid discussions with heretics," Beth told me as I closed the bedroom door. "Nothing but misfortune can come from it."

"So, Brother Woodrow didn't make a favorable impression on you."

"It's not my place to judge him. But nothing fruitful can come from talking to him."

"He means well in his own twisted way."

She quoted a verse in Greek and then translated it for me, "There is a way which a man thinks is right and that way leads to death."

Then she began to explain to me, "Jesus appointed Apostles to proclaim His message, and they ordained bishops in the various churches. Each bishop had authority only in his church. When a bishop died or was martyred, another was elected from his peers. In Greece we trace our bishops all the way to the Apostles. When the various heresies overtook the Church, like Arianism or Iconoclasm, they were always forced upon the Church from the top, and when the heretics tried to enforce their doctrines on the entire Church, we resisted them. The Faith is never enforced from without. It is a matter of choice from within."

I had never heard her speak with such urgency in her voice. "All we can do is pray for them."

Then she opened her prayer book and began to recite her prayers. I stood watching her for a few moments and then resolved to talk again to my father.

A light drizzle was falling as I made the trek back to the fields where my father was stilling bouncing precariously on his tractor. I shouted at him, "Is everything OK?" I repeated it. Then, he turned off the motor.

"Do you want to give it a try?" he asked me.

"I don't think so."

"I estimate five to six weeks to finish the harvest. I could use the help."

"We're due back in New York in three weeks," I told him. "I can't leave the radio shop closed too long."

"You're selling radios?"

"And eventually televisions," I interrupted.

I could see he was amused by the idea.

"You think people will put these picture boxes in their houses?"

"Eventually."

"Sounds like a plan to brainwash us all, like some space motion picture."

"Don't be ridiculous. It's not Buck Rogers. I imagine it will just be a radio with pictures."

"I've never liked the radio. I want you to think about it before you give me an answer."

Then he turned on the engine again. I remember thinking how difficult it had always been to talk to him.

The tape clicked off.

The clock in the living room was chiming twelve o'clock, and Jim could see that both his father and Burgess were sleeping, his father on the sofa, and Burgess in an overstuffed chair. But he was unable to relax. The final two tapes stood on their edges on the table in front of him, and though feeling slightly fatigued, he was determined to finish them, to bring to completion Nigel's story in order to put it behind him and move on.

He turned off the lights in the living room and carried the player and tapes into the kitchen. He set them down on the table in front of him. Then, lifting the next sixty minute tape to his face, he stared at it a moment and pondered how this peculiar little device had made it possible for a man's voice to outlive him. Then he placed it in the player and turned it on.

Chapter 27

As we all sat down for our first formal meal together, my father and mother at opposite ends of the table and my brother Reginald and Martha across from us, I could sense the unspoken tension in the room.

My mother was unusually nervous, as demonstrated through her persistent straightening of a napkin on her lap. We sat quietly a few minutes, and then my father rose to his feet as was the custom of the house and said a short blessing. "For what we are about to eat, may we be truly thankful, though Jesus Christ, Amen." My mother responded, "Amen," and then he returned to his seat. Then we began to pass the food in silence.

I could remember hundreds of such meals, and our dinner conversation usually concerned some recent event, or some task to be completed. Never had there been silence like this.

"I see you have new milking machines," I commented, hoping to break the silence.

"We've had them about a year now," Reginald responded.

Then my father, still chewing a piece of chicken, began,

"Have you decided to help me with the harvest?"

"I don't think we can stay five or six weeks."

"You've been away for eight years. You can certainly spare a few weeks."

"I have a life back in New York."

"Selling picture boxes to the rich and idle. What kind of a profession is that? Here, we work the land and produce something for our labors."

"You're not going to demean what I do."

"And what will you accomplish once you've placed one of these picture boxes in every house? People will be sitting there mesmerized by the pictures, and will the world be a better place for it? I don't think so."

I was becoming agitated, yet I fought to control my tongue.

"I have to live my own life."

"By rejecting all the values you were taught to believe in?"

"John," my mother jumped in. "Let's talk about something else."

I was so excited that I slid the chair backwards and escaped from the table. I went outside to calm myself down, and my mother, with some hesitation, followed after me.

"He has no right to talk to me that way." I told her as she closed the door behind us. "I'm not some child any more."

I was pacing back and forth.

"He wants the best for you, Nigel."

"He wants to run my life. From the time I was this high, he has told me what to think and how to feel."

"You don't know your father then."

"You seem to know him so well. Explain to me why he won't let me live my own life."

"Because he's convinced you're making a mistake."

I could see the anguish in her face.

"I promised him not to tell you this." She continued. "He's dying."

My eyes welled with tears.

"Dying?"

"He's been sicker than you can even know. For three days he was in bed, and he forced himself to get up so you wouldn't see him sick."

"That stubborn fool."

"He doesn't want you to take pity on him."

There were so many powerful emotions rushing through me at one time that I felt explosive. I didn't know how to respond. I felt angry, because even in his death he pushed me away, and I felt the greatest sadness I had ever known, as though my heart had burst into pieces and my life blood spilled out on the ground.

"So what am I supposed to do?" I asked her. "Pretend he isn't sick?"

"Help him finish his harvest. Make his last days happy ones."

"But that could be weeks," I told her.

Then she told me something that tore me apart.

"Your father wanted to leave the farm, but times were tough and grandpa wouldn't let him go. They had bitter fights about it, and when grandpa laid up sick in bed, your father wouldn't even go into the room to talk to him. The two of them, stubborn to the end, wouldn't

even share one kind word with each other. And when grandpa died, your father felt the deepest regret, and it still gnaws at him all these years later. Don't make the same mistake, Nigel." She paused. "Let's go back inside and finish our meal."

I nodded in agreement and we went back inside the house. Inside, the others were eating quietly as though nothing had happened. My mother and I reclaimed our seats. Then, curling her lips into a half smile, she told my father, "It's all right, John." A few minutes passed without a remark from anyone, and in a more pleasant tone my father began to speak, "There's a get-together at the Griffin place after church on Sunday."

I remember the huge gatherings they had given when, as children, we would play chase through their grove of apple trees while our parents, sitting on huge tables spread out across the lawn, would engage in idle conversation or would play dominoes. The food was usually wonderful, with a wide assortment of cakes and pies, and various vegetables which we hated eating, of course. There were chickens roasted on spindles over an open fire.

"That sounds nice," I responded to him, and Beth acknowledged, "It will be good to go."

Then the table became silent as before.

"I'm sorry that I flew off the handle like that," I said. "I've had a chance to think about what you've said. I'll be happy to help you finish the harvest."

My father said nothing in response. But two small streams of tears began to drip down from the corners of my mother's eyes. Then, I thought of what an imposition it was on Beth to take her away from the church and New York for so long. But I knew she would silently endure whatever I asked of her.

The next morning, she arose early as always, and from the corner of my eye, I could see her making prostrations while my father, standing just outside the window, was watching. From the expression on his face, I knew he was confused, but he would never mention anything about what he saw. After she finished her prayers, she went to the barn with him, and there they milked cows. It would become her routine for the rest of our stay.

On Sunday morning after the others had left early to walk to the small brick church where Brother Woodrow conducted services, Beth and I remained at the house. At nine o'clock, she began a prayer service in our room. She prayed in Greek while I read silently from the small English prayer book she had given me. I kept thinking about my father. It seemed impossible that he was dying. The vigor, the stamina, the incessant hard work which had characterized him for as long as I could remember were being sucked from him as one might suck soda through a straw. I didn't know if I could endure witnessing this debilitation and decay.

When everyone returned around noontime, we began to make preparations for the gathering. My mother made two apple pies and my father prepared two chickens for the roasters, though I could see from the strain on his face it was difficult for him to complete the task.

The gathering went pretty much as I expected. The children were playing games in the apple orchard, and the men were playing dominoes on tables on the lawn. Beth sat quietly among a group of young women, all engaged in the superfluous conversation which characterized much of the discourse in our county. I knew she felt out of place, that she would rather be engaged in a discussion of religious virtue or theological insight, but she endured it all for my sake.

At one point during the afternoon, Mary Parker approached me as I stood watching the men playing dominoes.

"Nigel," she began. "You're looking well."

"I've been all right."

"We missed you at church this morning."

"Beth and I prayed at home."

"They say you've joined her strange religion."

"Yes, I was baptized."

"And you bow down before pieces of wood and do other strange things."

The manner in which she described it made us seem like witch doctors.

"It's different, Mary. But it's still a Christian church."

I lacked the theological expertise to give a defense of what I had done, and I felt disinclined to explain myself or to justify my decisions.

"You've changed so much, Nigel," she observed, and I could see she wanted to say more, but she restrained herself.

It had been an awkward situation from the beginning, and I felt as if more should be said to all parties, but I couldn't find the right words.

I spent most of the afternoon darting from place to place, like a hummingbird hovering from flower to flower. I couldn't engage myself in any activity, and I found the conversations trivial and uninteresting. I wanted to talk about my father's illness, about the mystery of death, but it was one subject strictly forbidden.

I found my father talking to two men about farm equipment, and I attempted for a short time to participate in the discussion, though my mind was too distracted to focus on plows and milking machines. Finally, I found myself standing by Beth and listening to the young women discussing quilt-making.

"You should put the stitches one-sixteenth of an inch apart," one girl explained.

"No. That's too close together," another disagreed.

"But you shouldn't penetrate the padding," a third contributed.

Beth quietly listened, trying to fit in. But I never felt more out of place. There was a distinct incongruity between my interior reflections and the reality of my exterior circumstances. But that had always been the case.

While the women were discussing how one could sew a cloth so that it appeared seamless, it struck me that this was an apt metaphor for the philosophy of the whole community. Everything had been centered on the proper appearance. But for Beth, it was a different matter altogether. As she had told me many times, the most important concern was the inner life, those things which the naked eye could not see which were hidden in the human heart. The virtues of compassion and patience and mercy do not manifest themselves in the outward trappings of custom and social convention, but express themselves in ways often impenetrable to the human eye. And she once explained that we fool ourselves in thinking how much control we have over our external circumstances when we only have control over our inner life, over our growth into vice or virtue. It is a lesson that has taken me nearly fifty years to learn.

At three o'clock, as we all sat down to dine on all the delectable foods, I could see my cousin, Michael, talking with two young women, both obviously having designs on him, but he deflected their advances with the skill and charm of a diplomat. Then, he approached the table where Beth and I were sitting.

"I know it must be difficult," he began to tell her, "to be so far from

home, to be among people whose attitudes and beliefs are often hostile to your own. It takes rare courage. I just thought that I should tell you that." Then he turned and walked away. I didn't know how to take what he said, and Beth seemed equally confused. Yet, this was the Michael I like to remember, before the media managers and power brokers would mold him into what he was to become.

Beth ate very little of the feast that was spread before her. Having grown accustomed to the austerity of her fasts and finding the seasonings unfamiliar to her palate, she nibbled at a variety of vegetables, but found only the string beans to her liking.

"Is the food all right?" I asked her.

"It's fine."

"You haven't touched much of it."

"I was thinking about your cousin."

"He's always been an enigma to me."

"Was he trying to praise me?" she asked me.

"It seems that way."

"He disturbs me."

I snickered a moment and replied, "Oh, he's harmless."

Yet I could see from the expression on her face that she was not persuaded.

"Michael used to follow me around all the time and ask me questions. He's incredibly bright. I'm like a big brother to him."

She didn't say anything further about him, and later that evening when I pressed her to share her thoughts, she declined, saying, "It's not my place to sit in judgment of anyone."

The days that followed were surfeited with the most strenuous work of my life. We rose early and barely finished after sunset, and Beth labored with a stamina surpassing any man's. And my father, for whatever reason unable to dismiss his pretense, insisted on working beside us, though it was obvious the work was taking its toll.

I never understood what possessed him to continue this charade, when its obvious cost was hastening his death. But I could not bring myself to betray my mother's confidence and tell him that I knew, until, of course, his illness became so obvious that he would have no choice but to admit it. I often pondered whether this pretense was his own method of denial, of refusing to face his own mortality.

I can't remember how long it was before the strain of work became more than he could bear, maybe three or four weeks. The days blended together like a watercolor splattered with raindrops. But one day it came. When Beth went out to the barn as she had done every morning with my father, she went alone, and I could hear my father coughing in his room.

"He has a cold," my mother told me when I got up to see him, but I knew she lied. Then when the doctor came that morning and spent over an hour alone with him in his room, I knew it was far more serious than a cold.

"Is he OK, Doctor?" I asked him. He whispered something into my mother's ear, and she nodded.

"I'd like to take him to the hospital in Green Bay."

"He won't go," my mother responded. "He doesn't want to die in the hospital."

"Maybe, I can talk to him."

"No. He doesn't want you to know," she urged me.

"This is ridiculous. If he needs treatment, he should go to the hospital."

"He's a stubborn man," the doctor interrupted. "I've spent almost an hour trying to convince him."

"He's a stupid man." I felt terrible after I said it, but I could not believe he would refuse proper medical treatment.

I went into the room to talk to him.

"How do you feel?" I asked him.

"It's a little cold. That's all."

"I know you're dying."

He seemed angry at my acknowledgment. "Who told you?"

"That's not important. I came to tell you that you should go to the hospital."

"I don't want to die at the hospital, all alone without my family around."

"They'll give you proper treatment there."

"It's too late for that. There are some battles you cannot win, and a courageous man faces that."

"But I don't want you to die."

The sadness seemed more than I could bear, and the tears swelled like ripened oranges and rolled down my cheeks.

"I wanted this to be a happy time for Elizabeth and you, not filled

with sadness."

Then I hugged him for the first time in years. It was an awkward moment. My father being unaccustomed to such an open display of affection was first inclined to push me away, but I held him so tightly, that I don't think he had the strength.

"Go to the hospital," I told him. "We won't let you die alone."

But not even I could persuade him.

'What possesses a man to deny himself medical treatment?' I remember asking the doctor after I left the room.

"I don't know," the doctor answered me. "But I've seen it many times before."

I struggled with this problem the rest of the morning but came no closer to understanding it.

"Life is something to be struggled for," I kept reiterating in my mind. With every muscle and sinew, I fought the thought of death.

When Beth returned later that morning from the barn, my father was resting quietly in his bed. She noticed immediately how nervous I was, and she asked me, "Is something wrong, Neilos?"

"My father is sick, and he refuses to go to the hospital."

I began pacing back and forth across the kitchen floor.

"I'll talk with him." she told me.

"It won't do any good."

She smiled and then disappeared into the bedroom. When an hour passed without a sound, I wondered what they were talking about, and I grew more anxious as each minute passed. And then about one o'clock, she opened the door and came outside.

"Neilos. Go get the truck. We're taking your father to the hospital."

I was flabbergasted.

"What did you tell him in there?"

She placed her finger to her lips and told me, "I'll speak of it later. Help your father with his bag."

Then I returned to the bedroom where my father was packing, and I stood there a moment watching him as he struggled to close his bag.

"Can I help you?" I asked him and he nodded in acknowledgment. Then after approaching from the opposite side of the bed, I snapped the bag shut and lifted it by its worn leather handle to my side. It was heavier than I expected.

"What do you have in here? It feels like an anvil."

"Just some personal things," he responded.

"What did she tell you?" I asked him. I could see he was fighting back tears.

"I can't talk about it."

He was firm in his unwillingness to talk about it.

"You've made a complete about face."

But as much as I pressed him, he would not reveal a word of what they talked about.

It was a two-hour trip by car from the farm house to Green Bay, and I drove with my mother sitting beside me and my father beside her. We said hardly a word to each other for most of the trip, and I kept puzzling over what Beth could have told him to make him change his mind. From my own experience, I knew she could be persuasive, but my father was accustomed to having his own way, and I had never seen him more firm in a decision.

I remember the irregular rhythm of the bag as it bounced against the metal bed of the truck. At first it annoyed me with its incessant thumping, but when the trip began to grow monotonous after about an hour into the drive, I began to concentrate on the thumps, as if trying to predict when the next one might come. It was a mental exercise which took my mind away from the seriousness of the situation. My father was dying. This man who had intimidated me most of my life with the strength of his personality now seemed weak and frightened, as frightened as I felt most of the time.

When we arrived at the hospital, it was nearly dark. I could hear the sound of motorcars, a noise which I had taken for granted in New York, but which stirred in me all the memories of the past eight years, of my struggles to make a life for myself. It seemed ironic that as my father's life was coming to an end, mine was just beginning, and I felt a little guilty about it.

After filling out the necessary paperwork, we took my father to his room, where I chatted with them both for a short while. But then as my mother wished, I left them there and drove back to the farm alone.

It was nearly midnight when I arrived at the farm, and the house was almost completely dark except for a light in the kitchen where I hoped Beth would be waiting for me. Instead of entering through the front door, which might have disturbed their sleep, I walked around the back and entered there. I could see Beth sitting alone at the table and reading. Once she saw me, she opened the door for me.

"Did everything go well?" she asked me.

"As well as can be expected. Mom's going to stay with him tonight."

"How are you feeling?"

"The truth?"

"Yes, the truth."

"I almost wish we never came."

"You can't mean that."

"I know we never agreed on much, but he's my father, for God's sake. I can't deal with this."

"I made some soup for you," she told me. "Would you like a bowl?"

"Sure," I responded. *Then it occurred to me that I hadn't eaten anything since breakfast.*

She set a gray porcelain bowl in front of me, and then with a wooden ladle, emptied it three times into the bowl.

"I also have some Greek tea."

Then she poured me a cup.

"What did you tell him?" I asked her. *Then she smiled in her own disconcerting way.*

"I listened to him."

And I thought about all the customers, who, as though enchanted, would sit down across from her and then unwrap themselves while she listened earnestly to their deepest secrets.

"He's a lovely man," she told me. "In Greek we call it 'Atholos', without guile." *She paused.* "He thinks he's failed you. That's why you ran away from him."

"I didn't run away from him."

But I could see she didn't believe me.

"Alright, maybe a little."

"I talked about my father and my brother Pavlos."

"I don't remember him."

"The one that went to Athos," *she explained.* "They fought, and when Pavlos left, my father would not see him off. My father never forgave himself."

"And what am I supposed to do?" I asked her.

"Forgive him, Neilos, for whatever he may have done."

That night I had a succession of nightmares, each waking me in hour intervals throughout the night. At one point Beth awakened and said that she'd pray for me, and I vaguely remember her kneeling at the foot of the bed and praying, but I was too exhausted to acknowledge it. When morning came I was more fatigued than when I went to sleep.

"You had a bad night," she told me as I sat down at the kitchen table.

"The worst."

"Sometimes the demons attack us when we sleep. You should pray the evening prayers with me and you will have no more bad dreams."

"I don't believe in demons."

From her expression I could see she thought me foolish, but it had taken a radical metamorphosis for me to believe in God. Believing in demons seemed inconceivable.

"Oh, you must believe in demons."

I didn't want to argue with her, so I responded, "Of course."

After sipping the soup quietly for a few minutes, I told her, "We should see my father," and she nodded in agreement.

When we visited my father in the hospital, I found it difficult to look at him, his face transparent with his agony. The complexity of human suffering, of its inexplicable pervasiveness, had never touched me as personally or as profoundly. I had never lived very deeply, content to ride passively on the crest of life's wave. I had not learned that compassion entailed co-suffering; that in each man's life there is a cycle of crucifixion and resurrection, and that often it is only in the midst of suffering that we become fully human. All these lessons I had yet to learn, and lacking the tools to deal constructively with his death, I rebelled against it.

Beth was always nearby, encouraging him with her comforting voice, while I stood off at a distance, often looking out the window to the traffic beneath us. When he tried to make conversation with me, I was unconnected, for whatever perplexing reason unable to engage myself.

When he had a good day, Beth would invariably tell him how well he looked, and on the bad days she would quietly pray for him while counting out prayers on her prayer rope. Oftentimes when his face felt ablaze with fever, she would gently wash it with a small cloth and basin of water, all the while singing the same Greek hymn. She once tried to explain the words to me, but I was too agitated to listen.

All I could think about was his death and how angry it made me.

"Damn it." I wanted to shout at him. "Don't do this to me,"
as though he had some final control over it all. And I remembered every argument we had shared and how pointless they had all become.

"How can you be so calm?" I had once asked Beth. "He's dying for God's sake." And she smiled in her often disconcerting way as though mildly amused by my question.

"You must pray for your father," she told me.

For her, the reassurance she needed rested firmly in her faith. But for me I could not be as certain.

For my mother, the strain seemed more than she could bear, and though she heroically tried to mask her apprehensions, I could see it was too much for her. The only man she had ever loved was dying, withering like the winter corn after harvest. She sat nervously fidgeting with her fingers the whole time she was with him, and when my father would call for her, and she'd respond, "Yes. John," her voice would betray her anxiety. Not even her religion gave her comfort. It was difficult to learn what my mother was feeling about it all because she refused to talk about it. While at the hospital she was always preoccupied with making my father more comfortable. When we were home, she would close herself off in the kitchen as though it were a private fortress and there she would spend hours cooking, as though the proper mixture of spices would enchant away his death.

But despite it all, each day brought his death ever closer, and we began to feel its palpable presence as though it were sitting in the room with us.

When my father died I was not with him as I would have wanted. Beth and I were alone at the farm. At about noon, I could see my uncle Peter running up the footpath between our properties, and I could hear him shouting something in the distance.

Beth and I ran out of the house and met him on the way.

"Your mother called me from the hospital," he began to explain. Having the only telephone for miles, he had often played county messenger. "Your father's dead."

The news hit me like a storm, and Beth, falling to her knees, began to pray as fervently as she had the first night we met. I didn't know how to react. I remember shouting in an almost childlike rage, and I too fell to my knees, but instead of praying, I kept hitting my fists on the ground and screaming, "No! No! No!"

I remembered the last words he had spoken to me, not so much because they were particularly profound, but because they were his words. He had lifted his head from his pillow, with great effort, and in almost a whisper told me, "Live a good life, Nigel, and have no regrets." And now, nearly fifty years later, I realize I heeded nothing of what he told me. I rushed headlong into a life which has destroyed nearly everything that was dear to me, and regret has become one of my most intimate companions.

The tape clicked off.

Chapter 28

Jim removed the cassette from the player and flipped it over to the second side. But before he could turn it on, Burgess came into the kitchen to get a glass of water and interrupted him.

"You're still up. What time is it?" he yawned

"I don't know."

"Still listening to the tapes?"

Jim nodded and replied, "Have you ever pondered what it is like to die? What happens in those first few moments when the breath leaves us?"

"Another one of your morbid thoughts."

"No, it's an ever-present reality which hangs over us like the sword of Damocles. Remember what you were saying before about space and time being a continuum? If what science tells us is true, every event of our lives is continually present, woven forever into the tapestry of time. And, in fact, we've already died. We are simply waiting to discover the way it ends. Then, it can be argued that our whole lives are an expression of how we face this end."

His thoughts gained more coherence as he spoke. "Are we going to spend our lives somehow trying to cheat this death, either by living dangerously so that every time we face the danger and survive, it gives us confidence of facing the final danger? Or by accumulating things in the hope that they will somehow buy us time? Or by violence—if I have the power of life and death over someone else, then maybe I have the power over mine?"

"I came for a glass of water. Not to talk about death right now."

"That's precisely the point. We don't want to talk about it. We don't want to face it. This fear of death is all pervasive."

Burgess swallowed the remainder of the water in one huge gulp and set the glass down on the counter top.

"I'm too tired to deal with this right now. Jim, Go to bed."

Burgess went back into the living room to resume his sleep. But Jim was too agitated to think of sleep. Though he was unsure of the time, he knew it was late, maybe two in the morning. Still, he was determined to hear it all despite his fatigue.

When Beth and I returned to Brooklyn, it was late October. A trip which was to be only three weeks was almost three months, and I hadn't a clue what we would find when we returned. After the funeral we had tried to convince my mother to come with us, but she refused. I don't think she had the heart to leave everything that had been so dear to her, and a change of scenery, she insisted, would only intensify her grief.

During the train trip back, the one image which I could not seem to push from my mind was my father's casket being lowered into the ground and the dirt shoveled into the hole on top of it. I just couldn't accept that life ended this way. Nothing had been as I expected it.

When we returned to the neighborhood, everything was exactly as I remembered it, and I was surprised that the radio shop was still standing with my sign, though weathered and wrinkled, still fastened to the door.

During the course of the next few weeks, we both worked diligently to rebuild the business. And each day which passed brought greater anticipation of the arrival of the television sets, though when they were to arrive, I hadn't a clue.

Beth, as always, enchanted all who met her. And she soon had regained her role as the social center of the neighborhood. Over the years she never seemed to lose her capacity to endear herself to people. And even Brother Woodrow warmed up to her in the end.

I can still remember her childlike smile as she graciously attended to our customers. Pouring them coffee, ringing up the register, she seemed intent on making them feel welcome as though they were in their own homes. And she always remembered their names. Once I had ventured to compliment her for how wonderfully she treated them, and she chided me for praising her, "I only do what is expected of me. I must learn to see Christ in them." And she meant it.

It was early November when the first televisions arrived. It had been bitter cold, and I remember how the wind whistled in the canvas covers above the shop windows. At about one o'clock, a delivery truck stopped in front of the store, and two men dressed in blue overalls dashed frantically to our door to escape the piercing wind.

"We're here to deliver some televisions," one muttered in an almost unintelligible Russian accent.

"They're here, Beth, the televisions," I shouted.

I propped the door open with an old Victrola and they proceeded to unload five large boxes, each labeled in the corner with "Jamison Electronics." My heart raced like a child's at Christmastide as they placed each one on the cluttered floor.

"Beth," I shouted. *"Beth, come here."*

She emerged from the back, still carrying the rag she had used for cleaning.

"They're here, Beth, the televisions."

She smiled and set the rag aside.

"Go in the back and get me a knife to open one of the boxes."

Then one of the workmen had me sign an invoice, but I didn't even look at it.

Beth returned a few minutes later with a small razor knife which I used to meticulously cut open a box.

"They're smaller than I expected, Neilos."

"They're big enough."

I cleaned a shelf near the front windows and with great difficulty carried the television there.

"You'll hurt yourself," she told me as I wobbled like a penguin across the floor.

"Please find me an extension cord," I asked her. We plugged it in and turned it on and then, as if by magic, light danced across the screen.

"And people will watch this little box?" Beth seemed perplexed.

"They'll worship it."

She made a cross in front of my lips.

"Don't say such things."

"I was only joking."

It would be months before anything like regular programming started, but even without pictures it possessed a powerful attractive force. People would come from blocks away just to stare at it, and once regular programming started, they'd hover around it like moths drawn to a flame. I'd often observe them standing mesmerized, watching whatever was on. I became convinced that Leonard had grossly underestimated its seductive powers and that it would become *even more successful than he had ever imagined.*

At first business was slow. Most people seemed content to stare through the windows, as shoppers might on Fifth Avenue at Christmas time. But then two proprietors of neighborhood taverns, each believing a television might increase customers, came into the store and purchased one of the sets. From time to time in the ensuing months, I'd see them both walking and they'd thank me for my contribution to their growing success. And in gratitude, they'd send me customers to purchase their own sets.

It was like autumn when the first leaves begin to change, until one by one they paint a colorful tapestry on the ground. Soon, I could hardly keep enough in stock to keep up with the growing demand.

I'd like to say I took success humbly, recognizing its fickle affection, but each new purchase only emboldened me, and soon ambition became my driving force. Beth would tell me in her gentle way, "Every blessing comes from God. We must accept it with a humble spirit." But I saw none of this. Becoming intoxicated with success, I had plans, great plans, of expanding the store and opening others. By February 1948, this had grown into an all consuming passion.

But for Beth, as always, things were different. As I toiled tirelessly to build the business, she labored loyally and silently beside me. Yet, I could sense she had misgivings. Her faith had been the center of her life since childhood, and though she never uttered a word to discourage me, I could sense that she believed something unseemly about the whole enterprise, and that my almost religious zeal disturbed her.

She would often during the course of the day stand quietly praying, counting each prayer on a rope around her wrist. About what she prayed she wouldn't tell me, and the image today still haunts me.

In late March or early April, David Atkinson came down to see the store. I remember how satisfied he seemed when he saw how lively business had become. Beth, as usual, was pouring coffee and chatting with customers while I gave him a grand tour.

"I just had to come and see it all," he told me. "And bring you this."

He handed me an envelope.

"What's this?" I asked him.

"A royalty check."

"You could have mailed it to me."

I opened it and discovered a check for five thousand dollars, which I folded and put into my pocket.

"We've been keeping our eyes on you," he told me. "There are big things in the works."

I didn't know quite what he meant by this, but I didn't sense anything foreboding about it. After he left, Beth took me aside and told me, "I don't like this man. He frightens me." But she wouldn't elaborate further about him.

In the weeks that followed, as I began to nurture the business like a first-time father, Beth began to yearn for her own child. I could see it in her face whenever customers with young children came into the store. She would delight in their small round faces, and even when they seemed unruly, she was amused by them. Once when a couple came in to buy a radio, their young daughter, who was no more than four years old, kept following Beth around the store and playfully stopping a few inches behind her as though she was a shadow. After almost ten minutes of this game, when the young girl least expected it, Beth grabbed her and lifted her into the air, and then both of them began laughing intensely. She didn't have to tell me what she wanted. Though, I was unprepared to start a family, afraid of the responsibility it entailed, I couldn't have ever refused her something that she truly desired, though we had yet to understand how difficult it would be for her to bring a child to term.

When she finally had confirmation in early August that she was in fact pregnant, I remember the joy which like a light shining over her face seemingly illuminated any room when she entered it. But from the onset there were complications.

Whether from a genetic defect or some trauma in early life, her womb seemed unable to hold the child. When she miscarried the baby in early October, she became convinced it was a punishment for past sins, that God was calling her to repentance, and she prayed even more fervently afterwards than before.

I thought it senseless to blame herself for some obvious physical defect, but when confronted about it, she would simply reply, "God gives us temptations to test and to strengthen us. He is teaching me patience."

"I don't believe in a God who causes miscarriages," I would retort.

"God doesn't cause the suffering which comes upon us, but He allows it for our spiritual benefit."

I saw little philosophical distinction between the two positions. It seemed more a semantic difference than a substantive one, and her persistent defense of this assertion only served to alienate me from her religious perspective. But I could see she was struggling to understand the loss in the only terms she knew how, like all of us.

As a way of consoling her, I assured her we would try again as soon as she felt ready, but she insisted she must pray and fast with greater fervor, and she began to live with an austerity and asceticism that I had never known.

Often when we would return late in the evenings from the store, she would not have tasted food all day, and she would prepare boiled rice and vegetables, which she ate without seasoning, and she would sit stoically reciting her prayers in Greek. Whenever I tried to interrupt her to tell her how ridiculous it all seemed to me, as though hypnotized, she would not respond until after she had finished, and then would usually tell me, "I must be more fervent."

"God doesn't expect this out of you," I remember responding to her. "If you're sick, you see a medical doctor."

It was in those moments I realized I had no inkling of how she saw things, because my own cultural conditioning prevented me from understanding her.

I often became angry because she expected the same austerity from me, and I remember on several occasions snapping back at her when I found the same ascetic cuisine upon the table.

"I'm sick and tired of eating like this," I scolded her. "I can't work without more food."

I know it must have been difficult for her, having grown accustomed to a particular lifestyle and set of circumstances and then finding me challenging her almost every day, and I found myself growing ever more isolated from her church, attending more out of obligation to her than conviction. The glamour and prestige of television proved too seductive for me to resist. In a subtle way it was transforming me much as it was transforming the world, and soon Beth made it obvious that this disturbed her.

I remember how fervently I fought to buy this red sports car, and how earnestly Beth argued against such ostentation. But I was immovable and bought it despite her objections. Then, I drove it at speeds both reckless and unwise. It was as though something outside myself had taken control of my will and was remaking me in its image. I became arrogant and self-important and carried myself as though I were a demigod, and Beth witnessed this transformation with anxious impotence, unable, despite her character, to bring me to my senses.

As the weeks drew into months and business at the store began to exceed its capacity, I became more convinced an expansion was in order. But I needed a more visible presence to accelerate my growth. I can't recall who proposed it, or whether it was self-originated, but the idea occurred to me to advertise, but not in radio as some had recommended, but in the very same medium I sought to promote.

When I contacted the various agencies to determine cost, and I realized how expensive they were, I resolved to produce the spots myself. But I had to come up with some gimmick to make my commercials memorable. I remember struggling for days to come up with just the right slogan, just the right approach, but I had never been very creative and after countless attempts at writing a commercial, I began to realize that it wasn't as easy as it seemed. There were reasons the agencies could charge what they charged! I remember late nights as I struggled with the finances, trying to be both bookkeeper and entrepreneur. Beth told me, "You're working too hard. You must rest." Many times she found me asleep at my desk, and she'd struggle to carry me back to our bed. Often I could see the concern in her eyes and from the fervency of her evening prayers, how much she worried about me. But convinced success is only born in great struggle, I persisted.

I knew we needed a store in a more visible location, somewhere in midtown where tourists might see it. But our finances precluded this. "Patience," I kept telling myself. "Have patience." Yet it seemed an impossible virtue to cultivate.

Beth kept telling me, "Maybe it's not God's will that we be larger than we are. We should be satisfied with what we have." But I didn't believe this, no more than I had believed my father when he talked about the farm. I wanted more, much more, though I couldn't have said why. It was in one of these moments of agitation, too fatigued to work and too wound up to sleep, that the idea came to me about the commercials.

I had an image regurgitated from my mind reading days as though looking at myself from a distance. How ridiculous I looked, how awkward a spectacle, and I started to laugh at myself. "Why not resurrect the mind reader?" a voice seemed to be coaching me.

"But as a symbol of farce."

And I began to imagine myself standing in costume and pointing at televisions, and it amused me. The more I thought about it the more it amused me. It was cleansing, almost like purging myself. So I set about to find out how I might make a television commercial. It would be the next logical step in my determined self-promotion.

Even though the spots were to last no more than a minute or so, it was a minute which stood between me and success, and before I stood before the cameras, I knew I had to be prepared. For many nights prior to my first attempts, Beth stood by with a watch timing me as I went through my routine, sometimes as much as thirty to forty times.

I remember one of the first spots I did for a children's show on Saturday mornings. All television was live in those days, and when I arrived at the studio about half an hour before the show began, I was extremely nervous. The studio reminded me of a cattle market with people running in all directions, some pulling large equipment from place to place, and others scattering like mice, like when a cat rushes into the room. I kept pacing back and forth in the midst of it all, wearing a robe and turban with a fake goatee glued to my chin. Almost chanting, I went through my lines, "I'm Max," I rehearsed, waving my arms as I had practiced. "It doesn't take a mind reader to see the power of television." Several people stopped to stare at me as I went through my routine. "But I can see a television in your future."

I felt ridiculous, and when several of them began to chuckle, the embarrassment proved unbearable. I remember walking timidly to a chair near the back of the studio and sitting there until the director gave me my cue.

"You're on in five," he told me and I staggered from nervousness to my mark.

Then, I stood beneath the hot studio lights and was bathed in sweat as they counted down my cue.

"Five. Four. Three. Two. One," a technician counted. "You're on." Then a camera turned toward me and I began.

I really don't remember what I said. I was like a trained parrot mouthing words I had been rigorously taught, and when I finished, I felt tremendous relief as though the executioner's hand had lost its grip. It was a terror which never abated in over a hundred times in front of the cameras. Afterwards, the director came to me and told me, "You can stay and see the rest of the show, if you like." But I was anxious to get home again and diplomatically declined.

When I returned to the store, I found Beth quietly cleaning.

"How was it, Neilos?" she asked me.

"I don't know. It was all so new to me."

It was obvious that she felt apprehensive about what I was doing. I could see it in her eyes, but she never spoke a word of criticism, though there would be times I wish she had.

The first few times I did these commercials, I couldn't see a noticeable improvement in business. We sold many more radios than televisions, and I found myself repairing everything from old Victrolas to cuckoo clocks. But after the fourth or fifth, customers came in joking about the advertisements, and I could see it was having a beneficial effect. Through the remaining months of 1948, I produced ten such commercials and I saw a threefold improvement in sales. It was in mid-December that I again approached the banks about getting a loan.

I remember sitting nervously, waiting impatiently for this loan officer to finish with another customer. He had this serious look with his reading glasses balanced precariously on his ears, and he reminded me of those Norman Rockwell paintings from the Saturday Evening Post.

"You're that Max guy," he told me when I took the seat across from him. "I saw you on the television."

"Yes, I am."

"My children really get a kick out of you."

I could see that he was likewise amused.

"I can see a television in your future," he made a caricature of my speech.

"Do you own a television?" I asked him.

"No. But my sister does. The price is still too steep for me."

"It's a matter of volume," I responded. "The more we sell, the lower the price."

He explained to me how to fill out the loan application.

"Do you plan on making more of those television commercials?"

"I don't know, I haven't much thought about it."

I was surprised at his adulatory response to me, as though I were some sort of celebrity.

"You forgot to write what you want the loan for."

I quickly scribbled, "Midtown T.V. Store," in the blank.

I was surprised how quickly the loan was approved. Then it became a matter of finding the right place. I resolved to begin looking the following Saturday.

Early in the morning, Beth and I took the subway into the City, and we walked for three hours from Park Avenue and Thirty-fourth to Sixth Avenue and Fifty-ninth. Staring into windows as a tourist might, I tried to imagine televisions and the same crowds of people staring in at them. But Beth seemed more interested in window shopping.

When we stopped beside a window filled with baby furniture, I watched her staring expectantly into the window.

"I think I'm ready to try again," she told me.

"A child right now?"

"Yes, now."

There were a hundred reasons I could give for waiting, each seemingly more reasonable than the last, but I could not deny her heart's desire, so I responded succinctly, "Alright." As we continued walking down Fifth Avenue, she squeezed my hand tightly in hers.

"Why not there?" she pointed to an empty store front sandwiched between two clothing stores.

"It's a little small," I responded. "But it's probably what we can afford."

I jotted down the number from the "For Lease" sign. And it finally was this store we leased at the corner of Fifth Avenue and Thirty-Ninth Street.

It was around Christmas time in 1948 that I first opened the store on Fifth Avenue. In many ways it resembled the store in Bensonhurst, with its rows of radios and a T.V. in the front window, but I had a sign custom made and hoisted above the front doorway. It read "Max's" in huge letters nearly a foot high, and I had a caricature of myself in goatee and turban painted beside them. This I did in tribute to the commercials because they had made the new store possible. This caricature I would later register as a trademark and it would appear in the signs of all thirty-five stores, on our stationery, and in all our printed advertisements.

As I worked unceasingly toward my goal of selling ever larger numbers of televisions, Beth prayed earnestly and humbly for a child. As I grew more confident through each new success, I could see her disappointment etched as though in glass across her face.

"Neilos," she had often told me. "Each child is a blessing from God." I nodded in acknowledgment, seemingly unable, despite my successes, to give her what she truly desired.

"Who am I to question God's wisdom?" she once told me. "He has his reasons." But I could see in her face as always she blamed herself. Each day her prayers seemed to go unanswered only seemed to make her more zealous in her faith.

From 1949 to 1953, I saw my business grow tenfold. Two stores had grown into seven, with plans of opening seven more. I saw my net worth grow to nearly a million dollars, but even then I could see it was becoming too much for me to handle.

The tape clicked off.

Chapter 29

Jim held in his hands the last cassette, the one he hoped would give closure to this story and make sense out of everything which had come before. His fatigue was incessant, but he knew the foe which awaited him was more relentless than fatigue, and he forced himself to concentrate. He looked inside the cupboard to see if he could find some coffee, which once found, he placed inside a coffee maker atop the kitchen counter. As he filled the pitcher with water at the sink, he stared outside at the dimly lit garage behind the house, and he remembered the tortured car which was hidden behind its enameled doors. So much about this house had not been what he anticipated. He was afraid, as afraid he had ever been, because he knew Wilson was laying a trap for him like a python encircling its coils around him and in its slow compression squeezing every breath from him. As the coffee pot began a low-pitched hiss, he again turned on the player, while watching the pot drop-by-drop begin to fill with coffee.

In early March of 1953, my mother wrote me from Wisconsin that my cousin Michael, who had been working as a prosecutor in Green Bay since graduation from law school, was restless to move on, and would I object to finding him something to do in my television business. I wrote back that I'd be glad to have him, but that I really didn't need a lawyer. This would later prove to be another bitter irony.

Over dinner one night I told Beth about their plans.

"My mother wants my cousin, Michael, to help me with the stores."

"I don't know about him, Neilos. He unsettles me."

"I know he's intense. He's always been intense."

"It's like there is a fire inside of him," she continued. "You can see it in his eyes."

I thought it silly at the time. But I could sense, despite her misgivings, she saw in him a competent reinforcement who might make it possible for me to slow down.

"Where would he stay?" she asked me.

"Why he could stay with us," I proposed.

"No. It would not be good."

"Then I will find a place for him."

She nodded in assent. That Michael only saw us as a stepping stone to greater glory, I hadn't considered, because I hardly knew him before he arrived.

It was sometime late in April or early May when he arrived by airplane. I drove out to meet him in a brand new blue convertible, while Beth remained in Bensonhurst working at the store.

When I saw him standing at the ramp with a black duffle bag hung over his left shoulder, he looked afraid. In all the years, it was the only time I could recall him ever looking afraid. What was going through his mind, I could only guess. When I pulled up beside him, he smiled at me, but with the same disconcerting smile that characterized his later years.

"Well, I'm in the Big Apple," were his first words.

He tossed the duffle bag into the back of the car and hopped over the door into the seat next to mine.

"Where to first?" I asked him.

"I'd like to see the Empire State Building."

It seemed a rather odd request upon just arriving.

"Alright," I responded. "I'll take you there."

Then we drove from the airport and crossed over to Manhattan on the 59th Street Bridge.

Once on the observation deck on the 102nd floor, he made several rotations, looking across Manhattan in every direction. He seemed obsessed as though earnest to study every minute detail.

And then after about an hour, almost as abruptly as we had arrived, he told me, *"OK. I've seen enough. Can we leave now?"*

"Sure."

And without a word of further clarification, we were on our way down the elevator.

"Is everything all right, Michael?"

"Of course."

"What were you looking at up there?"

"I was memorizing it all."

On the half hour ride back to Bensonhurst, I struggled to extract meaning from his statement, but he confounded me. I was beginning to *realize Michael's mind did not operate like anyone else's, that coursing beneath the surface of what he was willing to vocalize were complex currents of meaning that only he understood. When I took Michael to the small studio apartment which I had rented for him, he seemed disconnected. He didn't say a word until I opened the door for him and gave him his keys.*

"I hope it is sufficient for your needs," I told him.

"We all have great needs," he responded. "And we struggle with insufficiency."

I didn't know what to make of the remark, whether he was just trying to be odd or joking in some way. I stood for a moment thinking he might clarify himself, but he said nothing else.

"Here is the address where my offices are and our apartment is only two blocks from here. You're welcome to come over whenever you like." I handed him a piece of paper with all the relevant information which he folded awkwardly and stuffed in his pocket. Then he grinned for the first time, saying, "Tell Beth thank you for everything." We shared an awkward handshake, and I departed. The whole experience unsettled me.

When I returned to the Bensonhurst store, Beth was pouring coffee and talking to customers. She smiled when she saw me.

"Well, he's here," I told her.

"You took him to the apartment?"

"Yes, but first he wanted to see the Empire State Building." I paused. "He unsettles me."

"It's difficult to be so bright," she explained. "Temptation is all around him."

"He said to tell you thank you for everything."

The next morning I took him around to see several of the stores, and finally to the office I had rented downtown on Court Street. When I opened the doors of my small cluttered offices, it was obvious he was disappointed. He had expected a secretary and a well-decorated suite, but I had papers everywhere, several broken televisions on shelves, a small brown toolbox opened with tools scattered around it, and the robe and turban hung on an old coat rack in the corner of the room. His eyes seemed fixed on the coat rack.

"This is where you work?" he asked me.

"Yes." In a small way it was reminiscent of the shed where I spent

so many hours as a boy.

"Who keeps your books?" he asked me.

"I do."

He walked around the office, apparently taking inventory of everything in his mind.

"Where do you keep your incorporation papers?"

I looked at him in bewilderment.

"You don't mean to tell me you're not incorporated after all these years?"

"No," I responded. "I'm not really a business man."

He put his hand to his chin and I could see in his eyes that he wanted to tell me something, but was restraining himself.

"You must know the benefits of incorporation."

"I hadn't really thought about it."

Then he began to explain to me in excruciating detail all the advantages of incorporation, from revenue and tax benefits, to legal protection of my private assets. But I found none of this important.

"All I'm really interested in is selling televisions," I responded to him.

From his posture and the way he moved his arms I could see he was impatient with me, but I didn't want to argue with him. Though ten years my junior, he obviously believed himself a superior businessman, and partly because I wanted him to be useful to me and partly for my mother's sake, I acquiesced. "Alright. Let's incorporate." It would be the beginning of an ongoing struggle over which direction the business should take.

During the next few days as Michael painstakingly pored over my books, I began to rehearse for another series of television commercials. I hoped these would push us over the threshold to even greater exposure.

"You really should have an accountant go over these books," he told me one morning. "I can't make sense out of half of these entries. And what are these asterisks you keep putting here?" He pointed at the books.

"Those are loans I've made to various employees. Advances on salaries and gifts."

"You can't be operating as a loan company for your employees. There are regulations. And it simply doesn't make business sense."

"I'm making money. Am I not?"

"Of course, but you could be doing substantially better if you just used a few accounting principles."

I sensed he must have thought me incompetent because he kept pointing out more efficient and business-wise ways to do what I was doing, but he didn't understand I was living a dream, in a way trying to keep Leonard's dream alive. I didn't want to feel constrained by a rigorous adherence to standard business practices.

"If you can tighten up the finances, Michael, you're more than welcome."

"I'll do what I can."

Within a week he had composed a ten-point list of recommendations for improving efficiency in the stores, and after a cursory glance at these recommendations, I approved them all.

Even then, one could see the powerful intellect which would often characterize him in his later years. But despite the fact I had given him an almost free reign to make whatever changes he deemed necessary to improve our performance, I could sense in him the same restlessness that my mother had written about in her letter. He was never satisfied with whatever situation he had in life, and he was constantly looking for greater opportunities to satisfy this sense of insufficiency.

I remember a dinner we shared together only a few weeks after he had arrived in New York. Beth had labored feverishly to prepare a wide selection of Greek delicacies, and when Michael finally arrived at our apartment, he spent most of the evening sitting in a chair, staring almost trance-like into a religious painting which Beth had placed on the table.

When she approached him to encourage him to come to the table to eat, he seemed unable to hear her, his mind apparently focused on the painting. She shook his shoulder to arouse him.

"Michael, is everything all right?" She asked him.

"This isn't like life at all. It rejects two thousand years of history of art in the west."

Beth smiled.

"It's like the perspective is inverted," he continued.

"It's how God sees us. Icons are like windows into heaven." she explained to him. "Michael, come to the table and eat."

He laid the painting aside and walked stoically to the table. He kept this demeanor throughout most of the meal.   Several times Beth attempted to coax him out of himself. She asked him questions about law school, "How was it? Did he find it difficult?" He seemed reticent to answer her. She asked him about his work as a prosecutor. He seemed willing to discuss important cases he had won, but not his personal feelings about them. She even asked him, "Are you seeing anyone in New York? Do you have a girlfriend back home?" She seemed determined to make him reveal himself, but Michael evaded all her inquiries with consummate skill. By evening's end, we knew no more about his personal circumstances than when he arrived.

As the weeks progressed into months, and Michael began to work at reorganizing the business, I could see an obvious improvement in our finances. And I decided to use some of the extra money to finance more commercials. It had been over four years that I had been playing "Max" in exaggerated style, mocking myself as a mind-reader and each slogan had become second nature to me.

"I can see televisions in your future."

"Max knows as only he can know that you need a TV."

"Come down to Max's. We always have the lowest prices, because we know our competitors' prices before they do."

I would stand before the cameras and recite these lines in abject terror, counting the seconds before the cameras went off. But this character had become so integral to the mythology of the stores, I didn't see how I could extricate myself from him, though I wanted to.

As Michael set about to reorganize everything in the stores, it became obvious to me that we had very different visions for the business. He wanted exponential growth with numerous new stores, in a word, an empire. But I was satisfied with the status quo, to be a small voice among many. Day by day, step by step, I could see that he was challenging my authority and usurping my position. I don't know if it was conscious on his part, or if he needed control so desperately that he couldn't help himself, but I began to believe that I had to put the brakes on his ambition, or I'd find myself pushed out of my own business.

I remember lamenting to Beth one evening, "Michael doesn't even consult me before making decisions anymore."

"Then talk to him about it," she told me. "He can't know where the boundaries are, if you have not set them."

"He's smarter than I am and better educated."

"It's your business, Neilos." She paused. "I shall pray about it."

But I didn't think prayer could solve the problem.

In Mid-June, David came from the city again to check up on me, and I introduced him to Michael. I hadn't foreseen the easy rapport that would develop between them. Within half an hour, they were conversing with such animation that one could easily see they were kindred spirits.

"You should come to lunch in the City," David told him. "I can give you a tour of our operations."

"I've been very busy with the stores," Michael responded. "It's difficult for me to find the time."

"Certainly, Nigel can give you some time off," David told him as though I were the cause of his zeal.

"Alright, next Wednesday," Michael proposed.

David smiled and agreed, "Next Wednesday."

In temperament, in outlook and in background, they seemed more suitable companions. Michael would find in David a more powerful mentor and David in his younger protégé an avid disciple. It now seems inevitable what would later come to pass.

For months, I had been dissatisfied with Michael's handling of the business, though I couldn't bring myself to confront him about it. Of course, we had become more successful, more than my expectations, but in his gradual encroachment of my space, he had pushed me out of the day to day details, and I felt consigned to only superfluous tasks, such as making the ridiculous television commercials. The culmination of this process came when he pushed me out of even that.

I came into the office one morning and found Michael sitting and talking with another man whose face seemed eerily familiar.

"Good Morning," Michael greeted me. "This is Tom Jacobson." He paused. "Nigel Fox."

We both shook hands.

"He's an actor, Nigel. I've hired him to do the television commercials, to take the pressure off of you."

"This man is going to do my commercials?" Then I realized he resembled me.

"Yes. You told me you never liked doing them. I thought it a suitable solution."

"No, no way. I do my own commercials."

"It's really not appropriate that the head of this corporation should be making a fool of himself this way. If I had my way, we'd stop doing them altogether. They're redundant."

"Do I have any say left in my own business?"

"Of course, Nigel. I'm just trying to help you."

I was overwhelmed. Then I took the actor aside and told him, *"Could you please step outside a few minutes."*

He got up and left the room and I closed the door behind him.

"I can't do this any more." The words just popped out of my mouth. *"You're fired."*

"I'm family for God's sake. I'm not some employee. You can't just fire me."

"I can, and I do. I don't want you here any more. Take your things and go."

I was afraid I'd say something worse.

"I don't know why I've bothered with you. There are certainly greener pastures elsewhere, and I don't have to work in this penny-ante television business." He paused. *"You don't have to fire me. I quit."*

He grabbed his overcoat and bag and left the office, slamming the door behind him. Standing outside in the hall, the actor was obviously stunned by the whole encounter. I came outside and told him, *"I'm sorry about the misunderstanding. But I really don't have need of your services."* Then we shared an awkward handshake, and he departed. Afterwards, I felt terrible.

I remember staring for what seemed liked hours at his empty chair in the corner and pondering if I had made the right decision. That I was throwing him into the waiting hands of Jamison and the others, I hadn't even considered, nor could I have possibly known what that would entail. I was too wrapped up in my own concerns to even think about it.

When I went home to Beth that evening, my feelings of remorse had not abated, and Beth, as always, could immediately sense something was wrong.

"What happened, Neilos?" she greeted me at the door with a kiss on the cheek.

"Michael and I had a disagreement, and I fired him today."

"Let him go. It's better for him."

"All I wanted him to do was give me my space. Maybe I should go over and talk to him."

"He has his own path to take." Then she said something in Greek which I did not understand. *"Please, Neilos. Sit down,"* she told me, and she led me to the kitchen table where she had placed two slices of cake and had poured two glasses of wine.

"What's going on here?" I remember asking her.

"Sit down," she encouraged me.

I slowly lowered myself onto the cushion of the chair and propped my elbows upon the table top.

"I'm pregnant." She told me. At first, it didn't register.

"I'm going to have a baby."

Her face was ebullient, even ecstatic.

"You're sure about this?"

"Of course, I'm sure. I saw the doctor today."

I could see in her face the fulfillment of seven years of fervent longing, as though God had vindicated her in the end, and two small pools of tears, like soup bowls toppled over, poured down both of her cheeks. I remember she embraced me and told me, "I shall not lose this baby." I was so surprised. I didn't know what to say.

That evening, she was the happiest I'd ever seen her and she began to make plans about what she would buy for the child. There would be cradles and rockers, and diapers, and eventually a house where the child could play.

The next morning, I went to Michael's apartment to see if I could talk to him, and I found it vacant with a note posted to the door. "Thank you for everything you've done for me," it read. "But I must find my own way, Michael."

The finality of it all unsettled me, and I remember walking through the apartment and thinking how empty it seemed, but with an emptiness, as though its soul had dissipated. Then when I returned to the office and again saw his empty chair in the corner, I felt regret, the deepest regret I had ever felt. Now I often wonder what would have become of Michael if I hadn't shoved him out the door.

The weeks which followed were filled with restless anticipation. As Beth began to struggle with what would become a difficult pregnancy, I began to sort out what Michael had left me. There were so many decisions he had made without advising me that for three weeks I found myself floating on a sea of paperwork without a clue as to what he had done. Between the assorted bills and invoices, I found three new store leases, two in North Bronx, and one in Bayside Queens. And I found the incorporation papers.

For curiosity's sake, I decided to drive out to Bayside to see what type of place that Michael had leased. It was over an hour drive, and I could see the city melting away into a sea of small detached houses lined in neat rows like children's blocks. When I arrived on Northern Boulevard, I found a suburban, almost rural environment with natural trees and well-trimmed lawns. It was just the type of place I knew Beth would like, and I remember sight-seeing a few minutes while I struggled to find the address. When I found the building on the corner of Northern Boulevard and Bell Boulevard, I realized it was a perfect location, and I began to imagine hundreds of the surrounding houses with families gathered around their televisions, my televisions. And I realized what a stroke of brilliance Michael's choice had been. This store would prove to be the most successful of them all.

I remember walking around the inside of the vacant store, staring outside through the front windows at the traffic on Northern Boulevard, and thinking how marvelous it was. I felt part of something bigger than myself, as though I were a channel through which this powerful transforming force was pulsating. But of course, I couldn't see the end-product of it all.

Afterwards, I drove around the area. I stared at houses like a real estate broker until, almost unconsciously, I found myself passing in front of the house which would later be our first home. There was a 'For Sale' sign on a stake hammered into the ground, and I pulled up to the curb and stopped. I remember climbing out of the car and walking up the lawn toward the house. I had this eerie feeling of connectedness, as though somehow it all made sense; and I must have stood on the lawn with my eyes transfixed on the house in front of me. Like everything else, there seemed this spooky familiarity about it all, almost like a memory, but with only partial recognition. I struggled to connect it to something, like a photograph I may have seen, or some image I may have imagined, but it only felt more dreamlike. Finally, I jotted down the phone number from the sign, and I resolved to bring Beth out to see it as soon as possible.

On the car ride back to Bensonhurst, I kept thinking about the house, as though it were a puzzle I was determined to unravel, but despite my intense analysis, I could not string it all together. I decided to set it aside for further reflection.

The next day I brought Beth out to see the house. By this time, she was five months pregnant and was just recovering from a two-month spell of morning sickness. When she saw the house, I could see it pleased her.

"Well, do you like it?" I asked her.

"Yes." She paused. "Very much."

"Then we can buy it?"

"Of course."

Then she hugged me. After we walked around the house for a few more minutes, we climbed into the car, and I still felt the same sensation of familiarity, but I pushed it from my mind. It would be months after we moved in before I was finally able to piece together where I had seen the house before. It was in those vivid and horrifying nightmares I had experienced after I was struck by the car. In the background, behind the field of weeping corn, stood a house very much like this one, though I didn't understand then why this was significant.

As I made final preparations to purchase the house, Beth began diligently organizing everything in our Bensonhurst apartment. I had never seen her happier, and it seemed as though our lives were gliding effortlessly toward inevitable comfort, like a sailboat blown by the wind. I remember thinking at the time how fortunate we were. After having known struggle and uncertainty for most of my early years in New York, I began to feel complacent and I liked it. I knew that television was becoming ever more successful. I could see the evidence of its pervasive conquest in something as simple as antennas mounted like religious artifacts on the rooftops.

In mid January of 1954, just as we were beginning to move, a terrible snowstorm came. On the farm, they would have thought it an omen, but I had long before dismissed such superstitions. By eight o'clock that evening, six inches of snow was on the ground and more was falling.

With furniture and boxes scattered throughout the house in random chaos, Beth began to search for the box of religious paintings. Once she found them in the hallway, she set about finding appropriate places to hang them.

"Is it necessary you put up these paintings now?" I remember asking her.

Jim arose from the chair to stretch his legs. He could feel the weight of the night upon him, but was determined to hear it all despite his fatigue. He began to look at the religious paintings hanging in the kitchen.

"They're icons," she responded. She pronounced the 'i' like a long 'e'. "They're not paintings."

I picked one up to look at it, and I remembered what Michael had said about the perspective being all wrong.

"They are painted, aren't they?" I remember playing with her. But she took the subject with total seriousness.

"Icons are written," she explained. "They're images. Like windows into heaven."

"So when I look at one of these, what am I supposed to see?"

I held it out resting on the palm of my right hand.

"Resurrected humanity."

"Then it's a little like cosmic television."

I could see she didn't find my humor amusing.

"You shouldn't joke about such things."

"I'm sorry."

But humor had become a way I dealt with the constant stream of religious information. That night she prayed as fervently as I had ever seen her pray, largely, I believed, because of me. I'm sure I must have seemed to her the most reckless of pagans.

During the next couple of weeks, as one snowstorm followed upon another, Beth began the difficult task of putting the house in order. Though nearly seven months pregnant, and obviously struggling just to move, she found the strength in herself to unpack, while I spent the evenings moving furniture, carrying boxes upstairs, and papering the walls in what was to become the baby's nursery. All this we did in the evenings while during the day I was struggling with my own chaos in the Bayside store.

In February, she ordered a walnut cradle similar to the one she had seen in midtown so many years before. And one evening I came home to find her with screwdriver in hand attempting to put it together on the living room floor.

"What's gotten into you?" I remember scolding her. "You're not supposed to be putting together furniture."

"Don't worry, Neilos," she responded to me. "I'm not pressing myself too much."

She seemed determined to have everything ready in time, and I could see she was completely carried away in her excitement. When the weather cleared for a weekend in mid March, she insisted that we go out and purchase sheets, diapers and linens for the nursery, and I remember how she almost fell to the ground on a patch of ice, and how I zealously rushed to catch her before the slipped onto the ground. The last month seemed to be the most anxious of them all.

In early April, as the first buds began to push themselves outward from the branches, for the first time in years I began to take notice of Spring. On the farm, I couldn't help but be in harmony with nature's rhythms, when springtime meant escape from the prison of our houses. But in the city, nature proved much easier to ignore, and I had ignored it, aided and abetted by technology.

At the store in Bayside, despite the winter, business had been brisk with sales consistently reaching twenty sets a week, and as the weather grew warmer, it had grown to thirty sets, and with combined sales of the other eleven stores, I was easily becoming the largest distributor of televisions in the metropolitan area. That such an empire had grown from such modest beginnings, I owed largely to Michael, but he had been as silent after his departure as before.

I remember the day the reporter came to interview me. It was two weeks before Beth's due date and I was busy in the office in Brooklyn, trying to coordinate the opening of our thirteenth store in Paramus, New Jersey. He knocked softly on the door, and smiled.

"Mr. Fox."

"Yes," I answered.

"I'm Frank James with the Daily News. *I called you earlier in the week about an interview in our 'Profile' section."*

I searched my desk and found his message buried beneath a stack of invoices.

"Yes, it's here."

"We have an appointment at three o'clock."

He could see I was very distracted.

"Look, I see I've come at an inopportune time. We can reschedule this."

"No. Please sit down. It'll be just a few more minutes."

He seemed no more than twenty-two when he took a seat across from me.

"As I told you on the telephone, I'm doing a series on television and I thought it would be a good idea to get a profile on the distribution side."

I had completely forgotten about our conversation.

"So, what do you want to know?"

"Everything," he answered me.

"Everything about television distribution or everything about me?"

"Everything. Just tell me how you got involved in the television business."

The prospect of distilling so involved a story frightened me, but I resolved to tell him as much as I could remember. For nearly an hour and a half, I related how I met Leonard, our early days in the radio shop, the radio training during the war, and culminating with the distribution contract with Jamison Electronics. He took copious notes, while nodding in acknowledgment to the host of points I made, and when we finished I felt a genuine rapport between us. When the article appeared a couple of weeks later, Beth was very close to delivering the baby, and I took only a cursory glance at it. Overall, it seemed quite positive, and I could see he even put a short discussion of my involvement with Leonard Matthews. I hadn't a clue what I had set in motion.

Jim was taking deliberate sips of his second cup of coffee when the tape clicked off. His eyes were slipping in and out of focus, and he began to rub them. He sensed it was around three in the morning, but he didn't have the strength to look at a clock to verify this. More than anything else, he wanted to sleep, but he was determined to hear everything before morning. With his hands shaking from exhaustion, he flipped the cassette over and turned it on.

Even though it was difficult for her, Beth insisted that April that we attend as many services as possible for Easter, or as the Greeks called it, Pascha. I could have argued with her. I certainly had enough work at the stores to keep me busy, but her silent persuasiveness, as always, prevailed.

"Neilos," I remember her urging me. "We must pray fervently for our son's health."

How she knew he was a boy still bewilders me.

During Holy Week, we attended all of the services from early Monday morning to late Friday night. In the space of those few days, I learned much about the Christian Gospel, more so than in the years which passed in between, but I still was unconnected to it, unable for whatever reason to completely commit myself to it.

I remember Beth trying to explain to me every aspect of the services, how the ritual, symbolism, and theatrics of it all were designed to involve the whole person in the events being depicted in order to make the events of two thousand years before as real and immediate as though we were really there. "This is the goal of our worship," she earnestly explained to me, "to involve all of the senses, to create a community through our common worship together."

It seems quite obvious to me now that this was what television was doing—creating a community in much the same way, using much the same methods.

I remember that Pascha, when at nearly midnight, with the whole congregation of faithful standing outside the front doors of the darkened church and each holding a candle like the myrrh-bearing women first arriving at the empty tomb. The priest began to shout, "Christos Anesti." which means "Christ is Risen." And the congregation responded, "He is truly risen." And then they began to sing the familiar Greek hymn, announcing his resurrection. It was at this moment, as Beth was shouting near the top of her voice, "Alithos Anesti" that her water broke.

"Neilos, it's time," she told me.

I was so caught up in the moment that I didn't realize what she was saying. Then I could see from her expression that something was wrong.

"Neilos," she repeated. "It's time."

I could see the pool of water on the ground. I remember helping her to our car and then frantically driving her to the hospital. All the while, she held her prayer rope tightly in her fingers, patiently counting out her prayers.

"Are you all right?" I asked her.

"I'm having a baby. Please let me pray."

Then she continued praying more fervently through each painful contraction. When we arrived at the hospital, I left the engine running and rushed inside.

"My wife is having a baby. Please, someone help me," I was practically shouting. And a young nurse approached me.

"Where is she?" she asked, apparently thinking I had forgotten Beth somewhere.

"She's outside in the car."

When we returned together, Beth was still praying, her face contorted by the pain, and the nurse helped me take her out of the car. Then someone else brought her a wheelchair, and they wheeled her away between two large double doors. I stood there a moment in a dream-like haze, until someone led me away into a small waiting room where a half dozen other expectant fathers were anxiously waiting out the news.

I could see the others pacing nervously, some smoking cigarettes while the mystery of birth was hidden behind closed doors. One man, apparently trying to occupy his mind with some diversion, turned on a television that was in the room and he began to watch whatever was on. Soon we all were watching it as though hypnotized. I thought it strange how little television I could remember watching, considering how I made my living, but I found little time for leisure. In fact, the television sitting in our parlor had been on only a handful of times since the day I brought it home, and, as far as I could remember, Beth had never watched it. But there in the hospital, I was captivated just like the others, finding myself laughing at all the same well-worn jokes, until it came time for the commercial spot, and of course it had to be one of my commercials. Having carefully evaded all prior broadcasts, I faced for the first time how ridiculous I looked, and I was never more grateful when it was finally over.

Then I remember how this man kept staring at me afterwards, as though he was trying to place my face somewhere. Finally, I admitted, *"Yes, I'm that crazy man from the television,"* and he turned his head away from me.

Three hours passed and I sat staring at a clock on the wall and watching each new father disappear as a nurse called him out of the room. Four times, I jumped up thinking she had come for me, only to *be disappointed. It seemed as if time itself had ceased and was trapped in the immanent present without reference to what had come before or after, and every noise in the room seemed amplified, from the sound of magazine pages being rifled, to the* click, click, click *of the second hand on the clock, and to my heartbeat and breathing. I thought of praying, but when I struggled for religious words, my mind drew blank; the only thought I could imagine was Beth alone in some sterile room, enduring the trauma without me, and this thought, over all the others, tortured me. Then finally, the nurse came for me.*

"Mr. Fox," she greeted me. I was disconnected.

"Mr. Fox," she repeated. "Your wife has had the baby."

"Is she all right? Did everything go well?"

"She's fine, and the baby's fine."

"Can I see her?"

"She'll be in recovery for about an hour. You can see her after that."

"And the baby?"

"Come, I'll let you get a peek at him." She led me down a hallway into the nursery, and there I could see them weighing him, and I couldn't help but cry.

Later, the same nurse took me to Beth's room where she was resting quietly in bed, her prayer book opened beside her. She looked tired, but I had never seen her happier.

"How do you feel?" I asked her.

"Exhausted," she answered. "But isn't he beautiful? Thoxa to Theo." She crossed herself. Then when a nurse brought the baby out to her, an expression of expectation illuminated her whole face. Then, holding him for the first time, she began to sing to him a lullaby in Greek.

"Let's call him Michael," she told me. "After my father."

"Whatever you want," I answered.

And she continued singing. That this light of joy would all too soon become extinguished, we could not possibly foresee.

I remember how excited she was the day we brought Michael home from the hospital. I had carefully re-papered the walls in this steam engine motif, and had repainted the trim sky blue. In one corner sat the walnut cradle with a down pillow and comforter and in another, an oak rocking chair with a dull red foam cushion. She had directed me where to hang icons throughout the room, and this huge one of Christ was mounted in the center of the eastern wall. Surrounding it were smaller icons of various saints and a larger one of St. Michael the Archangel, and in the right corner was this huge empty space where she hoped to hang a crucifix which she had ordered from a monastery in Greece, but which had yet to arrive.

From the car, she brought the baby into the house and then gently carried him up the stairs and laid him in his cradle. Then with her head only a few inches from the cradle, she began to sing to him again, this time the hymn to the Resurrection, which I remembered from the Easter service. Her voice glided gently through its cadences surfeited with tenderness and compassion.

In the days that followed, as we struggled to adjust to a new set of circumstances, I could see Beth flowering, opening as a blossom in the warm spring sun, and I didn't think I could love her more. She took to the task of being a mother, joyfully and patiently, as though some huge hole in her had been finally filled. And I remembered something my mother had said about children renewing her strength and making her useful because of their helplessness. Beth would say God gives us children to teach us to love.

Six weeks passed as quickly as a summer storm, and soon Beth began to make preparations for Michael's baptism. There were invitations to send, and a baptismal gown to buy, and a reception to arrange. She set about each task with great enthusiasm, while I labored till late at night to give order to the business.

I was beginning to disdain it—too many decisions to make and too many invoices to prepare. All the day-to-day details which Michael had managed while I pursued more creative outlets confronted me now each morning as I walked through the door. It no longer felt like living a dream, but more and more like a job. And I began to realize, as Leonard's memory was fading, that the stores had been my way of keeping him alive. In the void which Michael left me, I finally had to come to terms with Leonard's death.

In mid July 1954, we baptized Michael at a small ceremony at a Greek Church in Flushing New York. A young Greek Priest named Father Constantinos, who had just been ordained, performed the ritual. And I remember how worried Beth looked when he immersed Michael three times in the baptismal font, and Michael was screaming so loud that the glass windows of the church rattled. Afterwards, there was a small reception in the basement of the church.

After following behind all the others with my camera in hand, I remember turning my head and discovering that my cousin Michael had come. I had heard from someone that he had found a place in the City, and that he was working for Jamison Electronics, but I didn't know in what capacity, and I was deeply surprised at his sudden reappearance after what had been months of silence. I remember approaching Michael to talk with him.

I told him, "I'm sorry for the way things worked out. It wasn't the way I wanted it to end."

"That's all water over the dam," he responded. "I've found a new niche for myself."

"What are you doing with yourself?" I asked him.

"As much as possible." He paused. "A few of us are going down to Mississippi to register Negroes to vote. There are many changes coming."

"I heard you were working for Jamison Electronics?"

"I am. But Jimmy and I are taking leaves of absence to work for civil rights."

I didn't know who Jimmy was, but I could see Michael seemed sincere.

"How did you find out about the baptism?"

"I have my sources," he laughed. "Beth sent an invitation to the offices." He paused. "I have something for you." He reached into his pocket and removed a small gift box which he handed to me.

"Open it."

For the first time, I noticed the ring on his finger with the same triangular emblem which David Atkinson wore. I opened the package, and inside I found this small locket, a religious medal of some kind.

"Open it," he encouraged me. And when I opened the locket it played Brahms' lullaby.

Jim stopped the tape. He was stunned. He remembered how many times he had held his locket open in his hand while it played Brahms' lullaby. But he was still not convinced. Then he turned the tape back on.

I took the locket to Beth and showed it to her, and she smiled. I opened it to show her how it played. Then she approached Michael and kissed him on the cheek.

"Thank you," she told him. "I will always cherish it."

Michael would linger there only a few minutes more, and then with an awkward goodbye, he would soon depart. It would be the last time we saw him for years to come.

I can still remember that reception like a snapshot in my mind's eye. Beth was laughing and talking to Evgenia and Demetrios, while the baby, like a prized trophy was passed from person to person, each one anxious to hold him. Finally, someone passed him to me, and I lifted him into the air with his feet dangling beneath him.

"Be careful with him, Neilos," Beth exhorted me. "He's a baby."

Then she took him in her arms and nestled him.

For the next few days after that, I spent long hours in the Brooklyn office while making preparations for the arrival of a new model of Jamison's televisions. It was while in the office on August the second that I received the fateful phone call.

"Neilos," Beth was crying, obviously distraught. "They've taken him."

At first it didn't register.

"They've taken him," she was shouting. "I went inside the house to answer the phone, and when I came outside he was gone."

"Who would have taken him?"

"Neilos, they've taken him," she was almost hysterical.

I ran out of the office and down the hallway, and at a full sprint from the elevator, I dashed into the parking lot. I remember driving the car at speeds unheard of, thinking the whole way that it was all some big mistake, that when I arrived home, I would find her happily rocking Michael in her arms. But instead, I found her crying in the kitchen with the small cradle nestled like a baby.

"I put Michael outside with me to hang out some laundry," she began to explain. "I put the locket which Michael had given us around his neck, because he likes the music. Then the phone rang and I came inside, and when I came out, he was gone. My God, Neilos. They took our baby."

The phone was ringing in the kitchen, and I answered it.

"Hello."

"Mr. Fox. Nigel Fox," a harsh voice began to thrust at me.

"Yes."

"We have your baby."

"What do you want?"

"We want five hundred thousand dollars. We'll call you later with instructions where to deliver it. You mustn't call the police." He hung up the phone.

"It's the kidnappers," I told her. "They want five hundred thousand."

"Give it to them."

"I don't have five hundred thousand dollars just lying around. I'd have to sell the stores."

"Let's sell them," she pleaded. "Give them whatever they want. He's our baby."

"No, Beth. We have to call the police. They know how to handle these things."

I was determined to remain calm despite the horror of it all.

Within a half hour after calling them, an army of detectives descended upon the house and a special agent named McCracken took charge of the operation. He seemed cocksure and self-important, marching around the house while a team of technicians began searching the premises for clues. He kept assuring us that he had handled four such operations before, and in each instance, they had recovered the child. But I could see in Beth's eyes that she didn't believe him.

A younger special agent named Walter Bartholomew took me into the kitchen to ask me some questions.

"Mr. Fox," he began. "Do you have any enemies? Anyone who might want to take the child?"

"No," I responded. "There's no one I know who would do this to us."

"Any business rivals? Anyone to whom you owe a large sum of money? "

"Not that I can see."

"Think, Mr. Fox," he exhorted me. "Any information however trivial or unimportant could be the clue."

I stared into his boyish face and he reminded me of Leonard.

"It might be the loan shark." (This was the first time I had thought about it since the war.) "Leonard Matthews and I had a business *partnership before the war. We owed a loan shark a substantial amount of money, which I don't know if Leonard ever repaid."*

"Do you have Mr. Matthew's address or his telephone number?"

"He's been dead over seven years."

For the first time it occurred to me who might have murdered him, and I began to construct a complex chain of consequence inside my mind.

"You don't have any idea who this was?"

"Only Leonard knew." *I paused.* "I don't even think they knew who I was."

While we were talking in the kitchen, the technicians had placed a tap on our phone and we all waited anxiously for the next phone call. McCracken came in later with a brown attaché case, which he opened to show us inside.

"Our plan is really a simple one," *he began to explain to us.* "This case will carry the money. Inside is a small radio transmitter, which by triangulation we will use to track the kidnappers, eventually leading us to where they have the child."

"And you're sure this will work?"

"Of course," *he answered.*

I was dazed, my emotional responses muted by terror and disbelief. I could see Beth praying quietly, her face broadcasting her anxiety, but we were still hopeful it would all work out.

About two hours passed before the kidnapper called again. This time in a voice more demon-like, he began to rage, "I want no police. No publicity. You betray us and we'll make you pay. Leave the money at six o'clock P.M. at the entrance to track five at Grand Central Station. If we see any signs of the police, we'll forget it, and you'll never see your son again."

Agent McCracken put down the phone on which he was listening, while a technician who apparently was trying to trace the call shook his head to convey he had been unsuccessful.

"Why don't you just grab whoever gets the bag," *I remember suggesting to him,* "and just compel whoever it is to give up the information?"

"No. They must believe they've been successful. We have sophisticated electronic equipment to track them."

I knew from my years in the Navy that what was commercially available was often the lowest level of a given technology, and that the FBI had available to them the most sophisticated of equipment, but I still doubted the efficacy of their plan.

By four o'clock, I had managed to arrange the acquisition of the five hundred thousand. It seemed the easiest thing in the world to relinquish so much money, and despite assurances from the detective, I was prepared to lose it all.

At four-thirty, two radio trucks arrived up front, both disguised as phone company trucks. While I watched from the windows, as McCracken went outside to consult with the drivers, Beth was in our bedroom praying a paraklesis, *a long prayer exhorting the Virgin Mary to pray for Michael, and I moved to the bedroom and stood watching her, while a half dozen agents were combing the backyard for clues. One man apparently excited about something, held up for the others a short gold chain, which I recognized as the chain from the locket which Michael had given us. I could see him discussing it with several of his colleagues. Then he opened a small brown envelope and placed it inside.*

"These are the best men in the business," Bartholomew spoke and startled me. "You'd be surprised how many clues we can find, little things which the criminals often overlook."

"I don't care about clues. I want my son back."

"We'll get your son back."

But I didn't know if I could believe him.

At five o'clock, I left the house with the handle of the leather satchel held tightly in my hand. I climbed into the car, backed out of our driveway between the two parked trucks, and began the anxious drive into Manhattan. I remember staring as though hypnotized at the satchel sitting beside me, unable, despite intense effort to keep my eyes away from it. I kept thinking about how it resembled my father's bag which we had brought with him to the hospital, and a dozen intense emotions consumed me simultaneously.

As I crossed over the 59th Street Bridge in Long Island City and saw Manhattan rising like the Emerald City in front of me, I felt certain it had all been some huge mistake, that my father had been right after all.

Once on 42nd Street, I drove around the terminal in concentric circles, looking for a place to park until I found an open meter three blocks away. Then with deliberate and angst-filled steps, I entered into the cavernous terminal with my heart pushing blood in powerful surges through both temples. Then I walked to the entrance of track five and I stood like a reed against a river of rushing humanity coursing down the steps. Holding the bag close to my chest, I scanned the crowd of commuters in the irrational hope I might spot the kidnapper among the sea of faces. Then at a few minutes before six, I set the bag down beside me, and with an ambivalent gait I walked away from it. Within minutes it was gone, snatched by someone in the crowd.

And then the chase began. From every corner of the terminal I could see men running. One was carrying a field radio, and three others converged upon the entrance of track five. Then I saw a half dozen men converging on the front doors, and I reasoned they must have spotted him. I remember floating as though somnambulant toward those same doors when someone tapped me on the shoulder.

"Mr. Fox," he told me. "We've spotted him. He went outside through the front doors."

Then he led me outside to one of the radio trucks where we both climbed inside. It seemed almost surreal, with flashing lights and ringing bells, and technicians looking insect-like with their headsets pressed tightly against their ears. I can't adequately describe the pandemonium which surrounded me, but the agent assured me everything was under control.

Inside the truck ten minutes passed, and then I heard one of them acknowledge to another that the suspect had climbed into a cab on 61st Street. Then I felt the truck begin to move, though in the windowless box I could only guess our destination. We drove around for nearly thirty minutes while one of the men stared intensely at what looked like a radar screen in front of him. No one said a word to me. From the tone of the discourse of one the radio operators, I could sense that something was wrong, what I would later learn but could not see was that the taxi cab they were following was driving in erratic circles all over Manhattan. Finally, one of them blurted out the horrible realization, "He must be on to us. He's leading us around in circles." And from the expressions on their faces, I could see their plan was self-imploding. Then I felt the van pull to a stop, and the senior agent opened the doors.

We climbed outside. The taxi was parked a hundred yards away, and we both rushed toward it. Inside through the windows, I could see the open satchel emptied of the money and a typewritten note lying beside it. I stuck my head inside the open window but could not read it. Then the agent reached into the window with a pair of tongs and took it out.

It read, "Mr. Fox, we told you not to call the police and you betrayed us. We could kill your son and it would be over, but we've decided not to kill your son. Instead, we will insure he grows up somewhere and you will never know him."

I was consumed with rage.

"You bunch of damn incompetents," I began to shout, the words just pouring out of me. "You should have grabbed him when you had the chance. But no. Like a bunch of overgrown children, you had to play with your expensive toys."

"It isn't over yet," the senior agent assured me. "We have other resources to find the boy. We'll find him, Mr. Fox."

"I don't believe you. You couldn't find your way out of a paper bag." I paused. "Take me to my car. Just take me to my car."

Agent McCracken arrived a few minutes later with his team of investigators in tow, but I was too upset to talk to him. He read the note and examined the bag, and I could see that he was pleased with so many obvious clues, but I had lost my son, and I couldn't find any excitement in that. A few minutes later, one of the agents offered to drive me to my car.

When we arrived on 42nd Street and the agent stopped the car to let me out, he tried to console me, "Every resource at the Bureau's disposal will we utilized to find your son. It's not as hopeless as it might appear." But I knew with every muscle and sinew that he was mistaken.

The drive home to Bayside was the saddest in my life, and I cried as intensely as a child, and when I walked into the front door of the house, Beth came immediately from our bedroom to meet me. She could see that I was crying, but I couldn't bring myself to say it. I shook my head. Then she began to cry as passionately as she cried the night her brother died.

"Then it's God's will," she told me trying to regain herself. "Somehow it is His will."

"Damn it," I shouted. "It's not God's will that our child be

stolen."

And I stared into the living room at the television sitting on the floor and rage controlled me.

"It's all because of the television," I shouted.

Then I picked up a vase sitting on the mantle and tossed it through the screen. The picture tube shattered and shorted out. Then I grabbed the set and with almost superhuman strength carried it outside and threw it onto the back lawn, and I kicked it. Beth followed me outside, watching me in horror as I demolished it.

Then I told her, "Beth, I promise you, as God is my witness, every dime we have left, every ounce of strength I can muster, I'll use to find him and bring him back to this house. I don't care how long it takes me. We'll get him back."

And we hugged each other, but I could see from the expression on her face that she didn't believe me.

The tape clicked off.

PART IV

For we wrestle not against flesh and blood, but against principalities, against powers, against the rulers of the darkness of this world, against spiritual wickedness in high places. (Ephesians 6:12)

Chapter 30

Jim was fighting back his tears, though he tried to rationalize that they were the result of his fatigue and not because of what he had heard. 'Is this the conclusion?' he asked himself. 'This can't be the end of it all.' He wondered if he had misplaced a tape somewhere, and he went back into the front of the house to search for his bag. After finding it on a small table in the living room, he took it into the dining room and zipped it open atop the dining room table. He felt a surge of adrenaline rushing through him as the clock was chiming four o'clock. Both his father and Burgess were still asleep—his father stretched out on the sofa, and Burgess with his legs drawn up near his chest in an overstuffed chair.

He counted the tapes carefully, and then looked at each label. He remembered what he had heard on each one. After a few minutes of anxious investigation, he resolved he had heard them all. Yet so many questions still remained.

Intellectually, he still rejected the assertion that Nigel was his father. Despite a string of improbable coincidences, he found no compelling evidence, nothing that shifted the balance or which could not be explained away. But emotionally, his resistance was weakening, and he could feel a shift inside himself, like a sand sculpture washed away by successive surges of cresting waves.

He returned to the kitchen to drink another cup of coffee, which he poured and swallowed in one continuous motion. Then after turning off the lights, he stood motionless, staring out the kitchen window to the dim backyard in front of him. 'This is where the drama had unfolded over forty years before,' so began the argument in his mind. He tried to conjure up the scene, but in his fatigue, his mind was not focused. 'If Nigel was my father,' he resolved. 'Then I was stolen from that backyard' and at this thought his emotions swelled up inside of him. "God, I don't know what to believe anymore."

He lingered anxiously, thinking out methodically the ramifications of this assertion. Each successive step in the argument brought unexpectedly greater clarity, and he began to seriously consider its possibilities, but before he could pursue them, he noticed something strange in the back yard.

Near the garage, almost imperceptible in the darkness stood a figure dressed in black. He rubbed his eyes a moment to see if the fatigue was somehow tricking them, but the figure still remained. He could see it apparently trying to break into the garage. He went into the living room and shook Burgess to awaken him.

"Jim. What in the hell are you doing? What time is it?" Burgess snapped at him.

"It's a little after four."

"Look. Let me get some sleep."

"Someone's trying to break into the garage."

"You're sure about this?"

"Come and see for yourself."

Burgess struggled to his feet and followed Jim into the kitchen where both of them stared out the window at the ghost-like figure jimmying with the lock.

"What do you want to do?" Jim asked his friend.

"Call the police."

"No," Jim snapped back at him. "He could be gone by the time they arrive. We should go out there and apprehend him."

"Yeah, sure. He could be armed and the two of us, like chumps, go out and get ourselves shot."

"We'll have an element of surprise, and I know some karate."

"And when did you take karate?"

"In college, you remember. I took a couple of semesters."

"That's twenty years ago." He paused. "We came here to write a story, not to play Starsky and Hutch."

"Look. You yourself have said that this house has been picked over. Maybe they've been looking for something, and they haven't found it. That's why he's come to the garage. I think that's what Nigel is trying to tell me. We shouldn't let him go."

"I think this is what lack of sleep is trying to tell you."

"Then I'll go by myself."

"OK. We'll go out there. But if we see any sign of a weapon, we turn around and run back inside."

"Agreed."

Both of them left quietly from the front of the house. When they reached the side of the house, they could see the intruder, kneeling at the front of the garage. He was apparently trying to pry open the lock on the double doors.

Jim gestured for them both to kneel and they dropped down to the ground.

"I suggest we rush him. You run from one side. I'll run from the other."

"And he'll hear us."

"Not if we run quietly."

Burgess shook his head in disbelief.

"I can't believe I'm going along with this."

"OK, on five. One, two, three, four, five."

The two of them rushed toward the garage, and Jim jumped the masked intruder and threw him to the ground. The intruder pulled out a small nine millimeter pistol from his belt and began to swing it in the air, relentlessly attempting to point it in Jim's direction. Burgess attempted to grab it from the intruder's hand while the two of them wrestled on the ground. Finally, he was able to pry it loose, taking both the gun and the man's black glove. But the intruder bolted from them. He hopped over a fence and they could see him running down the block until he disappeared behind a line of trees.

Burgess was breathing heavily.

"This was the dumbest idea you've ever had, Jim. We both could have been killed. And what did we accomplish? We got his gun."

"Didn't you see his right hand?"

"No, I was too busy trying to keep from getting shot."

"He had the ring."

"What ring?"

"The Brotherhood ring."

Jim reached into his pocket and removed the ring from it.

"This ring." Jim held it up to him.

"Is there a key to open this garage?" Burgess asked him.

"I think it's hanging in the kitchen somewhere."

Burgess rushed back into the house and returned a few minutes later with a set of keys.

"I must warn you," Jim told him as he struggled in the darkness to find the right key. "There's this horrible car wreck in there."

Burgess found the key and snapped open the door lock. Then he lifted the large double door. Almost immediately, Jim noticed only the BMW was there. The wrecked car was missing.

"My God. It isn't here. How do you steal a wrecked car out of a closed garage?" Jim was bewildered.

"You don't," Burgess looked at him incredulously.

"I'm not going nuts. It was here."

Jim struggled to determine when they might have had an opportunity. But nothing came to mind.

"So what do you think we're looking for?" Jim asked him.

"How do I know?"

Burgess flipped on a light switch and began to look intensely around the interior of the finished garage. Then he backed off about ten feet away from the entrance and stared inside.

"Do you notice the slight difference in coloration on the wall there?"

"No. I can't see a thing."

"Come out here and look."

Jim came outside and stood beside him.

"It looks like it's been repainted," Burgess explained.

Burgess returned to the garage and began to pound on the wall with a fist, while putting his right ear up against the wall.

"What are you doing?" Jim asked him.

Burgess continued the pounding.

"See if there is a tire tool in the trunk of the car."

"You're not going to start ripping walls out."

"Just get the tire tool."

Jim opened the trunk of the car and found a three-foot tire tool, which he handed to his friend.

"Where did you get this expertise on walls and paint?"

"My father had a remodeling business when I was in high school. I must have painted or patched hundreds of walls. Believe me, you get to know all of the secrets."

Burgess pried open several boards and revealed something hidden beneath them.

"Just as I thought."

"What is it?"

"We'll soon see. But it looks like a briefcase."

"Why in the hell would someone put a briefcase inside a wall?"

"Come. Help me with this."

Both of them began to pry open several more boards until they were finally able to free a brown leather briefcase which Burgess yanked out of the wall.

"Let's take the gun and this inside," Burgess proposed. He tried to open the briefcase, but he discovered it was locked. Jim carefully lifted the gun from the pavement and put it in his belt, and then turned off the light in the garage. After closing and locking the double doors, he followed Burgess back into the house.

"What do you suppose is inside of it?"

"We'll soon find out," Burgess responded. He turned on the light in the kitchen and laid the briefcase down on the kitchen table.

"Jim, find something I can pry this open with."

Jim began to search through drawers until he found a hammer and a screwdriver which he brought to his friend. Then placing the screwdriver under each latch, Burgess hammered them until each one popped open, and he lifted the top open to reveal its contents.

"Well, what is it?"

"A manuscript of some type."

"Let me look at it." Jim turned the briefcase toward himself and discovered a bound manuscript about an inch and a half thick with the familiar Brotherhood symbol embossed on the top page. Beneath the symbol it read, "Interim report: Status of Infiltration and control over primary institutions."

They were both puzzled with what they were seeing,

"What is it?" Jim asked rhetorically.

"I don't know."

Burgess lifted it out of the briefcase and set it down on the table.

"It looks like a business report of some kind."

"This is not a business report," Jim intoned. "It's from The Brotherhood, some type of intra-organizational report."

Burgess rifled through the pages and scanned the long lists of names and institutions categorized according to degree of infiltration and ranked according to a nine level hierarchy, each rank indicating the level of the operative who had infiltrated the organization.

"This must be some kind of a joke. Look at the names of some of these institutions."

Jim took the manuscript from him and began to scan it himself. "Burg, if we can believe this, we're in over our heads, way over our heads."

"Who can believe this? It's like the most ridiculous of paranoid conspiracy fantasies."

Jim's father was standing in the doorway and interrupted them both.

"What are both of you doing up so early?"

"Oh, we've had an exciting morning," Burgess explained to him, his voice filled with sarcasm. "Wrestling with burglars, and taking briefcases out of walls in the garage, and now we're involved in a conspiratorial fantasy about secret cabals taking over the world."

"What do you mean wrestling with burglars?"

"I saw a burglar attempting to break in the garage," Jim began to explain. "Burg and I went outside to confront him."

"That was stupid. What if he had a gun?"

"He did." Jim paused. "Don't worry. We're both fine. We searched the garage and found a briefcase with a document inside."

"Is this the document you found?" Jim's father questioned, pointing to the manuscript on the table.

"Yes," Burgess answered.

"Let me look at it a second."

He pulled the document toward himself and sat down with them at the table. For fifteen minutes, he studied it, turning the pages slowly and skipping ahead to pages in the middle of the manuscript. He finally closed it and set it down in front of them.

"Well, what do you think?" Jim asked him.

"I can presume Nigel must have hidden it in the garage. We have no reason to believe otherwise."

"Do you think it's legitimate?" Jim pressed him for an opinion.

"Though I'm not an expert on such things, yes, I think it is legitimate."

"What about this nine level hierarchy? Doesn't that seem a little nuts?"

Jim was struggling to find a reason not to believe.

"It sounds nuts. But these are probably code words for levels of initiation. Perhaps like in freemasonry. But more pernicious."

Burgess seemed ready to burst out laughing.

Jim's father continued, "Everything inside of me wants to disbelieve it because I want to somehow believe in the sacrosanct nature of our institutions. We like to delude ourselves that it can't happen here. It can happen everywhere else, but not here."

"So what are you saying?" Burgess interrupted him.

"I'm saying that if we can believe this document, and I don't think we have much choice but to believe it, this group has infiltrated most of the positions of power in this country."

"Come on people," Burgess interjected. "This is just a few pieces of paper anyone could have written up on his home computer."

"You're an intelligent man, Burgess," Jim's father answered him in a professorial tone. "With what has happened thus far, can we really believe that? Honestly?"

After a few moments of anguished silence, Burgess finally responded,

"No."

"Then we have to act as though it were true, which means the three of us are targets now, just like the others."

"You're scaring the hell out of me," Jim finally spoke out.

"I didn't take this thing out of the wall in the garage. But now we have to deal with it. We have to carefully consider our alternatives."

"What alternatives?" Burgess questioned him.

"One advantage to being in possession of a document such as this one, it tells us what institutions they've successfully infiltrated, and those they have not infiltrated. We should start with those."

"What should we start with those?" Jim interrupted him. "I'm not getting involved in a confrontation with an organization as large as this one. They'll squash us all like ants."

"We're already involved in a confrontation with them."

The truth of his father's remark immediately deflated him.

"The best we can do is find allies who might insure the possibility of survival. The more we know about this group the better our chances."

"The only one I know who knows anything about these groups is Dr. Harvey at Columbia, and he's already said he won't talk to me any more."

Burgess proposed, "Take the manuscript to him and have him look at it. Maybe that will change his mind."

Jim was beginning to question every decision he had made since his arrival in New York, and he seriously doubted his own judgment. "I'm not so sure being combative with them is the best alternative," he began to lay out his argument. "Perhaps we should just give it back to them."

"You mean just turn it over to them without a fight," Burgess recoiled. "How can that help us? To give away our bargaining chip?"

"And you really think you can make a deal with these people? Or mount any credible threat to their position?" He paused. "No. As much as I hate to say it, I'm going to give it back to them."

The words left a bitter residue in his mouth, but he was not prepared to confront Wilson on the Brotherhood's terms. "In fact," he would argue to himself. "I'm not prepared to confront him on any terms." He began to yawn, feeling the deprivation of sleep suffocating him until he felt light-headed.

"I'm going to have to get some sleep, at least a couple of hours. I'm sorry."

He stumbled up the stairs and down the hallway toward his bedroom. Finally laying himself down on the bed, he pivoted his head backwards on the edge of the mattress and within minutes he was asleep.

When Burgess began shaking him to awaken him, he did not know how long he had been asleep and he fought consciousness.

"What time is it, Burg?"

"Ten o'clock." He paused a moment. "Julie is downstairs. She wants to talk to you."

"I'm in no condition to talk to anyone. Tell her to go home."

"I can't do that."

"Alright. Alright. Give me a few minutes. I'll be down in a few minutes."

He threw himself forward, his knees locking in place once he was standing, and then he lumbered zombie-like toward the bathroom at the end of the hallway as Burgess returned downstairs. Once in the bathroom, he turned on the water at the sink, adjusting the hot water until a cloud of mist rose ghost-like from the basin and he splashed this hot water into his face in successive salvos. After nearly five minutes of this ritual, he turned off the water and dried his face with a hand towel which he tossed precariously into a hamper on his way out of the bathroom.

As he descended the stairs, he could see Julie sitting on the sofa in the living room with a manilla envelope laid across her lap. Her face became animated when she saw him.

"You look terrible, Jim. Is something wrong?"

"I feel terrible."

He could see from the expression on her face that she was disturbed with him.

"I have your article," she began. "I got a copy of it this morning from production."

"It's not my article."

"I have to talk to you about some of the things you've written."

"I haven't read it."

"Don't be flippant with me, Jim." Her voice became harsher and more accusatory as she removed the papers from the envelope.

"How could you say that Nigel was a fraud? You say here," and she was about to read a section to him, when he blasted out, "Go home, Julie. You don't want to be involved in this."

"You can't treat me like I'm some sort of schoolgirl. You're going to talk to me about this."

"For God's sake, Julie. Just go home."

But she seemed more resolute the more he resisted.

"You're going to have to tell her," Jim's father interrupted them. "I don't think there's any other way."

She seemed pleased to see Jim's father, and her expression momentarily changed from agitation to expectation.

"Tell me what?"

"I don't think she'll believe me." He paused. "And I don't want to involve her in this."

"She's already involved. I'm sure they're watching the house."

"I'm sitting in the room," Julie interrupted. "You can talk to me."

"I don't know where to start," Jim began. He quavered at the prospect of distilling the events of the last days into a few salient points. But he continued.

"Has your father ever mentioned anything about belonging to a club or group which works behind the scenes?"

"No," she responded.

Burgess entered the room carrying the manuscript under his arm.

"Has he said anything about a secret society?"

"Of course not."

"That's why they call them secret," Burgess interrupted them. "They don't talk about them."

Jim struggled to find just the right words.

"You've heard of the Rosetta stone discovered in the early 1800's which allowed westerners to finally understand ancient Egyptian hieroglyphics. It opened up a whole mysterious world which finally became understandable."

"If ever there was a cryptic allusion," Burgess jumped in sarcastically, "Jim can pick the most esoteric. What he's trying to tell you is that your father and Michael are part of some super-secret group called The Brotherhood, whose goal is to infiltrate major political and economic institutions and finally rule the world."

She began to laugh.

"Oh, don't laugh, Julie. This is deadly serious."

"Who's been filling your heads with these ridiculous ideas?"

She paused. "Jim, I suppose. He read six books on the JFK assassination, and he was ready to accept almost any paranoid fantasy."

"Show her the ring, Jim," Burgess encouraged.

He pulled the ring out of his pocket and handed it to her.

"This is their ring."

She looked at it and seemed even more amused.

"This is a corporate ring. All the upper management of my father's company wear this ring. Who's been telling you these things?"

"Dr. Harvey at Columbia," Jim responded.

"I told you when I called you about him that Dr. Harvey is a nut. He makes his living spreading suspicions about these groups. I would seriously question anything that man has to say."

Burgess seemed ready to thrust the manuscript into her face when Jim stopped him.

"You're absolutely right, Julie. We've let the speculations of this man cloud our judgment and create a huge misunderstanding."

She began to relax.

"As for the article in *Newsmaker*," he continued. "I'm sorry. I did it for the money. And I regret having done it. And if you have any anger at me for this, I understand. "

"Jim, how could you?" Her voice began to heighten. "How could you betray him like this? I thought maybe you had changed, but you're the same self-centered man you've always been."

She hesitated. "I'm sorry. This was a mistake." She turned toward the door. "I have to go before I say things I'll regret."

She walked out the front door and closed it soundly behind her.

"That was quite a performance," Burgess commented. "From the way you behaved, I'd think you care about her."

"I do," he responded. A lump swelled in his throat. "I do."

He walked to the windows and watched her as she climbed into car which was parked at the curb.

"I still think you should take it to Dr. Harvey and have him take a look at it."

But Jim wasn't listening. His eyes were transfixed on her as the car disappeared down the block.

"I've made too many mistakes, Burg, too many bad decisions. And I have this sinking feeling there is coming some cosmic settling of accounts."

"I hope you're not getting religion on me."

"I'm getting something."

He walked away from the window and sat awkwardly on the edge of the sofa.

"So what have we decided to do?" Burgess opened the subject again.

"I don't think we've decided on anything," Jim's father answered him.

"I think I'm going to take up Burg on his proposal. I'll take the manuscript to Dr. Harvey and see what he has to say."

"You're sure about this?"

"I'm not sure about anything, but it seems as good a plan as any."

Chapter 31

"You're sure you don't want either of us to go with you?" Burgess reiterated through the open driver's side window, as Jim began to back the BMW from the garage.

"No. It's better if I go alone. I'll call you as soon as I get there, if I can remember Nigel's number."

"You don't want the gun?"

"I hate guns."

He began to back the car out of the driveway while Burgess opened the gate for him at the street. He took one last look at his friend before putting the car in drive and beginning to accelerate down the block. The manuscript was in his satchel sitting in the passenger seat.

He didn't know what he would tell Dr. Harvey once he arrived at Columbia or even if Dr. Harvey would talk to him. He hoped that it all would prove some elaborate hoax that once the professor saw the manuscript and burst out laughing, the raging conflagration within would instantly subside. Yet, Jim recognized this improbability as a peculiar lucidity seized him.

As he began to drive down the block, a strange impulse of heightened curiosity overcame him, and he had to stop the car at the corner and take one more quick peek at the document. Fanning it slowly, he stopped on a section entitled "False flag operations," but couldn't bring himself at that moment to read it more meticulously. He flipped through the pages quickly to the end, catching glimpses of titles such as "population goals" and "education agendas." Frustrated with his indecisiveness, he set the manuscript aside, restarted the car and continued on this way.

When he arrived at Columbia, it was almost noon. He circumnavigated the university several times before finding an open parking space, and after parking the car and opening the door to climb outside, he was overcome by a feeling of trepidation. As he reached over to grab the satchel, he couldn't keep from thinking that someone was watching him, but he resisted these thoughts, determined not to betray fear to any would-be pursuer.

He entered the university through its western gates on Broadway, pacing himself in his strides, conscious not to display panic when with each uncertain step he grew more anxious. He continued rehearsing his argument, struggling to find just the right words, but all his words seemed inadequate to convey the fullness of his ruminations.

When he reached the front of the history building, he stopped a moment and took several deep heart-wrenching breaths before opening the glass doors to go inside. He thought of looking over his shoulder to see if anyone was following him, but restrained himself. In the elevator, he stood like a sentinel watching the panel count out each floor, and then the doors opened and he reluctantly stepped outside.

First he went to Dr. Harvey's office in the middle of the long corridor. He found it empty with the lights turned off. Reading the schedule on the door, he determined Dr. Harvey was not in class, and he debated whether he should wait for him or go to the department office to learn where he might find him. After a few wavering moments, he resolved to ask the department secretary.

When he stopped at the office, he could see several people talking. One young woman was obviously upset.

"I was wondering if you can tell me where I might find Dr. Harvey?" he asked.

The department secretary turned her head away from the others and responded to him, "Dr. Harvey is dead. He was found dead in his apartment this morning."

"What happened to him?"

"They think it's a heart attack." She continued talking to the others.

"Did he have a history of heart disease?" He was devastated by the news.

"Who are you?" she rebounded.

"I'm sorry," he apologized. "I just wanted to talk to him about something."

He turned around and exited the office, his heart racing in his chest. Once outside, he found a pay phone and he dialed Nigel's number. The phone kept ringing without an answer.

"Damn it. Someone answer the phone."

After nearly ten rings, he finally heard Burgess' voice.

"Hello."

"Burg, why did it take you so long to answer the phone?"

"The police are here, Jim. They have a search warrant and they're tearing the place apart."

"What did you tell them?"

"We haven't told them anything. How did it go with Dr. Harvey?"

"He's dead, Burg. They say it's a heart attack."

"I can't talk to you now."

"I'm going to talk to Wilson. I'll call you when I have a plan." He hung up the phone. But he was too consumed with alarm and uncertainty to think about a plan.

When he returned to the car, the meter had expired and a parking ticket was stuck beneath the wipers, but not caring about the ticket, he tossed it inside the car once he opened the door.

'I don't know Wilson had anything to do with Dr. Harvey's death,' he fashioned the argument inside his mind. 'I can't let whatever fear I'm feeling cloud my judgment." Yet it was another in the series of coincidences which were steadily destroying his defenses. He didn't want to give into a pervasive paranoia nor minimize the dangers confronting him, so he resolved to give himself time to think.

When he pulled the car from the curb and entered traffic, he had no point of destination clearly in perspective. He allowed the moment to control him, and he let the traffic take him wherever it willed. He drove up Broadway into Harlem through Washington Heights to 180th Street; then he turned the car around and came back the opposite direction toward midtown.

He kept thinking about everything that had happened, about the shadow of death which seemed to follow behind him; he remembered every far left fringe opinion he had ever entertained and how they all seemed believable in comparison to what he had recently learned.

"God, I've been mistaken about so many things."

He yearned for the bliss of ignorance, of self-deception, of his provincial life in Hadleyburg, where white was white and black was black and the only grays were at the edges. But he knew, as one knows the rhythm of his own breathing, that whatever opinions he might have held before had become like dreams which fade upon waking and are soon obliterated by consciousness, and as much as he wanted to nostalgically revere his previous life, it too had been obliterated, and for the first time he understood what drives a man to drugs or drink.

He was driving almost unconsciously, making random turns, not knowing where he might be next, and he kept thinking about the manuscript. 'How can I hope to fight them?' he began his anguished argument. "If they can kill with impunity, without risk, as casually as someone changes socks? But if I toss it in the river, or dispose of it some other way, how can I prove I disposed of it? I'd be forever looking over my shoulder to see if they would come for it. And if I give it back to them, I expose myself and all the others to accidental death, to heart attack, to suicide, to the hundreds of convenient demises which feed the suspicions of paranoia?"

He wished he had never taken it from the wall, wondering how he could ever close this Pandora's Box or quarantine such a pernicious contagion. He was forever changed by it, and this truth possessed him. But still the only thing that made sense to him was to give it back, to render to Caesar what was Caesar's and to plead for mercy.

When he passed the port authority bus terminal, an idea jumped into his head. He turned the car into the parking lot, and parked it there. And then carrying the bag with deliberate steps, he entered the terminal and began to look for lockers, or somewhere he might store the bag. Once he found them, he hastily placed the bag inside and locked it there. Then memorizing the locker number, rehearsing it like a mantra, he rushed out of the terminal and back to his car.

He did not know what he had accomplished in this exercise, but it felt therapeutic, as though he had purged himself, and as he started the car and he began to drive out of the parking lot, he felt as though a tremendous burden had been lifted from him. Then he resolved to call Burgess again.

He stopped the car on the corner of 5th Avenue and 66th Street, and rushed to a pay phone standing on the corner. He found his last quarter and he again called Nigel's number.

"Hello," he heard Burgess' voice again.

"It's me again, Burg."

"Where are you?"

"I'm still in Manhattan. What about the police? Are they still there?"

"No, they left a while ago." He paused. "They want to talk to you."

"About what?"

"You're in some serious trouble," his friend's words pierced through him. "It seems they have a witness who claims you had an argument with this David Fox, and he claims you threatened him."

"He's full of it."

"They also have the gun."

"What gun?"

"The gun. The one we wrestled away this morning,"

"And you just gave it to them."

"Of course not. But they have it, and both our prints are all over it."

"You told them what happened?"

"Of course. But I don't think they believe me."

"I had nothing to do with it."

"We know that. I just think someone is trying to intimidate us."

"They're doing a good job."

"I'd ditch the car as soon as possible. I'm sure they're looking for it."

"I don't feel safe on foot."

"Also, stay away from the house for a while, at least until this blows over."

"How's my father doing?"

"He's all right. Do you want to talk to him?"

Jim's father came on the phone.

"Yeah Jim. Are you all right?"

"I'm breathing." Then after a moment of anxious silence, he went on, "I'm going to talk to Michael Wilson."

"I don't know how prudent that is under the circumstances."

"It's the only way. I've left the manuscript in a locker at the port authority bus terminal. Locker 6519. If anything happens to me, you can find it there. Remember, Locker 6519." He paused.

"I'm going into the belly of the beast. Wish me luck."

He hung up the receiver.

He walked across the street to go into a deli in order to get more change for the phone. He suspected that he was being watched, but he didn't want to become paralyzed by such feelings of paranoia. He bought a soda and a small bag of potato chips with his last twenty-dollar bill, and he carefully watched the clerk as she counted out his change. On the counter next to her sat a small five-inch television which she was watching out of the corner of her eye, and he could recognize the familiar Jamison label and its corporate logo which resembled the emblem on the Brotherhood ring. "Have I created this whole scenario in my mind?" he reflected. "Was it a corporate ring after all?" But the uneasy feeling in his stomach convinced him otherwise. After opening the chips and soda, he loitered a few minutes in front of the store before finally steeling himself for the bitter task ahead. He crossed the street and set the open can inside the phone receptacle, and then he began to search his pockets for the small piece of paper on which Dina had scribbled the governor's number. It took him several minutes before he finally found it, and he laid the crumpled paper beside the soda can.

He sighed and then began to dial the number, his fingers hesitating between each digit. As the phone began to ring, he fought the impulse to slam it down.

A woman finally answered. "Yes," she spoke in a staccato burst.

"Yeah, this is James Jacobson. I need to talk to Governor Wilson concerning a very important matter."

He tried to choose his words carefully not to betray his anxiety.

"The Governor is unavailable."

"It's absolutely essential that I talk to him."

"He cannot be disturbed."

"Where is he?"

"He's preparing his speech for tonight," she answered. "I'll take a message."

"Tell him to call me at 555-1819," he read the number off the telephone. "That's a Manhattan phone number."

"It will be later this afternoon or this evening."

"I'll wait."

He hung up the phone.

The prospect of lingering there for an extended period of time frightened him, but he was anxious to bring it to some sort of conclusion. Ten minutes passed, then a half hour, and he rocked robot-like on the concrete, alternately shuffling from one foot to the other. He kept scanning the surrounding buildings and watching for signs of a pursuer, but aside from pedestrians strolling on the paved walkway beside the park, he saw no one. He began to consider whether he was creating a false hysteria from an overactive imagination, and he began to relax. An hour passed without incident and several police patrol cars drove by without even slowing down, and he began to laugh at himself for fearing them. Then finally the phone rang.

"Hello," he answered.

The governor's voice was strident.

"I'm very busy," he began. "I hope this means you've reconsidered my offer."

"I think I have something which belongs to you."

There was a portentous silence at the other end.

"And what is that?" he finally questioned.

Jim was reluctant to tell him anything, but he chose his words carefully.

"It's an interim report," he answered cautiously.

Again there was silence at the other end.

"I want to make a trade," Jim told him.

"You're in no position to negotiate."

"Just get the police off my back."

He heard a snicker at the other end.

"I'm not putting the police on your back."

"I had nothing to do with David Fox's death. So call off the hounds."

"Look. I don't know what you're talking about."

But Jim didn't believe him.

"Do you have this report with you?"

"No, I have it stored for safe keeping."

"And who else knows about this?"

"I don't care about your brotherhood," Jim railed against him. "You can take over the whole world for all I care. All I want is to be left alone."

"Where are you now?"

Jim didn't answer him.

"Just bring the manuscript to the Javits Center. I'll have someone let you in."

Then Jim could see a car stop on 5th Avenue not far from him and suddenly three men jumped out and began to run toward him. One he immediately recognized as Marcus. He dropped the phone and dashed across the street between moving cars, several dodging him to keep from striking; then he ran into the park.

Jim rushed past several vendors selling hot dogs and ice cream. He could hear the men gaining on him. A juggler dressed in blue with orange suspenders was tossing bowling pins into the air and then long knives, and Jim sprinted past him, his lungs chastened by the cold air. He could not recall when last he had run as vigorously, his mind blurred by the sense of immanent danger, though he realized how flabby he had become when each struggled stride brought radiating pain up each calf and thigh. For him, the choice was a simple one—to endure whatever pain it brought to accomplish his escape. He ran between trees, his face twitching from the stress, and he could feel the muscles in his ankles twisting like knotted rope around his metatarsals. He ran as though he had become accustomed to running, his stride rhythmic and regimented. He could hear his name being shouted, but he blocked all noise from his mind.

"Give me strength. Just give me strength," he muttered. It was the closest thing to a prayer that he had ever vocalized.

Five minutes passed, yet it seemed like thirty, and each stride brought him closer to the western edge of the park. He ran beside picnickers spread out on the Great Lawn, and he could see Belvedere's Castle rising from the pale greens like an English estate house. Unconsciously, he rushed toward it, his face sweating profusely and the taste of salt bitter on his lips.

He sensed the men behind him had split up, but he was too afraid to slow down long enough to look behind him.

"I must be stronger," he coached himself, with his muscles surging from left to right. He felt a queasy lump inside his stomach. "I'm too old for this," he blasted out as though divided, and then he stumbled.

For a moment he lay stunned upon the ground. He could feel his forehead bleeding and death seem to rush over him. He pulled himself to his feet and in an awkward limp began to stride again, his forehead throbbing in pain, and he could see the western edge of the park with traffic moving down the street. He resolved to steel himself to sprint with all his strength the last hundred yards. He dashed toward it, with his pursuers no more than ten yards behind him, and he bolted into the street while searching his pockets simultaneously for a subway token, and he ran down the steps of a subway station, almost hopping with his legs throbbing in agony, and he pushed himself between the other commuters.

"Let there be a train here," he chanted almost religiously and he could see the open doors of an A train on the platform. Running with a subway token held between his fingers, he pommeled himself through the turnstiles, and then in a huge missile-like lunge forward he tossed himself through the closing doors, his pursuers safely barricaded behind him, and then he collapsed exhausted on the subway floor.

"Are you all right?" an older woman asked him as he painfully raised up from the floor. She handed him a piece of tissue.

"Yes, thank you."

He patted the blood a moment and then held the tissue on his forehead. He felt elation in the midst of physical agony. Every joint was traumatized and every muscle throbbing, but he escaped somehow. And then for the first time in years, he felt deeply alive.

Chapter 32

The subway train was rocking and twitching, its lights flashing on and off in random spasms, as he began to consider carefully his options. He knew that they would be looking for him, at every stop if possible, so he resolved to change his train. At 96th Street he exited and crossed over to the southbound platform. Then he waited, trying to conceal himself behind a cluttered newsstand until the next train arrived.

His heart was racing, pushing blood in powerful pulses to his smallest capillaries, and he thought of this as he moved the fingers of his right hand in an anxious frenzy, clenching a fist and then relaxing them.

"I must be calm," he tried to control himself. "I cannot let this panic me."

But he had already abandoned all pretense of sensibility. It was too incredible a circumstance to calm himself.

At that moment, he remembered every trauma he had known and how each had affected him in similar ways, as though inside his mind's eye they had become immanently vivid before him—like sixteen screens flashing at once; car accidents, broken bones, high fevers, the host of suffering were playing out like a well-worn videocassette with unrelenting cacophonous noise.

"I must remain calm," he struggled to regain himself to silence the demons inside his head, and when the train arrived, he stepped inside, one among a hundred, and in the presence of so many faces, he felt an awkward security.

He held the iron bar tightly with his right hand as a wall of human flesh surrounded him. It was suffocating! His forehead still throbbing, he twisted a moment to make himself more comfortable, though in such a cramped space he found it difficult to move.

A conductor announced each stop along the way. He struggled to hear the muffled words through a malfunctioning intercom.

"59th Street," he barely recognized the words as the train pulled to an erratic stop, and then the doors slid open.

"Let them off first," he could hear the conductor shouting. "Let them off first." Then a stream of riders pushed and shoved themselves outside the doors. Breathing deeply the perspiration tinged air, he moved further inside the train and tried to focus on his next course of action.

"They want the manuscript. I'll give it to them, but on my terms."

He carefully studied a mounted subway map, and when the doors opened on 42nd Street he disembarked. Following the signs to the Port Authority Terminal, he strolled briskly down the long corridor. Both knees were sore and he was limping slightly in his left leg. As he approached the entrance, he hastened his stride, almost sprinting up the steps until he reached the mezzanine.

When he found the locker, he opened it and removed the bag which he flung over his right shoulder. Then he resolved he would call Michael Wilson again. He dialed the phone more deliberately and waited while it rang.

The same woman answered, "Hello."

"Is the Governor there? This is James Jacobson."

"He's still unavailable," she sarcastically answered.

"Put him on the phone or tell him I'm going to the press with it."

A few anxious moments passed, and Wilson came to the phone.

"You can't be so foolish to think that anyone would publish it. Where are you now?"

"So you can send your thugs after me?"

"No one is going to harm you, Mr. Jacobson. They only wanted to talk to you."

"Well, talk to me. I'm listening."

The governor was silent.

"I want some assurances or I will go to the press with it."

"You are like a mosquito trying to take down an elephant. They can crush you in an instant with no remorse." He paused.

"Bring the manuscript to me at the Javits Center, and I'll see what I can do."

"I want assurances."

"What assurances? I can assure you that if you don't bring it to me, it's out of my hands."

"So you'll murder me like all the others."

"I haven't murdered anyone." He laughed. "You think because of my little demonstration in the car that I want to harm you? That was only an educational exercise for you to understand the stakes involved. We're going ahead with the article."

"You're a snake."

"I'm a pragmatist." He paused. "I'll be waiting for you, Mr. Jacobson."

He hung up the phone.

Jim felt ambivalent about his decision. A part of him wanted to follow through with his threat, if only to spite Michael Wilson, but he knew that he could not let his emotions control him. On a practical level, he realized that Wilson was right. He could not hope to mount a serious threat to the Brotherhood's position. If they had in fact gained effective control over key institutions, all resistance to them would be ultimately self-destructive, but he was still not prepared to accept total surrender.

He was reluctant to linger much longer at the terminal, but he was anxious to talk to Burgess and his father again, if only to confirm they were secure. He placed another coin in the pay phone and dialed Nigel's number. The phone began ringing. Immediately, he noticed a perceptible difference in the tone of the ring, but he didn't know what this meant. When three, then four, then five rings passed without an answer, his intestines began to knot. He sensed something was terribly wrong, but he wanted to dismiss such sensations as products of his imagination. It rang over ten times and then he began to count each unanswered ring. By fifteen rings he was overwhelmed with worry. He slammed down the phone.

"Damn, something must have happened to them."

He checked his watch. It was nearly five o'clock, and he began to calculate the time it would require to return to Bayside by subway and bus. It was too long. He resolved, as risky as it might be, that he had to return to the car and drive back into Bayside.

He took the shuttle from Times Square into Grand Central and the Number Six train uptown to 68th Street. When he arrived on 66th Street, he could see three men, whom he did not recognize, loitering near the car. They were all dressed in dark blue business suits. One was smoking a cigarette and resting his hand on its hood.

He realized he couldn't risk approaching them, so he decided to take the subway train back into Flushing and from there take a bus to Bayside. It would be a long excursion, but he didn't believe he had another choice.

On the platform at Grand Central, he waited on the long narrow slab of concrete while a local train hissed past him. He tried to call his father and Burgess again while holding the phone against one ear and his finger in the other. Again, there was no answer.

When the express train pulled into the station and its brakes squealed in an earsplitting pitch, Jim slammed down the phone and stepped inside the subway car. He began to chide himself for self-delusion. He had no compelling reason to believe anything was wrong, but he had to silence the voices of paranoia shouting inside his head.

When he arrived at Main Street Flushing, he lingered in the car a moment after everyone had exited. His mind overwhelmed with impulses, as though the synapses were firing randomly, and when the doors began to close on him, he rushed out of them and up the stairs. At street level, he hailed a taxi, and asked the driver to take him into Bayside. He didn't even ask how much it cost.

He sat nervously on the edge of his seat with the backpack balanced awkwardly on this lap. He zipped the bag open a moment and peeked inside at the cause of his anxiety. Then he took it out a moment to look at it.

He again read the title, "Interim report: status of infiltration and effective control over primary institutions." He was beginning to understand the methodology, but he was mystified as to their ultimate purpose or what ideology they espoused.

As the car moved down Northern Boulevard, he stared nervously at the chain of the houses and small stores which were strung as paperclips on each side of him, and when the car turned left on Bell Boulevard he noticed a vacant store on the southeast corner, and he pondered if this was where Nigel's store had been.

On 212th street, the muscles in his throat grew taut and he had difficulty swallowing, and then he realized what was wrong—Nigel's house was burning. He was overcome with emotion.

"Stop the car," he shouted at the driver as he handed him a ten dollar bill. Then he rushed out of the car, and he ran toward the house. Two fire trucks were parked on opposite sides of the street while firemen were battling flames shooting from the roof, and two ambulances were parked behind the fire trucks. His first impulse was to find his father and Burgess. He dashed toward the first ambulance and found it empty. In the second, he found a fireman breathing oxygen and he immediately thought the worst, that both were somehow trapped inside the house.

"No, no, no," he began to shout, and then he discovered his father and Burgess huddled beneath two blankets while they watched the conflagration in front of them.

"Thank God," he shouted and ran toward them.

"What happened?"

Coughing a few moments, Burgess responded, "I don't know. I smelt smoke and in minutes the house was in flames."

Jim's father sat in a stunned silence, breathing short shallow breaths, as he watched the firemen struggle to contain the flames.

"Two minutes later we both would have been overcome by smoke and died," Jim's father finally articulated, his voice quavering.

"Damn him, Wilson."

"We don't know he had anything to do with this," his father argued. "It could have been an accident."

"An accident?" Jim grew more agitated. "How can any of this be an accident?"

His father seemed dazed.

"You shouldn't be here, son. The police are still looking for you."

"Well, did you give him the manuscript?" Burgess asked him.

"No, I still have it." He paused. "What about the tapes?"

"I'm sorry, Jim. We were lucky to get out with our lives."

He was unable to respond, his eyes fixed with a childlike wonder at the dancing flames. He realized that Nigel's voice was forever silenced, and two rivulets of tears slid down each cheek.

"What are you going to do?" Burgess asked him.

"I don't know. But one way or another, he is going to pay for this."

He was filled with rage.

"Don't do anything foolish, "his father counseled him. "We don't know this was arson."

"I'm all right," Jim responded, though the tone of his voice and his phrasing suggested otherwise.

Jim recognized he had little room to maneuver. He was not prepared to mount a credible challenge to Michael Wilson, because he doubted its efficacy.

"Can I borrow a few bucks?" he asked Burgess. "I'm going to take the train back into the City."

Burgess retrieved his wallet from his back pocket and handed him a five dollar bill.

"Can I have another couple of dollars for a subway token back?"

"Sure." Burgess reached into his pocket and removed two dollars.

"I don't have time." Jim could see a police car approaching and he began to shuffle from side to side.

"I probably should be leaving," he acknowledged.

"That's probably wise," his father responded.

He reached over to shake his father's hand.

"What the hell?" He hugged him for the first time since his mother's funeral. When he released him after a moment, he turned to Burgess.

"Don't go hugging me!" Burgess snapped at him. Jim shook his hand.

"Wish me luck!"

"You'll need it," Burgess told him, and then he ran in the direction of the train station.

As he was running, the bag was bouncing erratically on his back and his mind was filled with sensations. He felt a panoply of emotions simultaneously, from anger, through fear, to anxious anticipation. When he reached the platform, he could see a train pulling into the station, and he bolted down the stairs, rushing into an almost vacant car as it closed its doors.

He found a seat near the back of the car and slouched down there while the conductor made her way from the front of the train toward him. He set the backpack down beside him.

"Tickets, please," she was chanting, punctuated by the sound of a hole punch.

He pulled the money out of his pocket, and she punched a ticket for him. He attempted to calm himself as she handed him his change.

Impressions overwhelmed him, like images painted starkly on glass. From the hospital room filled with flowers, to Nigel's grave with its red-brown earth, to Dr. Harvey's closet filled with its electronic toys, one perception crowding another almost like commuters on the subway. He couldn't make sense of them, nor of the tumult which raged within him.

His mind fixed for a moment on the image of the flames like arms thrusting out from the windows, but this soon blended into a continuous montage with a host of other memories. He could not hold onto any one of them, nor to the emotions which surfeited each one. Like a dam bursting, the cumulative effect of this erosion had disintegrated his defenses.

He knew it was foolish to give the manuscript back to Wilson, and that he had no reason to trust him, but despite his misgivings he remained committed to its completion, as though his destiny demanded it. He didn't know why he felt this way.

Something Julie had told him at dinner kept replaying inside his head, "The person I was to become was trapped inside the person I am." It was an odd paradox, seemingly a nonsense verse, but it had an otherworldly appeal to him, as though it described a reality beyond its simple words.

"The person I am to become," he repeated the words to himself, metamorphosis, transformation, regeneration, could this adequately describe the war within himself? *Who am I? Where have I been? Where am I going?* Like a children's game, these queries shouted at him, and suppliantly he acquiesced to them.

"Am I the sum total of all my experiences, the cumulative result of billions of random firings of neurons, or is there an 'I' which transcends this physicality? Which can survive the destruction of my neuron net?" Never before had he asked such questions of himself, but never before had he faced death as palpably.

"Penn Station. Next Stop Penn Station," the conductor announced through the loudspeaker, and he could feel the train slowing to a halt. Then the doors opened on Track 21, and he awkwardly stepped outside.

He had only a vague impression where the Javits center was located, so he found a subway map and stood a moment to study it. He discovered it was only a couple of blocks from the station. Then without much further reflection, he began his ascent up to street level to find his way. It was darker than he expected, and the wind had picked up, and he felt small wet droplets, like pellets, bouncing off his forehead and ears. In unconscious response to the cold, he lifted his shoulders and began to walk briskly toward the corner, and then down 34th Street toward 8th Avenue. It was a long block beside warehouses and a vacant department store, and he saw no one on the street. Despite his apprehensions, he resolved he had to continue. He was almost half way down the block when he heard a whimpered scream, almost catlike, from the far end of the block. He turned his head toward it and he could see a woman was being assaulted at the corner.

He didn't know what came over him. If he had a chance to think rationally, he would not have intervened. But he wasn't thinking rationally. He began to run toward them, and then he could see the woman struggling with the assailant, while he threw her from side to side. Jim found himself shouting, "Leave her alone, leave her alone." and then with almost Olympian energy, he found himself struggling with the assailant as he thrust toward him a long serrated hunting knife.

For what felt like five minutes Jim struggled with him, pushing him, kicking him, knocking the assailant's hand against the ground until at last he knocked the knife from his hand and tossed it into a storm drain. The young woman sat stunned, bleeding from the mouth, paralyzed by fear, and then the assailant, as though in slow motion, pulled a small pistol from his belt and shot Jim twice, once in the forehead and once in the shoulder. Then he grabbed the backpack and the woman's purse and ran down the block.

Jim grew faint, wavered a moment and then staggered into a television store at the corner, and there he collapsed on the floor beside a wall of televisions, every screen flashing the same program. He lay in a daze, the room spinning around him, and he could hear the words of the television screen as a reporter began to speak.

"This is Arnold Almanzar, reporting live from the Jacob K. Javits Center. Former Governor Michael Wilson has just finished his speech before the packed Economic Summit, and as his aides have been hinting to us all day, he is prepared to announce his candidacy for President of the United States."

There was a camera shot of Wilson standing at the lectern while applause was rolling across the auditorium.

"As many of you know, I have often desired to return again to public life," Wilson began to speak. "Well, I have been encouraged by my peers to put my name in contention for President of the United States, and I have decided on this occasion to announce my intention to seek the Democratic Party's nomination beginning with the primary in New Hampshire."

There was a raucous round of applause and whistling.

"It will be a difficult task to regain the Party's momentum. But I know that with persistence, we can accomplish anything."

There was more applause.

And then Jim heard the sound of two gunshots in quick succession, and pandemonium ensued as Michael Wilson grew rigid and then collapsed on the podium.

"The Governor's been shot," The reporter began to shout, losing his reporter's decorum, and then the camera began to move erratically across the panicked crowd. At this moment Jim murmured, "Oh God, please save me," and lost consciousness.

Chapter 33

A dim light surrounded Jim and he could only make out the edges of objects. His eyes burned a moment as he could see the light growing brighter and a figure dressed in black standing in front of him, but it was still only light and shadow without contrast or definition. As the image grew focused at the edges, it became a man. Dressed in long flowing black robes with a black skull cap on his head, he could see the boundaries of his charcoal beard and the folds of full unkempt black hair shooting out from beneath the cap.

"Am I still alive?" he asked the figure, feeling tingling in his extremities. And then the details of a room began to come in focus and he heard the figure reply with a chuckle, "Of course you're alive."

"Thank God."

Within moments he realized he was in a hospital room and he struggled to lift his head a moment, but he didn't have the strength.

"Save your strength, Michael," the figure answered him.

"Who are you? And where am I?"

"You're in the hospital."

"How long has it been?"

"A week." He could feel the taut bandages around his scalp, and he lifted his right arm to touch them, but his hand was too weak to reach his forehead.

"My head feels like hell."

"You're a fortunate man, my friend. The bullet hit in just the right place."

"I asked you who you are."

"You should know that. Think about it."

But he couldn't think, as though from intense fatigue.

"What's the last thing you remember?"

"I remember collapsing in a television store and vaguely something about Michael Wilson."

"Yes, the Governor's dead."

Jim's mind grew clearer, and he struggled to swallow, but his throat felt rigid. He could see the IV like a power cord rising up beside him.

"Where's my father and Burgess?"

"I sent them to a hotel to rest. They've been here for days."

Jim struggled a moment to speak, but he could not find the words.

"And Julie's been here for five straight days, and I finally sent her home."

"Who are you?" he repeated.

"You know who I am."

He was annoyed that this stranger spoke in riddles. Then the words just popped into his mind, "You're Father Michael, Julie's Father Michael."

"Yes, I'm Father Michael." He paused. "But more than this. Who am I?"

"I don't know."

"Do you remember the plane ride to New York?"

Jim struggled to focus his mind, though his head was throbbing. "Vaguely."

"I was there. Remember you picked up my prayer rope for me."

"You were there in Hadleyburg?"

"Yes. I left the cassettes on your doorstep."

"The tapes," Jim grimaced, sending a sharp pain down both ears. "They were destroyed in the fire." His memories came rushing back at him.

"Yes, those were destroyed in the fire, along with much of the house."

"Am I all right?" Jim asked him.

"You're a blessed man, in more ways than you can ever know."

Jim found this a perplexing paradox. Then Father Michael leaned toward him and grabbed Jim's right hand tightly in his.

Then he began to recite a verse, "I love the Lord because He has heard my voice and my supplications, because He has inclined his ear to me, therefore I will call upon Him as long as I live. The snares of death encompassed me, the pangs of Sheol laid hold on me. I suffered distress and anguish. Then I called on the name of the Lord. O Lord, I beseech Thee, save my life."

The sensation, the pain, the strangeness of it all was more than he could bear. He stared trance-like at the ceiling trying to collect himself.

"The police are not going to arrest me then?"

"Arrest you?" He paused. "You're a hero, Michael."

He pulled out a copy of the *Post* with a banner headline across the page, reading "Hero!" with Jim's photograph beneath it.

"In a moment of selflessness, you saved yourself."

"Why do you keep calling me 'Michael'?"

"Should I call you Jim Jacobson? You must know that's not who you are. Like Joseph, we are all children stolen from the kingdom, and sold as slaves, all of us longing for redemption."

"I don't know what to say."

"Your mother prayed for you fervently every day of her life. She asked God to protect you, to sustain you for one day to come when you learned who you really were. After the accident when she lay so near death at the hospital, her last words to me were: "Please continue to pray for Michael.""

He paused.

"I don't know how to respond. I'm still not convinced."

"I'm afraid I've been a little disingenuous."

"Why?"

"I made copies of the tapes. So they're not destroyed." Then he reached into the pocket of his cassock and removed two more cassettes. "And I kept the last ones." He paused. "I kept hoping you would figure it all out and come and ask me for them. You see, Nigel wanted me to hold the last two until a time when I felt you were ready to hear them."

He sat the cassettes down on the hospital tray beside the bed.

"But we'll have time to hear them. I know you must have questions for me."

A nurse came into the room to check his vital signs and she could see that he was conscious.

"I've come to take your blood pressure and temperature. It's good to see you're finally awake."

She took his blood pressure and temperature.

"Am I going to make a full recovery? How long am I going to be here?"

"Relax. Mr. Jacobson. You're in very capable hands."

Father Michael moved toward the window and stood motionless staring down to the street below.

"Alright. I'm finished."

She folded up the blood pressure gauge and put the thermometer away.

"Dr. Giordano will be in to see you later this evening. But everything looks OK."

"What day is it?" Jim asked her.

"It's Monday."

He again tried to lift his hand, but it felt like a hook was holding it down. Father Michael turned around and faced Jim again. His head was throbbing in pulses from the top of his scalp toward each ear.

"You said that Michael Wilson is dead. Who killed him?"

"A white supremacist named Abel Clarion, if you believe the official version."

Father Michael laid out a copy of *Newsmaker* on the tray. Jim stared at the cover a moment with Wilson's photograph and the headline, "Murdered!"

"And you don't believe it?"

"It could have been anyone, including you."

Jim pondered the implications of his words.

"You think they were trying to set me up?"

Father Michael stroked his beard a moment and then put his right hand on the edge of the window sill.

"It's a fascinating scenario, if one begins to think it out. But it's not important. What is important is regaining a life and that is what we can talk about."

"Why are you taking such an interest in me? What's in it for you?"

Father Michael laughed. "Ever the cynic. After all that has happened, can't you release it? Turn it over to God, and let Him take care of things. We are not meant to have all the answers. You remind me very much of myself before I became a monk. I had to have all the answers. I had to always have the last word, because basically I was afraid of life—too afraid of life to live. I built walls all around me, and I was surprised how easily they were breached." He paused. "You've been given a tremendous blessing, a second chance at life. Have the courage to take it."

Jim had never had anyone speak to him this way, and he could see that Father Michael was a man of serious conviction. But despite what had happened, he was still afraid of vulnerability.

"I'm sorry. I know I should be grateful for having survived. But I'm afraid."

"I've been afraid," Father Michael responded. He spoke with tremendous compassion in his voice. "The Fathers say that the fear of death is the beginning of all evil. It hangs like a shroud over all the earth, blinding us to the light of God. How many fortunes have been made? How many pleasures have been sought? All in the hopes of somehow cheating death."

With a strenuous thrust of his arm, Jim reached up and awkwardly snatched the cassette and brought it back to his chest.

"Could you bring me a player? I'm anxious to hear what Nigel has to say."

"Certainly."

"What were you able to salvage from the house?" He paused. "Were you able to salvage those religious paintings? What do you call them?"

"Icons," Father Michael responded. "Yes. Most of them were not destroyed."

"You know, so much has happened that I haven't had time to absorb it all. I feel like a whole lifetime of experiences have been squeezed into the space of a few days." He paused. "Why didn't he tell me at the hospital that he believed he was my father? He had the chance."

"I suppose he didn't think you'd believe him, or he was afraid, or he thought he had more time. We even discussed not telling you at all because he was afraid the knowledge might destroy you."

"And you're convinced he was my father?"

"He was your father, Michael. Of that I'm certain."

"For over twenty years I have stared into the mirror, and I've wondered who I am and what my life would have been like had my mother not abandoned me. In Hadleyburg, I simply stopped caring because it hurt too much to care." His eyes filled with tears. "God. What a fool I've been."

"Do you want me to tell you why I'm certain?"

"Of course."

Father Michael reached into his cassock and removed a worn photograph, yellowed at the edges, which he handed to Jim to look at. Jim saw a young man who bore a striking resemblance to himself.

"Who is it?" Jim asked him.

"It's your grandfather, Beth's father. The one you're named after."

"Where did you get this photograph?"

"You're like Thomas. You have to touch the wounds before you'll believe."

Then Father Michael reached into a bag lying beside the bed, and he removed the same worn scrapbook that Jim had seen at the hospital in Hadleyburg.

"Where did you get this?"

"I gathered the things up from Nigel's room. I was going to give them to you at the proper time." Father Michael set it on Jim's chest and opened it to show him the page from where he had taken the photo.

"Could you turn the pages for me? I'd like to see it again."

Father Michael opened the book to the first page, and Jim remembered it. But now the pages evoked intense emotions, because he finally understood what he was seeing. Page by page, Father Michael revealed its contents and on each page Jim discovered another palpable symbol of lives once lived. Photographs which before were lifeless images became enlivened, filled with meaning. Finally on a page near the back of the book, he found photographs of a baby, and in one of them, he could see dangling from the baby's neck a locket just like his. And he began to cry uncontrollably.

"Please close it." He told the priest, who set the book aside. "I believe you, God, I believe you." He paused. "How did he find me, after all these years?" He tried to regain himself, but he couldn't control his emotions.

"Look at me. I've completely lost it."

Jim began to breathe deeply in order to relax, and struggled to return the cassette to the tray.

"Why didn't you approach me sooner?" He asked the priest.

"Julie told me she tried to get you to come up to the house, but you refused, and I didn't think you'd be receptive to a visit with your attitude about religious people."

"I'm sorry."

"I have something for you. I brought it from the house. It was something Beth kept for you."

He reached into the bag and removed an icon of St. Michael the archangel that was burned on the edges, and he propped it up on the hospital tray.

"It's your patron saint." He paused. "I know you're not into religious artifacts, but it's something your mother wanted for you."

Jim looked a moment at the picture.

"It's all right. Thank you."

"Unfortunately, I have to be going now. There is so much work to be done at the house. I'll be in again tomorrow to see you."

The priest gathered together his things.

"I'll bring a player so you can hear the tapes."

Then Father Michael left the room, while Jim, unable to take his eyes away from it, stared intensely at the icon.

Chapter 34

Jim was lingering at the cusp between waking and unconsciousness when he vaguely recognized someone standing at the foot of his bed. With intense effort, he lifted his head and began to focus his eyes.

"You needn't wake up on my account," a voice broke into Jim's awareness, and he could recognize a doctor standing at the foot of his bed, though from his countenance the doctor seemed no more than thirty years of age.

"I'm Dr. Giordano," the man answered.

"You're my doctor?"

"I'm your neurosurgeon. " He paused a moment. "I know, I look too young to be a neurosurgeon. But believe me, I am."

"How am I, doctor?"

"For a man who's been shot in the head, you're doing remarkably well."

"I have this ringing in my ears, and it seems a tremendous struggle for me to make the most simple movements."

"There is much redundancy in the cerebral cortex, and the brain is a tremendously resilient organ."

"Will I be able to walk again?"

The doctor chuckled a moment at the question, then answered him, "Of course."

"How long?"

"Always the same questions. I perform minor miracles through the use of these two hands, and people want to know how long till they can go out and get themselves in trouble again. How long? Five to six weeks, three months, six months, who knows?"

"I've never been incapacitated for that long. What am I going to do with myself?"

"I can put you back together as best I can. I can't tell you what to do with the rest of your life."

At this moment, he could see out of the corner of his left eye that Julie had entered the room. Her face seemed animated when she saw that he was awake.

"They told me that you had regained consciousness, so I rushed down here to see you."

"I thought that you would never talk to me again after that article."

"It was never printed. After the assassination, that's all the magazine has been interested in, and your father told me how you were trying to protect me. I'm sorry."

Doctor Giordano excused himself from the room.

"My father," he expressed with a cornucopia of emotions realizing that the statement could never be understood in the same sense as it had been understood before Nigel had come to Hadleyburg and he knew he could never look upon his adopted father in the same way ever again.

"Father Michael left a scrapbook belonging to my mother on the floor near the bed. Could you get it for me?"

"Sure," she walked over to the side of the hospital bed, found the scrapbook, and handed it to Jim.

"Please open the pages for me. I don't have the strength."

"Alright." She leaned over toward him and opened the first page.

"Did you know Father Michael was in Hadleyburg when Nigel was there?" He asked her.

"No." Then she asked him earnestly, "How do you like him? I think he's wonderful."

"None of this has turned out as I expected."

"You didn't answer my question. How do you like him?"

"I like him."

"Good," she told him. "So what do we want to look at?"

She began to turn the pages.

"I want to see the baby pictures."

She flipped the pages until she found them, and then he asked her, "Please hold it closer so I can get a good look at it."

He stared closely at a picture of Beth holding him in her arms. Then he lifted his right hand with great effort, and began to touch the picture.

"She was a beautiful woman, wasn't she?"

"In every way."

"Did she really walk all the way across North Africa?"

"Yes."

For a moment he seemed lost in his own thoughts, unresponsive and impenetrable.

"Father Michael said he brought some things for me. Could you look in the bag on the floor and see what he brought me?"

"Sure." She lifted the bag from the floor and began to remove its contents. Inside she discovered a small Greek prayer book, a prayer rope, a Greek bible and a small porcelain doll dressed in Greek costume. She laid these beside the icon on top of the tray.

"These must have been Beth's," she reflected.

Jim carefully scrutinized each one of them, and he remembered what Nigel had said on the tapes about each one, all except the doll.

"You know, I've never believed in anything except unredeemed chaos. It seemed the most rational explanation for so much of the evil in the world." He halted a moment. "But now I'm not so sure any more. I'm afraid I'm going to have to rethink everything."

"Is there anything I can get for you?" she asked him. "Something to read?"

"No, my head is throbbing too much to concentrate."

"I'm sorry. I didn't think about it. This must be difficult for you, talking this much."

"I'm fine, Julie. Please stay with me a while. I don't want to be alone." It was the first time in years he allowed his true feelings to find expression.

She pulled a chair sitting near the window closer to the bed and then sat down beside him.

"I'm very tired," he told her. "I'd like to sleep for a short while."

He closed his eyes and within minutes drifted into an awkward sleep, while Julie, taking the scrapbook into her lap, began to examine it. She sat quietly, poring over each photograph and memento as Jim, apparently dreaming, mumbled in his sleep. Nearly an hour passed, then Burgess and Jim's father arrived at the doorway of the hospital room.

"How is he?" Jim's father asked her.

"He's been awake," she replied. "We had a good talk."

Burgess moved to the foot of the bed and stood clasping the cold metal bed rail.

"He had to play the hero," he told her. "He couldn't leave well enough alone."

When Jim heard his friend's voice, he opened his eyes, and after a moment of myopia, his eyes began to focus.

"I couldn't let him hurt her," Jim responded.

"Yeah. But you lost our only proof of the Brotherhood's existence."

Jim began to chuckle a moment and the chuckle deepened into a laugh.

"What's so damn funny?"

"I was thinking about the irony of it all. They struggle so hard to locate it and keep it out of the wrong hands, and now it's probably sitting in a dumpster somewhere, tossed there by a mugger who didn't even know what he had." The image was as clear in Jim's mind as though he had seen it there himself. He continued, "What was it the poet said about the best laid plans?"

"How do you feel?" Jim's father asked him.

"I could be better." He paused. "But considering what could have been, I'm grateful."

These were words he was unaccustomed to saying. For so long he had been submerged in an endless cycle of self-fulfilling defeat and disappointment that he had forgotten what it felt like to be grateful.

Burgess came closer toward him and began to examine the religious artifacts lying in the tray. He lifted the porcelain doll and gave it to Jim's father to examine as well.

"What's this stuff?" he asked. "Don't tell me you're getting religious all of a sudden."

"They were my mother's."

"So, you're finally convinced," Burgess half-chided him. "The long lost kidnapped son is returned."

"You make it sound so melodramatic," Julie jumped in.

"It is melodramatic. The only connection Jim has with this woman is that she gave birth to him. Any woman can give birth to a baby. The hard part is raising one."

"I can't believe you're telling him something like this," Julie chided him.

"I just don't want him to lose sight of reality. Whatever connection he has to Beth and Nigel Fox, he was raised by Thomas and Helen Jacobson. I think this other information, however compelling it might appear, is irrelevant, unless, of course, he wants to go on Oprah, or on one of those theme shows about adoptive children discovering their birth-mothers."

"Burgess, please," Julie pleaded.

"I can't believe how willing you are to encourage him to forsake everything he was raised to believe. This is not some alternative universe where Jim was raised in New York by a super religious mother." Then he directed his remarks toward his friend. "I don't see how you can slight your father, after he has come all this way to see you."

"Do you think I've slighted you?" Jim asked his father.

"Yes, a little. Whatever mistakes I've made, I don't want you to forget I'm still your father. I just hope that in these moments of self-revelation, you don't forget what place I had in your life."

"Look. If this is going to turn into one of those Hallmark moments, I'm leaving the room," Burgess snapped.

Then Julie said, "Maybe we should both go, Burgess, and let them have a chance to talk."

She set aside the scrapbook and grabbed Burgess's arm. Then both of them left the room. Once the door was closed, Jim struggled to turn his head toward his father and told him, "I'm sorry, Dad. I guess I've been self-absorbed. I haven't thought at all about how you might be feeling." He paused a moment. "How do you feel about all this?"

Jim's father, never easily expressing his emotions, appeared to struggle before he found the right words.

"It's been difficult."

Jim sensed the fullness of emotion pregnant in this short sentence.

"I'm sorry things turned out this way. I know it must be close to time for finals, and this has taken so much of your time."

"I'm not concerned about my classes. I feel terrible about all of this and somehow responsible. Because of my complicity, my impatience, I was a co-participant in this horrible tragedy. It makes a mockery of everything I've stood for."

He never heard his father speak with such vulnerability in his voice.

"We adopted you because we wanted to bring love into a life. When your mother discovered she could not have children, I saw this adoption as a way of filling the void inside of her. Now I'm only confused."

"You can't blame yourself. You didn't know where I came from."

"I didn't want to know." He paused. "Now I'm torn in half. I think I'm losing you and I'm not even sure I should try to hold on. It's like desperately trying to hold onto your mother."

"We can't hold onto the past."

"You know, I've always tried to look at things in economic terms—margins of utility and the market. But it just doesn't make sense any more."

"I didn't want to cause a crisis of faith."

"By my age, one is supposed to have it all figured out. I'm a respected economist for God's sake."

"I've always thought, of all people, you knew what you believed. I didn't often agree with you, but I always knew where you stood."

"This past week, as I've sat here watching you, wondering if and when you'd ever come out of your coma, I couldn't recall more than five conversations we have had in the last five years, and I realized you were lying here, possibly silent forever, because you acted on my words, on my values I had encouraged in you as a child. And I reflected on what a hypocrite I've become, railing against the establishment, speaking of economic equity, while I remained secure and sheltered from any of the market's debilitating forces, in a tenured position at the University. If faced with confronting that mugger, I don't know if I would have had the same courage."

"It was nothing. An impulse. You shouldn't be so hard on yourself."

"No. I should be even harder. As an educator and a role model, I need to be more."

"Whatever mistakes you've made, you've been a good father to me. Thank you for coming here. Thank you for staying with me."

Jim chuckled a moment.

"What a pair we make," Jim observed. "You paralyzed by self-doubt, and me, well, paralyzed."

In an odd way, it seemed an appropriate completion to everything that had gone before.

"Dad, would you mind raising the back of the bed a little? I simply don't have the strength to push the buttons."

His father rose up from the chair and approached the bed. Fumbling a moment with the controls, he finally pressed the right button and Jim's head began to rise until Jim was almost sitting up.

"That's much better. Thank you. Also could you ask the nurse when I could get something to eat? I'm starving."

"Sure." Then his father left the room.

There were a host of questions that Jim wished to ask his father about the fire, about the outcome of David Fox's murder investigation, about Michael Wilson's assassination, but he sensed these questions could wait for more opportune circumstances. For the moment he struggled with his dependency. Never before in his life had he felt as helpless, as vulnerable, as incapable, yet, instead of feeling more desperate and cynical, as he would have expected, he felt strangely unfettered, as though in his immobility, his psyche had found its liberation.

With intense effort, he began to move his fingers and toes, at first only slightly, and then with greater control. As he watched his fingers moving, he lay awestruck, pondering the odd coincidence that any thought produced a movement and marveling at the magnitude of engineering involved in even the smallest gesture. He remembered what Leonard Matthews, while sitting there as though hypnotized and staring at his hands, had told Nigel on the train. "What a remarkable feet of engineering," Nigel had related his words. "Because man can do this, he developed technology." And he struggled to fold his thumb across his palm, all the while thinking about the host of technologies which surrounded him and sustained him, and how they all had been built by human hands, and how each of them had first begun as a thought inside someone's head, and then he thought of Dr. Giordano's hands, carefully extracting each tiny bullet fragment from his own head, and he immediately thought of pianists and violinists and conductors and painters and watchmakers and mathematicians writing out their complex formulas with pencils held in hand, of the cornucopia of creativity which had sprung from human hands, and on the other side, the gun makers, the assassins, the torturers, each using this remarkable feat of engineering, which he could barely move.

When Jim's father returned to the room, Jim was sitting serenely, his eyes unfocused as though lost in his own thoughts.

"There's so much we take for granted," he began to murmur to himself.

"You're right," his father caught his attention.

"I'm sorry. I was lost in my own world."

"I could tell."

"Do you remember that baseball game you took me to when I was about eight or nine."

"I took you to a number of ball games."

"The one where you got hit in the head with a foul ball."

"Yes. I remember."

"You were knocked unconscious and I thought you had died."

"I remember the headache I had for a week after that."

"I was so afraid. I couldn't move, standing there as though paralyzed while you were slouched in the seat beside me. I kept thinking it was my fault that you had died, because I had begged you so hard to take me to the game."

"What prompted this reminiscence?"

"I was sitting here thinking how utterly powerless I feel, unable to even pick up a pencil. And I was trying to remember if I ever felt this way before. (He hesitated a moment.) When you finally came to after a couple of minutes, it was, I think, the closest I ever came to near-perfect joy, until now. God, it's good to see you." His eyes filled with tears. "I know it probably doesn't change a thing, but I love you."

He could sense his father was uncomfortable with such an outward display of emotion, but Jim couldn't contain himself.

"I've been a jack ass for such a long time. I'm sorry."

A nurse carrying a tray of food came into the room. After removing the objects sitting on the tray beside Jim's bed, she positioned the tray in front of him.

"It's a few soft foods," she began to explain. "Mashed potatoes, some soup, some chocolate pudding, until you get used to eating again."

Jim struggled to pick up the spoon, but he couldn't close his hand around it. The nurse helped him close his fingers and then he lifted the spoon with his had shaking erratically until he dropped the spoon into the potatoes, and then continuing to shake, he lifted the spoon toward his face until as a toddler might, he thrust the spoon into his open mouth.

"At this rate, it will take the whole day."

"I could feed you a few minutes," the nurse volunteered. But Jim answered, "No. I'll manage somehow."

Jim could see his father was at the cusp of crying.

"What did they find out about the fire?" Jim asked his father.

"They say it was a faulty wire in the boiler, and not arson."

"And do you believe it?"

Jim thrust a second messy spoonful into his mouth.

"I don't know what to believe."

"And David Fox's murder?"

"They don't know. The gun you found didn't match."

"So, I'm off the hook for that as well."

"It appears so."

"Why do I have the sinking feeling it could have easily worked out differently?"

"Burgess has a theory about it all," his father responded.

"Burgess always has a theory." Jim paused. "This Father Michael insinuated they were setting me up to take the blame for Wilson's assassination. Do you believe that's possible?"

"It is a distinct possibility."

"Then what made them change their minds?"

"You weren't there."

"So, all that stopped me from becoming the next Sirhan Sirhan was this mugging? I don't believe it."

"You didn't believe Nigel was your father either."

"Why do you suppose they killed Wilson?"

"Burgess believes there must have been a power struggle within their organization, and Wilson was on the losing end."

"Sort of like a mob war," Jim interjected.

"I suppose. But I doubt we'll ever know the complete story."

"I wish I could have had a chance to study that document."

"It's better this way. We're less of a threat to them." His voice halted a moment. "I should tell you, the press wants to talk to you and the mayor's office called. He wants to give you a commendation."

"I don't want to make a big deal out of this."

"In a world which is notably lacking in acts of heroism, people like to make a big deal out of these things."

Jim continued to struggle with the spoon until he finally dropped his hand in frustration.

"I can't do this, dad. Could you please feed me?"

His father drew closer to him and took the spoon from his hand. He began to feed him as though he were an infant. For Jim, this was the most humbling experience in his entire life.

Chapter 35

The strain of trying to feed himself had exhausted Jim. Shortly after finishing his chocolate pudding, he drifted into a restive sleep. Jim's father slid his chair back toward the windows, and had begun to read a magazine, when Father Michael returned to the room.

"I know Michael is anxious to hear the last cassettes, so I bought a player for him."

"He's asleep."

The monk removed the player from the small canvas bag he was carrying and set it on the table beside the bed.

"I brought a few things for him to listen to."

Jim opened his eyes when he heard them speaking.

"I didn't mean to wake you. I'm sorry," Father Michael apologized.

"That's all right. Could you tell me what time it is?"

"It's about ten o'clock," his father answered.

"I brought this player and a tape of the liturgy of St. John Chrysostom in Russian. I know you're uncomfortable with religious things. But it's music by Tchaikovsky, and I find it relaxing."

"Thank you."

"Unfortunately, I have to get back to the house. We have a food run tonight. So I'll see you again. Sometime tomorrow or the next day."

Then the monk left the room.

"Dad, could you put the next tape in the player and turn it on for me?"

His father rose up from the chair, found the cassette labeled number sixteen on the table beside Jim's bed and placed it inside the player. Then he turned it on. There was an audible hiss for about a minute until Nigel's haunting voice began.

> *"I know it must be difficult for you, but eventually you'll get over it," I remember a young woman telling Beth as a way to console her on those first weeks after the kidnapping. But her words of sympathy served only to open the wound anew, and I could see in Beth's face the*

same agony as vividly as the day it happened.

No, you never get over the loss of a child, as though it were some illness or malady. It casts a long dark shadow over one's entire life.

Nothing could console us. No words, no flowers, no promises of prayers could make sense of the senselessness, and the fervent assurances of Special Agent Bartholomew that he would recover our son seemed only empty and hollow promises.

I can't begin to describe the unrelenting rage which consumed me afterwards. I stood there staring at the broken television scattered in barren pieces on the backyard lawn, and I was scorching. But it was undirected, out of focus. I had no object for the enmity except myself. And when the detectives returned in their caravan and began immediately to recite their alibis, I couldn't bear a word of it.

I knew from their blank faces that they couldn't comprehend my destruction of the television, but no one said a word about it. Instead, we filed back inside the house and sat down inside the living room.

"I assure you," Agent Bartholomew began, "This is not the end of it. Every resource at our disposal will be utilized."

And his colleagues, like a chorus, added in refrain, "The agency has a thousand resources we haven't even tapped."

And Beth sat quietly, as always, counting out her prayers.

"Lord Jesus Christ have mercy on me," I could hear her chanting almost inaudibly in Greek, but mercy seemed impossible.

As he went on to explain the exact course of action he would take, I couldn't concentrate on his words, and after only a few minutes, I interrupted him.

"Could you please just go away and leave us alone? I can't stand to hear another word of it."

And one by one they filed out of the house and climbed into the vans until at last we were alone, facing a loss which neither of us could bear.

"Would you like something to eat?" Beth asked me, fighting back her tears. "I could make some Greek coffee."

"If you like." And then we embraced each other and began to cry.

"I'm sorry, Beth. I'm so sorry."

"Not even a sparrow falls without God's oversight," she told me. "If God desires us to suffer, it must somehow serve our benefit." But I couldn't see how it could benefit anyone to lose a child.

In the days that followed, I could hardly get up in the morning, subdued by a depression as intense as in those first months in New York when I had seriously contemplated ending it all. But Beth immersed herself more deeply in her faith, rising early in the morning to do long morning prayers and reading the scriptures in the afternoon. I could sense she was struggling to make her peace with God when her heart was seemingly broken beyond repair.

Then I went to work at the Brooklyn office, largely out of habit and because I couldn't bear to be at home. But never again did I feel the same way about television.

The joy, the awe, the sense of excitement which had characterized those early years had dissipated, and I continued out of obligation to those who worked for me, as Beth would say for compassion's sake, and not because I cared to succeed. In fact, I didn't care much for anything any more. An all-pervasive nihilism had subdued me.

I remember coming home one evening in those first few weeks after the kidnapping and finding Beth, as always, praying before her icon stand.

"Come and pray with me, Neilos," she pleaded. But I was in no mood for prayers and lashed back at her.

"Don't you get it, Beth? Don't you understand? Did all those prayers save your family? Did they save your brother Demetrios in London? God doesn't give a damn about our sufferings, if he exists at all."

"Don't say these things," she entreated me. "We shall be judged for every idle word."

"Then let him judge me. God put us in this veil of tears, where the innocent suffer and the guilty prosper. Why would this all powerful, all loving God you pray to allow our child to be stolen? Who can believe in such a God?"

"You don't mean these words," she countered. "You can't mean them."

"I don't know what I mean any more. This God you believe in, I just can't see Him."

As each new day surrendered to the next, and the days eroded into weeks, and the weeks into months, we somehow endured. Though I didn't have the heart to tell Beth, I knew that no amount of prostrations, of candles or of fervent prayer could alter the unalterable reality of our loss. He was gone, and if this helped her cope, so be it. I coped in the only way I knew how—I threw myself into work.

Over the next two years, the business grew largely on its own momentum, from fifteen to sixteen to seventeen stores. In March of 1957 we opened our first store in Newark New Jersey, and we finalized our plans for our first trip to Greece later that summer. I met the prospect with some trepidation, largely because of language difficulties. Though Beth tried incessantly to help me master simple grammar structures and basic vocabulary, at least enough to be able to order food and ask directions, she was unable to overcome my inherent weakness in languages. Like many Americans, I rationalized that the peculiar particularities of English were difficult enough to conquer without trying to master another language. It would be years before I grasped the inherent simplicity in the modern Greek language or understand the pervasive influence of Greek vocabulary on English vocabulary.

Sometime in mid June, I can't quite remember the exact date, we boarded a plane at Idlewild Airport and began an eight-hour plane flight to Athens. We flew in one of the new jet airplanes built by Boeing. I remember thinking at the time how quickly technology had progressed from the small crop dusting planes I had first seen as a boy, and I thought of Leonard for the first time in over a year. I recalled something he once told me while we were sitting in our first radio store on a hot August afternoon.

"We will be able to see farther, fly higher. We will look to the farthest edges of the universe or to the smallest components of the atom, to smaller than the protons, neutrons and electrons. We will be able to imitate the vast panoply of engineering marvels in the natural world, and even fly to the moon and back."

I pondered if he would be pleased with the way things had progressed, how technology had become both a blessing and a curse, and how these advances made it possible to destroy whole cities with impunity.

"What are you thinking about?" Beth asked me as I stared trance-like out the airplane window at the ground beneath us.

"I was thinking about Leonard."

She squeezed my hand.

"What about Leonard?"

"I was thinking what he said about seeing. He said technology would make it possible for us to see all the secrets of the universe."
She chuckled.

"Eye hath not seen, nor has ear heard, nor the human mind understandeth what the Lord has prepared for those who love Him. There is a seeing beyond human seeing, Neilos. Seeing directed away from God leads only to blindness." She seemed amused with my speculation.

She reached into her bag and removed a book called The Way of a Pilgrim *and handed it to me to read. It recounted the story about this Russian peasant wandering from town to town while practicing the Jesus prayer, and I struggled to make sense out of it. Did this simple prayer recited continuously really have the power to transform the psyche? Did its most ardent practitioners really see the uncreated light? To my rational mind it all seemed impossible. But much of what she told me about Christianity seemed as foreign to me as Hinduism, certainly completely unlike the Christianity which Brother Woodrow preached in Wisconsin, a Christianity which I had rejected as a boy.*

"Well, what do you think?" she asked me at one point halfway through the flight.

"I don't know what to think."

"Can't you see the power in it?"

"People can write anything in a book. I can't accept what they're saying simply because it is written down."

"No, it's something you must try for yourself." Then she said, "Faith is not something in the mind." She said this in Greek and repeated the same thing in English.

When we arrived at Athens airport, we greeted sixteen of her relatives, mostly distant cousins, many of whom had driven from Arnos to meet us. They greeted us both with the customary three kisses, as she once explained to me, one kiss for each person of the Trinity.

I felt awkward again as she began to speak to them in Greek, while I struggled to say, "Good day," or "How are you?" or to answer simple questions which they directed toward me. Only one of her relatives spoke English, a cousin named Emmanuel, about thirty years old, and I gravitated toward him when he greeted me with a simple, "Good day."

"How far is Arnos from Athens?" I asked him.

"About five hours by car," He answered me. *"This is my brother, Demetrios."* He introduced me to a boy of about twelve. *"We were so sad to hear about Michael."*

His remark only opened the wound anew.

"Where did you learn English?" I asked him.

"In Athens University. But my professional degree was in architecture. I hope someday to work in America."

After retrieving our bags, Beth's cousin, Petros, drove us to his house in a suburb of Athens where they had prepared a sumptuous feast for us. There were the normal Greek specialties, dolmadas, souvlaki, and a small lamb roasting on a spit over a fire. They sat us both down at the corner of a long rectangular table and poured each of us a glass of red wine. Beth sat across from a cousin named Maria who was six or seven months pregnant, and I could see the sadness spread across Beth's face when she first saw her cousin.

"Elisavet," her cousin greeted her in the traditional Greek pronunciation. I had never called her anything but *"Beth"* and she had graciously accepted this Americanization, much as I had accepted being called *"Neilos."*

A priest named Father Nectarios, who had been wandering around and speaking with everyone, and to whom Beth had briefly introduced me, finally gave the blessing and we all sat down to eat.

I remember thinking, as I sat detached watching all of them, about the magnitude of what faced us the next day. Beth was returning for the first time in sixteen years to the place of her family's murder, and though she was reluctant to talk about it and always projected a courageous face, I knew in my gut it was tearing her up inside. Several times in the weeks prior, I had tried to dissuade her from making the trip so soon after Michael's loss, but she was unmoved.

"You know we could stay here for another day to rest," I proposed at one point in the meal.

"No, avrio," she responded. *"Tomorrow."*

"This reminds me of those big picnics we used to have in Wisconsin."

"Yes," she nodded.

"I always liked those picnics. My idea of heaven would be a huge picnic."

I sensed she wanted to say something in response, but she

restrained herself. The remainder of the evening, we spent on the veranda behind her cousin's house. We could see the Parthenon and the Acropolis towering above us in the distance, and in the presence of something so old, I felt insignificant.

Beth's cousin Petros and his wife spent over an hour in animated discussion with Beth, while I sat quietly and allowed my mind to wander from thought to thought like a feather tossed in the wind. I thought of Odysseus and Homer, of the pantheon of Greek gods and goddesses, of a hundred random thoughts of what I knew of ancient Greece. I thought of the Greek War for Independence, of Lord Byron, of the Greek alphabet. No coherent thread tied these impressions all together.

At ten o'clock, Beth's cousins both excused themselves, leaving Beth and I to sit alone outside. Then for fifteen minutes we endured an awkward silence which Beth finally broke.

"Emmanuel will drive us to Arnos in the morning."

"You're sure you want to do this now? We could spend a few days in Athens, see the sights like tourists, and then go to Arnos."

"No, I must face it now. My family would want me to."

"Is there something you're not telling me?"

She nodded. "I can't. Not yet. I'll tell you tomorrow."

At eleven o'clock, we went to bed in separate rooms for the first time since we were married. As I lay restlessly atop my burnt red blankets, I could hear Beth chanting her evening prayer in the next room. "Thoxa patri ke eeo ke agio pnevmati, neen ke aee ke ees toos eonas ton eonon. Glory to the Father and to the Son and to the Holy Spirit. Now and ever and unto ages of ages."

We rose early the next morning at six o'clock, and Emmanuel met us at eight with a dark-brown 1955 Studebaker. Beth had prepared a picnic basket with sandwiches, olives and oranges which we planned to eat once we arrived in Arnos.

Our drive was pleasant and relaxing. I kept busy by watching the countryside and counting churches scattered like wild flowers across the hillside and standing like fortresses in the valleys. I must have counted a hundred of them by halfway through the trip, and there were several roadside shrines, a few no bigger than the car. Four times Beth insisted we stop while she went inside to light a candle and pray.

"What are these chapels?" I asked her.

"They're shrines to various local saints," Beth answered me.

"I've never seen so many churches. How old are they?"

"Many were built in Byzantine times," Emmanuel interjected. "I've made an extensive study of Byzantine architecture."

Beth began to speak to him in Greek.

"Elisavet is criticizing for using the word "Byzantine.""

"Why?" I asked him.

"Because there was no Byzantine Empire." He paused a moment. "Before the Greek revolution in 1822, all the Christian peoples which inhabited what is now the Balkan peninsula, Greece and Turkey called themselves "Romi" or Romans, and they called the language they spoke Romaiki or the language of the Romans. In order to get military and financial support for our revolution from western powers, we had to agree to call ourselves Greeks or Hellenes and our new state, Greece or Ellada," He paused. "What is a name? A rose by any other name would smell as sweet."

"It's all the fault of the Masons," Beth answered him.

I had heard the talk of Freemasonry before. They were blamed for everything from the American Revolution, the French Revolution, the Communist Revolution, to the rise of Adolph Hitler. But I was unconvinced. They seemed convenient bogey men when people wanted simple explanations. If Beth wanted to believe they were behind the Greek Revolution as well, I felt no need to dissuade her.

About midway through the trip, while Beth and Emmanuel conversed in the front seat, I sat pensively in the back. I decided to remove the pilgrim book from Beth's bag to take one more stab at reading it. I had read as far as this part about a Russian monastery and the value of the Philokalia, *a collection of Greek spiritual writings, when Emmanuel suddenly stopped the car, which tossed the book out of my hands.*

A horse and wagon was blocking the road. An older Greek man was shouting at the horse and yanking his reins, but the horse was immovable. After fifteen minutes of anxious waiting, Emmanuel finally got out of the car and went toward them. Then both of them together began pulling and coaxing, but the horse kept shaking his head and stomping his rear hooves and would not move.

Beth looked at me expectantly and I sensed she wanted me to do something. Reluctantly, I climbed out of the car to see if I could help.

When I approached the horse, he seemed agitated. Almost instinctively I began to stroke his forehead. I remembered seeing Mr. McIlhenry doing the same thing. "It's all right," I spoke barely above a whisper. Then I began to rub the bottom of his neck. "Calm down. Calm down." And then I grabbed the reins, and with deliberate steps I began to pull the horse, and we walked slowly step-by-step until the wagon was off the road.

"Efcharisto, Efcharisto," the man kept saying.

"I'm impressed," Emmanuel told me. We climbed back into the car and continued our journey.

It was three o'clock when we arrived in Arnos. We drove through a large olive orchard, and I could see flocks of sheep grazing on bare hillsides in the distance. When Beth first saw the village church with its dark green rotunda, two streams of tears ran down her cheeks. There was something eerily familiar about the place, but I couldn't put the thought into words.

We stopped the car in the center of the village square, and Beth climbed out. I could see a pallette of emotions painted in course brush strokes across her face.

"Are you OK?" I asked her as I placed my right arm around her shoulder.

"Thoxa to Theo," she crossed herself. Then she bent down on the uneven pavement stones and prostrated herself. Emmanuel opened the trunk of the car and removed the picnic basket while I stood restively with my eyes scanning across every building and landmark in the village. People were beginning to come out of their houses and shops to see who we were. Then I noticed a large plaque standing at the corner of the square, which listed over one hundred names.

"Elisavet," an older woman began to shout and wave her arms. Then she ran across the square and embraced Beth who was rising to her feet. Soon others arrived, embracing and crying, and I too began to cry. After several minutes of this nexus of intense emotion when I thought I couldn't bear it any more, she walked over to the plaque and began to read their names, one by one, touching the names of her family who had died that day sixteen years before.

I, too, was overcome with grief.

I approached the plaque with all the others and asked her, "Won't you read it for me?"

She read it first in Greek and then repeated it in English, "To all those who sacrificed themselves in the defense of the Gospel of Christ on June 30, 1941. May their memory be eternal." On the bottom right-hand corner beneath three columns of names read a date of June 30, 1946.

Eleven years had passed and nearly twelve years since the end of the war. Still, the memory of it cast a palling shadow over everything. How many dead? Twenty million, fifty million. Six million Jews. A million Serbs. The numbers were so staggering that we became inured to them; and to think it all began in the imagination of one man. His "kampf" had become the world's "agonia."

Though we had originally planned to spend only a few hours in Arnos, after we had eaten our picnic lunch, the people were so hospitable and so eager to spend time with Beth that we agreed to remain through the night. They invited us to a local tavern where they had laid out for us an opulent feast, which I knew, given their humble means, must have been a tremendous sacrifice. Three local musicians began to play bouzoukis, and a clarinet and a young woman sang in accompaniment. Greek music had always sounded unusual to me with its irregular cadences and its middle eastern inflections, but on that evening with all its enthusiasm, I enjoyed it.

Later in the evening, three men began to dance shoulder to shoulder, and soon others joined them, until twenty-five people arm in arm were dancing in near perfect synchrony across the irregular pavement stones. Several times, Beth encouraged me to join them, but I felt too uncomfortable. At one point, I looked over at Beth and she seemed happy for the first time in two years, as if for those few hours the yoke of grief had been lifted from her shoulders. "This is her world," I remembered thinking, and in her world I was clearly an outsider.

When the music subsided and everyone began to eat, Beth took me around and introduced me to people. "Anthras mou, Neilos, Amerikanos," she told them, and I shook hands in the American way. Then she asked them every detail of what had transpired since the war. She explained to them about her last sixteen years, and when she told them about Michael's kidnapping, without exception they said, "Thoxa to Theo," and crossed themselves. "We shall pray for his safe return." After several exchanges, I began to recognize the Greek words.

When she told them I sold televisions, many of them didn't know what they were, and others, when she explained it to them, seemed perplexed that anyone would want one. When one man challenged me by saying in Greek, "Tell me one benefit of television," I couldn't bring myself to give even a half-hearted apology for them because my heart wasn't in it anymore.

"What were you going to tell me today?" I asked Beth after we finally returned to our seats.

"I was going to tell you about the day my family was killed."

"You told me about it."

"Not everything." She paused a moment, then calmly and without modulation in her voice, she said, "I didn't tell you why they were killed."

"Why?" I responded.

"Because we gave sanctuary to several Jewish families, and someone in our village informed on us."

"Why didn't you tell me this before?"

"Because many of my people collaborated with the Nazis. I'm ashamed of it."

"You didn't do anything wrong."

"God allowed this to happen because we turned our backs on him and sought the things of the world. Sometimes a nation must pay for its sins."

"God didn't allow any of this to happen. Things just happen." I paused. "Did God allow the Turks to kill over a million Armenians because of their sins? Did he allow the city of Smyrna to be burned to the ground because of its sins? I refuse to believe in a God who uses rape and murder as a means of disciplining his children." I grabbed her hand and said, "Beth, I love you. None of this has happened because of anything we did wrong. Please trust me on this." But I could see in her eyes that she didn't believe me.

About eleven o'clock, the party began to break up. Then one by one, and in small groups, people began to return to their houses. By midnight the square was empty, except for Emmanuel, Beth and me. I seriously considered asking Emmanuel to drive us back to Athens, despite the late hour. The emotional intensity of the place was more than I could bear. But Beth looked exhausted, and after a few moments of hesitation, I told her, "Please go to sleep. You look tired. I'll be along in a little while." She reluctantly went off to rest in Theophania Christopoulos' house, where accommodations had been graciously offered.

"What are your plans?" Emmanuel asked me after Beth had departed the square.

"I don't know. But I'd like to leave tomorrow."

"You don't much like Arnos then?"

"It's not so much Arnos. It's the feeling of death I sense in this place."

"You can feel it too?" Emmanuel acknowledged. "Every time I come here, how you say it in English, it gives me the creeps."

"Perhaps it's because I feel personally attached to this place," I speculated.

"Because of Elisavet?"

"Yes. But there's something else. Even though I've never been here, this place seems hauntingly familiar." I paused. "How many massacre sites like this one are there in Greece?"

"I don't know. But we have relatives in Belgrade, and they say there are hundreds of them in Yugoslavia. Others are scattered throughout Greece, Bulgaria and Romania. It depends on how stridently they resisted Nazi and fascist occupation."

"Most people cooperated, then." I asserted.

"Not everyone. But at the point of a gun, most people choose life over death."

"You speak English very well," I told him.

"Thank you. But I don't get much practice." Sounding very much as though he wanted me to hire him, he continued, "I'd love to work in America." But business was the furthest thing from my mind. When he could see that I was not going to pursue it further, he said, "We really should be going to sleep soon."

"I am tired," I responded. Then both of us went off to sleep.

When we arrived at Theophania's house, Beth had already gone to bed. Theophania escorted us into her small parlor, where she had set up two cots side by side. They looked like army issue cots, not very comfortable, and with some reluctance both of us lay down on them. It was a precarious balancing act, and I was afraid of falling out of mine. Theophania provided us with two olive green wool blankets and small red pillows for our heads. "Peaceful sleep," she wished us in Greek, as she extinguished two oil lamps on her parlor hearth. There was electricity in the village, but not in every house, and not in Theophania's house.

Early the next morning, Beth was up for religious services. When she shook me about six o'clock, the cot wobbled unstably. For a moment I had forgotten where I was, and in that nexus between unconsciousness and waking, I had an intense recollection of my Navy days, dreamlike but as vivid as consciousness. I remembered a cot where I had slept during March of 1945, while we were working on encryption devices in one of the base's electronics labs. I felt the same acute pain in the small of my back. When Beth finally awakened me, the sight of Theophania's modest cottage startled me.

"Neilos," Beth was imploring me. "Wake up. We need to go to liturgia."

"Let me rest a little longer."

"No, Neilos," she spoke with more resolve. "We must pray for my family."

I struggled to my feet like an exhausted prize-fighter and went to the privy to wash up. I was annoyed that Beth didn't feel the same need to rouse Emmanuel, who was still asleep on his cot when I returned.

After dressing, we walked to the village church which stood atop a small hill on the east side of the village. I could hear the sound of the Byzantine chant through the carved wooden doors, though, since my discussion with Emmanuel in the car, I didn't know what to call it anymore. The church was almost empty except for ten to fifteen old women, several of whom were sitting in benches along the wall. There were no pews and most were standing. There were no men except for the cantor and Father Andonios, who looked nearly eighty and was chanting petitions from the altar with his hands in the air.

As Beth prayed earnestly beside me, I felt disconnected. My mind was unable to focus on the service as I reflected on the past ten years, on every decision which had led inevitably to that moment. There seemed a logical progression to everything which had happened, as predictably as a circle returns to itself. But I was unsatisfied with this conclusion. I felt as though I was losing myself. I wanted to cry out, "This is not who I am! This is not where I belong!" But where did I belong, and who was I? I surmised that most people were content with who they were, when I seemed to be displaced, no matter which path I chose to walk. Or did I choose it? I longed for reconciliation with myself.

After the service ended, Beth and I went to greet the priest. We kissed his right hand in the customary fashion and he blessed us.

"Pater," Beth introduced me in Greek. "My husband, Neilos."

I nodded in acknowledgment.

When we stepped outside the church, I told her, "Beth I'd really like to return to Athens today."

"I know it is uncomfortable for you. But I have one more favor to ask of you."

She reached into her bag and retrieved a letter.

"This is for my brother, Father Niphon," she told me.

"The one on Mount Athos?"

"Yes. I'd like you to take it to him. You know I can't go there."

The last thing I wanted to do was to take a pilgrimage to Athos. But when she looked at me expectantly, I begrudgingly agreed. "Alright, for your sake."

"Efcharisto. Agapo se." She kissed me on the right cheek.

That afternoon over lunch she also implored Emmanuel. From a comfortable distance, I could see he was putting up some resistance, but he too succumbed after a half hour of her persuasion.

"It seems we're going to Athos," he later approached me and told me.

"It appears that way."

"I'm not very religious," he confided, "and these monks can be very strict."

"Neither am I."

Later that afternoon, after we had finished visiting several old women in their houses, Beth asked me to walk the three kilometers to her family's farm. Everyone we visited had offered us very strong Greek coffee, and I felt wired from the caffeine.

She grabbed my hand as we began the journey, squeezing it tightly as though to gain strength from me. After a few hesitant steps down the brown gravel road, she suddenly stopped and looked at me. "Thank You, Neilos, for being with me. You don't know what a blessing it has been." As we continued walking, she began playfully swinging my arm. We traveled nearly a kilometer more and she stopped again. "Courage," she told me and released my hand so that she could cross herself. By this time I could see the burnt brown farmhouse standing in the midst of a grove of olive trees. There were grape vines laced through a large wood trellis which rested right up against the southern side of the house. It was not large, with perhaps six or seven rooms, and I could see blue curtains through one set of windows. It was the same blue as the blue on the Greek flag. I remember the piquant odor of basil from a dozen bushes planted on all sides of the house. As we approached closer, I noticed two worn wooden wagons, one with its left rear wheel missing and the other obviously still in use. Then I could see for the first time a small wooden barn, newly painted, maybe a hundred yards from the house at the edge of a shallow ravine. Beth looked nervous. She began to squeeze my hand more tightly as we came nearer to the house. I remember wondering who was still living in the house because everything seemed to be well kept.

When we approached within a hundred yards of the house, a young man in his twenties came outside and began to walk toward us. I searched my memory to see if I could recognize his face from those I had seen the night before, but came up blank. Beth released my hand and then gestured for me to remain where I was. She rushed up to meet him. I could see from his physiognomy that he was disturbed about something. Then he began to speak Greek in staccato phrases, punctuated with forceful hand gestures, while Beth stood passively and spoke more slowly and deliberately in response. After a few moments of this intense interchange, the young man returned to the house and after a minute or two, both he and an older man, who from family resemblance I presumed was his father, came out to confront her.

When the two men began to raise their voices, I became anxious and began to move toward them. But Beth gestured with her hands and said, "Ochi," or "No." At one point she bent down on her knees and kept saying, "Sygnomen," which means "forgive me." I began to understand why she had said, "Courage." Finally after fifteen minutes, both men returned to the house.

"What was that all about?" I asked her.

"They think I have come to reclaim the farm. They say it's theirs now."

I was confused. "How is it theirs?"

"No one was here to claim it after the war. So they took it."

"No one was there because they were all murdered," I responded. "And what did you tell them?"

"I told them I don't want the farm. I only want whatever things of my family were left in the house. I don't think they believe me."

After fifteen anxious minutes of waiting outside, the young man returned and gestured for us to follow him. I heard him say something under his breath, but the only word I recognized was "Ebraios." Then he began to lead us toward the barn.

He went inside alone and after a minute or two returned with a wooden box one foot by two feet by three feet, covered with a blanket. He set the box down on the ground in front of us. Then Beth reverently lifted the blanket to uncover what was inside.

She found a small porcelain doll about nine inches tall and dressed in a traditional Greek costume. As she carefully lifted it out of the box, I could see tears pooling in each eye. She discovered service books and a wooden cross and an icon of St. Michael, which she crossed and kissed and then set aside. By this time tears were flowing in rivulets down each cheek. There were photographs tossed in the bottom of the box, which she lifted up one by one to her eyes. She kissed each one like an icon, and I could see she could barely control herself. Then, as carefully as she had taken everything out, she returned each item to the box. "Efcharisto," she thanked the young man and then gestured to me to lift up the box. Then side by side, we walked back the way we came.

"He said something under his breath. What was it?" I asked her.

"Eseis Voithisate tous Evraios," she repeated. "You helped the Jews," she translated.

On the way back to the center of village, I struggled continuously with the wooden box. I started and stopped a number of times to re-balance it or to get a firmer grip. A couple of times, I stared down into it and thought of my own collection of objects at home, how each was invested with a treasury of memory, mute until my mind gave it voice.

Beth was still crying. I could see she held in her hand a worn photograph of a young child who bore a striking resemblance to our Michael.

"Who is it?" I asked her.

"It's Dimitrios," she responded. "He looked so much like Michael." She began to weep uncontrollably, and I set the box on the

ground and embraced her.

"You shouldn't do this to yourself," I tried to console her. I wanted to shout, 'Wasn't it enough, God, that you took her family? Must you take her child as well?' But I held my tongue. At that moment the world seemed a hellish place.

Then she began to chant, "Kyrie Isous Christe eleison eme."

"Lord Jesus Christ have mercy on me." Repeating it again and again, counting the prayers on a knotted bracelet around her wrist. I picked up the box and we continued our pilgrimage back to the town.

When we arrived, it was about four o'clock and Emmanuel was pacing nervously across the square.

"There was quite a commotion here while you were gone," he told me. Then he began to speak in Greek.

"What happened?" I interrupted him.

"The military police came and made an arrest."

"Why?"

"A suspected communist."

He continued to speak to Beth in Greek, and I could sense from the timbre in his voice that he was disturbed.

"Ochi, Ochi," Beth kept repeating to him. "I'm not leaving now. I want to see my family's graves."

"Alright," he acquiesced. "Let's go see the graves."

I was confused. As the three of us began to walk toward the cemetery at the far edge of the village, Beth kept stopping along the way to pick wild flowers, which she carefully arranged together in her left hand. She removed a rubber band which was holding her hair in a small pony tail and wrapped the rubber band around the stems. Her black hair then draped over her shoulders.

When we reached the cemetery, she rushed ahead of us and began to search earnestly through rows of small stone crosses for the names of her family members. After about fifteen minutes, she found her parents' graves. She threw herself to the ground, laying the flowers down beside her. Then nearly a half an hour passed as she prostrated herself, praying and kissing the crosses, one by one, on all their graves.

"Alright, I'm ready to leave now."

"Where to now?" I asked her.

"We're going to Thessaloniki to stay with friends of mine."
Emmanuel answered. "Then you and I are going to Athos."

"We could stay longer," I proposed.

"No. I've had my goodbyes. Efcharisto."

"Parakalo," I responded.

It was another two-hour drive from Arnos to Thessaloniki, and Emmanuel seemed anxious to begin our journey. We spent an hour making our goodbyes. Theophania told Beth that she hoped we would return again under happier circumstances. She gave us a basket filled with fruit, olives and Greek sausages for our journey.

I remember thinking, as the car began to pull away, as I turned around and looked out the rear window, what a cleansing experience the whole last day had been, or as Beth would say, "Katharsis."

The tape clicked off on its first side and Jim lifted his hand and tried to open the cassette player. But his hand missed its target and toppled the porcelain doll into his lap. He struggled to lift it from his lap and place it back on the table, but his hands wouldn't do what he asked of them.

"Let me help you with this," Jim's father interceded for him.

He lifted the doll and placed it on the table for him.

"Could you turn over the cassette for me?" he asked him.

"Of course."

"Thank you. You know you could go home and rest."

"I want to hear the rest of the story. I need to hear the rest of the story."

As they both stared a moment at the doll, they knew that they would never again look at it in the same way.

We arrived in Thessaloniki at about seven o'clock in the evening. It had been a beautiful drive through a mostly flat plain, punctuated by a number of small hills. The city sat in a valley between a series of hills, whose name in Greek I have forgotten. Our plan was to stay overnight with Emmanuel's friends and then in the morning, Emmanuel and I would leave for Athos.

Athos is technically a peninsula jutting out into the Aegean sea. At an elevation of five thousand feet, it is one of the highest points in northern Greece, hence its name Athos, or the "high place." Atop its summit are twenty monasteries scattered across an area of 75 square kilometers. Some of the oldest monasteries date to the ninth and tenth centuries. Beth's brother Father Niphon was an archimandrite, or priest monk, at one of the strictest monastic communities named

Esphigmenou.

At about seven thirty, we arrived in the center of the city, driving passed a number of modern buildings that had been built since the end of the war, and Emmanuel pointed out various sights as we passed them, including an old Jewish synagogue, one of the oldest in Greece. The prewar population of Jews in Thessaloniki had been over fifty thousand, but had been decimated by the war.

Panayoti and Sofia Papageorgiou, Emmanuel's friends, were living in a new high rise apartment building near the docks. We stopped in the front of the building, and Emmanuel exited the car. He stood a few moments by the doorway until a young woman, about twenty-five, carrying a baby in her arms, opened the door and came outside.

"Yasou, Emmanuel," she greeted him and kissed him on each cheek.

He took the baby out of her arms so she could approach the car and meet us both.

"Yasou," she reached through the window and embraced Beth. Beth reciprocated.

"My name is Sofia," she said in Greek.

"Elisavet ke Neilos."

Then we both climbed out of the car and followed Sofia back to the building. When we reached the front doorstep, Emmanuel told her something in Greek, and she reclaimed her baby. Then Emmanuel left to find a place to park the car.

As the elevator rose to the fifth floor, Beth and Sofia conversed enthusiastically. Though I understood only a few words, like "baby" and "nine months" and "Grigorios," I could deduce the general parameters of the conversation, but not the details.

Their apartment number, 505, was small but elegantly decorated. After opening the door for us, Sofia set down the baby in a mesh-lined playpen and went into the small kitchen to prepare us some tea. I watched as Beth bent over the playpen and stared tenderly into the infant's face.

"May I pick him up?" she asked in Greek.

"Malista," Sofia called from the kitchen.

Then, as delicately and tenderly as though he were her own, Beth lifted the child and cradled him in her arms.

"Ti Kaneis?" she kept saying playfully while poking her finger at his chin. *"Ti kaneis, pethiaki?"*

Then she began to lift the child into the air and rock him in her arms. It was the first time I had seen her genuinely smile in months.

Sofia soon returned with four cups of tea and honey, which she placed on small trays and carried out for us.

"My English is no so good," Sofia told me in a deep Greek accent.

"My Greek is worse."

"Panayoti working," she struggled to tell me. "He be home about nine o'clock."

"What does he do?" I asked her in English and Beth translated.

"Architectoniki," she responded.

"Architecture," Beth translated.

"So he was a classmate of Emmanuel's?" I deduced.

"Ne, ne," she responded.

Then our conversation was interrupted by Emmanuel's bell and Sofia rose up to let him in.

"She seems very nice," I told Beth after Sofia had gone.

Beth nodded in agreement.

"Can I hold him now?"

Beth carefully handed me the baby.

"Be careful with him, Neilos."

As I bounced him on my right knee while holding his torso between my hands, I could see a wave of sadness spreading across her face.

"I'll never see Michael again," she said. Her voice betrayed her melancholy.

"Don't say such things. When we get back to New York, I'll double my efforts. I promise you."

When Sofia and Emmanuel returned to the apartment a few minutes later, Sofia took the baby from my arms and carried him back with her into the kitchen. Then Emmanuel sat down beside me on the sofa.

"Nice place, isn't it?" he told me.

For the first time I closely examined the decor. I discovered two hand-woven tapestries, one depicting the fall of Constantinople and the other a view of the Acropolis and Parthenon. I also noticed pen and ink drawings hanging in several places around the apartment. One drawing of a beetle on a wooden log immediately caught my attention.

"They are very good, aren't they?" Emmanuel observed.

I arose to examine it more closely.

"I've been encouraging him to have an exhibition somewhere. But he doesn't think he's good enough."

His drawings revealed a precision and attention to detail I had not seen before, except perhaps with Leonard's sketches, or with some drawings I had seen in the Metropolitan Museum of Art. One particularly horrific drawing of the Crucifixion hung outside the doorway to the kitchen. It frightened me to look at it. When Sofia returned from the kitchen carrying a tray of pisticcio, a casserole of large macaroni, cheese and ground meat, she noticed me staring at the drawing. Then she spoke to Emmanuel in Greek.

"She says she has asked Panayoti to take it down because it keeps scaring the guests," he translated. "But Panayoti says they need to be scared."

Sofia set the tray down on the dining room table and began to cut the pisticcio into two inch squares. Then Beth came over to assist her. Beth removed the Greek sausages from the basket we had brought and began slicing them as well.

"I have a diagram of Athos," Emmanuel began to explain to me. He removed a folded piece of paper from his trouser pocket and unfolded in front of me. "It's rather crudely drawn." He continued.

"You drew this?" I asked him.

"Yes, largely from memory. I went there once after the war. But let me continue. This is Esphigmenou." He pointed to an "X" marked on the northeast side of the peninsula. Down here are Pantocrator, Philotheou, St. Paul, and many of the other monasteries.

There is no direct route from here to here." He pointed to a town marked as Ouranopolis and then to Esphigmenou. "We would take a boat from Ouranopolis and travel around the coast, stopping at every monastery along the way."

"And how long does that take?"

"I don't know?" He paused. "Sofia, echeis to photographia tou Esphigmenou?" he called out.

She left the kitchen, and went to a bookshelf in the parlor, where she removed a book from the shelf, leafed through it a few moments until she found a photograph of Esphigmenou, and set the book down in front of me. She then returned to the kitchen to resume what she was doing.

"Efcharisto," he thanked her.

The monastery was built in the shape of a square doughnut with a small basilica in the center. I counted five floors and four towers.

"*Have you been there before?*" *I asked him.*

"*No, but I saw it at a distance. The roof you see here in gray is a burnt orange.*"

"*How many monks are living there now?*"

"*I don't know. But numbers have declined.*"

By nine o'clock, Sofia had finished preparing the table, set elegantly with five place settings, including special salad forks. She had fed the baby and put him to bed. All we awaited was Panayoti's return. At nine thirty when he had not arrived, she proposed, "*If you are very hungry, we could begin the meal without him.*" *We all agreed to wait.*

At nine forty-five, she explained in Greek, "*He has a special project at work. I'm certain he will be home soon.*"

"*It's no problem,*" *Beth answered her. Sofia seemed more anxious than the rest of us about his delay.*

At ten o'clock, the door finally opened and Panayoti stepped inside.

"*Sygnomen, Kali Nichta,*" *he said. He was thirty years old, about six feet tall with auburn hair. I could see an incredible intelligence in his eyes.*

"*Ti kaneis, Emmanuel?*" *he greeted his friend and kissed him on both cheeks.*

"*Kala,*" *Emmanuel responded.*

"*I hope you are not waiting for me,*" *he spoke English with a strong Greek accent.*

"*You speak English,*" *I responded.*

"*A little,*" *he answered, holding his thumb and index finger of his right hand about half an inch apart.* "*Not as well as my friend, Emmanuel.*" *Then he began to speak to Emmanuel in Greek.*

After a few enthusiastic exchanges between them, Panayoti pointed to the chairs around the table and spoke, "*Kathete. Sit.Parakalo.*"

Each of us sat down at the rectangular table, Beth and I beside each other and Emmanuel across from me.

"*What work do you do?*" *Panayoti asked me.*

"*I sell televisions,*" *I responded.*

He looked perplexed.

"*You know television, the device which allows you to see moving pictures at a distance."*

"I know television." He paused a moment and then spoke, "Cosmas Aitolos."

"I'm sorry. I don't understand."

Then, he began to speak in Greek and Emmanuel translated.

"Cosmas Aitolos was a saint of the church who lived nearly two hundred years ago. He predicted that men would be able to speak from one side of the world to the other as though in the same room. He predicted there would be great black birds raining fire from the sky. He said it all would be inspired by demons."

As he spoke, all I could think of was Galileo being condemned by the Vatican.

"Panayoti, Ochi," Sofia rebutted. Her expression betrayed her annoyance with him.

"The demons give knowledge," he continued to speak, "But always at great personal cost."

Sofia grabbed his hand and squeezed it.

"I don't mean anything personal," he spoke slowly in English. "Just something to think about." He smiled.

If he had spoken these words before the kidnapping, I was certain I would have been deeply offended, but at that moment it didn't seem to impact me.

"I should have told you Panayoti always speaks his mind," Emmanuel attempted to diffuse the tension in the room.

"I'm not upset," I responded. "I have no profound commitment to the business any more. But I am responsible for those who work for me." This was the only defense I felt comfortable offering.

"Phagete," Beth gently interjected. "Let's eat."

Panayoti rose to his feet and gave a short blessing. Then, we all crossed ourselves and sat down to eat.

As we dined, the conversation became more ebullient, and Panayoti, despite his initial burst of intensity, actually became quite affable. I tried to follow the conversation. Most of it was in Greek, of course. But my attention slowly drifted to other thoughts. I remembered something Beth had said on the drive up from Arnos. "Thessaloniki is one of the oldest Christian communities of the world, dating from those communities founded by St. Paul." For some odd reason the image of Brother Woodrow popped into my head. I could almost hear him giving another of his bombastic sermons on Paul's First Book to the Thessalonians. I struggled to push his image from my mind.

"Neilos, we were talking about New York," Emmanuel began to speak to me in English. "How many people live there?"

"I don't know exactly. Six million, maybe seven million."

"How many televisions?"

"I don't know. But we are selling close to a hundred a week in most of our stores. I think we sold close to a hundred thousand units last year. Why are you asking me this?"

"Panayoti wants to know, how you say it in English, pervasive they are."

"They are quite pervasive," I retorted, "For good or evil. But I really don't want to talk about the television business."

"Sygnomen," Panayoti began to speak in Greek and again Emmanuel translated.

"He's sorry. He didn't mean to imply that you were personally inspired by demons. He believes television could be a Pandora's Box. All manner of evil comes out of it and hope remains locked inside."

I remembered the story of Pandora's Box from high school, and I could see from Panayoti's expression that he was pleased with this choice of metaphor.

"Sygnomen," he repeated. "Ego eime amartolos. (I am a sinner.)" I understood him. "I understand. So am I."

The rest of the meal progressed without incident. Television, Cosmas Aitololos or demons did not come up again. I spent most of my time trying to subdue a growing trepidation about the pilgrimage planned for the next day. I was not religious, or so I assured myself. The trappings of religion, its rituals, its disciplines, I had come to tolerate solely in order to be with Beth. I rationalized that I loved her in spite of them, that her unconditional love for me arose not from her religious conviction, but from her inner soul, which would have been the same no matter the particular circumstances into which she was born, be it Greek Orthodoxy or Hinduism or Buddhism. And all this talk of demons and technology I also found unconvincing. I believed, taken as a whole, technology had been good for man. 'Think of life without indoor plumbing, without refrigeration, without electricity, without penicillin,' I proposed to myself. 'Were we better off without these things?'

"What are you thinking about?" Beth asked me as I sat as though in a trance lost in my own thoughts.

"I was thinking about the journey tomorrow." I responded.

"Don't be afraid, Neilos," she encouraged me. "No one is going to coerce you into a monastic life. God loves us where we are. He understands our weakness." She paused a moment. "The church is a hospital for the sick. We are all in the need of its therapeia." Then she said something to the others in Greek.

After we finished the main course, Sofia brought out a tray of baklava and some Greek cookies made with orange juice whose name I have forgotten. Then Emmanuel pressed Panayoti to show us some of his ink drawings.

Panayoti went into the bedroom and returned a few minutes later with a brown leather portfolio measuring three feet by three feet square, which he zipped open on a table in the parlor. It revealed over a hundred drawings in a stack nearly two inches thick. Carrying our desserts on small porcelain plates, we all followed him into the parlor to look more closely at his drawings.

Then the baby began to cry in the bedroom, and Sofia left us to tend to him.

"What is this?" I asked him as I looked at the first drawing of a large basilica, very precisely drawn.

"Agios Dimitrios," he answered in Greek.

"Dimitrios is the patron saint of Thessaloniki," Emmanuel explained. "I should take you to see the cathedral after our visit to Athos."

Beneath it were several other drawings of landmarks including the "Levkos Pyrgos" or "White Tower", one of the tourist sites in the city. I had seen the tower when we first entered the business district.

"When was this built?" I asked them out of curiosity. I was stunned at the detail of the drawing.

"It was built by the Ottomans," Emmanuel answered. Then Panayoti began to speak in Greek. He spoke quickly for over a minute in what seemed a long disputation.

"It was once part of the fortress walls which guarded the city. It has been called the bloody tower," Emmanuel translated. "The Ottomans used it as a place of execution and as a barracks for the Janissaries.

Have you heard about the Janissaries?"

"I'm very ignorant about much of history, but you can educate me."

"The Janissaries were conscripted from the first born of every conquered Roman family. They were taken to Constantinople, forcibly converted to Islam, then sent back to Roman lands to act as executioners against their own people," Emmanuel explained.

There was indignation in his voice and he seemed to emphasize the word "Roman", rather than using Greek or Byzantine.

"They stole our history from us," Beth interjected, "First the Ottomans and then the Franks, even imposing on us German kings after our liberation."

I found it difficult to understand this personal connection to events several hundred years past. But then, America was a young country, not even two hundred years old, and by these terms we had so little history to remember.

Beneath this drawing were other sketches, more personal and intimate, several of Sofia and the baby. Each one, he lifted tenderly and set aside. There were landscapes of such exacting detail I could see the blades of grass and almost sense the wind blowing in the trees.

"These are more than good. They're wonderful," Beth spontaneously interjected.

Sofia returned to the parlor carrying the baby in her arms.

"Avtos echi charismata," Beth told her. I somehow understood, "He is gifted or very talented."

"Malista," Sofia responded.

Each successive drawing brought greater admiration from his already awestruck audience, as one by one he lifted them and revealed his depth of competence.

"I could find a gallery in New York which would gladly show these," I spoke and Emmanuel translated.

"Ochi, Ochi," he paused. "No, No."

"You're certain?"

"Ne, I'm certain," he repeated.

After letting us examine close to a hundred sketches, he carefully lined up the edges of the papers, placed the stack inside the portfolio, closed it, and returned it to the bedroom. It was nearly eleven o'clock. Beth could barely keep her eyes open, and Sofia had fallen asleep in an overstuffed chair with the baby asleep in her lap. Panayoti gestured for Emmanuel to help him, and the two of them pulled a full-sized roll-away bed from out of the closet, which they carefully unfolded. They found three pillows and blankets and prepared the sofa and bed for us to sleep. By midnight, all of us were asleep in our beds, with Emmanuel on the sofa and Beth and I on the full-sized bed. It was the first time we had slept together in days, and it felt good to hold her in my arms again.

But it was a restless sleep which followed. Several times during the night I was awakened by vivid dreams, those kind of dreams which have the feeling of consciousness, but whose subtle inconsistencies betray that one is dreaming.

One such dream concerned the farm. My father and I were sitting on two tractors, painted not red as I remembered them, but green, looking almost like two huge grasshoppers, when suddenly a butterfly, whose wingspan must have been at least ten feet from tip to tip, flew up in front of us. It kept flapping its wings with such intensity that the tractors began to fly backwards.

"What do you see?" a voice like my mother's began to shout from inside the butterfly. "What do you see?" sounding like chanting. And my father turned to me and began shouting back, "we're all going to die." Then almost like singing a round, the butterfly would chant "What do you see?" and my father would chant in response, "We're all going to die." The sound of the rush of air from the wings grew louder and stronger until it almost roared like a hurricane, and then the tractors began to rise in the air, tossed back and forth as easily as a leaf in the wind, until I could barely hold onto it. "Stop it. Stop it. This isn't real," I began to shout back. "This isn't real," until I woke up shouting.

"Neilos," Beth grabbed me. "You must pray before you sleep." She kept crossing me, saying, "Kyrie, Isou Christe Nika," till I calmed down and struggled back to sleep.

The next morning I awoke to the melodic resonance of Beth's voice as she chanted her morning prayers. Then for the first time in months, I joined her. Standing quietly beside her, I marveled as she recited these long prayers from memory.

By eight o'clock everyone was awake, including the baby. Emmanuel and I had completed our packing. Beth gave me the letter for her brother and entreated me, "Please ask him to come and see me. I so want to see him."

"Of course."

"Have courage," she encouraged us and kissed us both. "Have courage," I reflected upon her words, as we stepped outside the threshold and the door closed soundly behind us. "How can I have courage?" as a wave of fear swept over me. I sensed that from that moment nothing would ever be the same, that as a small boat is unmoored by torrential winds and is carried away by restless seas, I too was being propelled by currents beyond my control. The feeling became even more acute when we arrived at the docks of Ouranoupolis and I first saw the small sail boat which would carry us to Esphigmenou.

"I hate boats," I told Emmanuel as we stepped off the pier into the small deck. I had hated them since the accident. When the boat suddenly shifted beneath my feet, in a moment of anamnesis, when the past becomes as vivid as the present, I remembered that moment on the English Channel when that bomb, whistling as it fell, had struck the boat's starboard side. As I stumbled to my seat, I couldn't push the image from my mind.

"Are you all right?" Emmanuel asked me as I clung tightly to the vessel's rail.

"I nearly died in a boat," I told him.

"Sygnomen. I didn't know. But this is the easiest way."

The driver started the small single piston motor, unmoored the boat, and began to pull away from the docks. I crossed myself superstitiously.

"How long will this take?" I shouted over the loud choogah choogah *of the engine.*

"Eight hours, maybe more," Emmanuel shouted back at me.

He handed me a small guidebook to the monasteries. "I picked this up for you."

"Efcharisto." I opened the guidebook and began to skim through it.

"Do they know we're coming?" I shouted again.

"Of course, a message was sent to them yesterday. Father Niphon is supposed to meet us at the docks."

About an hour into the trip as the boat seemed to be moving at a snail's pace through choppy waters, Emmanuel shouted at me,

"Imagine, before they had petroleum engines, this trip could take two days." Though I thought eight hours was a long time to spend in such a small boat.

I had many questions about the monasteries, but the strain of shouting over the motor or of struggling to hear Emmanuel shout was too much to endure. I resolved to ask my questions when we stopped at the docks.

About two hours into the trip, Emmanuel shouted across to me, *"Do you feel any better about coming out here?"*

"I'm all right," I shouted back. We were passing cliffs nearly three hundred yards high where we could see a five-story stone structure at its pinnacle.

"We couldn't build these structures today. Too much money," Emmanuel shouted. *"To build this one alone could bankrupt a small country."* He paused. *"Most of them were financed by funds from the Roman Emperors; and it took hundreds of men to carry up each stone one by one."*

I pictured hundreds of men swarming like ants over the face of cliffs, then laying stones atop one another, while stone masons lined them up and mortared them. Then, I thought about how that once great empire that could muster the manpower and the monies to build such architectural wonders was no more, now a mere footnote in the history books.

'What is man that thou art mindful of him, or the son of man that you should take notice of him. For we are yet here a little while and then we are gone.'

We made our first stop about three hours into the trip. We stopped to leave off supplies at a small pier with a walkway carved out of stone, leading up toward the summit of a plateau. Two monks from the monastery Konstamonitou met us there, and we unloaded two cases of wine and a bag of charcoal. The monks gave us two boxes of beeswax candles and a small box of black prayer ropes which the monks had apparently made. We also gave them a hundred pound bag of flour. Then, Emmanuel and I stepped off the boat for a few minutes and stood on the pier.

"Can you afford to be taking this time away from your work?" I asked him.

"I work for myself," he responded. *"It is pleasure for me to do this*

for Elisavet and you."

We stood on the pier for a half an hour staring out into the ocean while the captain of our small vessel spoke enthusiastically with the monks. I didn't feel like speaking. I didn't want to think. I wanted to enjoy the silence, the stillness. I could even hear my heart, or as the Greeks would say, "Akuo alithos karthia mou."

I was surprised how much Greek I was picking up in those past few days.

"I have a question," I turned to Emmanuel and told him.

"I don't know if I can answer it."

"I've been thinking a lot about why I have been so afraid of this trip, why every sinew in my body fought the thought of coming here; and I'm thinking standing here on this pier and looking out on this ocean in front of me, what scares me the most is not knowing the outcome. If you believe in God, then you must believe he knows the outcome of every life. What a tremendous blessing to know the outcome. You and I could climb back into this boat, go out into the sea and a storm comes, capsizing the boat and killing us all. But standing here on this pier, we don't know that, we can't see it. Do you think Adolf Hitler, if he could have seen the outcome of his life's decisions, if he knew that he would end his life by his own hand in a bunker in Berlin, his country destroyed and his name forever defamed in history as a monster, he might have altered his course? Don't you think if I had known what a tremendous cost I would pay for this success with television, that I would gladly have given it all back to have my son?"

After a minute of stunned silence, Emmanuel struggled to respond: "You have asked a question I could not in a lifetime hope to answer. I'm sure it's for our own good that we don't know the outcome."

When the driver gestured for us to return to the boat, I could see from Emmanuel's expression that he was still struggling with my question.

The rest of the morning followed the same pattern. We would stop at a pier, first leaving off supplies, then taking on boxes. By noon we had stopped at four more of them, and the boxes we were carrying had become over ten. With only a few more, we would soon run out of room for our feet. We spoke very little. I sat quietly and thoughtfully, reflecting on my entire journey from the moment I had stepped off the airplane in Athens to the present moment. For the first time, I also began to think about my business. I had hired capable managers, men whose judgment and character I trusted, but an ambiguous uneasiness settled over me concerning what to expect when I returned. I rubbed my forehead with nervous strokes.

"You seem unsettled again," Emmanuel shouted to me.

"I have this problem with control. I want to be in control of every aspect of my life."

"I have the same problem. But we both need to learn to relax. Athos is about Isychia. Silence and stillness. That's why they call them Hesychasts, those who have mastered the art of silence."

Beth had once struggled to explain to me this whole theology of silence, but I was too reluctant to listen.

At one o'clock we arrived at the port of Daphne about midway down the western side of the peninsula. We boarded a bus to Karyes, the capital of Athos, where we would apply for papers to stay on the mountain. We stopped at a small guest house and tavern, where they served us a small bowl of barley soup and a single slice of barley bread. When I gestured to Emmanuel if I could ask for more, he shook his head, no. After we finished, we sat quietly across from each other. When I began to speak something, he put his finger over his mouth to silence me. "Not now," he mouthed without saying it.

Nearly an hour passed before the official returned our papers, and I could hear my stomach growling from hunger. He gestured for Emmanuel to approach him, and Emmanuel rose up from the table and met him near the doorway of the guesthouse. After a few minutes of barely audible interchange between them, Emmanuel returned to the table.

"Is everything in order?" I asked him.

"It's fine, I think. Athos has been self-governing since its inception, and since the treaty of Lausanne in 1923, it operates as its own little country."

"So what are we doing now?"

"We're going back to the boat. It should be another four hours. We should be at Esphigmenou by vespers."

The next four hours seemed to pass more quickly than the first four. I had inured myself to the rhythmic roar of the motor, and I resolved to relax and try to make the best of things. The scenery was magnificent, the steep jagged cliffs, the green foliage scattered like patches on a dark brown blanket, and the water was as clear and as blue as the sky it reflected. I could see reflections of the white stone monasteries vibrating like a canvas shaken by the winds. I leaned over the edge of the boat and peered down into the water, and I could see hundreds of fish moving in intersecting waves beneath us.

"Quite a view." Emmanuel told me as he approached and leaned over beside me. "Makes you feel very small, doesn't it?"

"Like so much cosmic dust." I responded. I remembered that Leonard had said this once, though I couldn't remember the context.

"What exactly can we expect when we arrive?" I questioned.

"Silence," he responded. "Silence and austerity."

"Isychia ke askesis," he repeated in Greek.

The tape clicked off on its second side.

Could you put the second tape on for me? "Jim asked his father who had returned to the room.

"Of course," he responded. He took the second tape and placed it in the player and turned it on.

Chapter 36

When we arrived at Esphigmenou, it was nearly eight thirty and almost completely dark, and I noticed, standing on the small pier, a short, slender monk, nearly fifty, with a full graying beard and long hair tied behind his back. He carried a small oil lamp in his left hand, and in his right hand he seemed to be counting prayers on a long knotted rope which hung halfway between his waist and feet. The captain of our little boat waved to him and he waved back to us, and for a moment, a large gold cross which dangled from his neck, brightly flickered from the reflected light of the lamp. Our driver turned off the motor and began to row the last few yards into the dock.

"Kali Nichta," the driver greeted the hieromonk once he had docked. He kissed the monk's right hand, and the monk blessed him.

Then, Emmanuel and I followed suit.

I felt awkward. When I raised my head after the blessing, I looked into his eyes, and it felt as if they were piercing through me and exposing my innermost thoughts. But he said nothing except a short sentence to Emmanuel in Greek, and then he gestured for us to follow him. I carried both of our bags as we followed him through two metal gates into the heart of the monastery.

"What did he say?" I whispered to Emmanuel.

"He said the monks are eating now, and we are welcome to join them."

He led us into a long room with three long rectangular tables, where nearly a hundred monks were eating quietly while another monk was reading aloud in Greek from a small lectern. I was immediately captivated by the antiquity of the surroundings, and I felt as if I had stepped back in time, though how far back I could only conjecture.

He led us to a table where three empty place settings were laid out for us. We took our seats and, as silently as the others, ate a bowl of lentil soup with an orange and a slice of bread. I gulped down a cup of water and waited for the others to finish. Though lightly seasoned, the *lentils tasted wonderful to me.*

After about fifteen minutes more, an older monk, whom I surmised must have been the abbot, stood up from his seat, gestured to the reader to stop, then said a short prayer of thanksgiving. After crossing themselves, the monks began to file out one by one until the hall was empty. Then the hieromonk gestured for us to follow him again. He led us up two flights of stairs, down a long corridor to a small room with two small beds, a table, a stool, and icon stand with icons and a small prayer book.

"Kali Nichta," he spoke. Then he said something in Greek that I did not understand. He closed the door behind us and departed.

"What was that all about?" I softly asked Emmanuel. "What did he say?"

"He said Orthros is at six o'clock tomorrow morning."

"Is that all he said?"

Emmanuel nodded and replied, "He probably doesn't have a blessing to say more to us. I told you, it's very strict."

"It's not very hospitable."

"Don't get the wrong impression. They just want you to know what kind of place it is."

We sat quietly across from each other for nearly an hour. I didn't know what to say. I had resolved to endure the experience through silence if necessary. I would deliver Beth's letter and make a request for her brother to return with us to Thessaloniki. I wasn't even sure if the priest who had met us at the docks was Father Niphon, and my Greek was too poor to ask him.

Another hour passed, and I began to drowse, when a small knock came at the door.

"Ellado," Emmanuel answered, and the monk slowly opened it.

Emmanuel rose from the cot and quickly approached him for a blessing. I, too, was rising up when the monk overtook me, kissed me on both cheeks, then pointing to himself said in Greek, "Pater Niphonos."

"Neilos," I responded. Then he began to speak to me in Greek.

"Lego oligo Hellenika (I speak little Greek)." My pronunciation was awkward. He pulled the small stool toward himself and sat down in front of us.

"You are husband to Elisavet?" He asked me in Greek. This much I

understood.

"Ne," I replied.

"Ti kanei avti? (How is she?)" he asked me.

"Kala."

"I thought she had died with others," Emmanuel translated his next remark.

Then, I went to my bag, removed the letter and handed it to him. When I looked into his face there was a softer, gentler pallor to his countenance, which I hadn't notice before.

He read the letter with quiet intensity, reverently turning each page of Beth's meticulous Greek script, until he finished it.

Then he folded it carefully and placed it inside his robes. He spoke something in Greek which I didn't understand, and Emmanuel translated.

"You've lost your son Michael? He asked you."

"Ne."

His words were few and well chosen—no more than were necessary, and no less were necessary to convey his meaning.

"God loves us," he continued, "loves us more than you or I could ever love a child. And we've all been kidnapped by the devil, stolen and raised as his own. We have forgotten God. This loss, Christ carried on the cross."

I was stunned by his words and began to cry.

"Sygnomen," he told us. "I will talk to you again."

He rose from his stool, crossed himself and then departed.

Once he had gone, I struggled to understand what he had said. I didn't know why his words had touched me, but in some irrational and inexplicable way in speaking them he had lifted a burden from me, and I felt more at ease. Emmanuel also seemed affected by them. He sat reflectively with his legs crossed and his hands cupped on his knees.

"Do you realize the full impact of what he was saying?" he asked me.

"Only vaguely."

"Let's lay aside the religious overtones for a moment. Let me speak philosophically." I could see he was trying to translate a complex thought in Greek into simple English words. "You have a word in English called estrangement."

"Yes," I acknowledge.

"It means to become a stranger after first being close to someone."

"I understand."

"In Greek, we say Xenon for stranger. In fact this room we are sitting in is called 'Xenona', a place for strangers."

I wasn't thinking about it philosophically. I wasn't thinking about it at all. My response to his words had been emotional and non-verbal. I struggled to listen as Emmanuel explained his philosophical insight, but I kept thinking about my own loss, my own sense of betrayal. I tried to imagine a God for whom these same feelings were appropriate. 'Would not an infinite God experience infinite loss and infinite betrayal?' I pondered. I found it difficult to believe in a God who felt anything at all. Human emotions, with all their imperfections and misapprehensions, seemed unfitting for an all-powerful deity.

"You understand what I'm saying," Emmanuel continued. "We have become strangers to God. We can't see him. We don't know him. We have lost the ability to even recognize him."

"None of this talk or this speculation is going to bring Michael back, nor bring me any closer to finding him."

"No," Emmanuel begrudgingly acknowledged.

After my remarks Emmanuel stopped speaking and a few hesitant minutes followed.

"I'm sorry. Go on." I finally broke the silence, but he was reluctant to continue after my interruption.

For nearly an hour more we sat quietly, each of us unable to broach the pregnant silence, when all at once he began to speak again.

"I've been estranged from my own father. I haven't spoken to him in nearly three years."

"Why?" I asked him.

"I don't know how to say it in English. We fight over religion, politics, over business." He struggled a moment to find the right English word. "He incites me."

"It's important to preserve our relationships," I responded. "They don't last forever. You may not have a chance to say goodbye."

After these words, I wondered if I sounded like a greeting card. Had my life become one huge cliché keeping me from dealing with the hidden truths of my own psyche?

"When I get home to Athens, I'm going to call him," he continued.

I didn't remember falling asleep. One moment I was contemplating the irony of my situation, how far I had come since my youth in Wisconsin. The next moment it was morning. I awakened to the sound of bells and Emmanuel shaking me.

"They expect us to be at Orthros," he chided.

"What time is it?"

"Six o'clock."

"I haven't been up at six o'clock in years."

"You are now," he insisted. He pulled me up from the cot, and I groggily placed my feet onto the cold stone floor. Throwing myself to my feet, I stumbled to the table in the corner of the room, where I used a pitcher and a basin to wash my face and hands. Emmanuel followed me.

I shuffled next to him as he led me down the corridor, down the stairs and through the quadrangle into the chapel.

When we entered the sanctuary, a deacon was chanting before the holy doors while holding a long sash in his right hand. The melodies were familiar to me, yet the mood was more intense than in any church I had attended in New York. When the choir began to chant in its irregular cadences, extending the syllables of words in long shifted flourishes, I wondered if I had gone completely mad. Here I was as far removed from American culture as Tibetan Buddhism is from rock and roll, and it had progressed as logically and as predictably as though it had been scripted for me, as though the paths I walked and the words I spoke were written by someone else.

I listened reverently to every kyrie eleison, *to every* Amen, *as the drama in front of me played itself out. When the liturgy ended at ten o'clock, everyone again filed into the refectory to eat. Emmanuel and I took our seats and ate quietly with the others. The abbot gestured for a young monk to begin reading from the lectern. Emmanuel removed a pen and small scraps of paper from his pocket and began to write on the papers in Greek. I pointed to one of them and he printed in English, "Dionysios the Areopagite on the Divine Names." A few other phrases he scribbled down and then quickly crumpled the papers. I didn't know who this was, nor was I motivated to find out, but it was a name which still stuck in my mind. After the meal, the monks dispersed each to his appointed task and Emmanuel, and I returned to our room.*

Again, we sat quietly. I removed my copy of The Way of a Pilgrim *from my bag and began to read it again, while Emmanuel occupied his time by tossing a coin into the air and catching it.*

"I guess we haven't mastered stillness," I broke the silence.

"Hardly," he responded.

"Do they ever speak?" I asked him.

"During confession or when giving spiritual counsel. But they don't engage in idle conversation."

"I could never endure this."

"Not everyone is called to a monastic life. Most of us have to live in the world." He paused. "In Greek, they are called moni *for one. Monasteries began as individuals like St. Anthony the Great went out into the desert to confront the devil alone."*

I was beginning to realize that Emmanuel had a preoccupation with the meanings of words. Perhaps because he struggled so hard to learn English and it made him more cognizant of vocabulary.

"It just seems too much for me."

Around noontide, there again came a soft knock on the door, and Father Niphon again paid us a visit.

"Evlogison Pater," Emmanuel greeted him as the priest blessed us both. Emmanuel pushed the stool for him to sit down.

"Elisavet said in the letter that you sell televisions," he began to speak as Emmanuel translated.

"Ne," I responded.

"She blames television for the loss of your son."

"Indirectly, yes," I responded.

I was certain I was about to hear another lecture about the evils of television, but he surprised me.

"Scientific knowledge is not evil in itself," he continued. "Man was given the ability to think by God. We have freedom as to how we use these gifts. (I recognized the word charismata.) Adam had many gifts before the fall which we no longer possess, among them a full functioning nous, that spiritual part of us which perceives uncreated realities. Much of scientific advancement has been man's attempt to regain those abilities without God. But the heart has not been cleansed. They become reflections of the evil which is in men's hearts. Television, if not subjected to the rule of God, will also become another means of expressing the evil in men's hearts. Scripture says the heart is inconceivably wicked. What we do here through this life of askesis, of prayer and fasting, through purification is to struggle to cleanse the

heart, to polish this lens of our spiritual eyes so that we might again see God."

"Why would Adam willingly give up these gifts?" I asked him.

"Adam did not have perfect knowledge. He could not see the outcome of his disobedience. He was created innocent like a child, and he was to grow into the perfect likeness of God." He paused.

"Come let me show you the library," Emmanuel continued to translate.

He gestured for us to follow him, leading us down a long corridor to a room where two young monks were working. The room was filled with books and ancient manuscripts stacked on four foot rows in every available inch of space. The monks were laboring silently, and when Father Niphon entered the room, they immediately sought his blessing. He waved them back to what they were doing.

Father Niphon was speaking barely above a whisper.

"Knowledge is one of the paths to God," Emmanuel whispered in my left ear. "Giving alms is another. The ascetic struggle is another. We are like athletes who discipline our bodies for an imperishable crown." He led us out of the library into other rooms. In one, two monks were making candles, in another, incense, in a third, these prayer ropes called, in Greek, komposkini. In a fourth room, we found an aging monk who was painstakingly painting an icon of St. George and the dragon. He held the brush firmly in his wrinkled hand and with gentle strokes, he daubed red paint onto the dragon's tail.

Father Niphon began to speak again. "Later you should take a walk to the summit of the mountain to watch the sunset. A fourth way to God is to look for him in his handiwork." After these words, he bid us goodbye and left us alone in the corridor.

"What do you want to do now?" Emmanuel asked me.

"Let's look around a little," I responded, recognizing a new freedom of movement. We walked from room to room, quietly and unobtrusively, hoping we might become invisible. Monks were working throughout the ancient edifice, and no one seemed to take notice of us as we passed from floor to floor, passed dozens of small monastic cells through corridors lined with the most impressive of ancient religious art. I was unsettled by the eerie quietude. I had grown accustomed to the din and chatter of New York, the sounds of sirens, of automobile engines, and the noise of a million voices rising heavenward like mist

on a hot summer day. This deafening silence, I had never experienced, not even on the farm where the myriad sounds of chickens, of cows, and other animals created their own unique symphony.

"I'm not sure I like the silence," I turned to Emmanuel and told him. "It reminds me too much of death."

"A monk's life is very much like death. He's dead to the world, its pleasures, its concerns, its passions."

"I'm not ready for death." I paused. "Let's take up Father Niphon's proposal and climb to the summit."

"That could take some time," he tried to discourage me.

"I'm up to it. But if it appears we are taking too long we can always turn back."

"Well, if that's what you want," he begrudgingly agreed.

We began the climb around two o'clock. I resolved to climb as far as we could by six o'clock and then turn back. At first we walked briskly from the shoreline where the monastery sat, through a series of small hills toward the northern summit. I could see small huts across the blood red stone, where hermits were living, some in no more than holes in the rock. As we climbed higher, the terrain grew more rugged and I began to doubt the prudence of our trek. But the walk seemed to invigorate Emmanuel, and I resolved if he could endure it, so could I. We began to follow a path hewn out of stone, which seemed to rise a hundred feet in front of us. Emmanuel walked ahead of me a few yards. Then I stumbled suddenly on loose stones and nearly lost my balance.

"You sure you want to finish this?" he asked me as he stopped to see if I was all right.

"Of course."

As the path grew steeper and more treacherous, he kept hesitating and looking back at me. His expression betrayed his concern for my fitness. For a half an hour more, I staggered over the footpath barely a foot wide, as we wandered our way nearly three hundred feet up a jagged embankment. When I stumbled a second time and scraped my right elbow. He rushed back to me.

"Elisavet asked me to watch over you. I don't want you falling off the mountain."

"I'm not going to fall off the mountain," I snapped at him. "I've climbed rocks before."

"Soon it will be dark and we shouldn't climb down in the dark."

"Don't make this a bigger ordeal than what it is," I told him. *"Isn't this better than just sitting in silence? We have a goal, and when reach that goal, we'll feel like we've accomplished something."*

I didn't know where we were going or when we would reach our goal, yet the uncertainty of our journey was quietly exhilarating. I was growing tired, and my muscles had begun to ache, but it was a fatigue born of striving, and I celebrated this fatigue.

By five thirty, it had become obvious that we were not going to reach the summit, and we both stopped on a small plateau to rest and catch our breath. There was a small hut about a hundred yards behind us wedged in a small crevasse of the rock, and at first it looked abandoned. But then as the light began to dim, I could see what seemed like a flickering candle and the sweetest smell, sweeter than any floral perfume, was wafting from the small carved opening. We both sat quietly, our hands wrapped around our knees, watching the flickering light as the sunlight slowly faded. By six o'clock, we were sitting in total darkness, though we were not afraid.

I could see a small figure of a man on his knees in a cell which was no more than five feet high. After nearly half an hour of deathlike stillness, we watched him as he slowly rose to his feet.

He looked nearly eighty, his hair snow white, and his robes were worn and torn in a hundred places. I could see one knee covered in wrinkled calluses, and his bare feet cut and scarred from a life long flogging. Then, he began to walk in our direction, really wobbling more than walking, carrying the candle in his right hand.

I did not think he could see us both. We sat motionless, trying not to be taken notice of. Even as close as five feet from us, we seemed invisible to him. But then the oddest thing happened to me. He stopped two feet away from me, slowly dropped to his knees, held the candle out in front of my face, his hand gently trembling. Then with a voice worn from age and disuse, he slowly spoke, *"Zitete avto en ton polin tou anemou."*

He then struggled to his feet and began his journey back to his cell.

"What did he say?" I asked Emmanuel in stunned paralysis.

"He said 'Seek him in the city of the wind.'"

"What does that mean? Seek whom in the city of the wind?"

An unsettling panic was sweeping over me. *"This is crazy, utterly and completely crazy."* I felt like rising to my feet, but the thought of *making one false step and falling off the mountain prevented me.*

"What do we do now?" I asked him.

"We wait till morning," he simply responded. "And then we climb back down."

The night was blacker than any night I could remember. But I was exhausted and too restless to sleep, and the stones were as cold and hard as a marble sarcophagus.

"I think this is insane," I murmured to Emmanuel. "He's been here so long babbling to himself, he has gone mad. I'd go mad if I had to endure much more of this."

Emmanuel did not respond to me. I slid toward him to check if he was OK, and he was curled up in a ball sleeping on the uneven stones with his bag propped beneath his head as a pillow.

I carefully slid back to my place and tried to position myself to be more comfortable, but no contortion seemed any better than the last. As my eyes grew more accustomed to the darkness, I began to recognize the outlines of objects, from trees to rock formations, to another hilltop in the distance. Beneath us, I could see the edges of the shoreline and the choppy waters of the Aegean Sea. Above me was a sea of stars, more than I had ever imagined. I struggled to remember the names of the constellations and to find the North Star. But it all seemed a blur of light to me with each star seemingly touching the next.

I don't know how long I sat there, gazing into the heavens and trying to make sense of everything that had happened. I remembered those summer nights in Wisconsin when Reginald and I would lie on our backs in the fields of rye and likewise gaze into stars. It was on these nights that I first contemplated leaving Wisconsin, beginning the long journey which would lead to this epiphany.

'The heavens declare his handiwork,' I vaguely remembered the line of a psalm. Was it not the heavens which forced Galileo to rethink the organization of the universe? Was it not the heavens which guided Columbus to the shores of this new world? Was it not man's dream to reach up and touch the stars? I stretched out my hand and imagined sweeping the stars to the edges of the sky.

'Seek him in the city of the wind,' I contemplated. 'But who could see the wind or find a city built there?'

I fell asleep shortly after this. I didn't know what time it was. I couldn't see a watch if I had brought one with me. I rolled over on my side, pulled my knees toward my chest and fell asleep on the open ground.

It was the deepest and most restful sleep that I could remember, with no dreams, no agitations. When I awoke, I was not sore or numb as I expected and a cool breeze was gently blowing, almost caressing my skin.

"You're awake," Emmanuel told me. He was standing over me and watching me as I raised myself up from the ground. I could see the morning sun out of the corner of my left eye.

"This is the first time I've slept outside on the ground," he told me.

"How was it?" I asked him.

"Surprisingly restful under the circumstances. And you?"

"I don't think I've slept as well in years," I replied, though my stomach began to growl in hunger.

"So what do we do now?" I proposed. "Do you want to continue climbing or go back to Esphigmenou?"

"I don't know."

I sensed genuine indecision in his voice.

"Let's go back to Esphigmenou," I resolved, and he agreed.

Our journey down was easier and less dramatic. We walked quickly, making the distance in a quarter less time. By eleven o'clock, we had reached Esphigmenou as the monks were leaving the katholika from liturgy.

I struggled whether I should tell anyone about our experience, but I knew that with the strict rule of silence, I would not have much opportunity. When we reached the courtyard, we filed behind the monks as they marched into the refectory. No one said a word to us. Only two young monks lifted their eyes to look at us as we entered the room. I noticed Father Niphon standing next to the abbot at the table where the clergy sat. He looked at me with acknowledgment. Then, the abbot gave his blessing and we all sat down to eat. A young monk, barely twenty, came toward us, and without speaking a word, gestured for us to sit down at the end of a long table. We sat like the others, eating quietly, while this same monk read from the lectern. After finishing our meal, Emmanuel and I again returned to our room.

"I certainly feel like a stranger. This room is aptly named."

"The monastic life is a renunciation of the world," he tried to make an apology, though I could see he was as uncomfortable as I.

"I understand that, but I just can't see the point in it."

There were a hundred other random thoughts which were rushing through my consciousness, from mundane ones like my feet being sore to reflective thoughts about my place in the universe, but I didn't feel like giving voice to any of them.

"What day is it?" I broke the silence.

"Thursday, I think, or maybe Friday," Emmanuel answered. "It's easy here to lose track of time."

"I don't see how you could avoid it," I paused. "How much longer do you want to stay here?"

"As long as you like."

"I'd like to leave today."

A knock again came on our door and Father Niphon entered the room. I reluctantly arose and received his blessing.

"Kathite," he told us, "Sit down."

"Did you walk to the summit?" he asked in Greek and Emmanuel again translated for me.

"As far as we could," I responded.

"And you spent the night on the mountain?"

"Ne," Emmanuel answered him.

"It is a holy place," he continued.

Emmanuel began to explain to him everything that had happened, including our encounter with the hermit. The monk simply nodded in acknowledgment when Emmanuel finished.

"Zitete avton en tin polin tou anemou," the monk repeated.

"What does it mean?" I interrupted him.

"You must figure that out," he responded.

"How could I do that?" I snapped back.

"Stay here with us, pray and fast, and maybe God will tell you."

But I knew in my heart of hearts there was no way I would stay any longer than I had to stay, and I could tell from his expression that he knew this as well.

"I have a gift for you," the priest continued. He reached into a pocket in his robe and removed a small pamphlet in Greek.

"I am sorry it is not in English," he continued. "But I am sure you can find someone to translate it for you."

"What is it?" I asked him.

"A prophesy of Neilos the Myrrh-streamer," Emmanuel translated.

"He wrote it over four hundred years ago."

I took the pamphlet and placed it into my bag.

"I believe this is the same Neilos for whom you were baptized," the monk explained. "Also, I have the blessing of the Abbot to return with you to Thessaloniki."

I was greatly relieved.

"So when do we leave?"

"Avrio," he answered. "I shall pray that God opens your mind and heart and allows you to understand his will for you." He bid us goodbye and then departed.

"Thank God," I exclaimed. "We get to leave tomorrow."

The rest of the afternoon, we wandered around the monastery, broadening our investigation to include the library where I haphazardly rifled through stacks of books, struggling to read the Greek titles to no avail. I felt as if a huge weight had been lifted from my shoulders, and I began to contemplate seeing Beth again and returning to the mundane world of television. At one point during our wanderings, we came upon two older monks sitting on the ground, their legs crossed and their heads bowed as though staring at their navels. They seemed oblivious to their surroundings and made no movement as we moved closer to them.

"What is this?" I asked Emmanuel.

"The Jesus prayer," he responded.

"I know about the Jesus prayer, but this seems unusual."

"They're supposed to sit, remove all thought from their consciousness, concentrate on their breathing, and through the rigorous discipline of their bodies, say the Jesus prayer with every breath, until it becomes second nature to them."

"It looks very strange."

"There was considerable controversy during the twelve hundreds," Emmanuel explained. "They were derided in Greek as the navel watchers. But Gregory Palamas came to their defense and the process was sanctioned by the Church as a path to glorification."

"You seem to know a lot about this."

"I know a little."

"I just can't imagine a God who would expect this from us." I paused. "Didn't Jesus say, 'Come unto me all you are heavy laden and I will give you rest. For my yoke is easy and my burden is light.'"

"*But they would also say his burden was the cross which he carried to Golgotha, and their lives are a type of crucifixion.*"

I was beginning to realize that the religious questions were far more complex and rife with paradoxes than I was willing to admit.

The remainder of the afternoon and early evening we spent in our room. I had given up trying to read The Way of a Pilgrim, *I couldn't focus on it for more than a couple of minutes. Too many thoughts, too many ambiguous and disconnected impressions were coursing through my awareness, bursting into my recognition momentarily and quickly dissipating. Emmanuel sat preoccupied with the pamphlet the priest had given me.*

"*What does it say?*" *I asked him, more out of idle curiosity than genuine interest.*

"*The Greek is very difficult, katharevousa or scholarly Greek. But it is talking about the Anti-Christ.*"

"*The Anti-Christ,*" *I repeated and then shook my head. I remembered all the frenetic sermons which Brother Woodrow had preached on the Anti-Christ, and I had always found them incredible.*

"*You know, I could accept the ethical framework of the religious life, and even some of the mystical elements, although I think this asceticism is too extreme. But do they have to mix this apocalyptic, conspiratorial stuff with it all? What does it say about the Anti-Christ?*"

"*It says people's appearance will change. Men and women will become indistinguishable from each other. There will be no respect for authority. Christian leaders will become vain men, incapable of distinguishing right from wrong. People will abandon modesty and decadence will reign. Lust, adultery, and all the other vices will be given free expression. It will be difficult to find any light at all. Because of science and the comfort it will provide, people will cease to believe in God.*"

"*A pretty dismal picture of the future,*" *I interrupted him.*

"*He blames it all on the deceit of the Anti-Christ.*"

"*I find it difficult to believe in the idea of an Anti-Christ.*" *I found it difficult to believe in the devil, despite my experience in the war.*

"*Why do you suppose people need to believe in an Anti-Christ?*" *I asked Emmanuel. "I think it's because they cannot live with the random chaos of evil. It's like a hurricane. Things operate on a set of physical principles, and the outcome is often destructive. But no one believes it has a personal volition to do evil. It just is what it is."*

"Then you don't believe in organized personal evil? You don't believe in the existence of conspiracies?"

"No, not really."

"Then, you're a fool."

These were the first harsh words to come from his mouth and it stunned me.

"All of human history," he continued, "has been an attempt by the Evil to destroy the Good. It rarely fights it directly out in the open, because it knows the Good is more powerful. It plans its assaults behind closed doors. In the cover of darkness, it attacks. It even masks itself as the Good to gain the trust of its victims. Four hundred years we were under the yoke of Ottoman rule. It was systematic. It was well-considered, and it was personal. (He took a deep breath.) Nazi Germany began with a few men sitting in a room."

I hadn't intended to incite this intensity in him, but I appeared to have struck a tender nerve.

"I didn't want to come here," he continued. "I had a hundred reasons for not wanting to be here. But last night, as we were sitting on the mountain, something happened to me. I felt a peace I had never felt in my life. Things are never going to be the same for me. As for what that hermit meant, for me it meant to seek God not in the mundane things of this world, but seek him in a city where the wind of God is." I could see he was struggling to find the right English words.

"I'm sorry. I didn't mean to make light of this experience."

But my apology rang hollow. I didn't understand how two people could share an experience and have such disparate perspectives about it.

After this discussion, the room felt claustrophobic. I knew I had to get away for a while, alone. I excused myself, mumbled something about having to pray, and then left the room. I rationalized that I had to endure only one more day of the place as I stepped outside into the corridor. I walked aimlessly, almost unconsciously, and after a few minutes, I found myself standing at the edge of the shoreline and staring out into the sea. I found a soft patch of wild grasses on the rocky ground and dropped myself down.

I don't know how long I was sitting there, tossing stones into the ocean, with my eyes fixed upon the rolling waves. I thought of little else. I remember the distinctive sound that the stones made as they skipped across the water and the smell of the wind in my nostrils.

"I'm sorry about calling you a fool," Emmanuel startled me as he sat down beside me.

"It's all right. I am a fool. I'm forty years old. Over half my life is over, and what do I have to show for it? Sure, I have the TV stores and a little money in the bank. But what did it bring me?" I paused. "You know I envy them in a way. It's all so simple for them. They know what is expected from them. Their path is laid out in front of them, and they just walk the steps toward their fixed destination. In the real world, unfortunately, it's not so simple.

"You don't think these monks suffer with the same doubts, the same questions about their decision that we in the so-called 'real world' do? The path toward wholeness is more like a ladder. They climb one rung at a time, conquering the passions, their own wills, until they reach the last rung. If they even begin to think they have accomplished anything, they fall back to the bottom and have to start all over again."

"It still seems too much for me," I was still tossing stones into the waters. "Did you know that there are over a hundred times as many species that live in the oceans than live on land? It's something my friend Leonard once told me."

"I didn't know."

"We should go back," I told him as I lunged forward and threw myself to my feet.

When we entered the rear gate of the monastery, evening prayer was beginning and the monks were slowly filing into the katholika. Emmanuel and I followed behind them and found a place in the rear of the sanctuary near a large icon of St. George. The prayers began with Father Niphon standing in front of the altar with his back facing us as a reader on a single note began to chant the evening psalm. Beth had once tried to explain the structure of the services to me, but I hardly paid attention. At several points throughout the service, the deacon came out from the altar and began to chant a series of petitions, all followed with a response from the cantors. There was censing and then processions, and all the other hallmarks of Greek Orthodox worship. After the service ended, as father Niphon stood facing us with a cross in his right hand, he began to speak slowly.

"Brethren," he began and Emmanuel translated, *"The Holy Fathers tell us that the Christian life is the acquisition of the Holy Spirit. The disciplines of fasting and of prayer, and the therapies which the Church gives us, are means to that end. Even the renunciation of the world, which we struggle to attain in this community, is not an end in itself, but a means to that end. Consider the parable which our Lord spoke of in the Gospel of the pearl of great price, which a man found in a field and sold everything he had to purchase. The Holy Spirit is that pearl. And just as a pearl begins as a grain of sand which is an irritant to the oyster, what seems difficult and impossible to us now, when it bears fruit in our souls, it shall be like the mustard seed which grows into a tree. The world offers us many pleasures now, but none of these compare to the gifts the Holy Spirit gives to those willing to receive them."*

He crossed himself and then began to bless the monks one by one as they approached to kiss the cross. Emmanuel and I stayed back, waiting for the others to finish. When we approached him, Father Niphon broke the silence once more, *"We shall all pray that you find your son."*

"Efcharisto," I responded.

We ate a small meal in the refectory, and then we returned to our room about nine o'clock. I was fatigued, and almost as soon as I laid my head on the cot, I was asleep. The next morning, I awoke to the sound of a soft knock on the door. It must have been five in the morning. It was pitch black outside, and the room was dimly lit by the flame of a small oil lamp. Emmanuel struggled to his feet and opened the door. Out of the corner of my eye, I could see Father Niphon standing in the hallway with a small bag in his hand.

"Kali Mera," he greeted and continued speaking.

"He says the boat arrives at seven o'clock. We should pack our things now."

"Sure."

I forced myself to my feet and grabbed the bag which I had brought with me. I took a soiled shirt and a pair of socks and stuffed them into it. I realized it had been days since I had bathed, and I looked forward to a hot shower again. When we arrived at the docks, the sun was just rising, and this brilliant red and blue hue was spreading across the sky. I could see clouds on the distant horizon, and the morning sky *turned bright blue almost instantly before my eyes.*

"*So it is with God's Energies,*" *Father Niphon began to speak and Emmanuel translated. "They fill, they permeate the whole created order. (Emmanuel was struggling to keep up with him.) Everything which exists, everything which lives, derives its existence from Them. St. Paul says in Him we move and have our being. How could God, who holds the universe together by His Will, allow any of us to perish? So, none of us need have a fear of death.*"

I could see from his expression, from his tone of voice and even from the way he held his hands that he fervently believed these words. When the boat arrived, my mind was filled with images of loved ones and friends who had died, of Leonard and of my father. I thought about how tenuous a grasp any of us has on life.

As I stepped into the boat, the muscles on my back began to spasm, sending pain radiating up my spine.

Father Niphon sat down across from me. His face was calm and placid. I could see his fingers rhythmically counting out his prayers.

"*What about hell?*" *I asked him.*

Emmanuel translated my question.

"*The fire of the Holy Spirit purifies the godly and is eternal Hell for the ungodly. Hell is the rejection of the love of God.*"

For me, this idea contradicted everything that I had been taught as a child, about redemption and damnation. Though I had rejected the Calvinism of Brother Woodrow, I had accepted the dichotomy that God loved the saved and hated the damned. What he was saying meant that God's love for us was not dependent on what we did or how we behaved. It was unsettling to my sense of justice.

"*It doesn't seem very just,*" *I responded.*

"*St. Isaac of Syria,*" *the priest continued, "says that God's justice is in his mercy. He shows compassion for both the worthy and unworthy.*"

His perspective was completely alien to my experience, and I was hesitant to accept it.

The journey back was much the same as the journey there, with the same loud engine noise and the same choppy waters. Though this time, I noticed the birds, dozens of them hovering as close as five feet from the boat. One settled a moment on the rail, wagged his head back and forth at me and then alighted. Another perched near Father Niphon who took a small slice of bread out of his pocket, broke off a piece and fed it to the bird. I was surprised how unafraid the bird appeared.

"Has Father Niphon been off the peninsula before?" I asked Emmanuel, who was resting against the opposite side of the boat.

"I'll ask him?" Emmanuel shouted to him and he answered.

"Several times," Emmanuel shouted back. "But not since the war ended."

"The world has changed a lot," I shouted and Emmanuel translated.

"Ne. And it will change even more."

The remainder of the morning I sat quietly, my mind dancing aimlessly. After a while, I drifted into an awkward sleep. When I finally awoke, we were in Daphne. I saw that Emmanuel and Father Niphon were engaged in an intense dialogue, but I had tired of spiritual discussions. I had pushed all questions of mercy and justice from my awareness and focused my attention solely on worldly matters.

We waited in Daphne for nearly an hour while supplies were loaded, and I occupied myself thinking about the business back home, worrying whether everything was in order in my absence, and picturing in my mind the arrival of the new color television sets to all the stores. We picked up another passenger, a young man in his twenties with light brown hair and glasses. He spoke a few words in Greek with a strong Slavic accent, perhaps Russian or Bulgarian or Serbian. I had known a few Russian emigres in New York, fervent anticommunists from Moscow and St. Petersburg, some of whom had fled Russia during the revolution. I had met several of them at an anticommunist meeting in Astoria, though I was reticent to become political and found their rhetoric uncomfortably incendiary. Emmanuel moved toward the young man and introduced himself. "Slobodan Bogdonovich," the young man answered, and from the sound of his name I conjectured he was Serbian. They talked for a short time in Greek. The young man spoke slowly and deliberately. He seemed gentle and soft spoken, projecting an aura of humility which I had rarely seen in young men. After about half an hour of discourse, Emmanuel moved back toward me.

"What was that all about?" I asked him.

"He's here for a week pilgrimage to one of the Russian sketes," he answered me. "He said he came to give prayer and thanksgiving for

having survived the war."

From his age, I surmised he couldn't have been more than nine or ten at the beginning of the war.

"His whole village was destroyed by the Nazis for giving sanctuary to an American flyer." he continued. "He survived by hiding in a sewer."

The image of this small boy huddled in a putrefying tank while the Waffen SS indiscriminately slaughtered men, women and children without remorse hung oppressively before my mind's eye. Later, I would learn that the Serbs saved five hundred and thirty one flyers and that whole villages were slaughtered rather than turn in one man.

"What does he do for a living?" I asked him.

"I asked him that. He said it's not important what he does. It's more important who he is inside."

I spent the remainder of our journey reflecting upon what Emmanuel had told me. I was coming to realize how fortunate I had been, despite the hardship I had experienced in my life. So many blessings seemed to have fallen undeserved into my hands.

When we arrived at the docks of Ouranopolis, it was nearly eight o'clock. I was sore and tired, but joyful to see the car again. Emmanuel lingered at the docks a few minutes to bid Slobodan goodbye, and I carried our bags back to the car. Father Niphon followed behind me a few steps, holding his small bag firmly in his left hand.

While I paced impatiently, he stood calmly, exuding the same peacefulness he had manifested at the monastery. Emmanuel eventually joined us, opened the trunk and placed our bags inside.

"We should be getting back about nine thirty," he told me as he opened both doors for us. Father Niphon seemed to prefer the back seat, moving in that direction and gesturing for me to sit down. But I insisted he sit up front, and he graciously agreed.

Emmanuel started the car, but before he began to drive, he turned around and handed me a small pamphlet in his right hand.

"It's a life of St. Sava, the patron saint of Serbia, in English. Slobodan gave it to me. Come on, take it."

I reluctantly took it from his hand.

"Slobodan told me something very interesting," he continued as we started to pull away.

"What kind of name is Slobodan?" I interrupted him.

"It means free man." He paused. "It turns out he's an electrical engineer. He works for a power plant in Paris. We talked about Nikola Tesla for a few minutes. He thought you might be interested in him."

"Maybe in passing," I responded.

My interest in Tesla was tertiary. Leonard had once tried to ignite an interest in his writing, especially his Colorado Spring papers, but I was unmotivated.

Emmanuel repeated his remarks in Greek for Father Niphon, who immediately responded.

"What did he say?"

"He said Tesla was the son of a priest who died rejecting the Church. It is better people don't follow his example."

"But he did bring us electricity," I retorted. "With no electricity, there would be no lights, no refrigeration, no radio, no television, no computing machines."

I imagined the whole chain of causality with electricity making possible all further advances in technology.

"Certainly, he must concede that life is better with these devices."

"There's no electricity on the Holy Mountain," Emmanuel explained.

Father Niphon did not respond to my remarks. He quietly counted his prayers on his prayer rope.

At about nine thirty, we arrived in Thessaloniki. The night sky was obscured by a ceiling of low flying clouds, and a mist was hanging in the air. Emmanuel stopped in front of the building and gestured for us to go inside. He pulled away from the curb to find a parking space. I would have gone immediately to ring Beth, but Father Niphon lingered at the curbside, apparently waiting for Emmanuel to join us. Ten minutes passed and Emmanuel came running around the corner.

"You didn't need to wait for me," he spoke in English.

"It's no problem."

He removed the phone from its small green box and placed it to his left ear. After a short interchange, he returned it.

"They're coming downstairs to meet us," he said and repeated the same thing in Greek.

I waited expectantly until Beth and Sophia arrived at the doors. Beth looked radiant with her black hair draped down her shoulders.

She was wearing a simple dark-blue dress which hung loosely on her torso, and she was cradling the baby in her arms. She smiled when she saw me. Sofia opened the front doors and was the first to come outside. After bowing down a moment, she received the priest's blessing. Beth did likewise, handing the baby afterwards to Sofia so she could hug me.

"I hope it went well for you," she told me as she embraced me and kissed me on my right cheek.

"I survived," I responded.

She hesitated a moment and then embraced her brother, her eyes immediately filling with tears which she wiped with her fingers.

"Sygnomen, Pater," she told him. He was the last living link to a past which had been stolen from her. She had come full circle in a journey which had taken sixteen years, from Greece to Cairo, to French Morocco, to England to New York and back to Greece again. I thought about these circles, how time itself and life with all its currents seemed as intersecting and sometimes touching circles, whether from birth to death, from war to peace, from the sublime to the mundane; these circles defined and demarcated every aspect of our lives. They gave us borders and brought order out of chaos. Countless examples came immediately to mind, each a living illustration of this impenetrable mystery, images of carousels, of the cycles of the seasons, of possession and loss, even of the silly zebra running in its circles. I became distracted by these thoughts as the others went ahead of me.

"Neilos," Beth called me. "We're going upstairs."

"I'm coming," I shouted and rushed up to join them.

In the elevator, they began to speak in Greek. Father Niphon listened attentively, but said very little as the small box rose. I was too distracted to pay attention to them. I had the strangest sensation, as though I were spinning around on a tilt-a-whirl and losing all sense of space and direction, as though I had for a few moments escaped this finite world of cause and effect, of sturm and drang, and for a small respite entered into eternity, no longer captured by the fixed boundaries of my perceptions, but in the presence of God himself who lives in an infinite circle.

The four of them were involved in an intense discussion, the topic of which I couldn't guess. I followed them down the corridor to the front door of the apartment, which Sofia opened with a key. She opened the lights to use the Greek vernacular, and I could see an elegant table was set with fruit and various vegetables and legumes, and large soup bowls with matching dinner plates.

"Panayoti Ergei," Sofia spoke. "Evlogison Pater."

He blessed the apartment and she brought a chair for him to sit in.

"What day is this?" I asked Emmanuel. I had lost all sense of time.

"Paraskevi," he answered, which means Friday.

I approached the sofa and sat down, leaning forward a moment with my hands cupped on my knees until Beth gestured it was time to eat and I rose up and approached the table. Father Niphon stood up a moment and then blessed the food. Then we all crossed ourselves and sat down. Sofia went into the kitchen and returned with a large pot of soup from which she served Father Niphon first.

"What is it?" I asked as I watched her fill his bowl halfway.

"Tahini soup," Beth answered. "A mixture of rice and ground sesame seeds."

It sounded awful, but I was hungry and would have eaten almost anything. She filled each bowl one by one, and then began serving vegetables and legumes. After she finished, I noticed that no one was eating. I twisted my spoon in my fingers, dipping it once in the broth and beginning to lift it to my mouth, and then Beth shook her head at me. When Father Niphon slowly and deliberately lifted his first spoonful to his mouth, they all began to eat.

I was surprised with my first spoonful of soup. It wasn't the most delicious taste I had experienced, but it wasn't that bad either. After a few spoonfuls, my palate began to adjust to the flavor and by the time I finished the bowl I had actually begun to like the taste.

"Can I have a little more?" I asked Sofia.

"Ne," she responded. "You like it?" She struggled in English.

"Ne. Agathos." I struggled in Greek.

"When is Panayoti coming home?"

"He has to work late tonight," Beth answered, and then she began to speak to Sofia in Greek.

Father Niphon didn't say anything as he slowly sipped soup from his spoon. I was finishing my second bowl of soup when he had eaten half of his small serving and hadn't touched his vegetables.

Beth asked him a question in Greek, and he set down his spoon to answer her. They began a long discussion which lasted nearly an hour.

I sat uncomfortably beside them, unable to understand a word which was spoken, remembering dozens of such conversations in New York, where not a word of English was spoken throughout a whole evening, and later I would press Beth to give me a synopsis of what was discussed.

"What are you talking about?" I finally interrupted them.

"Beth has been telling him how the family died," Emmanuel answered me. A lump immediately came into my throat.

I could see from her inflection and the way her voice quivered as she spoke that it was difficult for her to recount it all, even more difficult to translate into English.

"It's OK. I'm sorry I interrupted."

Beth rose up from her chair and went into the bedroom. She returned a few moments later with a small box containing some of the things we had retrieved from the farm. She gently laid the pictures out in front of him, sliding his dinner plates out of the way to make room. I could see how hard she struggled to control her emotions and keep from breaking down. Then she lifted the small porcelain doll from the box and also set it down in front of him.

"Do you remember this?" she asked him, and somehow I understood.

"Ne," he responded.

She started to cry. "Sygnomen," she pleaded as she tried to regain composure.

"I gave it to you," he acknowledged, "when you were about five."

Then, slowly and methodically, she pointed to the pictures, dozens of them, asking him to name faces she didn't recognize and tell her something about each of them. She even took a pad and pencil and began to write notes about what he was saying. Later, she would tell me she didn't want them to be forgotten.

After we finished eating, Beth and Sofia cleared the table, and we all moved to the parlor to drink Greek coffee, which Sofia poured slowly into small porcelain cups. About eleven o'clock, Panayoti returned to the apartment. He looked tired. His eyes were red from too little sleep.

"Yasou," he greeted each of us. Then he kissed Father Niphon on his hand and on each cheek.

"Ti kaneis? Pos eine O Agios Oros?" he asked.

"Kala," Emmanuel answered.

Sofia entered the kitchen and returned a moment later with a plate of vegetables and a bowl of soup balanced on each hand. She set them down on the table in front of him.

"Echeis spaniko?" he asked Sofia.

"Ne," she replied and returned with plate of spinach from which she took several leaves and placed them on top of the vegetables on his plate.

"Neilos," he began to speak to me. The only word I recognized was 'isychia'.

"Panayoti asks you," Emmanuel translated, "What were your impressions about the silence?"

I didn't know how to respond to him. Did I tell him how truly unsettling it was for me? Or out of politeness did I give him a diplomatic answer? I opted to tell him the truth.

"It was extremely unsettling for me. I don't think I could live with the silence on a long term basis."

"The mind is a very noisy organ," Emmanuel translated. "Remove the background noise, and we're faced with listening to the shouting in our heads. Most people would rather have the noise."

Panayoti began to sip the soup and nibble on the spinach leaves. I got up from my chair in the parlor and moved toward the table to speak to him. I noticed for the first time, as he was reaching across the table to get a shaker of salt, an ugly scar on Panayoti's left arm running from his wrist to his elbow.

"What is this?" I asked him.

"It's nothing," he responded in Greek.

"Panayoti was in a concentration camp during the war," Emmanuel explained to me. "He doesn't want to talk about it."

"I'm sorry."

"Thoxa to Theo," Panayoti responded and crossed himself.

He pulled down his right sleeve to show a number tattooed on his wrist. Then he spoke something in Greek.

"Whatever suffering I have had in this life will be to greater glory in the next," Emmanuel translated.

I wanted to ask more questions, but Beth shook her head at me when I started to speak and I stopped myself.

"The world thinks that suffering is a bad thing, that it should be

alleviated or pacified at all cost," Beth began to explain. "Suffering purifies us. It allows us to participate in the passion of Christ."

She repeated her words in Greek, and I could see from their expressions they were in agreement with her.

I responded, "I don't think suffering is necessarily a good thing. I don't want anyone to suffer. It's hard for me to imagine that God, who by your own admission is infinitely kinder and more benevolent than I am, would want any of us to suffer. I can imagine two different people afflicted with exactly the same degree and type of suffering. One becomes a saint, and the other a monster. I'm certain that this must happen. If we suffer, it's hard for me to imagine that God wants it so. This means to me that there are some things beyond his control."

In the terms of the Calvinism in which I was raised, this argument was heresy. Above all else, God was sovereign, not even a sparrow fell without his purview, but I had long stopped believing in an ordered universe. Chaos seemed to rule, if you could call it ruling, and the world more resembled a battlefield than a Swiss clock.

Beth seemed annoyed with my challenge, because I so obviously contradicted her in front of the others. Hoping that he might refute my argument and vindicate hers, she turned to Father Niphon as an arbiter.

"Who is right?" she ended her supplication to him.

He responded simply, "amphoteri," which meant "both."

"Amphoteri," she repeated. "Explain, Father."

He began to speak with deliberation.

"The world is a battleground," Emmanuel translated. "There are two armies fighting for the control of men's souls. God does not desire the annihilation or destruction of any of the combatants, but their conversion. In a battlefield, there is chaos. The innocent are killed, the guilty commit atrocities with seeming impunity, but the forces of Good will prevail in the end. The army of the enemy will be defeated." He paused. "God did not desire that there would be this rebellion. He did not desire that any of us suffer. He has entered into this suffering in the person of Jesus Christ. In this world, there is suffering, but through Christ it can be cleansing and not destructive."

I recoiled from these allusions to warfare and carnage. The images from the war were still vivid in my memory.

Panayoti had been quiet throughout our entire conversation.

Sipping his soup from his spoon and calmly chewing his vegetables, he lifted his eyes from his plate and stared at me, his eyes seeming to penetrate inside of me.

"I know something about you, Neilos," he struggled in English.
"What is that?"

"You are like Thomas," he continued. "You must see to believe. One day you will see."

Panayoti finished his soup and vegetables and pushed the dishes aside. He stood up, crossed himself and stepped away from the table. As I looked at him, I couldn't stop thinking about the marks on his arms.

Though it was late, almost eleven thirty when Panayoti finished eating, Beth implored Father Niphon to sing a small Canon with her. It was a service which took a little over an hour, and I wanted to sleep. He agreed and for the next hour I struggled to keep my eyes open while each of them sang the refrains and verses together. I could see in her eyes that there was true joy in what she was doing, and I envied her for that. At some point, I simply nodded off and fell asleep.

The next morning, I woke after all the others, still fully clothed, though someone had taken off my shoes. I didn't know the time, but I assumed from the intensity of the sunlight that it must have been mid-morning.

"Kali Mera," Sofia greeted me as I lifted myself up from the sofa and pushed a green wool blanket from my legs.

"Elisavet," she called and Beth returned from the bedroom carrying Grigorios in her arms.

"Kali Mera," Beth greeted and kissed me on my cheek. "We have decided to go to Athens together this afternoon."

"Where is everyone?" I could not see Emmanuel, Panayoti or Father Niphon.

"They've gone to the market to buy a few things for the journey," she answered. "I have something for you, which I forgot to give you last night."

She handed me a small package neatly wrapped in brown paper.
"What is it?" I asked her.
"Open it. You'll see."

"Is it something religious?" I asked as I began to rip the brown paper at the edges. She didn't answer me.

Inside, I found a small black box with a title embossed in gold letters on its cover. I opened the box and discovered a gold pocket watch with an engraving of the White Tower on one side and St. Dimitrios on the other.

"Open it," she told me. So I opened it.

I found engraved on the inside of its cover the words in English, "For Neilos, whose love for me has made the impossible possible. Thank you for coming home with me."

A lump formed immediately in my throat, and I fought back tears.

"You didn't have to do this for me."

"I couldn't have faced this without you." Then she embraced me.

About noon, Emmanuel, Panayoti and Father Niphon returned to the apartment. Emmanuel was carrying a bag of groceries and set them down on the table. Sophia and Beth were finishing last minute preparations, from packing sandwiches to making food for the baby.

I took a long shower, my first in days. As the warm water beat against my back, I thought of what awaited me at home. Our trip to Greece was almost at an end, two more days after this one and I'll be back in New York. Once home, I promised myself I would renew my efforts to find Michael. After thirty-five minutes, I emerged from the shower, war weary and purified. I was ready for another round of battle.

"We should be leaving shortly for Athens," Emmanuel told me as I entered the parlor from the bedroom. He was sitting at the table and sipping a cup of coffee.

"Where are Beth and Sofia?" I asked.

"They've gone to wash some clothing for the trip. They should be back any time now."

"And Panayoti and Father Niphon?"

"I don't know where they are."

"Can I ask you a question?"

"Sure."

"What camp was Panayoti incarcerated in?"

"Dachau," he responded. "His parents were Greek diplomats who were arrested for giving sanctuary to Jews and Gypsies."

"Does he speak German?"

"Like a native." He finished the cup in one huge gulp.

"And that scar on his arm?"

"They tortured him, more for the joy of it than anything else. His parents died in the camp."

"And he doesn't want to talk about it?"

"He doesn't dwell on evil memories. He says he has no malice against them, and to talk about it is only to tempt others to hate them."

"I certainly believe these monsters are worthy of hate," I countered.

"From a human perspective," Emmanuel responded. He arose and poured himself another cup of coffee. "But you have to think of them from God's perspective. He created each of us, including the devil and his dominions. If human mothers somehow love even the worst of criminals, how much more God loves every creature brought into existence through His Energies." He paused. "It's an odd paradox. You cannot hate the sinner without becoming like him. Only when he forgave them was Panayoti finally free of them."

About noon Father Niphon and Panayoti returned to the apartment. Panayoti was carrying a brown paper bag whose top he had folded into neat creases. From its size and shape, I surmised that it carried either books or religious artifacts. Emmanuel began to speak to both of them in Greek. Then Beth and Sophia approached Father Niphon for his blessing.

"Kali Mera," Beth greeted them both. She asked her brother something in Greek and she responded.

"What's going on?" I asked her.

"They went to St. Demetrios to buy a few things and there was another arrest of a suspected communist."

This was ten years before a military coup finally seized control of the government, all under the guise of dealing with the communist threat. I suspected that many of these so-called communists were merely political and personal enemies of the ruling aristocracy.

"What are we doing now?" I asked Beth.

"We're leaving shortly," she told me. Then she said something to Sophia in Greek.

"Can't I help you with something?" I asked Beth.

"You can take our bags to the car."

I picked up the two small suitcases, one in each hand, and began to move toward the doorway. Emmanuel, noticing I was beginning to leave, stopped his conversation with Panayoti and came to join me.

"I'll get the car and bring it to the front of the building."

He rushed ahead of me and was in the elevator before me. The doors closed before I could get inside. Ten minutes passed before the elevator returned. By this time the others had joined me, and we all entered the elevator together with Sofia carrying the baby in one arm and a bag of sandwiches in the other. I noticed Panayoti was clutching a small satchel in his right hand and a pad of sketch paper was precariously balanced under his armpit.

"Are you going to draw some pictures in Athens, Panayoti?" I asked and Beth translated.

"Ne, I will try," he stammered in English.

When the elevator doors opened, I could see that Emmanuel had already parked the car at the curb and opened the trunk for us. We unloaded everything into the car, and within five minutes were on our way.

The tape clicked off on it first side.

Chapter 37

Jim struggled for a moment to flip the tape over in the player and again his hands wouldn't do what he asked of them. His father rose up from his chair and flipped it over for him.

"I've never felt so helpless in all my life. Thank you."

Jim tried several times to press the play button, but could not.

"Could you please turn this on for me?"

His father turned on the player and it buzzed softly for a moment.

As I think I mentioned before, the drive from Thessaloniki to Athens takes about six hours. We left at close to one o'clock.

With a half hour stop for lunch, we planned to arrive in Athens about eight o'clock. Beth had called ahead to her cousin's house and they were preparing a nice meal for us.

As we pulled out on to the main highway, the strangest feeling swept over me. It was a little less than trepidation, not quite anxiety either. I wanted to rest. But when I tried to close my eyes, something would immediately stir me to consciousness.

About an hour into the trip, we had the first in a series of minor catastrophes. The left front tire blew out and Emmanuel nearly lost control of the car. I grabbed the wheel from the back seat and helped him bring the car to a stop. It took the three of us nearly thirty minutes to loosen the lug nuts and the jack wasn't working properly.

"I hope this is not an omen," I suggested as we finally got the spare tire on the car.

Nearly an hour later, we had a radiator problem, and we had to stop the car again to let the engine cool. Beth took the opportunity to take the food out of the trunk, and we ate our sandwiches using the trunk lid as a table. The baby was restless by this time, and he began whining in this almost unbearable drone while Sophia tried unsuccessfully to pacify him.

"I don't think were supposed to go to Athens," I remember telling

Emmanuel as he leaned against the left side of the car.

"I'm sorry about the problems with the car," he responded. "I had it checked by a mechanic before we left Athens."

"It's not your fault. The fallibility of human technology," I spoke with a tinge of sarcasm in my voice.

Then, it began to rain, at first as a light mist, and then as soft droplets, and then as a torrent, growing stronger and more violent with each passing moment. Soon, we were all huddled in the car as the rains of Noah encompassed us.

"I guess there will be locusts next," I shouted, trying to make humor out of the situation.

Beth shook her head at me.

"You shouldn't make fun of the wrath of God."

"This isn't God," I countered her. "This is nature, unmitigated and uncontrollable nature."

The winds were so strong that they rocked the car like a cradle. Emmanuel got out at one point and quickly slammed the hood shut. He was nearly soaked to the skin when he jumped back in the car.

"Think the engine has cooled now," he said and he turned over the motor. It growled several times before it finally started.

"I hope you're not going to drive in this," I told him.

"No, I'm turning the heater on for a few minutes."

Father Niphon seemed as calm as ever. He was counting out his prayers and didn't say a word to us.

"Father, can we pray," Beth asked him in Greek.

"Malista," he answered and he began to recite a prayer while the others repeated it after him. I pressed my right hand against the window glass and the raindrops felt like small needles bouncing against my hand.

The storm raged nearly an hour while they prayed in Greek. I tried to empty my mind of all impressions. Then almost as suddenly as it started, it stopped and the sun cast a long rainbow against the clouds.

"Does it rain like this often?" I asked.

"Sometimes," Beth answered me.

I remembered these late summer thunderstorms in Wisconsin which caused the whole house to shake and with rain so hard it sounded like the sound of a thousand rifles all discharging at once, or thousands of marbles bouncing off the barn's tin roof. Once when I was eight or nine, a twister came within a mile of the farm and my father carried us both down into the cellar, where we huddled together in the darkness, while this deafening roar filled the air around us. So many years later, the same feeling of abject terror returned to me in the car.

"I'm not much into omens," I told Beth. "But maybe we should consider stopping until tomorrow."

"We are under God's protection," she replied. "We really have nothing to fear."

"And were the martyrs under God's protection?" I asked to make a point.

"Of course," she responded. "Even unto death."

"My point exactly. I don't want to die before we get there."

"No one is going to die," Beth began to chuckle.

Emmanuel pulled the car out onto the highway, and we continued our journey. The remainder of the trip went without incident, and we arrived in Athens nearly three hours behind schedule at eleven o'clock that evening.

When we rang her cousins' doorbell, I could hear them running toward the front door. They quickly opened the door and embraced us all.

"Yasou, Pater," they said as they sought the priest's blessing.

When we entered the foyer, I could see that the table was already elegantly set with two small candlesticks placed in the center of the table. Each of them lit a candle and invited us to sit down.

"Kathite, phagomen," they said in Greek, which means "Sit down, let's eat." It was eleven fifteen.

I was exhausted and struggled to stay awake in order to finish the meal. Father Niphon sat across from me. He said very little, while I gorged myself on tomatoes stuffed with rice. I lifted my eyes a moment from my plate and noticed Niphon and Beth's cousin Petros sitting beside each other. The resemblance in their faces was striking.

I don't remember falling asleep. In fact, except for a few salient moments, the rest of the trip seems a blur to me now. We awoke early the next morning and attended liturgy at a small chapel near Beth's cousin's house. After liturgy, we ate a small lunch in the chapel basement and then we went to see the Parthenon.

Beth tried to engender in me an interest in these historical sights, but I only wanted to return to New York. As we wandered through the *ruins of the Acropolis, Beth and Sophia took turns in carrying the baby. I couldn't stop thinking of bagels, of hot cups of American coffee, of doughnuts, of the sound of subway trains, of the smell of roasting peanuts on sidewalk vending stands, and of hot dogs, which I seemed to miss most of all.*

"There used to be magnificent marble statues here," Beth pointed to the ruins. "But they were appropriated by the Europeans."

"You mean stolen," I acknowledged.

"Of course. So much of our culture was either stolen or supplanted."

"You think about it. Right here in pagan times, they engaged in human sacrifice," I said

"What a morbid thought," she retorted.

"So much of what the West celebrates as the height of Greco-Roman philosophy was satiated in moral debauchery and the blood of the murdered innocent." I paused. "I wonder if things have really changed."

"I wanted to enjoy this time with you, but you seem to be in one of your moods again. Can't you just release it all and take joy in this moment?"

"I'm sorry, but when I look at these ruins, I don't marvel at them. I'm satisfied, satisfied that the culture that produced them is no more. Given the choice of a culture which produces an Aristotle or a Plato at the cost of the murder of thousands of the innocent, and one where even the weakest finds justice and satisfaction and there are no great philosophers, I would gladly choose the latter."

"It's not that simple."

"It never is."

I felt agitated, though I didn't know why. For so long, I heard the claim that the Greeks were the cradle of civilization, that from them came all that was good about the West. I found it difficult to understand this clinging to the past, this looking backward rather than forward. But they were a people whose glory and dominance had faded, as photographs grow dull and yellow over the years. I sensed in their eyes that they knew this, that all the talk about a renaissance of Greek culture, of the restoration of the empire, was so much wishful thinking, as children amusing one another with grandiose dreams of greatness. The Greco-Roman world was no more, now only a footnote in the history books. Yet, who was I to deprive them of this one thread of dignity which unmerciful history had left them?

As the others had separated from us and were wandering over the ruins, Beth turned to me and bluntly asked me, "Can you tell me what's going on with you? You seem determined to be disagreeable."

"I'm sorry. I'm tired and I just want to go home."

"Has anybody been unkind to you? Has anyone shown you anything but hospitality?"

"Of course not."

"Then, why do you insist on speaking about human sacrifice on a sightseeing trip?"

"I'm sorry. It is the impression I have of the place. I have a very vivid imagination."

"We've talked about the dangers of the human imagination before," she told me. "About what the Fathers say about giving yourself over to every fantasy."

I remembered this long rather esoteric explanation she once gave me concerning the nous and the human imagination, how the mind now dumps all these images into the malfunctioning nous, and these images and impressions have become our fantasies and dreams. How in a unified person with a fully functioning nous, the imagination completely disappears and is replaced by direct vision of God's uncreated glory. But at that moment, I was not interested in another such conversation.

"The only nous I want to hear about now," I sarcastically rebounded, "is the one I feel tightening around my neck."

"What's gotten into you?" her voice raised in pitch and volume and she visibly projected her disdain with me. "Sometimes I think you don't love God at all."

"I'm sorry. It has all been very strange for me."

"Strange. Strange." she snapped back at me and the others began to take notice of us. "You make us sound like a circus side show." Tears began to stream down each of her cheeks. "Please, don't behave this way. This trip has been difficult enough for me. I need you."

Her voice betrayed a vulnerability which disarmed all my resistance. "I'm sorry, Beth. Please forgive me."

We spent a couple of hours more wandering over the ruins. At one point, as Beth was quietly talking to Sophia near two large stones which were once the base stones of a huge pillar. I stopped a moment at a distance and watched her. The way she held her arms and leaned toward Sophia as they spoke revealed her keen interest and compassion. Though she had ample reason to be bitter about her losses, she carried herself humbly and serenely, and I began to feel ashamed over my own selfish preoccupations.

I approached her again to speak to her.

"I'm so sorry for the way I have behaved. I've been a real ass."

"I've never told you why I love you so much," she responded. "That night after my brother died in London, I went home to my uncle's house and I cried for two days. I thought my life was a huge mistake. I was in a strange place. I couldn't speak the language. I didn't understand the culture. I regretted that I didn't stay in Arnos and die with the others. But then I thought of you. How kind you had been to me on that night. In a moment when I most needed someone, you helped me. I'll never forget those days. You were one of those blessings which God had given me to make my suffering bearable. I don't regret a single day I've known you."

I began to cry.

"Don't think I don't know what you've been going through. I know. I know."

I was too choked up to speak. I struggled to say inarticulately, "I love you so much." Then she embraced me.

"Come on, Neilos. Let's enjoy the remainder of our vacation."

She held my right hand tightly in her left hand and we began to walk toward the others.

"Ti kaneis?" Sofia greeted her.

"Kala," she responded and squeezed my hand.

Afterwards that evening, Beth's cousins took us to an elegant restaurant in the center of Athens whose name escapes me now. We dined on roast lamb and calamari, and Greek potatoes with lemon. Her cousin Petros ordered champagne and he toasted us all. "Long life and prosperity." He lifted his glass in the air.

"May God grant us all the fullness of joy," Emmanuel joined him.

It was the last evening we spent in Greece. The next morning, Emmanuel drove us to the airport with Beth's cousin's driving behind us. Before we boarded a Pan American flight for New York, we all embraced, and Father Niphon read a prayer of blessing for our journey. I can still remember them all standing behind the glass and waving to us as we entered the gate.

"Yasou, Elisavet," Sophia shouted.

"Yasou," Beth shouted back. We waved one final goodbye and boarded the plane. A lump grew in throat and my stomach knotted up.

Soon we were in the air, and I sensed this journey had forever changed me, but in ways I did not yet have the capacity to understand.

"When we get to New York, I will double my efforts to find Michael," I told Beth as we found our seats.

"It's all right, Neilos," she gently answered me and kissed me on the cheek. "Wherever he is, he is in God's hands. We must trust that He will watch over him."

When we arrived at Idlewild Airport, I felt this great sense of relief. I was back in familiar territory, with accustomed frames of reference. As the plane taxied toward the gate, I kept thinking about all that awaited me, from the two new stores, to a stack of papers to sign, to the awesome responsibility for so many employees. As we gathered our bags at the baggage pickup and loaded them in the taxi, I thought about the new line of color televisions I was expected to review and approve the next day.

I don't recall at exactly what time we arrived at the house. I had lost all sense of time, and I was only tentatively cognizant of which day of the week it was. Then, when we pulled up in front of the house, there was something eerily unfamiliar about it. Everything was exactly as we left it, except the colors seemed slightly shifted in hue. The greens seemed more yellow and the browns more red and the whites seemed closer to beige than I remembered them. The sense of proportion also seemed distorted to me, with the doorway a little taller and the walkway a little longer and the windows smaller than I remembered them.

"Are you OK, Neilos?" Beth asked me as I lifted two bags and carried them toward the front doorway.

"Things look a little different from how I remember them," I explained.

"Have you noticed how sometimes people's faces change after you get to know them?" she asked me.

"I've never thought about it before. But yes, I've experienced that."

"Perception is a very (I could see she was struggling to find an English word.) changeable thing. If we change, often our physical perceptions change as well."

I opened the door and left it open for her, and I returned to retrieve the other bags.

I had never really pondered it before, this malleable and capricious thing we call seeing, how dependant upon prejudice and subjective conditioning it is, and how we must learn to see as problematically as we learn to walk.

"Home at last," I said as I closed the front door behind us. I took one deep breath and released it.

That night it felt wonderful to sleep in my own bed again. I slept deeply and restfully and woke without a sore back for the first time in days. Beth prepared a good breakfast for me of pancakes and an omelet, and I drank a tall glass of tomato juice. By eight thirty I was in the car and on my way to Brooklyn. It was a routine which I had followed consistently for six years, but for the first time it felt uncomfortable for me.

When I arrived at the office, my secretary Patricia was already there.

"Good morning, Mr. Fox," she greeted me. "How was your vacation? "

"It was good," I responded to her. "But I'm glad to be home again."

I unlocked the door to my office and turned on the lights.

"You have an appointment with David Atkinson this morning at eleven o'clock, and Richard has already set up one of the new color sets for you to examine in the conference room, and I left some papers for you to sign on your desk."

"How long have you been with me now, Patricia?" I asked her.

"Three years, sir."

Though she was nearly thirty, she looked so much younger than I remembered her. When I entered the office, I stood in front of a mirror near a small wash basin in the corner and I stared at my face. My brown hair was beginning to streak with gray, and I had gone completely gray at the temples. Over half my life had passed and I felt even closer to death.

I approached my desk and tentatively sat down on the edge of my chair. Before me lay stacks of contracts to sign, invoices to review, and new brochures to approve. There were countless decisions I had to make about everything from paint colors to shelving sizes. I lifted two lease contracts from the stack, opened a drawer to find a pen, but for some odd reason I couldn't bring myself to sign them. I reached into my pocket and removed the pocket watch, which I opened and laid out in front of me on the desk. Then a knock came on my office side door.

"May I come in?" Richard Matheson, my assistant, greeted me. His white sleeves were rolled neatly up to his elbows.

"Certainly," I responded.

"How was Greece, as exotic as they say?"

"Even more so," I found myself unusually unresponsive.

"I've set up one of the new sets in the conference room. I'm sure you will be pleased."

"Alright, let's see it."

I rose listlessly from my chair and slowly followed him through the side door across the hall and into the conference room. There I found, sitting in the center of the room, the picture box, with its Jamison Logo and shiny new dials. He pulled a chair from the table and set it down in front of the set.

"Sit down," he coaxed me, and I begrudgingly sat down.

He pulled a knob in front of the set and a single white dot appeared in the center of the screen. Then, like a burst of fireworks, color filled the screen.

"We set a camera up in front of the Brooklyn Museum," he continued. "Just a small demonstration of the future. Isn't it impressive?"

The colors were as bright and sharp and crisp as a Technicolor motion picture as I watched pedestrians and vehicles pass before the camera's eyes.

"I'd be more impressed if it could show me the future," I retorted.

"We're working on that," Richard rebounded. "Well, what do you think?"

"I think people will become mesmerized by it, and if the price is right we'll sell a million of them." I paused a moment and looked again at the screen. "I've seen enough of it for now. Can you turn it off? I've got some work to catch up on. Maybe around one o'clock we can go get some lunch."

"Sure," he acknowledged and left the room.

I walked across the hallway and back into my office. When I closed the door behind me, I felt frightened, though I didn't understand quite why.

I must have sat an hour staring at the papers on my desk without the slightest movement in my fingers. I began to stare at the opened watch in front of me, watching its hands move from ten thirty to eleven o'clock. At eleven fifteen, Patricia broke my trance when she spoke through the intercom, "Mr. Atkinson has arrived. Should I send him in?"

"Go ahead, Patricia," I answered and I waited for him to come inside.

"It's good to see you again, David," I greeted him and reached out my hand to shake his. His grip was firm and strong.

"You're looking well, Nigel. I guess Greece must have been good to you."

He sat down in an oak chair across from me.

"It was intense," I told him. *"Not really what I expected."*

"I suppose Richard has shown you the new television."

"Yeah, he showed me this morning."

"We're very pleased with the way it has turned out." He pulled a cigarette case out of his pocket and removed a cigarette.

"Do you mind if I smoke?"

"Go right ahead." I reached into my desk and found him an ash tray which I placed in front of him.

"It's a nasty habit, I know," he spoke, dangling the cigarette from the corner of his mouth as he lit it with a silver lighter. *"But I can't seem to break it."*

He took two huge drags and dropped the ashes in the tray.

"I suppose you're wondering why I came over here today."

"I assumed you would get to it eventually."

"I have a proposition for you," he began. He balanced the cigarette on the edge of the ash tray. *"How many stores do you have now?"*

"Twenty-four, and I have leases to sign for two more."

"And how much inventory would you say you have?"

"Off the top of my head I couldn't say," I paused. *"This sounds like the beginning of an offer to buy me out."*

"We always were on the same page." He took another puff.

"Yeah, I've come to find out what you'd want for us to take over the stores. Certainly there must be a figure which suits you."

I began to chuckle enthusiastically.

"What's so funny?" he asked me.

"You figure, I've had two weeks of intensive anti-television propaganda and now is the perfect time to make an offer when I'm most likely to accept the lowest figure. I'm sure that you've done your homework. How much inventory do I have?" I paused. "If you offer me, let's say, five million, then I must presume it is worth ten times as much over the long run. And that's what we're talking about, isn't it? You must know that I don't care about the money. I sink almost every free dime I have into expanding the business and employing more people. It's these people for whom I am responsible. No, I can't sell the business, not for any price."

"You're sure about this?"

"For now."

"That's what I told them." He pulled a contract out of his vest pocket and laid it out on the desk in front of me.

"What's this? "

"It's the licensing agreement for the new sets."

I picked it up to look at it.

"Not now, have your attorneys look it over and send it back to me." He began to chuckle to himself.

"One day you're going to take my offer and sell me all the stores." He put the cigarette to his lips and sucked it again.

"How is Elizabeth doing? I bet it was hard for her going back home again."

"It was devastating, but she got through it all."

"People want to forget about the war. So we can offer them a little bit of fantasy in their living rooms."

"What are we going to do when everyone who wants a set has bought one?"

"We'll sell them a better set."

I snickered a moment at a passing thought.

"What's so funny?"

"It's something Leonard once told me. He said they'd figure out a way to make a television no bigger than a business card and people would carry them around in their pockets." I paused. "Eleven years

since his death, and it seems like yesterday."

"Look, I'm not going to keep you much longer," he told me. "But I do have one bit of good news to tell you."

"What is that?"

"We've appointed your cousin Michael to the board of directors of the corporation."

"I'm sure he's very pleased about it."

"So are we."

David soon left my office, and I placed the licensing contract on top of all the others for further review. A sinking feeling soon swept over me. I pondered that maybe I should have taken his offer, because my heart wasn't in the business any more. Over the next few days, the next few months and the next few years, I got up every morning and went to work more out of habit than anything else. I knew tremendous success in the midst of tremendous social and moral upheaval. In March of 1970, I had forty stores when I sold them all and finally ended my life as a television salesman. In the thirteen years which passed between, it seemed as if the world turned inside out. From the frivolity of "I love Lucy", to the McCarthy hearings, to the Quiz Show scandals, to the assassination, to the Viet Nam War, our self destruction was chronicled intimately and immanently in the picture boxes in our living rooms, and I often wondered what Leonard would have thought of it all had he lived to see it.

There is much that I could say about those years, about the powerful effect that television had in transforming our culture, but it doesn't interest me anymore. In fact, I haven't seen a television in twenty years. And this finally brings me to why I made these tapes.

Ten months ago before all this began, Beth and I were enjoying our waning years as best we could. She was working with the disadvantaged children and later with autistic children, something which she had begun shortly after losing our son, as a means, I suppose, of coping with the loss, and I was busy with various charities, from the Red Cross to a homeless shelter in Harlem. Each of us had carved out a niche, a place to occupy our declining years, and I suppose had it not been for the dreams, we would have continued on as we had grown accustomed to doing, until our eventual deaths. And despite the passage of time, I still thought often about Michael, and I pondered what he might be doing if he were still alive, and occasionally something would trigger a vivid memory, and in the mysterious way the mind often transcends time, I would relive those intense moments of anguish, as when the trauma was new and not accommodated. But the feeling would quickly dissipate, along with the intensity of the memories. I realized that, although I would never forget what had happened so many years before, I had finally accepted it. And then came the dreams.

Of course, I had always had vivid dreams, some of the most vivid during the Viet Nam war years. I remember a number where I found myself on patrol in dense jungle, struggling to move amid destruction and debris while the smell of napalm swelled my nostrils. Beth would wake me, striving to calm me while chanting a blessing in Greek.

"You must pray more fervently," she would invariably counsel me, but I lacked the self-discipline to keep her routine. And once awake, I quickly forgot them, writing them off as the byproducts of a fervent imagination or as indigestion. Occasionally, I'd revive the nightmare with the crying corn-stalks, rich with its symbolism and pomp, though I lacked the inclination to interpret these symbols, still unconvinced they had any real importance. My waking life seemed enough of a struggle. I would argue to myself that I spent so much of my time trying to integrate the chaos of my conscious hours into some coherent whole, how could I hope to integrate the madness of my dreams? And for most of my life, I found this argument compelling.

I remember the first of the dreams which began to shake my confidence.

I was standing in what seemed to be an industrial city in Japan. I recognized it from the architecture and the way the houses were squeezed together like children's blocks sitting side by side, though I had never been to Japan, nor could I recognize the city.

Suddenly, the earth began to shake violently, and within minutes buildings began to topple and total chaos ensued. Children were screaming. People were running; gas lines began to rupture and ignite. The whole horrible image of death and destruction played out in front of me as though on a movie screen, and I felt helpless, unable to move even my hands to gesture to the children running beside me, and not knowing Japanese, I couldn't understand what they were shouting.

I watched a three-story apartment house shake apart like paper mâchè, and I heard the sounds of panic and agony broadcasting

outward from within its walls, and then Beth began to shake me,
apparently because I was moaning in my sleep.

"*It was horrible,*" *I began to tell her,* "*horrible.*"

Then she placed her finger over my lips.

"*Do not speak of it,*" *she urged me.* "*Do not give it power.*"

Then she encouraged me to return to sleep.

But I couldn't push the images out of my mind. As I showered and
dressed that morning, I kept thinking about the children, their
anguished faces lingered with me as I began the mundane tasks of the
day. I went outside the house and picked up a copy of the Times and I
returned to the kitchen to read it while Beth poured me a cup of Greek
coffee.

When I slid the paper out of its plastic bag and folded it out in front
of me, a banner headline read, "*Earthquake in Japan, severe damage*
and casualties." *And beneath was a photograph of the same scene I*
had witnessed in my dream. It terrified me.

I immediately began to postulate a plausible explanation for what I
was seeing. '*Perhaps, I heard it over the radio and my mind created*
these images in response.' *But we had no radio in our bedroom and I*
had gone to bed early from fatigue. After fifteen minutes of such
speculation, I realized I could find no sensible explanation, and I
simply resolved to push it from my mind. Then submerging the
experience into my subconscious, I went about my regular routine
until three days later when the pattern repeated itself, this time with a
plane crash.

It was as though I were sitting on the edge of a wing; staring inside
the aircraft as it began to make a descent, I could see the flight crew
through the cockpit windows. Then something went terribly wrong—
the crew struggled to keep control of the plane as it began to pitch and
toss, like a boat on rough seas. The nose pulled upward and then
down, and the plane began to fall, spinning and tipping until it crashed
in a ball of flames. I stood motionless on the ground like a camera
recording it all. Then again the next morning, I went out to get the
paper and found a photograph on the first page which matched my
recollection. I thought I was going mad.

I sat down with Beth and tried to explain to her what had happened,
and she seemed annoyed.

"*Neilos, we all have dreams. The Fathers say we should forget them."*

"But Beth, I have to understand what's happening to me."

When the experience repeated itself a third time, with a dream about tornados in Kentucky, I decided to see a doctor.

I remember being tested for every conceivable neurological possibility, with MRIs and electro-diagnostic testing. And when the results were in, Dr. Berger called me into his office.

"I can't find anything wrong," he began. *"Everything checks out OK. We've run an MRI, various electro-diagnostic tests and they're all negative. There's nothing neurologically wrong with you except the effects that age has on all of us."*

"You're saying these nightmares have no neurological basis?"

"The human mind is a complex machine, Mr. Fox. We haven't even begun to understand all of its subtle nuances. Look, I have a colleague of mine who may be able to help you. He's a psychiatrist." He scribbled his name out on a piece of paper.

"I can see you're experiencing anxiety about these dreams. Perhaps, he can recommend a pharmacological solution."

"I'm not crazy."

"No one is saying you're crazy. But there are drugs which can suppress REM sleep."

He tore the paper from his pad and handed it to me. But I could see from his expression he thought I was overreacting. For my own sake, I wanted to believe him because any other explanation would prove beyond my capacity to accept.

A month passed peacefully after this. I had begun to accept that the dreams had been the result of a convergence between an overactive imagination and coincidence. There were certain logical boundaries which separated the dream life from the conscious life, and because of fatigue and old age, my mind had blurred these distinctions. I refused to think otherwise. But this fragile peace which I had brokered did not endure when a fourth more vivid dream occurred.

I was standing in the midst of a train wreck, and devastation surrounded me. I closed my eyes because the images were too powerful to bear, and I could hear a young child crying.

"Mama," he shouted, *"Mama,"* and with each anxious scream I found my heart breaking. I wanted to shout, 'Why do this to me?' For in a strange way I sensed I was dreaming. Then, I began to walk.

Surveying the damage which surrounded me, like a railroad inspector, my eyes darted across the ground. There were casualties everywhere and I averted my eyes to keep from looking at them. Amid the carnage and destruction which overcame me were newspapers and handbags and styrofoam coffee cups. I recognized a copy of the New York Times, *and a ski magazine, all poignant ancillary evidence of lives once lived. Then for some odd reason, I found myself reaching down to the ground to pick up a newspaper. I lifted it to my eyes and the caption read, 'December 27, The Hadleyburg Times.' I then folded it up and placed it under my arm.*

I could feel Beth beginning to shake me and her voice pierced through my dream, "Wake up, Neilos. Wake up. You're dreaming again."

And suddenly it was over and I lay almost rigid in bed.

"You must pray fervently. You must pray now," she entreated me.

"It's all right," I extolled her. "It's only a dream."

These were words which in their obvious simplicity, held the darkest of secrets. Within weeks, I would begin to believe they were much more than dreams and every assumption I had about time, about space, about continuity, would face serious challenge.

The dream about the train wreck repeated itself the following night and each successive night for a week, growing ever more detailed and place specific. As though working through a puzzle, I began to keep a journal, and upon waking I would jot down details in hopes to capture information before it dissipated in my consciousness. I began to recognize landmarks as I struggled through minute details to determine the location. It seemed familiar, almost as though I had been there before, as though I were somehow part of the place, yet I knew I had never been to this place. Then the craziest idea began to crystalize in my mind.

I became convinced that I was being carefully taught something, as when a schoolmaster through simple repetition drills a lesson into his reluctant pupils. But, of course, this implied a teacher. Though I was prepared to believe in God as an abstract first cause, to believe in a schoolmaster God who took a personal interest in the lives of his creatures was too difficult for me, even after forty years of Beth's constant example.

I can't pinpoint at which moment I began to believe that the dreams were some sort of premonition. It was more an emotional response than an intellectual one. But the force of my experience had conquered any intellectual objections I could raise, and as a man on a quest, I became obsessed to unravel them.

When I confronted Beth and began to explain to her what I suspected, her response was cautious.

"I don't think we should take our dreams so seriously. The Fathers say..."

"I don't care what the Fathers say," I interrupted her. "This is happening to me now, not sixteen hundred years ago. As mad as it seems, I believe it's a premonition. And if this is a premonition, maybe I'm supposed to do something about it."

"It's a temptation."

"Don't you think if there were any way I could discount these dreams, I would do so? I know I'm supposed to do something."

"Do what, Neilos? You can't stop a train crash."

"I can try."

Then I began the daunting task of trying to piece it all together and discover where it could happen.

I became a man obsessed, unable to sleep, to work, to eat without thinking about the dreams. I studied railway maps and atlases and picture travelogues. Laying them out on the living room floor like an odd mosaic, I moved on my hands and knees and pored over them with a magnifying glass. Beth watched this transformation in anguished impotence, as what seemed senile dementia had overtaken me. Four anxious days I spent in a state of heightened tension, barely sleeping, barely eating, in a struggle to attain recognition, before I collapsed in exhaustion and slept. Upon waking nearly twelve hours later, I lifted my head to see the clock as it was chiming on the wall, and it just popped into to my head where I had seen the town. It was outside Pittsburgh nearly fifty years before on that first train trip to New York.

I remember the morning of December twenty-sixth, I rose early and began to pack a bag. I planned to find a place to stay overnight and look for the location that day. Beth came outside to the garage and confronted me.

"Nigel, you can't do this," she began. "It's insanity."

"I can't let them die."

"You don't know from where these visions come. Maybe it's what

God wants for them."

"I can't believe that."

"If I could have saved my father, my brothers, I would have tried. But it was not His will. I watched the Nazis shoot them like animals. Nor was it His will that I see our Michael again."

"I'm going, Beth. I have to go."

"Things happen in this world. It's not our personal responsibility to make everything right."

"If this train crash happens tomorrow and I didn't try to stop it, I could never live with myself. It's about conscience. Pray for me."

I loaded the car and backed it out of the driveway and looked back and watched her a moment as she stood anxiously on the pavement.

Of course it's now old news what happened. I drove out to Pittsburgh, I found the correct siding, and in a heavy rainstorm I diverted a switch and kept the freight train from crashing head on into the passenger train. It was a two minute decision which would forever change my life. I had striven earnestly not to leave a trail of clues, nothing leading back to me, and when I read the Times *the following morning and read this small story of this minor miracle, as they called it, how some unknown angel diverts a train and prevents a massive train wreck, I was relieved it was finally over, of course never realizing in my ineptitude, I had left dozens of clues and within days I would be thrust into a media maelstrom.*

I remember when Frank Glen came to my doorstep. Buoyed by an overwhelming sense of his own investigative prowess, he knocked on our door in hopes, I surmised, of cajoling a confession out of me. I didn't know how he had found me. But lacking any competent criminal skills, I thought, I must have scattered a trail of fragments which he painstakingly followed until they led him to their source. But he was only the first, like a forager ant who sniffs out food and then brings hundreds in his wake.

"Mr. Fox," he almost shouted at me through the door.

"Who are you?" I asked him.

"I'm Frank Glen. I'm a reporter."

I cracked the door open for him and could hardly restrain him. "I know you diverted the train," he told me. "I've pieced the whole thing together."

"I'm sorry. You must be mistaken." And I closed the door between

us.

"Mr. Fox, eventually you'll have to talk to me. I won't be put off."

Then he sat on the front of our house for what seemed like hours, waiting for me to relent and to come outside and talk to him. When it became apparent that he could not easily be dissuaded, not even by a heavy rain which had begun to fall, Beth took pity on him and went outside to feed him sandwiches and cookies and to bring him an umbrella, which he accepted with gratitude.

I listened to them through the door

"Your husband did it, didn't he?" he asked her. "He saved all those people. My friend at the railroad tells me it would have been a fireball consuming everyone inside the train. Look, I know he doesn't want to talk to me, but if he did this thing it's important that people know about it."

I knew Beth believed the opposite, that the praise of goodness in this life destroyed its heavenly reward, but she didn't respond to him. When she returned into the house, she confronted me.

"Neilos, we can't let him stand outside in the rain. He'll catch a cold. I'm asking him inside."

"Alright," I relented. I opened the door and gestured for him to come inside.

"Thank you. Mr. Fox."

"You're all wet," I told him.

"Yeah, could you get a towel for me to dry up a bit?"

Then Beth went into the bathroom and returned in a few moments with a towel.

"Everyone thinks I'm crazy," he began to explain as he patted his face with the towel. "I know if you think about it, it seems off the wall. But things have been happening this last week that are really crazy. I met your wife three days ago at this school for autistic children. Isn't this an odd coincidence? If I told you how I put this all together, you'd really think I've lost my mind. But I'm convinced if you did this thing, it must have been because of some premonition. As crazy as it sounds, because of this autistic boy, I've come to believe in them now. How else could you know? It's tangible proof of some sort of paranormal experience."

"What kind of publication do you work for?" I asked him.

"Oh. It's not what you think. I'm not one of those paranormal

devotees chasing after ghosts. I'm a legitimate investigative reporter. The last piece I did was the effect of NAFTA on migrant farm workers." He paused. "I just think it would be nice to write a story with some transcendent theme for a change."

I don't know what it was about his words that touched me, but I found myself confessing to him everything that had happened, and he sat captivated by what I told him. Yet, I couldn't understand why he seemed to believe me when on the surface it seemed impossible. But I always underestimated people's capacity to believe.

I suppose if I've learned anything from all this pain, it must be what binds us to one another is often invisible. It transcends time and space and it begins in a capacity to believe the impossible. And that compassion always entails a payment, a rendering to God what is God's, and if we knew the cost before hand, we'd never care for anyone. It hurts too much. Yet somehow, despite all this, it's worth it.

Within days after this small interview, the chaos of media celebrity engulfed us. Our front lawn became an encampment of reporters, each competing for a cogent or not so cogent sound bite. The strain proved unbearable for Beth who summoned within herself the strength of will to shoo them off the lawn as though they were stray animals who had broken free from their owner's control.

"You people are crazy." I remember her shouting at the one pugnacious young woman. "Leave us alone."

"It's like the demons have made camp at our front door," she lamented to me once inside.

Then at considerable expense, we had a security company construct the security fence around the house to preserve what small amount of privacy we had been begrudgingly allowed. I couldn't understand what they expected of me and I began to regret that I had ever let Frank Glen into our house.

Even the telephone became a source of constant perturbation, from the desperate calling for some hopeful word from me, to police departments that thought I might be able to bring progress to unsolved cases. Each of them believed in my powers of premonition and sought earnestly for my assistance. I began to see myself through their eyes, as solely an object to gratify their desires to satisfy their needs. And this disgusted me.

We bought an answering machine and began to screen all calls, from old women who wanted me to find children they had given up for adoption to lottery players seeking the winning numbers. Even the terminally ill hoped against hope that I had healing powers in addition to a second sight. These calls unsettled me most of all because I had no magical powers to provide the remedies that they desired.

"Give me a sign," one young woman almost shouted into the phone. "Should I marry Milton or not?"

I wanted to lift up the phone and chastise her, but Beth's compassionate countenance dissuaded me. She communicated silently through her eyes to show kindness to them.

"Each of them in his own ignorant and often misguided way seeks God," she told me. "We must pray fervently that they find Him."

She began to pray for all of them, scribbling their names in long lists for remembrance in her morning and evening prayers. And often as someone was describing some heart wrenching problem, I'd find her prostrate and praying with streams of tears running down each cheek.

"We live in a world of such suffering," she once confided in me. "I'm certain Christ must continually be in tears."

This image of a crying Christ unsettled me.

As her list easily passed one hundred names, and we accumulated a small box of cassettes, I began to stop listening to the messages people left on the machine. Their earnest pleas disturbed me—until one evening in the midst of a dozen unrecognizable voices, Beth called attention to one voice, which sounded uncannily like my cousin Michael's.

"I'm sure you must be sick of the attention, Nigel. But I think that I can help you. I'll be in New York this weekend. You can reach me at the Plaza Hotel."

It had been over ten years since we had spoken to Michael, but I could never forget his voice. I reluctantly called him that weekend and agreed to meet with him the following Monday for lunch. But Beth had misgivings about him and refused to come along with me.

"It's good to see you again, Nigel," he greeted me and we shook hands.

"I often read about you in the papers," I told him.

"And I you," he responded. "That's part of why I want to talk to you."

I remember thinking how well he had aged.

"How is Beth?" he asked me.

"She's fine."

"I'm sorry she couldn't come."

"She doesn't like the City."

What I didn't want to tell him was she didn't like him.

"There's been quite a stir about these premonitions," he chose his words carefully and deliberately.

"It's been a circus."

I could see several people in the restaurant were staring at us as we talked.

"Look at them," I commented, "staring at me like I'm some sort of side show freak, it's ridiculous."

He smiled.

"That's part of why I'm here. I have a proposal for you."

He sipped a moment from his glass of wine.

"Would you object to giving a series of talks?"

"Where and for what purpose?"

"I've been considering the possibilities," he began to explain to me. "I would set up a number of lectures around the country. We would charge a nominal admission fee to cover rent of the facilities. Any profit above our expenses you can use for charitable purposes, and you could just talk about anything you like."

"And you think people will actually come to hear me talk?"

"Of course."

"And what would I talk about?"

"The dreams, for example, or other spiritual concerns."

"I refuse to feed any more of this hysteria," I interrupted him.

"I don't believe anything happens by chance, Nigel, and if you have these experiences, it is important you share them with others." He paused. "The implications of these experiences resonate with many, and it would be a shame to allow the tabloids to control the discussion about them. And I'm willing to risk my considerable reputation in the promotion of these talks."

"What's in this for you, Michael?"

"I see this as a culmination, a completion of much of the work I have done in these past few years. As you may know, I've been actively involved in the environmental movement, and these experiences raise profound philosophical questions concerning our relationship to the

world."

I didn't know what to make of his remarks. He continued, "I also have a profound sense we stand on the threshold of a great spiritual reawakening, and I want to be in the forefront of that movement."

I tried to read some ambiguity in his voice, but he seemed completely sincere.

"I'll think about it," I answered him.

"That's all I ask."

There was something enormously seductive in what he was saying, and the thought of traipsing all over the country at my age amused me. 'Could it become a way of redeeming myself, of finally having a discernible positive effect on the world?' I pondered as we quietly finished our meal. By the time the check arrived, I had almost convinced myself to go along with him, but I still had Beth to convince before I could commit.

"It sounds very interesting," I told him. "But I have to speak to Beth about it."

It seemed instinctive to me that she would object, but the depth of her objection I could not have anticipated.

When I returned home, I began to explain to her everything which Michael had told me, and Beth listened passively, without interrupting me until I finished my remarks with the statement, "I think some good can come from this."

She was silent a moment, apparently carefully considering what she might say to me and then she began.

"You remember your experiences with Michael the last time," her argument began. "He has the compulsion to control. I'm sure over these years it's become even stronger."

"He said I could say whatever I want."

"He says that now. But people change their minds."

"I talked to him, Beth. I have no reason to doubt his sincerity, and he's risking his reputation on this."

"I think it's a mistake to do this. You should seek spiritual counsel."

"You may be right. But I feel I have to do this. It's somehow expected of me."

She remained unconvinced, but I resolved to do it despite her objections, and I did.

I embarked on a series of talks beginning in Pittsburgh, which nearly became quasi-religious in tone. Michael would begin with a five minute introduction, usually touching on highlights of his own journey, and then he would paint a context for the dreams.

I remember one particularly vivid introduction in Cleveland. He began, "As many of you know, I had an early and active involvement in the Civil Rights movement. But then I saw it more in socio-political terms, not spiritual terms. Perhaps the single most important thing that can be learned from Nigel's experiences with his dreams is that the connections between past, present and future are not as finely demarcated as we so easily believe. Often, what connects events and people to one another transcends our pedestrian notions of time and space."

Then I approached the microphone and gave a more rambling and extemporaneous talk, dealing with my dream-life, my own struggle with spirituality. The small audience sat captivated as though hanging on my every word.

As we moved from auditorium to auditorium, I could see the audiences growing, but Beth continued her strenuous objections, refusing to even attend the talks and marshaling as her defense a list of Scripture references to support her position that I was violating God's will. But the attention and acknowledgment of the audiences proved too seductive for me to resist.

"You can't set yourself up as some kind of prophet," she almost shouted at me. "It's like you're changing into a different person."

I couldn't see what she was talking about and dismissed it as a product of her cultural conditioning. Upon reflection, I wished I had listened.

As one could have anticipated, both Michael and I received a substantial amount of negative press because of the talks. One conservative pundit's scathing critique began, "From Civil Rights to Second Sight: The devolution of the American Liberal, "and characterized the whole liberal movement as a fringe group consisting of UFO kooks and tarot card readers. But Michael took it all in stride as the number of our adherents seemed to be growing.

There was one particularly derisive cartoon, showing a caricature of me in my early years standing beside a television, and me as I look now with what looked like radio waves flying out my eyes and ears. The caption read, "From Mr. Television to Mr. Tell-a-vision."

Michael assured me such criticism would only enhance our popularity, and as always, his judgment proved correct. But it was beginning to get to me.

After the tenth or the eleventh talk, Michael persuaded Jim Jamison to join us on the dais. I presumed because of my connection to his father, or because I had sold his father's televisions during those first twenty years. Yet, I never felt inclined to ask him for a reason. It was as though I were enchanted and danced to the piper's tune.

In Boston, Hartford and Trenton, the crowds became so unruly that the police had to be dispatched and I had the first taste of the magnitude of their hysteria. Like a people long deprived of spirituality and overcome with a thirst for it, they clamored after any small taste. Their enthusiasm both repulsed and moved me.

I called Beth from every stop, to tell her how I was doing, but her voice seemed more distant with each call.

"Please, come home," she almost pleaded with me, when I called her from Omaha. "For your own sake, please come home,"

But it would be three weeks before I returned to New York, and when I finally walked through the front door of the house, I was tired, but relieved to be home. I could sense immediately something was wrong. Then I noticed there were two packed suitcases sitting on the living room carpet.

"I'm home, Beth," I shouted to her.

Then she walked into the hallway from the kitchen. She was dressed as though she were going out somewhere.

"What's going on here?" I asked her as I picked up the suitcases.

"I'm leaving you, Nigel," she firmly told me. "There's nothing you can tell me to change my mind."

"What do you mean you're leaving me? We've been married fifty years. You can't just walk out the door."

"This has been the most painful decision of my life, but I can't stand by any longer and watch you make a mockery of everything I believe."

She was fighting back tears.

"What are you going to do? Where are you going to go? This is insanity."

"I love you. But I have to do something to show you the magnitude of what you're doing."

"Alright, I won't give any more talks, if that's what this is about."

"It's not about you. It's about them. Can't you see what they're doing to you? They're making a fool out of you, Nigel." She paused. "I have to do something to bring you to repentance, to bring you back to the Church."

I began to shout at her, "How is walking out on me supposed to bring me to repentance? It hasn't been easy living with you either with the constant finger-pointing when I fall short of your expectations. I didn't ask for these dreams. You're acting like it's something I sought out. They came to me."

"Nigel, I don't want us to say things we'll regret. Please help me load the suitcases in the car, and I'll call you once I've settled."

Two streams of tears were running down her cheeks. Then I helped her load both suitcases into her car, and she climbed inside to back it out of the garage. Rolling down her window, she told me, "Please pray, Nigel." Then trying to hold myself together, I watched her back into to street. She put the car in drive and then disappeared down the block. It felt as though an anvil had been tossed onto my chest. Then I stumbled as though I were tranquilized through the back door and into the kitchen, and there I found her scrapbook on the kitchen table, like she had left it for me. I opened it and my eyes began to well with tears as I turned each page.

"My God, what have I done?" I pleaded.

When I saw our wedding pictures, it was more than I could bear and I slammed the book shut. But I couldn't put it down. I carried it with me into the living room, sat down on the sofa with it and began to cry. I cried until my eyes stung and every muscle ached until I fell asleep from exhaustion.

It was nearly midnight when the buzz from the front gate roused me from my awkward sleep, and I staggered to the front door to discover who was ringing.

At the curb, a police car was parked and two uniformed police officers were ringing at the gate. I buzzed the gate open and then watched them as they strode up the walkway. I had no idea what they could have wanted.

"Are you Nigel Fox," the first officer asked me once I opened the front door.

"Yes, I am."

"Do you have a wife named Elizabeth Fox," he continued.

"Yes. Is something wrong?"

"She's been involved in an accident."

"An accident? What kind of accident? Is it serious? "

"Unfortunately, yes."

"Where is she?"

"She's at the North Shore Hospital," the other officer answered me. "I'm sorry." He was obviously upset.

"How serious is it?" I asked them as I went to retrieve my overcoat.

"Very serious."

"What happened?"

"It appears someone ran her off the road and then left the scene."

As we drove out to the hospital in the patrol car, and I was sitting in the back where they normally carry prisoners, I felt like shouting, but I couldn't speak a word to either of them. I kept blaming myself, telling myself that I shouldn't have let her go, that I should have fought her more vigorously. And once at the hospital, I realized it was far more serious than I imagined. When I saw her lying in intensive care, with tubes and monitors touching her from all directions, like a rag doll tied with strings, I simply fell apart. I was crying uncontrollably while a young nurse tried to comfort me.

"It's all my damn fault," I kept mumbling. "All my damn fault."

I remember asking one of the nurses, "Is she going to make it?"

"We don't know," she responded.

"Then I need to call her priest."

I went out into the hallway to use the phone. I called her Greek priest, Father Nectarios, and I soon discovered he was out of town. So I called Father Michael from the homeless shelter and he advised he'd be there as soon as possible.

At three in the morning, she regained consciousness for a few minutes, and she squeezed my hand when she saw me.

"Neilos," she almost whispered. "I love you. Don't blame yourself for this. I had a full life, filled with many blessings. It is God's will."

At four o'clock, Father Michael arrived and asked to be left alone with her. He prayed with her and anointed her.

"She's not going to make it, is she?" I asked him once he left the room.

"I'm afraid not," he answered. "We must pray for her."

I went into the room and watched her as I had watched Leonard so many years before, and in my own inarticulate way, I struggled to pray. "Dear God," I stammered. "Don't take her away from me. It is for my sin she is suffering. I'm responsible for this." As I watched her dying and thought of all the pain which I had brought into her life, I cried. Then at five in the morning, she died in her sleep. It was the saddest moment of my life.

I remember her funeral as though it were a haunting dream, as hundreds of her admirers had come to wish her a final goodbye. So many lives, so many condolences, she had touched them deeply and profoundly, and they came to bear testimony to a life lived well, a transforming life which had touched thousands. From her great acts of kindness through the small things she had done, all her works became manifest among them.

And I couldn't count the hundreds of times someone would say to me, "What a tremendous woman we have all lost," and with each small word of condolence, I wept anew.

Then, I remembered how many times over the years she had tried to tell me how even the smallest acts of kindness have profound transforming effects. But I had become too cynical to take it seriously. Yet here before my eyes was testimony to its truth.

After the burial services at the cemetery, as I lingered to watch them lowering her casket into the ground, Michael approached me to talk.

"I realize this is probably not the appropriate forum for this conversation," he began. "But we do have a talk scheduled in Baltimore next month. If you don't want to speak anymore, I would certainly understand."

"There's so much she tried to tell me, but I never listened to her."

"We can talk about this later, of course."

"I'd do it if I could talk about her," I responded to him. "Otherwise, forget it."

"You can talk about whatever you want," he told me. "I told you that before we began."

"I can talk about her life? About the values that were important to her?"

"Of course."

"But this must be the last time. I wouldn't want to do it any more."

He nodded in acknowledgment.

I don't know why I agreed to give another talk, except that I sensed something cleansing about it, and in some inexplicable way it was a method of bringing things to closure, of purging from myself the whole terrible experience.

Then in Baltimore, Michael gave the same ubiquitous introduction and then sitting on a short stool on center stage, with a small spotlight shining on me, I began to speak, first in a muffled tone, but then more emotionally and with greater control.

"Many of you have come to hear me speak about the dreams, "I remember myself beginning. "But as most of you must know, my wife has recently died and I wish to talk about her instead." The audience quieted to a stunning silence. "It is difficult to talk about someone whom I have known and loved for over fifty years without breaking up about it. This sense of emptiness which has seized my soul seems beyond my capacity to describe." I turned to look to see if I could find Michael's face, but he stood off in the shadows.

"I could talk about my powers, about the dreams, but one small act of kindness has more transforming power than one hundred dreams which presage the future. This is the legacy I have learned from her life and now that she is gone, I don't know how I will carry on."

I sighed deeply and continued.

"I've seen hundreds of your faces, each of them longing for what I have longed for, hope, the feeling that our lives are more than the passing of time, and that the end is more than wasting away in the ground. I sense that's why you come to hear me, so together we can proclaim that life is more than the accumulation of inanimate objects, that what's important are those things which are invisible, which are mysterious, which cannot be explained away, like dreams, which can both frighten and inspire us.

In a world so often filled with unrelenting sorrow, of undeserved suffering, where the weak are destroyed and the strong destroy with impunity, we despair, wondering if there is any justice in this world, if any point of restitution can occur, if all our noble words of truth and beauty are but platitudes, the fantasies of childish minds, when the world is brutal, unfeeling and uninspiring. I've felt these feelings. I feel them now. They well up within my bosom, and like a fountain of sorrow they spill over and wash everything away.

Haven't you ever wanted to turn the clock back, to shout to the heavens, 'why dear God, why me?' And why must love hurt so damn much? I know we all know. I know we all share this common human condition. We love, we lose, we sorrow.

But what my wife's life and death has taught me profoundly is that what matters most is the kindness I have shown to others—this is all that lasts, all that transcends time and space, like dreams. And God knows I've loved not nearly enough."

At this moment, as I stopped to regain control of myself and catch my breath, a woman began to scream and run down the aisle toward me. She jumped up on the stage, shouting, "Please let me touch him or I'll die!"

Then Michael's head of security, an odd man named Marcus, gestured for his assistants to seize the woman and take her off the stage. She hugged me tightly, crying like a baby in my arms until they yanked her away. This convinced me I would finish with these talks.

After a few minutes of awkward silence, I tried to continue, but I couldn't. I apologized abruptly and left the stage.

"You can't just leave in the middle of the talk." Michael confronted me back stage.

"I can and I am. It's over."

"Go back out and talk about Beth."

"You go out there. I'm through."

I could see that he was holding a small package under his arm which he awkwardly tried to hide from me.

"Nigel, we have to talk about this."

"There's nothing to talk about. I'm going back home."

He gestured for Marcus to come with him and then told me,

"Please come with me into back room where we can talk, it will only take five minutes."

"You're not going to change my mind."

I followed him back into a small dressing room and Marcus closed the doors behind us.

"You will finish the talk, Nigel, and give any other talks that are required or they'll kill you."

I laughed at him as though it were preposterous.

"Or who'll kill me?"

"I've already told you more than I should."

"Or who'll kill me?" I began to shout. "Are you threatening me,

Michael? Is that what this is all about?"

"This is not about you, Nigel. It was never about you. It's about their agenda. You're just a pawn, like all of us."

"What are you talking about?"

"Surely, you must know something, Nigel. They didn't put you in the television business and nurture you into a comfortable life without expecting anything in return. Now has come the time for payback."

"I made that business. No one did me any favors."

"You were allowed to make the business. Nigel, open your eyes. Need I be more explicit?" He paused. "Let's say for the sake of argument this group of powerful men, a brotherhood, which controls almost every institution in this country, allows you, a lowly farm boy, to rise to the level you had. It served their purposes, and this continues to serve their purposes. It's about control, Nigel. It was always about control. Please leave us a moment, Marcus." Then Marcus left the room. "I have been instructed to give you a script for the next several talks." He opened the envelope. "Read it, study it. Learn it." He removed from the envelope a bound document and handed it to me.

"I'm not going to do this. I'll fight them."

"You can't fight them. You'd be like an ant trying to take down an elephant. They'll destroy you without a second thought."

"Who are these people? Give me names."

"That's not important. Do as you're told and you survive."

"How can you do this to me? After all I did for you?"

"I'm not doing this to you!" he shouted at me. "I'm a foot soldier. I do as I am told."

"No, no, no. I will not give in."

"Nigel, please listen to me. You cannot possibly win." His voice became softer. "I shouldn't allow you to see this, but I received it this morning." He reached into the envelope and removed another document.

"It's sort of a progress report. Study it a while. You'll see how hopeless it is to resist them. Nigel, I will go out and talk to the audience. Please return to the stage."

And he left me there with the document.

I opened the document to investigate it, and it took me only a few minutes to realize the serious implications of what I was seeing. But despite the obvious futility in resisting them, I resolved I would resist, and I would not return to the stage. Ten minutes passed, and then fifteen, and I sat there alone with the document on my lap. Finally, Michael returned to the dressing room to confront me.

"I'm not going back on stage tonight," I told him. "I don't care if they kill me."

He placed his hand on his forehead. "Alright, Nigel. I'll make up some excuse for you. "

He returned to the room about ten minutes later and told me, "We're going to the hotel."

Then he and Marcus and Jimmy began to escort me out the rear entrance of the theater.

"Consider carefully your alternatives, Nigel," he spoke to me as we walked. "Your life is in your hands."

I remember Michael was walking beside me on the left and Jimmy on my right when we noticed an older man, who had inexplicably broken through security, waiting for us at the rear door of the building.

"I need to talk to you, Mr. Fox," he told me. "It's extremely important."

Michael gestured for security to escort him out of the building and Marcus moved toward him.

"Let me talk to him, Michael," I encouraged them.

"In private please, if that's all right. It's personal."

"Certainly," I responded and led him into a small office near the rear of the building, while Michael and Jimmy followed us.

"Need they come with us," the man almost pleaded with me. "I'd like to speak to you alone."

"Michael, please." I entreated them both and they stepped outside.

"I'm very sick," he began to tell me. "Liver cancer they tell me, and I've probably got only a couple of months left."

I saw the disease painted in anguished pigments on his face.

"I'm sorry, but despite what people may think, I have no healing powers."

"I've done many things in my life for which I should be punished, but there's something I have to get off my shoulders."

"I'm not priest or a prophet. I can't grant you absolution for your sins. "

"I'm not seeking absolution Mr. Fox. You don't know who I am?"

"No."

"You talked out there about kindness, about one act of kindness having the power to transform a life." His eyes filled with tears.

"They were just words," I responded.

"No they're more than words. I've done many things in my life for which I deserve condemnation. I did them willingly and without remorse. But one thing has bothered me all these years."

"And what is that?"

"I took your son, Mr. Fox, and I know where we took him."

I was stunned.

"We sold him through a baby broker to some professor in Chicago."

"Thank you," I told him. "God bless you." And I embraced him.

When Michael opened the door and saw the two of us embracing in that moment of reconciliation, he must have thought it odd. Then the man left me as suddenly as he had arrived. It was as though, in the midst of great agony, God had blessed me with great joy.

"What was that all about?" Michael asked me.

"It was about his sickness," I responded. "He needs our prayers."

"These people really believe you're some kind of prophet. It's incredible."

And it was incredible. Like gullible marks, they were all being led to the sting, and I was the biggest dupe of them all.

I remembered what Beth had told me about Michael, what she had always told me about Michael. And here I was trapped in a net of my own making, like a fish caught for the hungry king, I squirmed mindlessly in the hands of my executioners. I had no idea what I was going to do, but somehow I would find my son.

I don't think Michael suspects a thing, how this whole excursion to Hadleyburg is a ruse to see my son, and how tomorrow I will renounce this whole affair. Finally, forty years of anxious wandering will come to an end, and I'm terrified.

What can I tell him? What can I tell you?

I've grown to believe in these past three months that Beth's accident was no accident, that Michael's brotherhood had something to do with it, perhaps as a way of weakening me for the kill. And it is likely that they will kill me as well. I wonder how many lives have ended at the hands of their executioners. It numbs me just to think about it.

And what can I tell you? How can I break through the wall of cynicism which lays siege to the best of us? And how do I convince you I am your father, as pathetic and foolish as I have become?

There is much more I hope to say to you tomorrow, and if God wills, in the following days. But if something should happen to me, and if I am unable to say these things, please know how much we both loved you. I hope, then, from these feeble words you might come to know me and through me your mother, so that whatever they might say about me should I die, you might know the truth. God bless you, and please forgive me.

The tape clicked off, and both Jim and his father were crying.

"They must have killed him when I left the room."

"You can't blame yourself for what others did to him. If they wanted him dead, then he's dead."

Chapter 38

Two television news cameras and six news people had squeezed themselves into Jim's small hospital room. They were all waiting for the mayor to arrive. Burgess, obviously amused by the whole spectacle, was standing off in the corner, while Jim's father sat awkwardly on the edge of a chair.

When the mayor of the City of New York entered the room, followed by one of his aides, one of the producers instructed his crew to turn on the cameras and both teams turned them on.

Two competing reporters gave short introductions, and then the cameras pivoted toward Jim, lying restless on the hospital bed.

"On behalf of the city of New York," the mayor began." I present you with this plaque commending you for your heroism in coming to the rescue in the face of a crime." He handed Jim a small plaque, which Jim, unable to hold, dropped into his lap.

"We all pray for your quick and complete recovery."

The mayor reached out his hand and Jim uneasily lifted his and awkwardly shook it.

"Thank you," Jim responded. "But I only did what I had to do. I'm no hero."

"In a day and time when heroes are sorely lacking," the mayor countered, "your courage in the face of danger is commendable."

Both producers gestured to turn off the cameras and each operator dropped his camera to his side.

"Again on behalf of the city, thank you. Peter, arrange a luncheon with Mr. Jacobson at the mansion as soon as he is able to ambulate."

His aide nodded in acknowledgment. Then, as quickly as he arrived, the mayor departed, along with his aides and the news people in tow.

"You've now had your fifteen minutes of fame," Burgess chided him.

"I don't know why they're making such a big deal about this. If you ask me, it was kind of stupid."

"They want to promote certain values," Jim's father interjected. "It's part of the social politic."

"They want to promote themselves," Burgess rebounded. "It's about politics."

Jim was gradually regaining the use of his hands. He lifted the plaque from his lap and laid it on the tray with the religious artifacts.

"If you don't mind, I'm very tired. I could use some rest. You don't have to stay here and baby-sit me."

"So you're running us out, Jim?"

"No, I just think you might want to see some of the city before you have to go back."

"I've had enough of the city," Jim's father replied. "But I guess we could eat something."

"Please eat. I'm not going anywhere."

Then Burgess and his father left the room.

A short time later, Dr. Giordano came into the room on his daily rounds and looked a moment at his chart.

"You're doing very well, Mr. Jacobson. Tomorrow, I'm releasing you to the rehab clinic."

"How long will I be there?"

"That's hard to know. But given your current rate of recovery, I'd say a couple of months."

"Is there anything you can do about these headaches?"

The doctor pulled out a small light and began to check Jim's eyes.

"I'll instruct the nurse to increase your pain medication. Otherwise, everything checks out OK."

A little later a nurse came into his room and checked his vital signs and scribbled the results into his chart.

"You've become quite a celebrity, Mr. Jacobson," she told him. She reached into her pocket and removed a stack of messages, which she laid out on the table beside him.

"It seems the whole world wants to talk to you. With things like political assassinations and acts of terrorism becoming the normal course of things, it's nice to have a story about heroism for a change."

Of course, Jim knew he couldn't tell her how inextricably linked both of his stories were, and he decided since the Brotherhood seemed to have left him alone, it would be best if he kept silent about what he knew, though he still wondered what had become of the manuscript after the mugger had snatched it from his arms.

He reflected on how much had changed, on how his experiences in New York had obliterated everything about his previous life, and he realized that in an inexplicable way, the wish he had made that restless night in Hadleyburg had been granted, like an answered prayer and he knew he would be forever changed by what had happened to him.

Epilogue
(Three Months Later)

Jim was standing in Flushing Cemetery at the foot of Nigel's grave. He was leaning on a metal cane while Julie held him up from the other side.

"It is a fitting tribute," he told her, both of them staring at a newly mounted granite gravestone.

"Julie helped me pick out the verse," Jim began to talk to the grave. "In the last days, I will pour my spirit on all flesh, your young men shall see visions and your old men shall dream dreams." He paused. "I'm here to tell you goodbye. I'm going back to Hadleyburg to put my life in order, to try and find purpose again. I don't know how I can thank you for showing me the things you showed me, or if you can forgive me for walking out on you like I did. I'm sorry for so many things. I wanted to tell you that Julie and I have decided to start seeing each other again. Of course, it will be difficult at first, the distances being what they are. But we hope to be together soon. And you were right after all about me. I've been a disappointed idealist. I love you, Dad!"

A light snow began to fall and Julie helped Michael as he leaned against the cane and began to slowly walk away from the grave.